BOUDICA
DREAMING THE SERPENT SPEAR

www.**books**at**transworld**.co.uk

MANDA SCOTT

BOUDICA

DREAMING THE SERPENT SPEAR

BANTAM PRESS

LONDON • TORONTO • SYDNEY • AUCKLAND • JOHANNESBURG

TRANSWORLD PUBLISHERS
61–63 Uxbridge Road, London W5 5SA
a division of The Random House Group Ltd

RANDOM HOUSE AUSTRALIA (PTY) LTD
20 Alfred Street, Milsons Point, Sydney,
New South Wales 2061, Australia

RANDOM HOUSE NEW ZEALAND LTD
18 Poland Road, Glenfield, Auckland 10, New Zealand

RANDOM HOUSE SOUTH AFRICA (PTY) LTD
Isle of Houghton, Corner of Boundary and Carse O'Gowrie Roads,
Houghton 2198, South Africa

Published 2006 by Bantam Press
a division of Transworld Publishers

A catalogue record for this book is available from the British Library.
ISBN 9780593048801 (cased) (from Jan 07)
ISBN 0593048806 (cased)
ISBN 9780593053218 (tpb) (from Jan 07)
ISBN 0593053214 (tpb)

Typeset in 11/13½pt Sabon by
Falcon Oast Graphic Art Ltd.

Printed and bound in Great Britain
by Mackays of Chatham plc, Chatham Kent

1 3 5 7 9 10 8 6 4 2

Papers used by Transworld Publishers are natural, recyclable products made from wood grown
in sustainable forests. The manufacturing processes conform to the environmental regulations
of the country of origin.

For Faith, with all love.

ACKNOWLEDGEMENTS

In this final book of the series, all thanks must go to the two women whose energy and inspiration made it possible from the start: Jane Judd, my agent, and Selina Walker, my editor at Transworld; both believed in the impossible so often that it became not only possible, but tangible, for which no written thanks is enough. Similarly, Kate Miciak and Nita Taublib held faith on the far side of the Atlantic; both gave time, effort, insight and encouragement that helped shape the series to be what it is. Nancy Webber and Deborah Adams have worked far beyond all reasonable limits to hold my copy-editing in line and, as ever, I am indebted to H. J. P. 'Douglas' Arnold for his accuracy of Roman thinking.

I am indebted also, at this ending, to my friends and neighbours in Moulton, who have taken care of me for the past twenty years: you are too many to name, but you know who you are, and that thanks are not enough. Those who had the courage to join me in the dreaming have been part of an extraordinary journey which has taken all of us beyond any boundaries we might have imagined to be real, while those friends who remained in consensus reality have been the bedrock of a stable life: Debs, Sarah, Jackie and my fellow Unusual Suspects. And to Faith, who began at the beginning – thank you.

CONTENTS

CAMULODUNUM – *Colchester*

MONA – *Anglesey*

CANONIUM – *Kelvedon*

CAESAROMAGUS – *Chelmsford*

LUGDUNUM – *London*
aka VESPASIAN'S BRIDGE

VERULAMIUM – *St Albans*

CALEDONII

BRIGANTES

MONA

ORDOVICES

CORNOVII

CORITANI

Approx site
of Fortress of
ixth legion

ECENI

CATUVELLAUNI

TRINOVANTES

SILURES

VERULAMIUM○

○CAMULODUNUM
○CANONIUM
○CAESAROMAGUS

○LUGDUNUM
aka VESPASIAN'S BRIDGE

N

ATREBATES

DUMNONII

BRITANNIA-RELEVANT TRIBES

*L*ISTEN TO ME. I AM LUAIN MAC CALMA, HERON-DREAMER, *Elder of Mona, guardian of those who wait in exile in Hibernia, and protector of the Boudica, who is our hope for the future. You who gather here will inherit that future, whatever it may be.*

We stand now at a crossroads in our history. Once, we were a proud people; we honoured our heroes for their courage in battle, and our dreamers for the wisdom they brought from the gods.

Our tribes were diverse in their customs and histories, we were famed throughout the known world for our work in gold and silver and iron; our horses and hunting hounds are sought from the far northern snows to the heat of Alexandria; our land was so fecund that Julius Caesar believed he had come to a place of the gods when he first sailed across from Gaul with intent to conquer over a hundred years ago.

In our diversity was our pride, but we held our gods in common and this was our strength. Each tribe sent the best of its warriors and dreamers annually to train here on the island of Mona, beloved of the gods and all people.

This heritage, and the island itself, is at last under threat. It is nearly twenty years since Rome sent her legions to conquer the tribes of the land they call Britannia, to take our gold and silver, our hounds and our horses, to tax our peoples for the right to farm our own soil and to take our youth into slavery.

Throughout those two decades, while the eastern part of our land has suffered under occupation, the west has resisted savagely and effectively. The high mountains and the fierce courage of the western tribes have kept safe the land they treasure and, most especially, have protected this gods' island of Mona.

For much of those two decades, I believed that whatever other crimes Rome might commit, Mona and all that it means to us was safe. This is no longer true. The new governor of Britannia, Suetonius Paullinus, is gathering two of his four legions off our coast, tasked first to invade, then to slaughter all those who live within the gods' domain and to erase for ever the dreaming from the earth. Such is Rome's fear of what we are and what we may be.

Our hope of survival lies now in the woman we know as the Boudica – she who brings victory – in those who care for her and keep her safe, and in the war host that gathers even now in her name. She is Breaca of the Eceni, once Warrior of Mona.

Breaca carries within her the strengths and reality of all that we have been. She is a warrior without match and has fought un-ceasingly these past eighteen years to clear Rome from the land.

While she remained here in the west, with Mona as her home, she was successful. But the east lacked a leader with the strength to raise the warriors from their slavery, and without an eastern uprising the war in the west was one of attrition, not of victory.

Three years ago, the Boudica took the decision to leave Mona and to travel east, to the lands of her birth, to the heart of the enemy's occupied territory. She arrived in Eceni lands with her daughters Cygfa and Graine, and with Cunomar, her only son. There, they found a once-proud tribe living in fear and humility with none willing or able to rise against the legions who surrounded them. Still, they set their minds on raising a rebellion and worked towards it.

Over three slow years, they settled into their birthright as the royal line of the Eceni, and with the death of Prasutagos, who had claimed rulership, began at last to raise the war host that might rid the land of Rome.

That might have been the end of it, or, at least, an auspicious beginning. But the emperor Nero, who covets gold above all else, and who had heard of the wealth of the Eceni 'king', sent his procurator, one Decianus Catus, to claim all that belonged to the Eceni in the emperor's name.

Catus was a tax collector, a man of mean mind and meaner spirit, who made himself safe with a cohort of paid veterans: men retired from the legions, who retained with their fighting abilities the legions' abhorrence of the native tribes.

They arrived in the Eceni steading to find the beginnings of resistance and insurrection. After a mockery of a trial, they found Breaca and her family guilty of treason and began the steps to execution. To this end, they flogged the Boudica and her son and then raped the two unmarried girls that they might not be slain while still maidens, this being against Roman law. Thus is justice prosecuted in the emperor's name.

One man prevented the inevitable progress to execution by crucifixion: the Boudica's brother, who had fought for fifteen years on the side of the legions.

Born Bán, and later called Valerius, this man's story is known to you all: his betrayal into slavery, his return to Britannia with the auxiliary cavalry, and his eventual betrayal by those close to the dying emperor Claudius, such that he was named traitor by Nero and became exiled, then, from both sides of this conflict.

Valerius has lived with the essence of despair, but he has also come to understand his birthright both as a warrior and as a dreamer. In his time with Rome, he was given to Mithras, the bull-slayer, hidden god of the legions' elite. Later, on Hibernia, he came to understand that he was given also to Nemain, god of the moon and water, she who walks most closely with the tribes, who sends the hare and the frog to be her messengers on earth. In the living history of our tribes, no-one has ever walked in the presence of two gods more disparate. It is a testament to his strength that Valerius can do so and live. That he can do so and retain his sanity and humour is exceptional.

Valerius was travelling east, bearing a message from Mona to the Boudica, when he learned of the procurator's actions and the imminent execution of his sister and her family. His enduring love of the prefect Corvus enabled him to ask that man's help in preventing the catastrophe; only an officer of highest rank in the *legions could have commanded the procurator to desist and his men to leave. This Corvus did, and then departed, to lead his men west to join in the preparations for the attack on Mona. Even now, he travels towards us.*

Half a month has passed since then. With the legions marching west, the Boudica's war host is in the best possible position to attack Camulodunum, the once-sacred settlement named by Rome as its capital city. To do so will not be easy: Camulodunum has been colonized by veterans of the XXth legion who were given land and holding as their pensions from the legions and will fight hard to keep them. Then, too, they must deal with the IXth legion, which has been stationed to the north of Eceni lands since the time of the invasion, to prevent just such an assault. At the first signs of insurrection, the IXth will march south to attack the war host from behind.

We are also uncertain of the strength of those who must bear the brunt of this war. In the month since the procurator's assaults, Airmid, dreamer, healer and the Boudica's first love, has worked day and night to restore those who were damaged.

She has succeeded in some measure. The Boudica's son, Cunomar, who lost an ear in battle and was later flogged, can fight again and, with the warrior Ardacos, is training his she-bear warriors. His sister Cygfa, who was raped by half a century of men, has taken up her sword and thrown herself into the war against Rome. Of all those close to the Boudica, she has taken most closely to Valerius, trusting him to train her in ways that will best defeat the legions.

We are left, then, with the Boudica and with Graine, her nine-year-old daughter, who is broken in body, but worse, is broken in soul such that she has lost her dreaming. Once, Graine would have matched the Elder of Mona. Now, she is a child who looks at the world with ordinary eyes. Breaca knows this and holds herself responsible.

It is this, I believe, as much as a premature effort to walk and to ride, that has set her into the fever that consumes her. She is beset by despair and there is no healing we can offer which will lift it. In the healing of her daughter is her own healing, and she knows it, but time is short: the legions already gather to invade Mona and in the east a war host gathers in her name, awaiting her leadership.

She is our hope; in her healing is the hope for the land. I leave you with the words of the long-dead ancestor dreamer who spoke to the Boudica in a cave on her first journey from Mona. They are as real now as they were then, and our future lies within them:

You are Eceni. It is your blood and your right and your duty. It is not too late to keep the children from weeping. Only find a way to give back to the people the heart and courage they have lost. Find a way to call forth the warriors and to arm them, find the warrior with the eyes and heart of a dreamer to lead them and you may prevail. At the last, find the mark that is ours and seek its place in your soul. Come to know it, and you *will* prevail.

PROLOGUE

A HAMMER, AN ANVIL, HOT IRON BEATEN BETWEEN. THE NOISE invaded her dying.

Nemain was close, a vague god-presence hazed in moonlight, felt but not seen. She said, 'Your brother makes you a serpent-spear. He believes it will hold you more strongly to life.'

Valerius; the lost brother of her childhood, returned to her changed beyond all measure. The sound carried his presence: a wild mix of despair and compassion together. There was more, but she was not able to read it. Even so, she did not want any gift that would hold her to life.

Breaca said, 'Am I not yet dead?' She spoke in her head, where only gods and the ghosts of the dead could hear her. The voice that might have reached the living had long since burned away in the fires of her fever.

The god was her mother, and then Airmid and then Graine. Their care encompassed her. It did not ease the pain of her body or her soul. As all three, the god said, 'You could be if you wished. Have you no reason to live?'

She wanted to say 'No', and could not. A single name sealed her lips, over and over.

Graine. Graine, Graine.

The anvil spoke it in the triple rhythm of making: a reason, the first and the best; the mark by which all else was measured. It came

15

as a gift from her brother. She drifted on the sound, and on memory, and the understanding of failure.

Nemain said, 'Your daughter's wounding is not your fault or your failure.'

'But can she be healed?'

'Perhaps. Nothing is certain. Would that be worth living for?'

'If you could promise it.'

She felt the light touch of a smile, and a kiss and the vagueness of presence, departing. The god's voice remained, hidden in the tap of the anvil.

'Nothing is certain except death, and the peace that it offers. War is coming, with the hope of victory. Is that alone not reason for life?'

Airmid came later, lover and dreamer, not god. She stood in a stippling of too-bright sunlight, bringing scents of rosemary and seaweed and lanolin and the touch of cool water and cooler hands that made the fever seem less.

She spoke to someone else, as if Breaca were asleep. Her voice carried over a quiet, where the ring of the anvil had ceased. 'If the flesh can't be made to cover the bone, then she will never wield a weapon again.' She was tired, and had been weeping, and was hiding both.

'Just now, I think we have more to worry about than weapons and their wielding.' Valerius spoke from the other side of the bed and it could have been another country and another language and another kind of grief. 'The legions flog men to punish, not to maim. This was done more savagely. It will take her longer to heal.'

'But she will heal?'

'I think so,' Valerius said. 'If she wants to badly enough.'

They left her soon after, these two who held her to life. The rhythm of the anvil began again. A hound remained, to lie by the bedside, and became two hounds that lay one on each side of the line between living and dying, so that she would have company whichever path she chose to follow.

I
SPRING AD 60

I

RAIN CLOUDS BRUISED THE LAST PALE OF THE SKY, LIT TO COPPER by the dying sun, and the ring of fires beneath.

Cunomar of the Eceni, only son to the Boudica, thrust a lit brand into the bundle of gorse and thorn and straw that lay close to the base of the legionary watchtower.

He waited, watching the clouds and the fire equally. A lifetime passed; time to be seen, for the alarm to be raised in the watchtower above, for a legionary standing on the ramparts to hurl a javelin into his unarmoured flesh, for a dozen of the enemy to burst from the gates with their blades unsheathed, seeking the life of the warrior who sought to burn them.

None of these things happened. He watched the nuggets of mutton fat wound in the centre of the thorn take light and flare, brightly. Three part-naked warriors ran in from his right and threw more bundles of fatted furze along the foot of the wall. Cunomar ran after them, lighting each one. He hurled the burning end of his brand into the heart of the last.

Straw and dry thorn blazed, belching greased smoke. He backed away, choking. Heat washed over him then, as if the need to succeed had kept him safe from the ravening power of the fire. Freed from that, he felt the skin of his forearms blister where burning tallow had sprayed onto them. The king-band on his arm grew dull in the heat and burned him.

'Cunomar! Here!'

He ran back into unseen shadows, blinded by the flames. Friendly hands caught his elbow and dragged him to shelter behind a short barrier of woven wicker palisades. Someone – Ulla, perhaps; she cared for him most closely – reached across to cover his head and shoulders with a cape of soaked rawhide, making sure not to touch the healing wound on the right side of his head where his ear had once been. Someone else passed him a scrap of wet wool and he pressed it over his mouth and nose. He tried to make his breathing shallow and could not; the run and the heat and the fire had taken that from him.

He breathed smoke and coughed again and was not the only one. His lungs ached. The bear grease about his torso and limbs became fluid in the heat. Battle marks in woad and white lime that spelled out his oath to the she-bear, to honour her in victory or die, smeared into meaningless swirls. His hair stood up like a cock's comb, a hand's length of stiff, white lime. He flexed his shoulders, and felt the heat equally on the old bear scars, cut with love by the elder dreamers of the Caledonii, and the new ones scourged by Rome. None of them matched the savage, perpetual ache at the side of his head where a hawk-scout of the Coritani in Roman pay had hacked off his ear.

Far faster than he had imagined, the flames engulfed the wood of the fort, except at the gates, where the timber was steaming, but had not yet lit. Following standing orders, the men of the XXth legion on watch inside had doused the gates with water before dusk. Even here, in the occupied east of Britannia, where there was supposed to be peace, the legions still protected their watchtowers nightly against fire.

Valerius had said they would do that, and that the men inside would be drunk because, orders not withstanding, the legionaries did not believe there was any risk of attack. He had said, too, that, drunk or not, they would still charge from the gates in a wedge as soon as the alarm was sounded.

Valerius knew too much and was too free with his opinions. On principle, Cunomar did not want him to be right.

He was thinking exactly that when the gates slammed open and the legionaries charged out. They were formed in a wedge, with their shields to the outside and wet leather draped about their heads as protection against fire and iron.

Cunomar's spear had already left his hand when the words he needed came to him. 'Go for their legs! Aim below the shields. Go!'

The night splintered apart. Two dozen greased, limed, howling bear-warriors threw down their wicker barriers and hurled their spears. Most aimed as they had been told and if they did not all hit flesh and bone, they caught amongst the ankles of men who stumbled into the night dazzled and deafened and drunk but still viciously able to fight.

'Break the wedge! Don't let them form a line!'

The battle rage had not yet come. Cunomar was intoxicated by heat and smoke and the heady release of action, but still able to think. He saw his second spear glance off the knee of the leading legionary. The man wore the helmet plumes of a junior officer but no leg greaves. Shocked, he looked up, drunk and sober at once. His eyes were black pits in a fire-red face. He was too young to be leading men alone.

His eyes barely changed as another spear struck him. He collapsed onto one knee, using his shield to push himself upright, and opened his mouth and shouted 'Hold the wedge!' and it was then, spurred by the angular grate of the Latin, that the bear took hold of Cunomar, filling his heart and his gut and his head with a vast, unstoppable fury, so that he no longer knew what he did, only that he needed to kill and to keep on killing until every thing of Rome had been broken apart and driven into the sea for ever.

He was of the she-bear; he ran to battle unshielded and un-armoured, fighting only with spear and knife. Bear grease was his armour, his rigid, white-limed hair his helmet. The king-band that encircled his arm marked him as the son of the Boudica, child of the royal line of the Eceni. His knife was a gift from his mother, made before the men of Rome had flogged her. He had made his first battle kills with it, in her company. As he had done then, he sought the song of the blade that he might bear a small part of the Boudica into battle.

Screaming her name, he smashed the cheek of the Roman officer with the knife's hilt, then stabbed at his eyes. The man's one good knee buckled. He crumpled to the bloody earth, too suddenly dead to cry out.

Exultant, Cunomar threw back his head and howled victory for the Boudica and the bear. If one of the enemy had struck him in that moment, he would have died. He knew it and did not care. He lived because the bear watched over him and was invincible. He shared a second kill with Ulla while there were still men alive to hunt and was sorry there were not more.

Afterwards, it was quiet, but for the spit and tumble of the fire.

Eight Roman legionaries and their officer had manned the watchtower, and all were dead. Of the two dozen she-bears who had attacked it, only Scerros, a red-haired youth of the northern Eceni, had taken any wound and that a shallow sword thrust to the thigh which would heal by the month's turn.

The enemy dead were stripped of their weapons and armour and their bodies fed to the fire. The flames reached up for the sky, bright as sun in the encroaching night. The heat was unbearable.

Cunomar walked back to the wicker palisades and began to stack them. From that distance, the fire was pleasantly warm, easing the transition to calm.

'It'll be seen.' Ulla spoke from the shadows to his right. Her kill had been first and cleanest, and she had visited the bodies of the slain afterwards, running her blade along each throat that the men might be assuredly dead before they were given to the fire.

Such an act was a mark of her care, or her hate; probably both. She, too, had been flogged by Rome, with Scerros and three others. These five made the tight, unyielding kernel of Cunomar's honour guard, and if Rome had had the choosing of them, still, he was glad of the choices. Nearly a month had passed since and they were recovered enough to move and to fight, but the scars would never go, nor the patina of otherness that set them apart even within the she-bear, which was already set apart from the greater mass of the Boudica's gathering war host.

Ulla was dark-haired and bright-eyed and she killed as a hawk does, with a fluid, savage beauty. She joined Cunomar in stacking the wicker barriers in a heap.

'The fire will be seen,' she said again. 'If a single sentry of the Twentieth is awake and even half sober in any of the other watch-towers, they'll light the signal chain and the whole of Camulodunum will know by morning there has been death in the Eceni lands.'

Cunomar hefted the topmost palisade, testing its weight. 'I would think so,' he agreed. 'Valerius said as much.'

Ulla met him face on, her lips set straight. 'He said it as a warning, not an invitation,' she said. 'He thinks we are not yet ready to take on the legions.'

'I know. I think he's wrong. Soon, we will learn which of us is right.' Cunomar hurled the wicker onto the flames. The fire coughed and stuttered and flared higher and brighter. He stepped back, smiling.

'Perhaps if we throw enough of these on,' he said, 'it may be that we can make the flames reach the clouds. However drunk they are, Rome's watchmen will find it hard not to notice that.'

Ulla was the closest of his honour guard, his sworn shield in battle; she had never yet argued against him. With the four others who had bound themselves closest to the Boudica's son, she helped him to throw the wicker onto the fire.

Before the last of the wood was alight, a pinpoint of flame blossomed to the south and west. For a moment it looked fragile, a dandelion puff fluttering in the wind. Cunomar turned to face it fully and spoke aloud the first eight names of the she-bear as he had been taught them in the caves of the Caledonii.

The night vibrated, richly. At the sound, the distant flame strengthened and held, and was joined, presently, by seven others, strung out over half a night's ride in a line that led directly south to the veterans' colony of Camulodunum, Rome's first city in its occupied province of Britannia.

II

T HE FEVER BROKE AT DUSK ON ITS TWELFTH DAY.
    Breaca woke to the smell of smoke and the quiet of an
    empty hut. The fire lay dead in its hearth and the sweat was
cold on the horsehides beneath her.

Her face was creased in a pattern of ridges. She moved and then
did not move, but simply breathed, because nothing else was
possible while the pain consumed her: great, mountainous, pounding, waves that crushed everything else to nothing.

The fever had been a gift, she had known that even at its height.
She tried to fall back into its oblivion and could not; the day was
too sharp and too present and her body would not let her go.

Other things made themselves felt.

Her feet were cold, that was the first thing, and the palms of her
hands too hot. Woven wool covered her, and paste had been
smeared over the worst parts of her back so that she felt the tickle
of the blanket through crusted remnants of dock leaf and
powdered clay. Her hair was not plastered to her face as it had
been when she last paid it any attention; someone had combed it
with care, and braided it back from her face, so that there was a
tightness at her temples and across her head. Airmid had done that;
the touch of her care was still there in the patterns of weaving.

Breaca had no memory of the paste, or the blankets, or the
combing of her hair. Her memories began and ended with Graine,

and the sounds of her screaming, and the brutal finality of the moment when it had stopped.

Your daughter's wounding is not your fault or your failure.

So the god had said. Breaca did not have to believe it.

On the third remembering, or perhaps the fourth, when the shock of the sudden silence was less, she realized that she could no longer hear the anvil, and that she had moved twice now, and no-one had leaned over to offer her a beaker of water and ask if she needed help to drink.

Confused, she stretched her mind beyond the confines of her body for the first time in days. Sage smoke drifted light on the air but the scent was old, with its sharpness long gone. The fire was dull and white ash lay cold on its surface. No-one sat with their back to the wall, ready to lay the small heaps of apple wood and pine chips onto the embers, to cleanse and clear the staleness of the room.

No-one was waiting, either, to change the wads of uncombed wool that had been propped under her armpits to keep her still in the turbulence of the fever, or to lift her head with quiet hands to offer her water and help her void urine into the clay pot that lay empty by the bed, or to kiss her, and smooth paste on her back and speak to her of the growing spring and the new foals in the paddocks and the whelps fathered by Stone newly born in the great-house and how the war host was in training, ready for her return.

She waited a while, and then turned her head and so found that she was, indeed, alone, without either the god or Airmid watching over her for the first time since the fever began.

The shock of that left her numb for a moment, like a plunge into cold water in summer. After, coming to herself again, she began to weep, slowly and silently at first, then later in great, heaving sobs, and the release of it, and the knowing that her grief was no burden to anyone, was as overwhelming as the pain had been, and made it less.

After that, she needed water, and so sat up, and drank on her own account from the beaker that was left by the bed. The water was cool and tasted of nothing more than the river, which was as telling in its own way as the silence.

It was a long time since she had drunk anything that was not laced with something bitter from Airmid's stocks, leavened with a little honey to disguise the taste. Those who cared for her, therefore, had known the fever was ending and had left her alone to find for herself the limits of what she could do. For that care, she wept again, briefly.

She lay back, and stared up into the reeds of the roof thatch and began systematically to take the measure of her life.

Am I not yet dead?

She was not. The gods wished her to live; she must, therefore, strive to do so, and to fight, if that were required of her, and to care for those whom she had loved, and did still, and all of this must be done amidst the despair of Graine's wounding, with no promise from the god that it would end.

But she will heal? Airmid had asked, and Valerius, in his wisdom, had answered, *If she wants to badly enough.*

To want to heal, one must first have a passion for life, and her passion was Graine, who was broken.

She faced the bleak prospect of a life without the fire that had always sustained her. Weakness said it was better to be dead than that, or at least lost again in the fever, but she was the Boudica and a war host gathered in her name. Five thousand warriors waited daily for news that she had risen and had taken up the serpent-spear her brother had made for her, and was ready to lead them to victory after victory against Rome.

She wept again, quietly, for the burden of that, and then drank and set herself to finding how she might manage this new life with all its limitations.

She was not without courage and with courage came a pragmatism that said she was surrounded by those who were fit and able and had not lost their passion for life and so it was not necessary fully to heal, only to be well enough to rise, and fight and lead the warriors, at least in name. That was as much as could be expected of her, and was enough.

Before all of that, there was a blade she must find which had been hidden, and before that, before anything else, she needed to find Graine, wounded child of her soul, and speak to her and hold her and find out if there was anything about her that could be mended.

Breaca put her fingers to her face. With care, she rubbed the crusted matter from the corners of her eyes. An early moon cast long angled spears of light through the part-open door of the hut. Silver splashed on her, and on the chestnut horsehide that pillowed her cheek, with its dribbles of old saliva and the crusting of white hairs.

She took a breath, and hissed it out, slowly. The pain was not unmanageable; nor, if she were careful, was the fractured gap in her soul.

On the second breath, for the first time in very much too long, Breaca of the Eceni, once of Mona, known to her world as the Boudica, bringer of victory, levered herself out of bed, put on her tunic, and went in search of the child whom Rome had broken.

'You can walk.'

The hut to which Graine had been moved was so new that the reed thatching the roof had not yet seen rain and shone dully green, like the hide of a frog. A low fire outside hazed the last of the evening light and cast dusty shadows on the clayed wicker of the walls.

Inside, Graine lay on a pile of sheepskins near the side wall, one hand flung loose over the blanket, sweatily hot. Dark, ox-blood hair lying in straggled knots about her head told its own tale of restless sleep. The bruises on her face and neck were not as marked as they had been when last Breaca had seen her. That had been in daylight, and the bruises had been muddy green puddles against the strained white of her face. They were less now in the kind, grey light of evening.

Carefully, Breaca eased herself down to sit on the edge of the hides. Stone, the crippled war hound who had been waiting outside the door to her sickhut, lay down with the same breath-held care near the bed, in a place where both mother and daughter might reach him.

Breaca said, 'I can walk, yes. It doesn't mean I can fight, but it's a start.' Here, in Graine's company, it was possible to acknowledge openly the mountain yet to be climbed. 'Can you?'

'I don't know.' Graine looked down at Stone. She combed her fingers through his ruff, teasing the hair straight and scrunching it up again. She said, 'Hawk won't let me go farther than the stream. He listens to Airmid and she says I shouldn't. She thinks that if I

27

sleep, I might dream, and that if I get up and walk about, it will stop me from sleeping. I think she's wrong.'

'Do you? She isn't often.' Breaca reached over and swept her daughter's hair out of her eyes. 'Is Hawk the Coritani scout who is sitting outside your door with his blade naked on his knees? The one who cut off Cunomar's ear?'

She had seen him and not thought much of it except that he still had both of his ears, which was surprising. She had thought the she-bear had cut them off in vengeance for Cunomar. Sometime in the fever, she was sure she had heard that was about to happen.

The youth had watched her walk into the hut and said nothing, only nodded to acknowledge her presence, and all that it meant. The shadow of a blood blister showed on his lower lip where Valerius had marked him with a knife, but he still had the easy, almost arrogant beauty that had been so evident when he served the Roman procurator. That had not changed, nor the blue lizard marks that crawled up the sculpted muscles of both arms as evidence of his clan ties and vows of vengeance to the ghost of his father.

Breaca had killed his father. Hawk had cut off Cunomar's ear and, later, had a part in delivering Graine to the hands of the procurator. She had no idea if those things balanced each other in his eyes or not.

Graine said, 'Yes. He and Dubornos both think they are to blame for . . . what happened.' The words came doggedly, one after another. 'They take turns to keep watch on me.'

Two men keeping watch over a child who had been raped by half a century of men. Whoever they were, however guilt-ridden or oath-sworn, Airmid should have stopped that. Breaca took her daughter's hand and turned it over, studying the bitten nails and the bony fingers and the marble-white skin with the veins running thinly beneath.

There was nothing to be read there. She folded the fingers closed and studied the lines of Graine's face instead. Grey eyes, the colour of clouds after rain, stared back at her, unblinking.

'Do you trust Hawk?' she asked.

'Yes. He has sworn to protect me, my life for his, as if I were his sister. He did it kneeling with his blade across his hands, before Valerius and Airmid and Gunovar of the Dumnonii who was tortured by Rome. They're all still dreamers and they all believed him. Why should I not?'

They're all still dreamers.

Such a barren phrase, so calmly spoken, so final. The small hands lay calm on the hound, held by an effort of will. Lifting one, Breaca kissed the blue-veined wrist, feeling the pulse run taut under her lips.

She was lost, searching for a way to mend the unmendable, when Graine said, 'Do you still wish the gods would take you from life?' It came as a whisper, so faint it could barely be heard.

'I didn't—'

'You did. I heard you say it to Airmid. That was before they knew you had a fever and moved me out of your hut.' The grey eyes were very wide. The self-control by which Graine had kept her hands still was abandoned now. Small fingers gripped Breaca's wrists, careless of the places where Roman cords had cut flesh. Their pressure grew with each word. 'It wasn't your fault.'

So Nemain had said. It came no easier from the living than from a god.

They waited, mother and daughter, in a place neither of them had thought to reach so soon or with so little warning.

Words would not come. Breaca eased her hands free and opened her arms, and Graine came to her with a small, wordless cry. They clung together as mariners drowning in a storm neither has foreseen.

Breaca pressed her lips to the crown of her daughter's head and blew gently down, sending her breath to ease away the hurt as she had always done when the child was sick, or had lost something precious. It was not enough, but it gave comfort to them both.

When she could speak, Breaca said, 'Will you let me believe that I could have protected you better? Or sent you away sooner? Or simply that, as a mother, I should have the power to change the world and my heart breaks for knowing that I don't?'

'You can still change the world. The war host is waiting for you to do exactly that.' The words came muffled and were sent straight into her chest.

'I know. And perhaps when the warriors are ready, I will be ready also. In the meantime, there's something else that must be done first. Valerius found my sword, the one my father made for me with the serpent-spear on the hilt. If I'm ever going to be able to fight again, it will be with that blade. He hid it in the woods the day he came to stop the procurator. I want to go out now and find it. If Airmid is wrong and sleeping will not heal your dreaming, would you come with me instead?'

The look on her daughter's face was enough. Breaca reached for the tunic that lay at the bedside. A thought gave her pause. 'Will Hawk let you get up if I ask him?'

For the first time, Graine's smile held some warmth in it, and the knowing of a child who sees things her mother does not. With exaggerated patience, she said, 'Hawk's only alive because you told Ardacos not to let anyone kill him. The she-bears would have slain him otherwise, or at least taken both of his ears. He owes you his life and his beauty and knows it. For the rest of his life, he'll do whatever you ask of him.'

'Then I'll tell him where we're going so he can tell Airmid and Valerius. We'll have to leave Stone; he isn't well enough to run beside a horse yet. Can you ask him to stay, do you think, so we don't have to tie him to the doorpost?'

III

THE HORSE PADDOCKS LAY TO THE WEST, A SHIFTING OF PURPLED
silhouettes, soft-edged in the dusk. Gorse hedges in early
flower circled the margins, showing flashes of acid yellow
amidst the greys. A wicker gate opened in one corner and a rope
halter hung on a hook beside it. A trio of long-legged fillies waited
there, huffing white breath into the dusk.

Breaca moved them back and slid the halter instead onto a solid
dun cob that had been her gift to Graine in the autumn before
'Tagos' death. It was the steadiest horse she had ever seen under
saddle, entirely safe for a horse-shy child who was lost riding the
battle mounts of her family. It remained steady at the mounting
stone while she lifted Graine up, then caught a fistful of coarse
black mane and hauled herself on behind.

They rode due west at a steady walk, into the setting sun. Breaca
held one arm round her daughter's waist, mourning the skeletal
thinness of a child who had never been warrior-fit, but had always
been healthy. The small head rested on her breastbone and she felt
her own heart rebound against the weight of her daughter's skull.

They had passed beyond the margins of the paddocks when
Graine said, 'We need to turn a little north of here, and go faster,
or we'll be lost in the dark.'

'Do we? I'm not sure I can ride any faster than this.'

A fragment of conversation, overheard, sounded again in her

ears. *Riding a horse after a flogging is not as hard as walking, and both are better than lying in bed.*

She had overheard Valerius say that to Cunomar, or Ardacos perhaps. He knew these things. He had been flogged more than once and had ordered it done to other men, and helped them heal afterwards.

On the strength of that, she nudged the cob into a canter. Three paces later, she stopped. Her brother was right in part; it was easier to ride than to walk. It was not easier to ride fast.

Tactfully, Graine said, 'It might be all right to go slowly.'

'I think so. Perhaps later, we can try going faster again.' Breaca quickened the walk, and turned a little north. Presently, she said, 'How do you know where we're going?'

'I was in your hut still when Valerius told you how the god came to him in the shape of the bull with the moon between its horns to guide him to where your blade was hidden, and how he had hidden it again himself afterwards, before he came here. You got out of bed before he'd finished speaking, and asked him to lend you his horse. You fell off and they brought you back and that was when the fever began and they thought you were going to die.'

'Is it? I'd forgotten that. I thought it was a fever-dream.'

'But you remember now?'

'I do, yes. Thank you.'

Already, the sun was a red nail paring on the horizon. Streaks of bloody light leaked into the uncolour of the night. Graine's hair was liquidly black, framing her face. The path along which they rode grew harder to see with each passing footfall, but never quite impossible.

They came eventually to an oval clearing surrounded by a clutch of hawthorn and hazel that had been coppiced at the edges and left to grow wild in its heart, for the gods of the ancestors, and all who followed after them. Deer tracks led through to the centre, narrowly, so that thorns tugged Breaca's tunic away from the ruined flesh on her back. Riding was still better than walking, but less so.

The dun cob stopped alongside a fallen oak. Breaca dismounted onto it. Her feet sank into rotting wood and the smell rose up around her, pleasantly mellow. She lifted Graine down and let her lead on, following the fine line of a path. From a little ahead, where clustering hawthorns snagged the light, Graine said, 'There's a stream here, about half a spear's length wide. Can we jump it?'

So small a thing to give them pause. A month before, either one would have crossed without stopping to think. Breaca stood at the stream's edge listening to the curdling water and wondered if Valerius had sent her this way deliberately as a test. In his own way, he was as hard as the ancestor dreamer.

From her side, Graine said, 'Airmid has always said that the gods answer certainty, not fear.'

Breaca made herself smile. 'Did I seem fearful? I'm sorry. I was wondering whether you wanted to jump with me or for me to carry you over. It might be easier to wade through.' That much was easy to imagine; the stream was not deep.

'No. I want to jump it, to know that I can.' Graine was already shifting her weight from one foot to the other, as if the distance from one bank to the other were three times as wide. 'I'll go on my own,' she said, and did so, unprettily, landing in a sprawl on the far side.

Breaca followed, having no choice. Breathing carefully, she crouched by her daughter. Graine was pale and her fists clenched tight. Breaca said, 'Are you hurting?'

'No.' The lie was not to be challenged. Frowning, Graine looked up through the trees to where the full moon made sharp silhouettes of the branches. She said, 'We should go quickly. The clouds will cover the moon by midnight.'

'You should lead, then. You can remember what Valerius said better than I can.'

The woods were quiet, as if their presence were unusual, and something to be watched. They walked a while along the water's edge and then cut inward, following a track through the thickening jumble of undergrowth to another, far older, clearing where ancient trees hung with scabs of lichen formed the margins. Here, the stream spread to become a small pool and a hazel grew up from the bank, dipping branches downwards to trail long-twigged fingers across the water.

Breaca caught hold of Graine's hand and skirted the pool to stand in the moon shadow of the hazel. The stream ran in slowly, filtered through sphagnum moss. The surface of the water was a languid mirror reflecting the tree and the night sky. The moon made an unbroken circle with the hare on its surface so complete as to be alive: creature of Nemain, made real on the water that was her domain.

Coming new to such a place, Breaca dared to hope; a dreamer could see the breath of the gods in a pool such as this, or a violated child, perhaps, who had lost her dreaming.

Because she knew her daughter very well, she felt the moment when exactly that thought occurred also to Graine. She felt the same hope, sharper and less curtailed, course through the small frame, and then the desperate, damaging disappointment at the recoil just after. She opened her mouth to speak and found no words and looked down at the child's blank mask of a face and was glad she had kept silent.

Graine found her own way out. The small, sweaty hand tightened in Breaca's, drawing her away from the water's edge. She said, 'The flat stone Valerius spoke of is nine paces west of the gods' tree. You'll have to make the strides. Mine are not long enough.'

'Come with me. You can count as we go.'

Counting aloud, they paced away from the pool towards the trees at the far edge of the clearing. Halfway between water and wood, they stopped. Dead leaves lay in flurries at their feet. Breaca knelt and swept them aside with the edge of her hand. Underneath, a flat plate of green-grey moss, longer than a man's arm and half as wide, showed where a stone lay flush with turf.

A winter's leaving of silt bound the edges to the earth on all sides. Valerius had said that he used his sword blade to lift it. Lacking a sword, Breaca slid her belt knife all the way round. Iron grated on stone but the gap was still not enough to hook in her fingers. She looked around for something else to act as a lever.

Graine, squatting beside her, picked at a corner of the moss. 'There's a carving on the stone's face,' she said.

'Is there?' A hawthorn branch lay nearby, split from the parent tree by winter storms and still green enough to be strong. Breaca hefted it and set her blade to sharpen the wider end. 'Can you clear the moss and see what it looks like?'

She whittled at the end of the stake until the density of her daughter's silence drew her back. Lifting her head, she said, 'Beloved, what have you found?'

'It's an altar, an old one, from the time of the ancestors.'

She should have known. Around them, a wood lay silent when it should have been most filled with life. A river whispered into the gods' pool and out again, leaving the surface undisturbed. Black as a hare's eye, as flawless and pure, the water caught the moon and held it fast in a ring of trees so ancient, so clearly god-filled, they had resisted even the Roman axes in a land starved of wood.

Slowly, carefully, Breaca laid her part-carved hawthorn branch on the grass. The hairs on her arms stood erect, pulling gooseflesh in their wake.

'Should we leave?' she asked. 'I think I can find a quicker way back to where we left your pony, one that doesn't take us past the pool.'

Her daughter shook her head. 'I don't think we need to do that. Come and look at the carving.'

Graine's fingernails were black. Moss lay in broken handfuls on the turf. The stone that had held it was gritty with mud and earth, smeared into arcs where a small hand had tried to scrub it clear and had instead forced the loam into the depths of the markings so that the shape carved on it stood out as if newly painted.

There, facing Breaca in the middle of the gods' wood, was the symbol that had followed her from childhood through all the disparate parts of her adulthood, as Warrior of Mona, as the Boudica, co-leader of the western tribes with Caradoc, as Breaca of Mona and, later, of the Eceni, as Breaca, mother to her children, as the Boudica, un-leader of a gathering war host. Through all of these the serpent-spear had been her mark. It came to her again now, on a moss-covered stone, in a form that was entirely new.

Kneeling, she traced a finger along its lines. A two-headed serpent looped back on itself, staring to past and future. A crooked spear lay angled across, joining the gods to the earth. Beyond it, the twin-headed serpent and the spear that crossed it were encircled by the most ancient of the gods' marks: a zigzag line with moon dots above and below that staked a claim to this one sign and made it far more than simply the mark of a god-gifted warrior, or even the dream of an ancestor, however ancient and wise.

Hoarsely, Breaca said, 'This is Briga's. The mark and the altar, both.'

She sat back on her heels. Pain and the crossing of rivers was forgotten. Her hawthorn stake lay untouched by her side. For years, she had believed the mark her own, a gift of the elder grandmother, and had painted it on her shield and on her horses in battle so that it had become one with the Boudica's name. Only later, in the year of Graine's birth, had she found that it had belonged to the ancestor-dreamer long before that.

It should have come as no surprise that, before all the others, it had belonged to Briga, mother to all the gods, holder of life and death, god of battles, of childbirth, of the smith's craft, of poetry; the god who lived as the serpent did, on the cusp of life and death, bringing one into the other, as the spear did in battle, as the serpent did, easing from one skin to the next, and one life to the next, leaving the ghost-shape of the old behind.

As a warrior, as a mother, as a smith, Breaca had lived her life in Briga's care. Even so, she had not expected to be so closely bound; a dreamer might be so, but she was not that.

She hissed air through her teeth. 'We should leave.'

'No.' Graine came round to sit beside her, taking her hand. 'Valerius has trained on Mona with Luain mac Calma and spent his long-nights in the dreaming chambers of Hibernia; he will have known what this was and he didn't think it was unsafe when he needed a place to hide your blade. I think you should lift the stone.'

The carved end of the hawthorn stake lay greenly white in the moonlight. Breaca jammed it under the long edge of the stone and used the hilt of her knife laid on the earth as a lever. Resisting at first and then easier, Briga's altar stone rose from the earth.

Mother and daughter worked together to free it. Graine stood on the end of the stake and Breaca moved to the far side to pull up on the long edge, straining lacerated muscles against the dead weight until it rose past the point where the earth drew it downwards and she could set it on end, balanced against the heel of her hand.

Underneath, a black cavity gaped. The air that leaked out was damp and earthen and sharp with the tang of forged iron. Graine lay prone on the earth and reached in as far as she dared, and came out with her hands full, and again, and again. One after the other, she drew out five long, slim bundles, each bound about with oiled linen and rolled birch bark and thongs made of red bull's hide. She laid them out in a line across the turf. A smear of mud marked her temple, the kiss of the god.

The closeness of the iron was dizzying, the smell of rust and raw metal and the songs of making and battle that were in it. Breaca leaned the altar stone against her knee and reached down to untie the bull's hide thongs that bound the bundle that was hers. The oiled linen was not yet stiff or mildewed by its time in the earth. It curled away in her fingers, laying a hand's breadth of bright iron open to the moon.

She needed two hands free. She lowered the altar stone to the earth. With the same quality of care she would have shown Graine in infancy, she peeled the rest of the linen from the blade that her father had made; his gift for the child-become-woman who was his daughter.

Eburovic had forged the iron and beaten it out over days, matching the length and weight to the woman she would be. Later, he had cast the serpent-spear in bronze for the pommel, knowing nothing more of it than that Breaca had seen the mark in the dreaming of her long-nights, and that it should be on her blade.

The sword that Briga's mark adorned was older than any of the Boudica's children, or any of her loves except Airmid, who had always been first. Breaca had borne it in battle for almost twenty years until it became a part of her, as necessary as the muscle and sinew and bone of her body.

It came to her hand like a live thing, keening. The scar on her palm itched and then burned and she welcomed the pain as she would have welcomed the soft bite of a lover; something sharp and familiar that promised more if she could meet and match it.

She was not at all sure that she could. The passion that was missing from her healing was exactly the part of her that had once most yearned to fight. Even now, she feared knowing the full measure of what was lost.

From her place by the altar stone, Graine said, 'The gods answer certainty, not fear.'

Breaca stood, letting her hand hang by her side with the weight of the blade drawing her arm down and out. She rolled her shoulders, loosening them. Then, under Nemain's moon, beside an altar to Briga, who ruled battle and death, with only her daughter as witness, Breaca of the Eceni, bringer of victory to her people, set out to test the true limits of what she could do.

Afterwards, she could not have said exactly when she became aware that more eyes than Graine's were watching her, only that there had been a sense of emptiness that was the gods' watching, which became less empty, so that she did what she could to stretch further, and sweep more cleanly, and pushed her breathing and her broken body beyond what she had already done.

Even so, there came a time when it was necessary to stop. She made the last block and strike and counter-strike and let the blade's tip fall slowly to touch the loamy earth.

Facing the place where the less-emptiness waited, she said, 'If I am not fit to lead the war host, will you do it in my place?'

It had been a guess and a risk in the asking and there was a long, sweating wait before she was proved right.

'It hasn't come to that,' said her brother. 'We have no need to discuss it.'

Her brother, Valerius, officer of the Roman cavalry, who had once been Bán of the Eceni. Her last clear memory of him was from the ground, as he sat the horse he called Crow and spoke in coruscating Latin to the Roman procurator who lay between its feet. Moments later, he had slain the man with the horse. Half of her fevered dreams had been of the implacable rage of that killing.

He stood now in the quiet light of the clearing and she looked at him properly for the first time. He was taller than she remembered, and leaner, but not as gaunt as he had been on the boat from Gaul, when she had wanted to kill him. His hair was long for a Roman, but short for Eceni, and he had not woven in the warrior's braid at the side as he might have done. He wore an Eceni cloak over a Roman tunic and the blade at his belt was of his own making, shorter and slimmer than the great-blade of the Eceni warrior but longer than the auxiliary cavalry swords of his legionary past.

His eyes were black, as they had always been, but far less troubled. He was a man caught on the dividing line between two worlds and he did not look badly for it. She remembered that he was given to Mithras, hidden god of the legions, as well as to Nemain.

The pain in her back was less now. She lifted her blade. 'Will you match against me? So that I can find how I might live, or die, in battle?'

It was a fanciful offer, only half serious. Valerius threw her a grin that was layered with too many meanings to be read. His blade came fast after it, before she was ready.

She swung her own blade up to block and braced herself for the pain of impact, but he was already gone, the iron flashing blue in the moonlight, a twisting fish that tapped her own sluggard sword and danced away, and tapped and away and again and again, fast and fast and too fast to follow, until she forgot herself and her pain and raised her own blade in both fists and brought it cleaving down towards his head, screaming his name as if they were in battle.

'*Valerius!*'

He did block that one, hard, slamming his blade crosswise against hers so that the jar ran from her wrists to her arms to her shoulders and on to the ruined flesh of her back. She stopped abruptly and was still, grinding her teeth and swearing aloud. Sweat poured from her as much as it had done in the fever. The sound of her breathing rasped between the trees.

'And so?'

Breaca lifted her head. Her brother was breathing a little faster than he had been, but had not broken sweat. He studied her and said nothing, only cocked one brow, dryly.

'If you can remember never to lift your blade like that without a shield-warrior on either side to protect your flanks, you will be perfectly able to lead. If you forget, then the first raw recruit with a javelin will run you through and our war of liberation will be over before it starts. Can you remember, do you think?'

'Maybe. If there's nothing else happening that might distract me. Which doesn't change the fact that I'm not yet fit enough to lead any army into battle. You're more than fit. You know Rome as no-one else does and you have led more men to victory than anyone else. You're the obvious choice.'

'Am I?' Valerius sat down suddenly, folding his legs beneath him. Turning towards the gods' pool, he said, 'Graine? We have nearly five thousand untested warriors who have gathered in the Boudica's name. Do you think I should lead them if your mother is not fit? What would your brother Cunomar say if I did?'

Breaca watched her daughter step over and sit beside him with an air of confidence and ease, as if she saw in him only the dreamer of Nemain, trained on Mona, and not the other, equal half, which was Roman.

Graine said, 'Cunomar remembers the prophecy the ancestor-dreamer made to mother. *Find the warrior with the eyes and heart of a dreamer to lead them and you may prevail.* The vision showed a warrior leading the final charge against Rome. My brother wants to be that warrior. He always has. Then you came and were not only the man who abandoned his father in Gaul, but now a warrior and a dreamer and brother to the Boudica – and you saved his life. He owes you everything and you are all he has ever wanted to be. How can he not hate you? Hating you, how could he follow you as leader?'

Valerius looked up. The irony and the humour were gone. 'Breaca?'

She took time to slide her blade back to its sheath and wrap the belt loops round it. 'I had forgotten that. I'm sorry. It seems I have forgotten a great many things that matter.' Her hands and the sword's hilt were greasy with sweat. She wiped the serpent-spear with the sleeve of her tunic, so that the metal returned to the dull matt her father had made.

After a while, when no-one had spoken to fill the silence, Valerius rose and went to kneel by the altar stone, and the hole that was under it. He leaned in as Graine had done, so that the upper half of his body was hidden, but delved deeper, digging his fingers through the earth in the floor of the pit that Graine had found.

He emerged some time later and sat still with his head bowed over the slim wrapping of birch and bull's hide that he had brought out. His hound was visible by his side then, and remained so afterwards through all that followed; the dream-hound that had been Hail and was still Hail, but no longer living.

'Could you come with me closer to the pool?' he said. 'I would have Nemain also bear witness to this.'

Breaca was still lost in the memories of Cunomar and his ambition. Even as she sat down and Valerius began to unwrap the thongs of the bull, sacred to Mithras and the birch, sacred to Nemain, she still had no idea what it was that he held.

Then he smoothed the linen flat and sat back and a new, quite different blade lay in the moonlight: her father's. Not the fast, light cavalry blade that he had made for her, but Eburovic's own sword, the great war blade of their ancestors, which had come to him down the lineage of warriors, passed from father to daughter and mother to son since the Eceni first came into being.

It was longer than her own sword by a hand's length, and broader at the hilt, and the balance was different: not an easy blade to use, but lethal in the right hands. The shape on the pommel was the feeding she-bear that had been Eburovic's dream long before Ardacos of the Caledonii brought the cult of the bear from the cold north to the eastern lands of the Eceni.

Breaca stared at it, empty. She wanted to feel something and could not, only thought that she had heard nothing to warn her, neither the song of the blade nor her father's voice, and both should have been there.

She said, 'Valerius? How did you come by this? It was hidden beyond any man's reach.'

'Eburovic led me to it. That is, his ghost did, and I had not time to ask . . . when did he die, Breaca? In the invasion wars, with Macha?'

'He was killed in the battle in which you were taken from us.'

She had forgotten that he would not know, that so much of his own history was missing from his life. She watched him take this fact, and fit it into the pattern of his loss.

More gently, she said, 'Has he given the war blade of the ancestors to you? That would be fitting. He raised you as his son, and felt for you as if you were. With that blade, you could lead the war host and be honoured for it.'

'Thank you, but no. The blade and the leadership that goes with it are, I think, for another.'

He stared out a moment at the moon's disc on the pond, and pressed the knuckle of his thumb to his breast bone. Quite close, an owlet screeched for its parents, and was answered.

Valerius said, 'The spirit of your father – of our father – gave the blade into my keeping only until such time as he should ask me to relinquish it. He has given no sign yet of whose it should be, but we're moving towards war which will take us away from Eceni lands. If we leave it buried here, we may never come back. I think it's time it had a new owner, who knows how to use it, and has the right. I don't want to lead your war host. With this blade as his gift, Cunomar may yet grow into the leadership of—'

'No.'

Graine and Breaca said it together, with one voice.

The owl chick screeched again, in underscore.

In the quiet afterwards, Valerius asked, 'Why not?'

'*If my grandchild ever wields my blade, know that the death of the Eceni will follow. I trust you to see it does not happen.*'

Breaca had not meant to say it with the voice of her father, but it came out so, echoing across the gods' pool.

In her own voice, she said, 'Eburovic's spirit spoke when we hid the blades. Cunomar was there; he heard it as clearly as any of us. One source of his grief is that he will never wield his grandfather's blade. If you tried to give it to him, he would refuse it.'

'And likely think I was trying to bring ruin on the entire Eceni nation, which would hardly improve his trust of me. I see.' Valerius pressed long, lean fingers to his eyes. Some time later, hollowly, he said, 'I have no sense, then, of what your father would have wanted. I can hear no word from him or the gods, except that we need to wait until his wish is made more clear. In the meantime . . .'

His hands had dropped from his face. His eyes were oddly amber. In quite a different voice he said, 'In the meantime, there may be more pressing things to consider and we may no longer be alive to consider them. There are fires lit in the east.'

Breaca turned as he had turned and looked at the place where the moon had been and where should now be black night and was instead pale, flickering light reflected off a boiling sky.

Dawn had come early, many dawns; she could count four smaller fires beyond the first and the greatest, four columns of smoke, which became white and black in steady rhythm.

She said, 'Cunomar,' because no-one else would, and then, 'He's attacked one of the watchtowers and set off a signal chain.'

Valerius said, 'He was forbidden to attack either the Ninth in the north or the city of Camulodunum to the south. We had not thought he would bring both on us at once.'

Very briefly, her brother was quite easily read: raw anger was followed by frustration and both gave way to the wry, dry humour that was his response to most things, except that, this time, a hint of astonished admiration coloured it.

Valerius whistled slowly, and ran his tongue across his teeth. To Breaca, thoughtfully, he said, 'We can't afford to be caught between the hammer of the Ninth and the anvil of Camulodunum. But the centurion in charge in the city has just lost three cohorts of fighting men to the western wars; he won't try to march his veterans out against us until he knows what it is he faces. What he will do, as soon as there's daylight, is send messengers north with all speed to the Ninth legion asking that they march down to assault us from the rear. If we can intercept them, there's a way we could yet make a victory of this.' His gaze took in all of her. 'Could you do that?'

'No.' The sweat was still wet on her face from their fight. 'We've spoken of this already. I can't ride a horse faster than a walk or wield a blade for the time it would take to fight a full battle. I'm not fit to lead the war host into conflict.'

'I know. But I have an idea, and if it can be made to work, there won't be a full battle. All you have to do is kill a messenger in front of the war host so that they can believe they've seen you fight. I'll be there, I'll call him in and, if necessary, I'll hold him for you. Will you trust me to do that much and keep you safe?'

He asked it lightly, this brother she had once tried to kill. He had not done so before, only offered her his service until the end of his days. There was doubt in his eyes that she had not seen before.

Breaca took his hands between her own. Close by, the owls hunted and a shrew died, shrilly. With no irony intended at all, she said, 'Valerius of the Eceni, I trust you with my life.'

I V

VALERIUS STOPPED THE MESSENGER. BREACA KILLED HIM.
Sedge grass swayed over the dead man's face, pushed by
the dawn wind. A skein of geese mourned him thinly,
forlorn echoes strung across the grey sky. Where he lay at the edge
of the marsh, the air was fresh with spring and the hope of
freedom. To the east where the watchtowers smouldered, greasy
smoke stained the skyline, delivering the smell of charred bodies
onto the wind.

Valerius lowered the body down from the horse, taking care not
to break the seal on the message pouch. The messenger had been
young and his face held no fear; he had believed Valerius a friend,
for the red cloak that he wore and the officer's plume in his helmet
and his easy, urbane, soldier's Latin that had offered security and a
better route past the wet fenland with the marsh to one side and
forest to the other and only an open unprotected pathway for a
man alone to ride through.

He had been terrified because all five of his companions had died
to Dubornos' slingstones and Ardacos' bear-spears and he was
alone and in need of a friendly face. Calling his welcome and his
relief, he had not known death was close until it claimed him. His
soul had departed quickly, called to freedom by the cries of the
geese.

Behind, nearly five thousand warriors of the Eceni, with a

44

smattering of others from as far north as the Caledonii and as far south as the Durotriges, stepped out of the forest. Their line extended from the marsh to the far horizon, a glitter of bright blades and spears and round, painted shields and the occasional shimmer of cavalry mail or legionary armour, stolen from other dead men of Rome.

They were as diverse as any group of warriors: their hair was red gold and bronze, with the occasional dark throwback to the ancestors, and braided high at the temple and left without ornament to show they had not yet killed in battle. Very few wore helmets; the Boudica did not, and never had done, and they had gathered in her name, answering her call, holding fast to the belief in her immortality, even when the rumours spread of her sickness and closeness to death.

She was not dead. She had killed a man cleanly in sight of them all, reversing in a single stroke their waning hope of the past thirteen days. That stroke may have lacked the brilliance that had always set the Boudica apart from the greater mass of warriors, but there were few amongst those watching who had the experience to understand the distinction between the mundane and the truly great, and fewer still who could see such a thing in the flash of a knife across a man's throat.

Valerius was one of those few, but he had already seen all that he needed in the brief contest by the gods' pool. The details of that were something private between them, shared only in outline with those of her closest circle who knew already the reality of what Breaca could do and what she could not, which was the greater part.

The challenge for all of them was to find ways to keep her alive until she could find her way back to who she had been; or it became clear that she would never do so. They had not yet spoken openly of that.

The warriors of the war host, who saw exactly as much as they were shown, stood in silence at first, in honour of the dead, and the gods' gift of the morning and the shedding of blood that signalled the start of the war for which they had gathered and trained. Then a woman among them raised her blade in one hand and her shield in the other and set up the war chant of the Boudica, that the oldest had heard first on the banks of the great river at the time of the legions' invasion and the youngest had only heard sung quietly, in secret, through all the years since.

The sound grew and grew and spread out across the marsh, silencing the wind and the geese, and became a roar that might have reached north to the IXth legion and south to the veterans of Camulodunum and west to the Roman governor of Britannia in his assault on Mona and all that was sacred.

Under the wane of it, Breaca said to Valerius, 'I should talk to them. Could you find a way to help me mount the horse? It'll be easier from there.'

The messenger's horse was a pale strawberry roan, trained to stand where its rider had fallen. It remained steady while Valerius knelt at its side and spread his officer's cloak wide, and removed his helmet with deliberate ceremony and offered his knee for Breaca to mount so that it looked to the watching warriors as if they had arranged it ahead to show how Rome must kneel before the Boudica's greater strength.

They cheered for that as well, and gave her time again to catch her breath.

She looked better mounted; she had always fought best on horseback. The morning sun caught the copper of her hair and set light to it so that even sick-grey and slick with the sweat of old fevers, with the mist leaching the colour from the air and a pale-washed horse beneath her, she shone as the watchers expected.

What followed had not been prepared at all, except that each of those who had cared for Breaca had imagined something like this, and had prayed for it, and had come ready to act if the moment allowed.

Thus, Airmid lifted up the torc of the Eceni, which had been saved from the procurator's looting, and set it about Breaca's neck so that it, too, caught the sun and blazed gold, marking her as royal and, more than that, lending her the strength of her lineage. Ardacos gave her a new shield painted with the mark of the serpent-spear in red on Eceni blue and Valerius passed her the blade with the serpent-spear hilt that they had retrieved from beneath Briga's altar.

'Warriors of the war host, you who have gathered in the name of victory . . .'

She could not be heard by the full five thousand, no-one

expected that, but she sent her words to reach the oath-holders and spear-leaders and clan chiefs who stood as of right in the front lines of the massed host and could be relied on to repeat her message, word for word, to their followers.

'As you know, the legionaries of the Twentieth have been ordered out of Camulodunum and are marching west to aid the governor's war against Mona. The time is ripe now to attack the city that Rome claims as her capital in our land. We have only to rid ourselves first of the Ninth legion, the legionaries who wait in their fortress to the north and will move swiftly to attack us at the first word of insurrection . . .'

It was better than Valerius had dared hope. He stepped back from the horse and listened to a woman who was barely fit to fight a full day's battle nevertheless speak of leading five thousand untrained warriors to war and victory as if these two were certain; who, better than that, was able to reduce to a few, crisp, god-filled sentences the arguments of half the previous night and make them sound as if they were planned policy, as if Cunomar's act of madness, and the risks that followed from it, were part of a strategy set in motion months, if not years, in advance.

'. . . my son Cunomar, who had the honour to strike the first blows of this war . . .'

She stretched out her arm and Cunomar came to stand beside his mother, a tall, lean youth, made taller by the hand's length of lime-stiffened hair set straight up from his head. He wore only a waist skin held in place by his knife belt and the marks of the she-bear were freshly painted about his body. Even for those who knew the ways of the bear cult, he stood apart as something new and different, or possibly very old, which was worth more.

The loss of his ear was part of that difference. He was no longer beautiful in the way he had been when Valerius knew him in Rome and Gaul. Then, he had been a bitter, clumsy child, living in the shadow of his father's genius, for ever striving to match the legend, not the reality. His beauty had been of the fragile kind that graced the Roman salons, so that only those who wished the best for him could have said there was a promise of strength at the core.

Valerius had not been one of those, and Cunomar's growth to adulthood had been the first of several surprises that had greeted his return to the Eceni.

The youth who had faced him in the meetings of the past month, who had returned the night before to the council circle reeking of smoke and victory, was not the child he had so pitied on a beach-head in Gaul.

The voice that had spoken against him until dawn was no longer strident with the arrogance of youth, but the clear product of Mona's training, incised with the clarity of rhetoric. More than that, somewhere in the harsh mountains and caves of the Caledonii, the elders of the she-bear had taught Cunomar patience and a quiet, prideful dignity that had given his words a weight beyond his years.

He stood now beside his mother in front of five thousand warriors, many of them older by a decade, and that same dignity let him bear the disfigurement of his wounds as if they were honour scars; his missing ear flowered in its ugliness at the side of his head and his back was a mess of part-healed wounds that would never knit cleanly and even so, there was not one amongst those watching who did not either wish him as a son or desire him as a lover.

'. . . we have languished twenty years under Roman rule, forbidden to train our warriors in the arts of battle. Thus we must find ways to confront them that allow the youths amongst us to learn from the battle-hardened. Above all, we must not, yet, face the legions in a full pitched battle. To give them such an advantage would be to wreak our own destruction and we . . .'

Valerius closed his eyes and gave thanks to both his gods. That had been the hardest part of the night: to sit in the presence of Cunomar and his smoke-filled victory and say over and over, 'The Ninth are behind us, Camulodunum in front. We cannot allow them to come at us from two sides and we cannot, we *must* not attempt to take them on in full battle. We are not yet fit. We never will be.'

Quietly, Cunomar had said, 'We are nearly five thousand, the strength of a legion, and growing daily. Soon we will outnumber them.'

'And we could be ten thousand, or twenty, and we would still lose. We are not the strength of a legion, we are five thousand poorly armed, untrained warriors fighting on tales of past glory. This is what Rome does best. This is what the legions are for; they train for it from the first day of their recruitment until the last day before they retire: to stand in line with their shields locked and their gladii in the fine gaps between and walk through and past and over the bodies of those foolish enough to think they can break a Roman shield wall. Even when they have civil war, their generals do everything they can to avoid setting one legion against another. To attack them with anything less is suicide. While I live, I will not see it happen.'

Valerius had been tired, still caught in the feeling of the gods' pool, or he would not have said that last. Cunomar had not challenged him on it, or offered combat to the death, only stared impassively from the far side of the fire, and touched a single finger to his missing ear. Even if Graine had not spoken of it earlier, Valerius would have known him in that moment as an enemy, and would have regretted it as deeply.

There was no time, then, to remake and mend a relationship gone sour, and no time either, now, before the war host, to question the wisdom of the Boudica as she stretched out her other arm saying, '. . . such a thing can only be done by my brother, Valerius, who was once Bán, son to Luain mac Calma, Elder of Mona, who sent him back to us to be our aid against Rome.'

He had no choice but to go to her side, to stand there with his Roman helmet on his arm and his Roman chain mail bright in the sun and let the gathered warriors make what they would of the contrast between the Boudica's son in all the naked glory of his wounding and her once-enemy brother who, almost alone of her council, was whole and unharmed by Rome's assaults.

Nobody threw a spear at him; that much was good. A great many turned openly to spit against the wind and more made the sign against evil. He might have stepped back, but that Cygfa came uninvited to his side, and the mood of the host changed again at the sight of her; even more than the Boudica's son, the Boudica's elder daughter was known to them all, and what had been done to her.

She smiled at him with evident warmth, as if he were a trusted friend, which was an entirely new experience. Through it, she said, 'Do as I do,' and began to unfasten her belt.

Caught, he did so, and hid his surprise when, in a gesture as laden with meaning as any that morning, Cygfa swept off her sword and handed it to him, exchanging her weapon for his.

The crowd approved that, if not rapturously, then at least without the frigid mistrust of before.

It was enough. They stepped apart and Cunomar was there, this time, to find a graceful way to help his mother dismount.

Left alone with Cygfa and the eyes of the host elsewhere, Valerius said, 'Why did you do that? You have as much reason to loathe me as Cunomar does.'

She tilted her head. 'But I don't want to lead the war host. And I do want it to be led by someone who understands what it is we face. I love my brother, and respect him as a warrior, but he is not yet fit to lead us to victory against the legions.'

Valerius said, 'Breaca will do that.'

'Perhaps.'

Cygfa was daughter to Caradoc, and bore his stamp far more than Cunomar. Her hair was the colour of the noon-sky sun and her eyes the grey of new iron. Nothing was hidden in them. She was in pain and had been and would continue to be; and it was overridden entirely by the strength of her hate.

She said, 'I saw you fight on the beachhead in Gaul,' as if that answered more than it asked.

Gaul: the land where her father lived in exile; the land from which Valerius had fled, taking Caradoc's place on the boat.

He said, 'I think Gaul is best forgotten.'

'Which is why it never will be.' Her gaze was not kind. 'You were half drunk and rotten to the core with self-hate. Half the time you were riding a horse you had never seen before and you had a child clinging on to your back and you still fought as if the gods inspired your blade. Breaca fights like that, when she has the heart for it. My father might have done once, before the emperor's inquisitors broke him. I have never seen it in anybody else. They say you are a dreamer, given to Nemain, but I think you are a warrior first and that you were born for this. You have lived with the legions and know them as no-one else does, and now you are here, bringing all of that knowledge to us that we may use it against them.'

'You trust me not to betray you,' he said, in wonder. 'There are very few others amongst the war host who do.'

'I have seen the lengths to which you will go to keep an oath. That, too, was a part of Gaul.'

Her horse was there, the bay colt he had begun to help her train. She mounted it neatly and swung it round to face him.

'If we did not need you so very badly, I might hate you, but Rome takes up all of my hating. I will do what I must, support whom I must, to rid my land of that evil. Afterwards, maybe, I can hate you. If I am alive to do the hating. If you are alive to take it.'

She gave the salute of the warrior so that all watching could see it and spun her horse away from him.

Valerius watched the place where she had been for a long time before he broke the seal on the messenger's satchel and read the message from Camulodunum to the legate of the IXth legion.

Presently, when no-one came to disturb him, he searched for and found the spare vellum and ink that was always kept in a messenger's pouch, knelt on a patch of clean turf and began to write.

The messenger lay at the edge of the path, stripped naked now, as the gods had made him. Cunomar and a girl warrior of his she-bear strapped stones to his elbows, knees and belly and lifted him up and swung him sideways. The marsh took his body, sucking it down to a cold and quiet rest.

Valerius listened for help in the soft sounds of the death-wash and offered the necessary prayers to both his gods, that carried in the wake of the dead, and might be more easily heard.

A horse shifted restively behind him. A shadow crossed his path. Without turning he said to his sister, 'That was well done. They're different when you're with them. If I don't return—'

'You said there was no risk.' There was a thread of fear in the bluntness of that.

He stilled the flutterings in his own belly. For Breaca, if for no-one else, he could be confident. 'There has to be some risk or your warriors will not believe I have offered my life in their cause. But I don't intend to die, I swear it; in you, in this war, I have found a reason to live that outweighs everything. The Ninth legion must be brought south by a route that leaves it vulnerable. That won't happen unless they are led into it by someone they trust.'

'And if they don't trust you? If they recognize you and crucify you for twice-treachery? What then?'

She had asked the same, with the same urgency, in the counsels of the night. The answer was no more easily found now than then. Valerius touched the crook of his thumb to the brand on his sternum that was his first link to the bull-god. He felt no warning

51

there, nor any intimations of death approaching unseen. The gods did not always show such things, but there was a measure of expectation which needed him to act with courage to sway the order of things.

To Breaca, quite reasonably, he said, 'You've just finished explaining to the war host how much honour this brings on your family. They'd tie me to a tree and throw spears at me for cowardice if I backed out now. For that alone, I can't. And I truly do think I am safe. Petillius Cerialis is legate of the Ninth and he has been in Britannia less than a year; he knows nothing of a decurion who once served in the Thracian cavalry. The men he leads have been stationed north of here since the invasion, keeping watch equally on the Eceni and on the northern tribes; they don't know any more than he does of the politics of Camulodunum and the west. I am nothing to them, just a messenger.'

He touched the vellum that lay drying on his knee. 'The message says what we need it to say. I've copied the best flourishes of the original. Listen—'

Valerius smoothed out the perfect, unblemished kidskin, best of the emperor's office, and read, '*From Titus Aquilla, primus pilus of the Twentieth legion, in the governor's absence acting commander of the colony of Camulodunum, site of the temple to the deified Claudius, site of our unblemished victory over the native Trinovantes* – et cetera et cetera. A man promoted above his abilities and certain of it, clearly – *to Quintus Petillius Cerialis Caesius Rufus, legate, the Ninth legion. Greetings.*

'*War is upon us. A watchtower is burning even as I write, the men within it dead and defiled. The emperor's procurator of taxes is missing and our veterans fear for his life. The Eceni king is dead, and his people remember who they were in the times before we blessed them with peace. We are not in a position to remind them of their folly. Camulodunum is stripped of its defences and its men. I have less than one century of acting legionaries, and three thousand veterans whose courage is beyond reproach but who are no longer young men, fit for sustained battle. If it please you to remember the emperor's justice, we will offer whatever aid we can.*'

With cautious optimism, Valerius said, 'The legate of the Ninth is known across the empire for his impetuosity. Men say he prays daily for the chance to march his men into battle. He'll weep tears of raw frankincense when he reads this. He'll offer his worldly goods to the gods as a mark of his gratitude. He'll have the Ninth legion at muster and marching down the ancestors' Stone Way before they have time to kiss goodbye to their lovers. All we have to do is contrive some visible injuries so that I look as if I've fought for my life. Could you bring yourself to hit me, do you think?'

V

I T WAS RAINING, AND THE MULE WAS STUCK.

The beast was young and had never been in a pack train before. Broken to harness at the end of autumn, it had spent the winter in the store paddocks at Camulodunum, knee deep in mud and snow, and fed on musty hay, with no exercise to keep it fit.

The recruits who drove it were every bit as raw and as green and they, too, were on their first campaign. They had no real experience of how to load the packs and the mule was lame on one hind leg and had open sores along its back where a pad had been badly placed.

To Titus Aelius Ursus, decurion of the second troop, the Fifth Gaulish cavalry wing, assigned to care of the men and their mules for the entirety of their month-long journey west to join the governor's campaign against Mona, all of these things were regrettable, but inevitable. None of them explained why the beast had planted its feet on the first planks of the bridge and was refusing to move.

'Hit the bloody thing. What are you waiting for?'

Ursus shouted it from half a cohort away, urging his horse past the muttering mass of men spreading out along the river bank. They were glad of the rest, and had broken formation, dropping their packs without orders. The indiscipline of it was terrifying; they were young and had been recruited straight from the back streets of Rome, which was a relatively safe place to live, and had trained in the east of Britannia, which was almost as safe, and had no notion of what it was to march through land held by un-conquered tribes, where the bones of legionary dead lay thick as pebbles among the heather.

A battle-served centurion stood on the far side of the river, marshalling the forty men who had already crossed. Tardily, he put his hand to his mouth and called back to the rest of his century: 'Get back in formation! I will personally flog any man who steps out of line!'

Men shuffled and cursed and picked up their packs and were no more ready to meet the enemy than they had been before.

Ursus was tired and saddle-sore and thick-headed from lack of wine. He had ridden for thirteen days in the wind and pissing rain, with poor food and his bedding rolls damp through the night and not able to drink into warmth and forgetting because his bastard of a prefect had forbidden them to touch the wine supplies from the moment they rode out of the winter quarters. He wanted either to be in battle or out of it; safe in Camulodunum or committed to the western wars, not babysitting a cohort of helpless, hopeless children, half of whom would be dead by the month's end.

He reached the bridge and let fly at the nearest of them. 'If you don't get that bloody beast moving, I'll have you carrying its pack for the rest of the journey west.'

The pink-faced boy who should have been across the bridge and halfway into the valley beyond raised the rod in his hand and the mule flinched and set its ears back and brayed as it had been doing for far too long, and Ursus finally came close enough to see the welts on its back and haunches where it had been hit often and hard, and so to recognize that hitting it more was not going to make any difference.

Cursing, he threw himself from his horse. 'Leave it. There's no point.' A junior officer stood close by, old enough at least to be shaving. To him, Ursus said, 'Has it done this before?'

'Never. We've never had any trouble. It's the bridge: it doesn't like it.'

Ursus rolled his eyes and sighed, pointedly. 'Obviously. They never do. Nobody with any sense walks onto a strip of swaying planks stretched over a twenty foot drop with rocks and running water below, and mules have their own weight in common sense. That's why you're here to—'

He stopped. Sweat pricked sharply along his neck. A horse was coming along the river bank at speed, from the left. He knew the sound of it as he knew the sound of his own heartbeat.

Without turning, Ursus said stonily, 'Stand to attention. That's the prefect. How he knows we've stopped is beyond me but you can pray now to whoever you like that his mood has improved since last night.'

Behind him, the incoming horse drew to a halt, almost within reach. A quiet voice observed, 'You've stopped.'

Quintus Valerius Corvus, prefect of the Fifth Gaulish cavalry, could cut a man's soul with the knife of his voice if he chose to do so, and he chose it now. Quietly, with balanced precision, the words were at once a question and an accusation and an assessment of worth, or its lack. Faintly, there was disappointment, which was hardest to bear.

'It's the mule. It won't . . .' Ursus abandoned the sentence, unwilling to state the obvious: that he was in enemy territory with a full cohort of untested legionaries and he had allowed a new-broken mule to halt the progress of his unit. He felt the prickle of sweat run to a scalding flush and hated himself and everyone who saw it, including – particularly – the prefect.

'Yes, I saw.'

Corvus had dismounted and was examining the mule. The god-forsaken beast had stopped braying, as if it were indecorous to holler in the prefect's presence. It stood mutely, watching with everyone else as the company's most senior officer knelt in the ooz-ing mud at the edge of the bridge and, laying his cheek flat, peered along the planks, then under them. Corvus sat back on his heels, ignoring the filth on his knees, nodded to something unseen in the damp air and then turned to Ursus.

'Find a man with a head for heights and have him look under-neath the bridge, about a third of the way along. Keep him well roped. I don't want to lose anyone now. And get the rest of your men into armed formation. This place is an ambush waiting to happen.'

'Sir.'

When he tried, Ursus could make things happen fast. When his

56

own men, the cavalrymen of the second troop, with whom he shared the shepherding of the legionary recruits, understood that his honour was at stake, they gave him their hearts and were glad of it. It was this that had won him promotion to decurion and might keep him that post now.

Flavius was there, the troop's standard-bearer, with two other junior officers. They had heard the prefect's order and knew how to bring their men most swiftly to battle formation. At Ursus' nod, each gave orders, quietly and crisply. Booted feet rocked the morning. The loose rabble of polished iron and helmet-bronze that had been their cohort became a shining line, not one man out of place.

Abruptly, the rain stopped and it was possible to believe that the gods approved of what had been done. The men certainly thought so; in the stillness of the lines, small handfuls of corn meal were scattered as offerings to Jupiter, Mars, Mithras and the more minor gods of hearth and home. Murmured sacraments hung like smoke in the air.

The danger of ambush became noticeably less. The three officers conferred and, soon, a dark-skinned lad of seventeen with curled, Hispanic hair and tendons that stood out on his forearms like pulleys had tied a rope round his waist and then pulled himself along under the bridge and back again. Standing to attention in front of Ursus and Corvus, he was white, and not from the height or the officers' presence.

'Someone's cut the bindings. The hide holding the planks has frayed almost to nothing. The ones who got across were lucky. If the mule had gone over, it would have fallen to its death and taken anyone else on the bridge with it.'

Corvus had seen it. Ursus should have done. The only grace was that it had been obvious from the moment the prefect spoke and Ursus had already thought through what to do. 'I have engineers,' he said. 'We can abandon this bridge and build a new one. It will take less than half a day.'

'I know. Thank you. Sadly we don't have half a day. The governor needs us with all speed for his assault on Mona and we have no remit to repair bridges that have been sabotaged by the enemy.'

Corvus was a compact man, slim and fine-skinned with no spare flesh or hanging jowls and only a salting of white at his temples and along the parting of his hair to show that he had aged since the first years of the occupation. There was an air of difference about him so that even now, under the mud and the stains of travel, with his officer's cloak hanging wet about his armour and his greaves polished to blind the sun, he did not look fully Roman. His nose was more Greek, or perhaps Alexandrian, and his eyes were wider and could hold the world. For nearly two decades, Ursus had felt himself drown in them daily and, daily, had levered himself out again, cursing.

Ursus was broad and tall and his hair was a very un-Roman pale brown, a legacy from a maternal great-grandfather who had been Batavian and had earned his citizenship fighting under the deified Caesar. He had survived a brief revolt by the Eceni in the east soon after the invasion and twenty years of savage resistance by the tribes of the west and was as good a field commander as any man of his rank. He could take anything the enemy warriors chose to throw at him; it was his prefect's opinion that made or broke his days.

'What then?' he asked, too shortly.

Corvus smiled and raised a brow. 'The next bridge is four miles downstream. It's intact; my troop and their legionaries are crossing now. Bring your men down and follow us. Keep to the rear; the snake will need teeth in its tail.'

It was an offering, of a sort. Corvus led all his own patrols in person, but he put his second most competent officer at the rear, so that the snake of his line, if cut, might yet strike fast and hard at any enemy coming from behind. It was a place of implicit trust, and assumed the good initiative of the officer placed there, who might well have to act alone.

Once, Valerius had been there. It was Valerius who had destroyed whatever little of the prefect's good humour had survived the winter in Camulodunum. Ursus hated him for both of these, but not enough to reject the gift that was offered.

'Thank you.' He bowed, as if in the governor's presence. Ahead of him, a horse shifted, restlessly. When he raised his head again, Corvus had already gone.

'Why did he do it?'

The shame of the mule was a passing shadow, almost forgotten in the routines of a night-time camp. Ursus lay on his back and asked the question of the tent roof above his head. Rain fell steadily, so that the words slipped into the drumming of the goat hide and were lost.

To his left, Flavius, his standard-bearer, shifted a little, making his camp bed creak. He laughed, sourly. 'Who, Corvus? Because you'd have lost two days building a bridge fit for the emperor himself and the governor would have flogged you afterwards for bringing his much-needed reserves late to war.'

From the dark, an older, wise voice said, 'He's not asking about that. He's asking about what happened a half-month back that has left his favourite prefect in a foul temper. He's asking about Valerius and the procurator. About why we lost half a day on private business that will see us all crucified if the governor ever gets to hear of it. He's asking why Corvus stopped the emperor's tax collector from collecting the emperor's taxes. Actually, if any one of us is honest, he's asking why did he commit treason?'

Sabinius, the third of the party, was nearly two decades older than his tentmates. He had been with Corvus from the first days of the Fifth Gauls, and was nearing retirement. His hair was greyer than the prefect's and his face more lined, but he carried less care.

As standard-bearer to the first troop, he was the most senior officer of the wing, under Corvus. He could have slept in a tent of his own with slaves to light the fires and keep his bedding rolls dry. That he preferred the company of his own kind on campaign created a patina of respect amongst the men that drew from them the extra effort required in war.

Sabinius, too, lay on his back with his fingers laced behind his head and his face turned to the rain-sodden hide of the roof. 'You're asking the wrong question,' he said mildly. 'It's not why did he do it; that's obvious. What matters is why did we let him? And why did we not and are we not going to report him to the governor?'

There was quiet, and some thinking.

'Are we not?' asked Flavius, thoughtfully. 'There's still time. It might save our lives.'

Ursus said, 'We're not. He'd be given his sword and an eye's blink to fall on it, and if he paused long enough to commend his spirit to the gods, they'd crucify him in front of the camp as a traitor and a coward.'

With surprising feeling, Flavius said, 'Good.'

Ursus snorted. 'Are you so tired of life? Corvus is the man who will keep us alive through this misbegotten war against sorcerers and warriors who fight with no fear of death. If he dies, who else is going to get us back east with our skins in one piece? In any case, it wasn't the wrong question. I still want to know – why did he do it?'

'For Valerius, you fool. Why does he ever do anything?' The other two heard Flavius turn over and rock the pan of hot stones lying in the centre of the tent that drove away the damp for the first part of the night. Temporarily, the air became warmer, and smelled of steam.

From the wet dark, Flavius said harshly, 'You were both in the Eceni steading. You saw him as well as I did. Valerius was there, alive, with his bloody killer of a horse and Corvus couldn't reach him.'

'Would he have wanted to?' Ursus was newer than either of the others. His gut was not yet attuned to the thoughts and senses of his prefect as theirs were.

Flavius snorted, 'Of course. Why do you think he hates so much coming west when the whole winter has been bent towards it? The light of his days begins and ends with Valerius and he thought the man was on Mona, or at least on Hibernia with the rest of the god-drenched dreamers. Now he knows he's in the east and may die with Corvus not there to help or to hinder or even to speak to him at the end and heal the damage between them first.'

The hot pan rattled a second time, less harshly. Sabinius, older and wiser, said, 'Don't listen to Flavius. He's bitter because he's been fifteen years with Corvus and the man has never yet invited him into his inner tent. And he's jealous of you in the newness and innocence of your love.'

Ursus blinked in the dark. He had not thought his love so widely known. 'But is it true?' he asked.

'Of course. Everyone knows that Corvus did what he did for Valerius and he would do it again tomorrow, were the cost twice as great. Both of you can smile at your beloved prefect until your jaws crack and your eyes leak down your face and it won't make any difference; his heart was long since given to a wild boy of the natives who rode a horse called Death and had the courage to face down the madman Caligula.' The bunk creaked and the voice was directed more at one man than the other. 'Are you happier knowing that than you were before?'

The quiet stretched longer this time.

Eventually, Ursus said, 'He loved the governor's son once. Scapula's eldest. That was after Valerius. I heard about it.'

'That wasn't love, that was anger and politics and an eye to the future. In any case, Scapula's son is dead, knifed on Nero's orders for being too beautiful and too brave and too decorated in battle. Which should be a warning to us all; you can be beautiful and brave or brave and decorated but the gods won't help you if you are all three. So all we have to do is stay alive and stay ugly and we're fine. The second is easy. The first will only happen if we get some rest. The dreamers and warriors across the straits on Mona will not give quarter just because you are love-sore and too tired to fight properly. Go to sleep. The world will be the same in the morning.'

A long time later, when the breathing of the others had settled to sleep, Flavius lay on his back, staring up at the sag of the tent roof and the rain. 'It still isn't too late to tell the governor,' he said, into the dark.

VI

'I DON'T CARE IF YOU HAVE TO SINK THE FOUNDATIONS PAST THE floor of the ocean and ship every godforsaken stone one at a time from Iberia, you will build the baths here and they will not slide into the sea at the first kiss of a winter storm. Do I make myself clear?'

It was shortly after noon and the sky above the fortress of the IXth legion was as grey as if it were dusk. The easterly wind knifing in from the sea was sharp with salt and it scoured equally the faces of Petillius Cerialis, legate of the Legio IX Hispana, the blue-lipped, shivering Iberian master mason who stood up to his ankles in seepage in the trench at his feet, and the five legionaries who stood behind, armed and ready to defend their general against everything except weather, leaking foundations and the intransigence – or stubborn common sense – of the province's only master stone mason.

To Cerialis' left, the winter fortress of the first three cohorts of the IXth legion, strategically placed at the northern end of the ancient trading route known to the local tribes as the ancestors' way, took command of what height existed in the flat lands north of the wash, spreading up and over the low crest of the hill. Thus advantaged, the watchtowers were given an easy view of the sea, and, regrettably, an equally easy exposure to whatever storms the gods might choose to visit upon the shores.

There were no storms on the day Cerialis elected to order the building of the baths for his men, only the knife-wind, and the beginnings of trade on the drove road below, and of work in the salt pans to the north, and a fishing boat newly set into harbour, mobbed by a havoc of screaming gulls.

The wind clearly carried the sound of the birds' hunger; they drowned out the master mason's answer entirely. By those watching, the man could be seen to open and close his mouth. He quite clearly shook his head. He spread his palms and raised his brows and began, soundlessly, to explain the details of engineering and bath house foundations to the legate – and then abandoned all effort, not for the gulls or the wind or the growing frustration on Cerialis' face, but for the hammer of hooves on the stone of the drove road, that became, even as he lowered his palms and turned south with the others to look, the stumble of cavalry horses driven past all endurance on rising turf, and then the shatter of chain mail such as a man might make who has ridden himself beyond exhaustion and whose legs will not hold him upright when he dismounts, so that he falls to his face at the feet of his legate.

Or, not his legate: the prostrate man was not of the IXth legion. The mason, climbing out of his waterlogged trench, recognized the goat-headed fish of the XXth on the bridle and saddle cloth of the spent horse that stood with heaving flanks ahead of him. Then, late, he recognized the encircled elephant that was the personal imprint of the governor of Britannia on the satchel that lay now on the rank grass of the hillside, its seal cracked open by the force of the messenger's fall.

The gulls were quieter now; a new boat had set out to sea and they followed it, spreading their noise elsewhere. The messenger's companion, a russet-haired cavalryman, dismounted more neatly into relative silence and stood behind his fallen comrade.

Petillius Cerialis, legate of the IXth legion, drew in a breath of brine-laden air and directing his voice downwards said, 'If you are not dead, perhaps you would care to stand and deliver your message?'

Valerius lay with his face pressed to the wet grass, and realized that he was genuinely winded so that rising was, for the moment, impossible. Through the tunnel of black that sucked at his diaphragm, he heard Longinus say, in thoughtful Thracian, 'You've ruined that horse.'

He had not intended to bring Longinus; very specifically, he had given the former cavalryman tasks that would keep him at the steading watching over the routes from Camulodunum by which a desperate cohort of veterans might march. The Thracian's name was not the first that had come to mind, therefore, when he heard the horse openly following him on the track north to the IXth legion.

Pulling the messenger's strawberry roan off the track, he had waited, and continued to wait while a riderless horse galloped past him. Then, understanding, had said aloud, 'Longinus Sdapeze. It's less than six months since you were half dead with a broken skull and that was my fault. I am oath-sworn to keep you from further harm. You are not coming with me to the fortress of the Ninth.'

'I would like you to explain how you can stop me,' Longinus had said, from behind his left shoulder. 'And you told your sister there was no risk. If they don't remember one decurion of the Thracian cavalry, I don't see why they should remember his successor any better.'

A little desperately, Valerius had said, 'They think you're dead. The veterans of the Twentieth held collections for your memorial stone. That kind of word passes.'

'Then we'll raise a wine jug to the incompetence of scribes throughout the empire and celebrate the fact that I am very much alive. I haven't been indicted for treason. If you're safe, I'm in no greater danger.'

So saying, Longinus had pushed out through the spring under-growth. He whistled and the horse, which had stopped, came back to him. Mounted again, he had grinned, and then stopped, and said, 'Do your gods see danger in this for you?'

'No. Not as long as I hold courage.'

'Do I lessen that courage?'

'Never.'

'Good.' Longinus' smile had been real for a moment, shorn of the dangerous hilarity with which he faced danger. 'Then we have a time to be together, before the real fighting starts. I, too, have things to prove to your sister's war host before they will believe I have joined their cause.'

He had swung his horse, and his mood had lightened. 'In any case, these horses are too good to waste. If I left you with that roan, you'd give it to the barbarian Batavians and they'd ruin its tendons in a month of bad riding. You need me there to keep it safe for you so you have something decent to ride back down on.'

It had been better riding north with company, particularly this company. Not for the first time, lying prone on the grass at the legate's feet, it came to Valerius that, alone of his sister's close circle, he had no honour guard that might surround him in battle, and nor did he want one; but that this one, solid, unwavering friendship, and the steady humour it offered, was a gift to be treasured.

It was a pity about the horse.

He could breathe again, which was good. He counted a few heartbeats longer, then pressed his palms to the turf and levered himself to standing. He swayed a little, and it was not all for show. His hand had a welt across the knuckles, as of a sword cut gone awry. His face, too, was bruised, as if he had fallen from his horse onto rough ground, or been hit a glancing blow by a club. Cygfa had done that, not unkindly, but perhaps with more enthusiasm than might have been necessary.

None of these was remarked upon by the legate and Valerius did not mention them, but retrieved from the wet grass the message-pouch that bore the governor's broken seal and was about to open it and read aloud the message, when he noticed the mason for the first time, and the slowly leaking foundations beside which he stood.

Beset by a new idea, Valerius knelt and dug his fingers into the turf, testing the quality of the earth between his fingertips. Rising, he said, 'This ground will never hold a baths; there's too much sand to support the foundations. There may be chalk under some of the other hills here, or clay on the higher ground inland. The mason might find it useful to know that.'

The legate gazed at him, flatly. 'You have been here before?'

'No. But I was present when the baths were built in Camulodunum in the year just after the invasion. The land is similar in some respects.'

'I see. Then you have been in the province as long as any man living, while I have been here a bare ten months. How clumsy of me not to appreciate that. And now you are a messenger. What were you before this, a centurion?'

'Almost.' Valerius allowed himself to smile. 'A decurion. I have only ever ridden for the cavalry. I served in the Fifth Gauls under the prefect Quintus Valerius Corvus.'

'Indeed? I have heard of him. He has a reputation for extraordinary valour.' There was a rim of yellow round the whites of the legate's eyes, as if his liver had rebelled for many years against the sharpness of his intellect. Tapping his forefinger to his teeth, he said, 'You stoop low, for one who has risen so high. Are there not others of lesser rank who could bear a message from one commanding officer to another in a province at peace?'

Valerius retrieved his message satchel from the ground. His fingers traced the outline of the beast that had been the symbol of Britannia's governor since Claudius first rode his elephant in through the opened gates of Camulodunum.

When he looked up, even the legate was shocked by the haggard weariness in his eyes. 'None that are alive,' he said. 'Five other messengers were sent ahead of me. None have got through – unless you know already that the Eceni lands are ablaze with the beginnings of insurrection?'

The Iberian mason knew himself out of his depth. He bit back an oath and cursed inwardly the ill-luck that had brought him away from the safety and warm winds of Rome to a land where the natives still resisted civilization and the generals in the army still believed there was glory to be won in war.

It was no secret that Petillius Cerialis, legate of the IXth, craved battle, and was sick to the back teeth of guarding a trade harbour and a drove road and the salt pans of eastern Britannia against a group of pacified client tribes who ventured no more than the occasional sheep-stealing from their neighbours.

Cerialis' gaze, resting on Valerius, became curiously fixed. 'And yet you are alive,' he said, slowly. 'Which is, in itself, an achievement.'

The wind blew straight from the sea, cold and damp and laden with salted mist. On the drove road, a wagoner paused to speak to the fisherman and then clucked his horses forward, heading south.

The legate watched the wagon begin to roll, then said, 'My

armourer buys iron from that man. Perhaps it would be of benefit to tell him that the Eceni are no longer at peace.' He turned to the russet-haired cavalryman. 'You are?'

'Longinus Sdapeze, decurion, the First Thracian cavalry.'

Cerialis nodded, curtly. 'Good. You will ride down and tell the iron trader not to leave until we can give him an escort. When you are done, see to your horses and then make yourself ready to ride. We set out today, to restore the emperor's justice in the lands of the east.'

Longinus turned his horse back down towards the trade route. He leaned forward to smooth a hand over the lathered neck and, in the lifting tone a man might use to encourage one more effort from his mount, said in Thracian, 'There is a man riding up towards us now on a flashy bay cavalry horse with too much silver on its bridle. He seems to know you. If you're in trouble, shout. I'll hear it.'

Longinus had never been afraid of combat. He turned to salute Valerius. His yellow hawk's eyes held all the light of battle and only a little of warning. Grinning, he set his horse down towards the trackway before Valerius had time to reply.

I don't intend to die, I swear it . . .

Valerius had said it to Breaca, truthfully. In his analysis of the possible dangers, he had not included the Batavian cavalrymen who were stationed with the IXth legion, for the simple reason that he did not think any would still be alive who might recognize him.

It was over twenty years since he had trained with the native tribes on the banks of the Rhine and the Batavians, of all those who fought for Rome, threw themselves hardest into the most dangerous conflicts, vying with each other to perform the most outstanding acts of bravery and self-sacrifice and so win a place – posthumously for preference – in their winter sagas. To die of old age was anathema to a Batavian and the overwhelming majority avoided it with a good two decades to spare.

Riding north into country policed by a wing he had once known was the kind of easy risk against which Longinus would have offered long odds and Valerius would have accepted with a light heart and the certainty of winning.

He would have lost. Julius Civilis, by order of the emperor

Caligula citizen of the Roman empire, had survived every battle and was enduring the curse of old age with commendable dignity.

Buffeted by a wind that had no care for rank or honour, he rode straight-backed up the hill towards his legate and the new visitor and it was impossible not to recognize him, however much the sun had leached the colour from his hair and the wind chiselled cracks on his skin.

Valerius was not as exhausted as he had made out, but nor was he as battle-fresh as he would have liked. He stood by his swaying horse and watched the slow approach of the man who had once named him soul-son and brother.

It was a moment's work to assess the sources of danger and put them in order: Longinus was his first concern. The Thracian was nearly at the bottom of the slope and had hailed the iron trader; he was thus beyond reach of the men on the hill and his horse had enough fire left to carry him into the forest and the safety of the trees if the need arose.

Of those who might have posed a danger to Valerius, and so, indirectly, to his sister's cause, the legionaries who formed the legate's guard were young and bored and more concerned by the blustering wind and the unexpected prospect of a long march down the ancestors' Stone Way with battle at the end of it than they were by any possibility of attack from the messenger who had just ridden in. They stood hunched against the wind, their bare forearms blue with cold and their noses dripping freely.

The mason posed no danger at all, which only left the legate. Cerialis was close enough to kill, and he had made of himself a gift; his sword was clipped into his sheath so that he might mount his horse smoothly without the risk of dropping it and his mind, unlike those of his legionaries, was reaching forward to the glories of combat and the planning required to bring it about.

What was left of the legate's attention was all for Civilis; his features had softened, as if the approaching rider were a distant grandfather, still remembered fondly from childhood.

Almost forgotten, Valerius tested the spring of the turf beneath his feet. The salt on the wind tasted sharper than before and the scudding clouds seemed more richly textured. The irony of that was not lost on him; the world always became most beautiful when death was closest. For so much of his life, the Boudica's younger brother had wanted to die. As the Batavians did, he had thrown himself into the hearts of uncounted battles and had killed and killed and mourned the fact that he emerged alive. Only recently had he discovered how badly he wanted to live, and only in the short time since his return to the Eceni had he come to understand how much he was needed, and that he had an obligation to live that went far beyond his own needs and wants.

The man who wishes most to live must abandon all fear of death. He had learned that long ago, in the days when Civilis' hair had been the colour of washed gold and the sun had blessed his face with freckles, not lines.

The old cavalryman was close now and the weight of his age showed more clearly, and the effort he was making to hide it. His hair was no longer flowing gold, but ice-white. Against all Roman law, it was bound up at the right temple in a warrior's knot, with the many teeth of his enemies plated in silver and left to dangle to his chin. His hands were cramped and rested on the pommel of his saddle; cold and sixty-five winters spent on horseback had cracked and swollen the joints so that holding the reins clearly pained him and it was the hours of training that had gone into his horse that enabled him to ride it so safely, not the strength of his grip.

The passing years had changed Civilis almost beyond recognition. There was the hope, always, that Valerius, too, might have altered; Breaca had once failed to recognize him, leaving room to believe that others might do the same.

Remembering late the role he had assigned himself and the lie within it, Valerius opened the messenger's satchel he held in his hand. Addressing the legate a little louder than was necessary, he said, 'The message from Camulodunum is written here in full. Would you have me read it?'

'Later.' Petillius Cerialis flicked a dismissing hand and gestured towards the advancing cavalryman. With uncharacteristic delicacy, he said, 'Julius Civilis has retired from service to the emperor, but he is still our best horseman and retains the respect and war oaths of his tribesmen. If he advises herbs or a hot mash for your mounts, do not refuse them.'

Valerius bowed. 'His name is known throughout the legions and your care for him honours you both. I would not dream of refusing him.'

He turned and saluted the oncoming rider. The beginnings of battle fever burned like old blood on his tongue, a welcome friend. His body prickled to the promise of violence in a way it had not done when Breaca had killed the messenger.

A lifetime of war had taught him that danger was better faced head on. True to that training, he stepped forward, saying, 'Julius Civilis, prefect of the Batavians, greetings. Your name is known from one coast to the other as the officer who led his men to swim the Great River and destroyed the Eceni horses in their lines.'

The horse picking its way with such delicate care up the tussocked slope stopped at the sound of the river's name. Civilis, once prefect of the First Batavian cavalry, tilted his face towards the man who had spoken to him. A chaos of memories swept his face. Tears sprang fresh to his eyes.

'There are not many who still choose to remember that. Were you there at the first battles?'

Civilis' voice wavered. His gaze focused only briefly on Valerius and then wandered uncertainly to the legate. There was no hint of recognition. Offering a prayer to the gods of poor memory, Valerius said, 'Not as closely as you were. I fought with the Quinta Gallorum, but not all of us were in the front lines.'

That much was true. Valerius stood very still, waiting. The Civilis of old would have known that a certain member of the Fifth Gaulish cavalry had not only fought in its foremost ranks, but had swum the river into the blazing core of battle with Civilis' Batavians.

A heartbeat passed, and a second. At the foot of the hill, Longinus had reached the iron trader and talked the man into turning his wagon round. The legate had stepped away, but was still close enough for Valerius' blade to reach. Civilis stood two paces away. He was neither armed nor armoured. His life could be measured in parts of a breath.

'The Quinta Gallorum? That was Corvus' wing. I served under him before they gave me my own command.' The old man's head lifted a little, as an old hound might at a distant hunt. He frowned and the crags of his face deepened. 'Then I should know you. There are too few of us left who fought in that battle to forget each other.' Rheumy eyes searched Valerius' face and slid away, finding more of interest in his horse. 'What's your name, boy?'

'Tiberius. I was named for the man who was emperor when I was born.' The deceit was slick, and hateful. The gods did not honour the makers of lies.

'Ah, yes . . .' The old man's larynx bobbed in his throat. 'I remember now. You served under Rufus on the Rhine. A good man, before the natives cut his throat. They carved their witch signs, too, on his chest. And cut off his . . .'

Civilis abandoned all attempt to remain in the present. His gaze drifted over all the men to a past horizon none of them could see. The waxen contours of his face melted. Spit gathered creamily at the corners of his mouth. It seemed possible he might weep there, before them all.

The legate stepped forward to hold the horse's bridle before the old man let fall the reins and the beast became unruly.

He said, 'Old friend, war is upon us. The legion must march south to Camulodunum to stem the rot of revolt. Your Batavians will accompany us as honoured escort. This messenger and his companion will ride as our guides. If your horse boys could take care of their mounts, it would speed our progress.'

'Their horses?' Civilis' gaze became noticeably sharper. He studied Valerius' strawberry roan and then looked down the hill to the place where Longinus was escorting the iron trader back towards the fortress. 'Oh, yes.' He nodded, thoughtfully. 'I expect we could take care of their horses.'

VII

'I TOLD YOU THEY'D TRY TO STEAL OUR HORSES.'
Longinus leaned peaceably against a wall at one end of
the covered barn that housed the Batavian cavalry's
remounts. Down the length of the line, horses by the dozen dozed
and ate hay and watched from their stalls the new men who had
come to disturb their morning's peace. Their breath warmed the
air, mellowing the scents of urine and horse dung, of leather oil and
newly cleaned harness mounts and the sweat of many horses
recently exercised. The beasts whose heads turned to look at the
incomers were sleek and well muscled and fit. Not one of them was
in any way broken in wind or limb.

Valerius stood a little further down the line with one foot hitched
onto a trough and observed the small flurry of activity taking place
in the stall ahead of him.

Without making the effort to turn, he said, 'They're not trying to
steal them, they're doing their best to make them fit to ride again
so they can take us safely south as you wanted. Myself, I would
have said we'd do as well if they'd give us one of theirs to ride
instead. Have you noticed that they're all bay?'

'Bay and big and they've been training all winter. Yes, I had. If
they kept them like that in Camulodunum, you might not have
crippled your pretty roan in that ride up the hill.'

'It was necessary. We had to be seen to be desperate.

72

And he might be saved yet. The horse boy knows what he's doing.'

With some interest, Valerius watched the care of the gelding he had taken from the dead messenger and then ridden into the ground to impress the urgency of impending war on the legate. In that much, he had succeeded; Cerialis had ridden back to his fortress and even now was issuing orders with a speed that unnerved his juniors, and set the legion abuzz with the foretaste of action.

The care of the horse was less certain. It was lame in both forelegs with heat and swelling in the tendons that could leave it lame for life if not treated with skill. Valerius had come to like it in the short journey north and was not proud of the damage he had done. Encouragingly, the beast was being groomed and fed and clucked over with much disapproval by a freckle-faced lad not yet in his teens who had Civilis' hawk-beaked nose and gold Batavian hair.

Civilis himself had gone to use the latrines, leaving them alone. The lad spoke to the horse and studiously ignored the man who had ridden it to such harm. Experimentally, Valerius tossed him a silver coin from his messenger's pouch and watched as the boy tested it with his teeth, nodded at the result, and then tucked it up between cheek and teeth for safe keeping. He looked no less wary afterwards than he had done before; certainly no more prone to idle conversation.

Valerius slid his back down the nearest wall until he crouched on his heels, hugging his knees to his chest. From that less threatening height, he said, 'Civilis will be with us again shortly. My soul-friend the Thracian and I will have to ride south again to show the legate where best to fight the Eceni. If your kinsman were inclined to honour us with fresh horses for the ride and for the battle after, which ones do you think he would give?'

He spoke in Batavian, the language of all sentiment, where soul-friendships were made between men for life and sealed in blood and the bonds of kinship were stronger by far than any oaths taken or given by Rome. One or other of these two facts reached places the silver had not touched. The boy's eyes grew round and then narrow in thought.

Newly shy, his gaze flickered down the horse lines to a certain place and back again. He grinned conspiratorially and, in well-schooled Latin, said, 'To give a gift honours the giver. The greater the gift, the greater the honour.'

'Indeed.' Valerius offered another silver coin and saw it taken with less mistrust.

He pushed himself away from the stall's edge and walked down the line. At the place the boy's gaze had alighted, the hindquarters of a horse faced the passage between the stalls.

Alone of all those around it, the beast stood facing the wall. Similarly alone, it was not the rich, red bay of every other horse in the barn, but the colour of aged walnuts, so darkly brown as to almost be black. At Valerius' approach, it snaked its head round and pinned its ears back, savagely. He stopped abruptly and stood in the alleyway between the stalls with his hands laced before him and his face wiped entirely of feeling.

A long moment passed. Valerius let out slowly the breath he had taken. A trivial comment to Longinus on the unruly nature of Batavian horses died unspoken in his throat. The world was very sharp, suddenly. He was aware of the beast's part-white ear flicking towards him, of the white splashes on its brow, of the individual strands of black hair in its tail, of the narrow stripes of black down all four hooves where ermine marks at its coronet no bigger than a denarius gave colour to feet that would otherwise have been completely white, as its legs were completely white, to knee and hock and above.

More than any of these, Valerius was aware of the tight, knotting pain that had taken hold of his diaphragm and all the hope and pain that it heralded. He took a hesitant step forward, extending one hand to the broad cheek and the wary, white-rimmed eye above. 'Tell me, son of a god, did your sire—'

The not-black horse pinned its ears again and struck at the stall's side. Teeth cracked on wood with a noise to shake the rafters. Throughout the barn, the quiet rhythms of eating ceased for a moment and then started again a little faster.

Valerius stood very still, watching the place where the teeth had gouged deeply into age-hardened oak. His face felt cold and slick and a single line of sweat ran down the centre of his spine. He was shaking, which was neither expected nor welcome. He realized it as Longinus reached him and saw the other man notice the fact and its reasons and choose not to speak and was grateful. He had forgotten how deeply they knew each other, he and Longinus. The remembering came in sharp counterpoint to the shock.

Longinus had stepped back to study the horse from a safe distance. He whistled, a low appreciative warble. 'You leave one mad horse behind with the Eceni and Civilis finds you another. Did he use the Crow-horse at stud all those years ago on the banks of the Rhine?'

Longinus had not been present on the Rhine, or even in its immediate aftermath, but he had listened to half-told histories and understood those parts that mattered most; and he had ridden the Crow-horse in battle, which no-one else had done but Valerius. For that, alone, he was unique.

Valerius said, 'One of Civilis' black mares threw a white-legged son by the Crow just before the invasion. I thought they had killed it as a four-year-old for being unrideable. I must have been wrong.'

'That horse would be nearly twenty. This is barely a six-year-old. It can't have been broken long.'

'I know. If I were to guess, I'd say it was born while I was in Hibernia. It could be a grandson, or great-grandson. Enough of the Crow has passed down the line for it to be that.' Valerius put a hand behind him and found a wall to lean on. Unsteadily, he said, 'Will you look at its face and tell me what you see?'

'Two eyes and two ears and a nose and a mouth?' Longinus regarded him curiously. 'What would you like me to see?'

'The markings. What are the markings on its brow?'

The horse had turned away to face the darkest corner of the stall. Longinus walked round to its head and back. When he returned, he was no longer grinning. He said, 'It has a disc on its brow in the shape of a waxing three-quarter moon and a flash like a falling spear above it. Julius, is that the horse of your dream?'

Julius: the intimate, personal name. Longinus only used that when they were alone, and then most often at night, in the extremes of love.

Valerius looked down at his hand. The tremor in it was less than it had been but still not gone. He said, 'No. I killed the horse of that dream on Hibernia, the day it was foaled. And the markings are not quite right. In the dream, the disc was a shield and the line of the spear passed diagonally across it, not above like this one.'

'And if I remember all that you said, in the dream you rode a gelding.' Longinus ducked down to peer under the horse's belly, confirming a thought. 'This is a colt.'

'Yes.'

'But a good one,' said a voice neither man fully recognized. 'You could do worse.'

They spun, together, reaching for blades that were extensions of living flesh.

'Longinus, no!'

Valerius threw an arm out, stopping a strike before it had begun. Hissing a breath through clenched teeth, he said to Civilis, 'Old man, you forget yourself. We're at war. We have killed warriors who crept at our backs in the dark as you have just done. If you wish to die before your time, don't leave your blood on my blade. I don't imagine the legate treats kindly those who slay his favourite horsemen.'

'I don't imagine he does, although he would have to move fast to claim your lives before my Batavians, and any death devised by Rome would be better than what they might offer, I promise you.'

Civilis stood three stalls away. Off his horse, he seemed less frail. His eyes focused without effort, and with some amusement, on the two men who threatened his life.

The freckle-faced boy stood at his side, grinning. The old man ruffled his hair with unfeigned affection. 'Gentlemen, I apologize. My courtesies have abandoned me. If you will blame it all on the curse of old age and a weak bladder, I would be grateful. In recompense, allow me to introduce my daughter's daughter's son, the first boy child of my line. There are nine women living who carry my blood and my name, and only this one boy, who will one day be a man and wield his great-grandfather's blade in battle. For now, he is the best healer of horses we have got. If anyone can make your gelding sound again, he will.' He patted one lean shoulder. 'Thank you, Arminius. You may go now.'

The boy wanted to stay. He shaped a plea, looking up at his great-grandfather. Whatever he saw in the old man's face led him to abandon it. He paled, until the freckles stood out like mud spatters across his face. Bobbing a bow to Valerius and Longinus, he ran for the door.

Civilis lowered himself to sit on the edge of a drinking trough. There was little about him now to indicate old age, but a residual stiffness and the silver of his hair. His gaze flickered over Longinus and returned to linger on Valerius. His brows were entirely white. The blue-grey eyes beneath seemed paler than they had, and sharp enough to strip a man to honesty.

'Tell me, you who are named for a dead emperor whom every man came to despise before his death, if you listen to the noises outside, what do you hear?'

Valerius leaned back on the nearest oak upright. The shaking had passed, for which he was grateful. He turned over one hand and studied the broken edge of a nail. He had played the board game of Warrior's Dance with lesser men than Civilis of the Batavians and, rarely, with greater.

The question was not a hard one to answer. The sound outside was one he had known from his teens, a noise unique to the legions that only thousands upon thousands of men can make, in their ordered urgency, preparing for war: the clash of armour and the random shouts of excited men and the holler of horses who feel the beginnings of battle fever that might, if everyone were lucky, last the duration of a march and into the battle beyond. The subtle nuances were unique to each cohort and each legion, but the broad press of it reached into parts of Valerius he had thought long dead, so that his hand came unasked to rest on the hilt of his blade and his blood thrilled freshly through his veins.

As much for that as for any instinct for the game, Valerius offered the truth, unadorned.

Looking the old man directly in the eye for the first time, he said, 'I hear horses eating hay that have been well cared for and know themselves safe. I hear harness being readied by men who know their horses as brothers and who savour battle. I hear part of a legion, but not all of it, preparing to march under a man who has kept it too keen for too long, so that the men have gone sour and cannot tell the real thing from a drill.'

'Indeed. You are at least part of what you say, then.'

'Am I?'

They were no longer playing. Each man of the three had lived this long because he knew the difference between threats and reality; because, in his gut, he responded to one and not the other. A pace further down the aisle, Longinus had not moved. Nothing about him had changed, and everything; his smile was as open, his yellow hawk's eyes as genial, his balance as good – and he could kill now, effortlessly, where before it had been only a thought.

Valerius had clear priorities: Longinus must not die, and the IXth must march down the ancestors' Stone Way into ambush; these two things mattered more than the life of an old man, however honoured in the past.

Rehearsing in his head the lies that would be necessary afterwards, Valerius judged the distance from himself to Civilis, and the moves it would take to grasp his head and twist until the sinewed neck had broken. Already, he felt regret at a needless death. He took a small step sideways, to find a place of better balance.

'Ha!' Civilis laughed aloud. With studied nonchalance, he leaned back on the stall and hooked his thumbs in his belt, then crossed his feet at the ankles. 'Gods, man, do I look like a fool? If I don't walk out of this barn first and free, both of you are dead men, in ways you have never yet dreamed of. The Batavians have their own honour, and while I may be retired in Rome's eyes, I am first rider until my death for my countrymen. Petillius Cerialis knows that. He needs us. As you need me – Valerius of the Eceni.'

The silence into which that fell would have brought lesser men to their knees. Down both sides of the line, horses stamped, restlessly. The white-legged colt with the moon and spear on its black brow kicked the sides of its stall, scattering splinters across the floor. Longinus caught Valerius' eye and stepped back three more paces, giving them both space in which to move. The quiet was broken by the whisper of iron on fat-softened leather as he drew his blade from its sheath.

'No. Longinus, put up. He isn't going to betray us yet.' A grain sack lay near Valerius' feet. He kicked it closer and sat down. Very carefully, he cupped his palms to his face, pressing the tips of his fingers to his closed eyes. When he was as certain as he could be that the turmoil inside did not show on his face, he let drop his hands and faced the older man.

'When did you know?' he asked.

The old man's smile held a hint of sadness. 'Son of my soul, how could I not know from the start? For twenty years, you were the son I never had, the younger brother of my fighting days. It grieves me to the core that you believe I could forget. I knew you from the moment I saw you ride that flea-bitten donkey of a messenger's horse up the hill. It was already foundering and you held it up for the last dozen strides.'

Civilis reached for Valerius' hands and opened the palms and read the scars there as if they told him as much as Corvus' letters. There was pity in his eyes when he raised them. 'You forget, the first time I saw you, you were riding the Crow-horse and he was trying to kill you. It is a good thing for a man to remember, particularly at the end of his days when the moments of true glory have been few and are to be cherished.'

'You do me great honour.'

What else to say? Valerius had come expecting physical danger, and had prepared for it. There was no preparing for this.

'Yes?' Civilis barked a short laugh. 'It would count for more if you had the decency to be honest and tell me that I am right in what my heart craves.'

'Which is what?'

'That you plan to destroy Cerialis and the Ninth legion in the way my kinsman, the hero Arminius, destroyed Augustus' three legions in the forests and marshlands east of the Rhine.'

It was exactly what he planned. Valerius said, 'Your heart craves the destruction of the legion you are sworn to serve?'

'I serve him who gives me gold to fight, that I may come to greater glory in battle. When the son of my soul returns to my life and is Arminius come to life again, gold is as nothing, or the legions' oaths. My ancestor, too, was sworn to the legions. He is not heralded in our winter halls as a traitor, but as one who outwitted Rome. I am old. I have lived through too many battles. Each winter, I fear the coughing fever and the loss of more teeth and the slow death of a body that has survived too long. For the past five years, I have prayed to the horse-gods at mid-summer that they send me one last, glorious battle, by which my name might be measured amongst the heroes. This year, they have answered. They have sent me you.'

Tears stood proud in his eyes as he spoke. With a terrible dignity, he said, 'I beg you, from the floor of my heart, let me come with you, to join in that which you plan.'

Valerius picked a straw from the floor, flattened it and folded it across and across. Studying the result, rather than the man, he said, 'I am not Arminius and this is not the Rhine. I have delivered an urgent message from Camulodunum, which suggests a route the legate might take to reach the city in time to relieve it. As a result, if and when it is asked of me, I will lead Petillius Cerialis and however many cohorts of the Ninth he can muster at short notice back down the ancestors' Stone Way towards the place where the watchtower was burned two nights ago. The track passes for half a day's ride between the forest and the marsh. If the legate is so foolish as to march his men down there without adequate protection, and if the Eceni warriors are waiting, with the she-bears and the newly sworn spears among them, then it may be that the Ninth legion will, indeed, be destroyed in the way that your great-grandfather's cousin destroyed Augustus' three legions.'

His gaze came up then, to meet the other man's, and the regret there was laid over other things, more complex. 'I will do everything in my power to make that happen. The future of this land is at stake, and all that comes after it for all generations. I will not let an old man, even one who rightly names me brother, put that in danger.'

'Am I a danger?'

'You may be. If you come, then the entire wing of Batavians will come with you. How many of those will agree with you that their oath to serve the legions is as nothing compared to a glorious death in battle?'

There was a pause, and time to reflect, then, 'Follow me,' Civilis said.

Pained joints cracked as the old man pushed himself to standing. He walked down the horse line to the white-legged descendant of the Crow. It did not pin its ears at him, nor threaten to bite. He lifted a soft leather rope from a nail and twisted it into a halter. The horse nodded its head to let him slip it over its ears.

The love with which the old man rubbed his age-twisted hands down the beast's face was displayed without shame. After a while, hoarsely, he said, 'The Batavian squadrons will ride with the Ninth anyway, whether I join you or not. You're right, I am old and they honour me, but at least half are blood-sworn to my nephew Henghes who is given wholly to Rome and cares nothing for the names of his ancestors. The other half, I think, will follow me. They would not fight against their fellows, but they would fight against the legions in support of your warriors if they saw me

80

doing the same. It is not what I would want, but it's the best I can give you.'

Civilis turned, holding out the halter. 'Except that I can also give you this colt. He is the Crow's grandson and he has some of his fire without all of his hate. He is not a match for the horse that holds your heart, but nor is he as difficult to ride or to handle. If I were your age, I would ride him into battle and feel honoured that he carried me.'

Valerius felt the drain of battle exhaustion, and had not yet fought. Without trying to conceal it, he asked, rawly, 'Civilis, I could not have hoped for as much. How can I thank you?'

'You walk with a god at either side of you, Valerius. Ask your question of them, not an old man who craves their company. Rome will brand me traitor, but the gods and my people will know that I have followed in the footsteps of Arminius, a man I admire above all others. What greater glory can there be than that?'

VIII

 A T DAWN ON THE FOLLOWING DAY, SIX COHORTS OF THE
IXth legion marched south towards Camulodunum, side on
to the salted wind.

Grey, blustery light rebounded off three thousand polished
helmets and raked across curls of strip armour kept free of rust by
daily attention. Four men abreast, with two javelin-lengths
between each row, and twelve between each cohort, the legion
marched fast and light, taking neither mules nor carts, but bearing
their packs with them, each man burdened with only enough food
and equipment for two overnight encampments.

The legion's eagle and the cohort standards crowded in a scarlet
and glittering forest in the early rows, flanked by the officers on
their horses with the cavalry, better mounted, just behind. These
first ranks departed at dawn. The last of the men, waiting their
turn, passed through the eastern gates of the winter fortress around
noon. In between was an unbroken snake-line of mounted and
unmounted men and the measured tread of their footfalls.

They marched south along the ancestors' Stone Way, a paved
trading route so old that a hundred generations of wagoners had
brought their raw iron and salt and copper and enamel along its
length from the southern ports of the great river to this sea port
with its access to snowbound lands across the sea, and carted the
hounds and leather and Nordic amber and walrus ivory and

mutton and bales of wool back south to the great river and thence to Gaul, the Germanies, Iberia, Rome and all the rest of the empire. The legions used the trackway, and had repaired it, but it was old when Rome was young and had been a trading artery when the ancestors still used flint to tip their spears.

A full wing of five hundred Batavian horsemen trotted on either side of the leading cohort, hooves hammering on the stone like the roll of distant thunder. They were big, broad-shouldered men, armoured in chain mail and bearing cloaks of undyed lambs' wool with green checks like studded emeralds woven along the hems. They rode into a possible war unhelmeted, with their gold hair tied up at the right temple and their arms bared to the sun, the better to show off the quantity of armbands in enamelled gold and silver that was their pride and their wealth.

Like their riders, their horses were big and bay and fit and uniformly harnessed in good oxhide with quantities of silver at the harness mounts. Each mount had its mane pulled newly short and its tail tied up to keep them from providing a handhold for the enemy in any battle. The Batavians were taught from childhood that if they had the ill luck to be unhorsed in battle, they should grab the tail of an enemy horse and swing themselves up by it to unseat the rider and claim the mount for themselves. Twenty years of battle amongst the tribes of Britannia had not convinced them that the warriors against whom they fought would never dream of grabbing the tail of a passing horse.

Valerius rode at their head with Civilis on one side and Longinus on the other and only the standard-bearers between him and the legate, Petillius Cerialis. His mount was the white-legged almost-black colt with the beautiful neck, whose mane and tail, at his insistence, had been left unpulled and untied.

Civilis had been blind to the vices of a horse he clearly loved, or was sweetening the truth when he made his gift; the beast was not significantly easier to ride than the Crow-horse, who had sired its sire, only younger, and less predictable. It shied and spooked sideways at patches of sunlight or grasses waving alongside the trackway; it napped at every lift of the wind and every crash of armour from the ranks. It had not bucked Valerius off on mounting, but only because he had been warned that it might do, and had the practice of sitting its grandsire.

As the morning progressed, a shifting, treacherous mist drank what was left of the light so that, by noon, they rode as though at dusk. Away from known surroundings, the not-black colt became more wilful, not less, sidling three steps sideways for every one forward. Men on either side gave it clear space, grinning. Valerius bit his lower lip and cursed at it roundly in Hibernian.

At a point when his horse had remained parallel with Longinus' for more than a stride, the Thracian said, 'You're enjoying that.'

Valerius arched a brow. 'Not as much as you think. If we get back to the steading alive, you can have him. I'll go back to the Crow-horse.'

'No thank you. Some of us like to ride without fear for our necks. I'm happy with what I've got. It's better by far than the one I rode in on.'

Longinus rode a bay gift-horse that was indistinguishable from any other in the Batavian cohorts. His only concern, voiced the evening before, was that it would respond to the Batavian battle calls, which were foreign to him, and that he might therefore find himself charging into the enemy at a time not of his choosing. Who or what the enemy might be had not been discussed: the two incomers had been dining as Cerialis' guests at the time, on wood pigeon roasted in honey with figs and olives and a quantity of good red wine and the only shadow on the evening had been Valerius' refusal to drink anything stronger than water.

Valerius had plainly not intended insult and made up for it later by acknowledging his position as a sworn Lion of Mithras. He had found himself therefore the highest-ranking initiate of the bull-slayer in the IXth legion, the centurion who had been Father having been swept to the god in an epidemic of pneumonia at mid-winter, and had spent the time between the second and fourth watches, two hours either side of midnight, conducting an initiation in the cellar-shrine beneath the quartermaster's stores.

Longinus, who preferred the moon-gods of Thrace over the Persian incomer, had not been privy to the underground rites, only seen the new peace in Valerius' eyes as he had emerged, so that it seemed as if a night of lost sleep might not have been a disaster.

Later, in the grey light before dawn, with the first dew beading the grass and cockerels calling, the pair had walked up into the horse paddocks to another shrine that Civilis told them of, where the sign of a running mare had been chiselled onto a rock above a spring. Above was a far older mark of a moon, and a hare, and the two men had poured water in libation for their respective gods, and for each other.

They had each poured, too, for Civilis, without either of them being clear what it meant. Thinking of that now, Longinus said, in Thracian, 'Your once-brother is old. This is his chance to seal his name in history. You have no need to feel responsible for it if he chooses an honourable death in battle.'

The track passed a small mere. A trio of ducks took flight in a clatter of wings and aggrieved honks. The white-legged colt spun on its hocks, wild-eyed and snorting. Valerius swore in Thracian, Batavian, Gaulish and Latin and fought it back into line. Breathlessly, he said, 'I am not responsible for any man's actions. Civilis' life is his own to treat as he will. If he endangers what we plan, I will kill him myself, I swear it.'

'I know. I've seen the extent of what you will do for the Eceni.' Longinus pushed his horse sideways to avoid a pothole that stretched half the width of the track, cursing idle Roman engineers and the ravages of winter. 'What are we going to do if his Batavians don't follow him as he has said?'

'Fight them, as we thought we must to begin with. If we get that far, which we may not. If you look up ahead, you'll see the legate has noticed the place where the forest kisses the marsh and the track squeezes through between. I think perhaps he has just remembered the stories he was told as a young tribune of how Arminius slaughtered three legions on the Rhine.'

Petillius Cerialis rode a blue-eyed white gelding with a splash of chestnut on one ear. It stepped high-legged at the front, and did not look as if it could sustain a man long in battle. Bending, he spoke at some length to the youthful messenger riding at his side, who turned out of line and dropped back to Civilis' side.

'His excellency wishes to point out to you the potential for ambush ahead where the track is constrained between the forest and the marsh. He requests that you call to your side the most courageous of your Batavian warriors and, taking with you the messenger of Mithras who has the skills of an engineer' – he favoured Valerius with a white-eyed glance – 'that you ride ahead to the site of the overnight camp, there to hold it secure against possible attack until the advance cohorts of the legion may join you. He further orders that if you are attacked, you are not to await commands but are to act on your own sense of battle, nurtured since the time of the invasion, to repel the enemy. I am to come with you, to learn the tactics of warfare.'

It was a long message, relayed in a voice that cracked near the end with the pressure of responsibility. The youth was high-born Roman, third son of a magistrate, and fired with the service of his emperor. He had been one of those branded with the raven of Mithras in the cellar at midnight and was white still, with smoke-reddened eyes and the simmering fervour of one who has seen the face of his god and may not speak of it except in the clamour of his own heart.

Civilis smiled for him with something of the soft indulgence he had reserved for the horse boy, Arminius, his great-grandson, named for the man who had destroyed three legions of Rome. He said, 'Thank you. My men are already chosen. They will do now as the legate orders. May he have long life and the close company of his gods.'

The old man raised a hand. If his salutation was ambiguous, neither the youth nor the legate commented on it. A Batavian in the line behind bore on his spear's neck a scarlet pennant marked with an oak tree in black. At Civilis' signal, he lifted it high with one hand and with the other raised a silver-tipped cow's horn to his lips.

The noise when he blew was not unlike that made by the ducks which had risen from the mere, but longer and louder. Valerius sat very still, waiting for the white-legged colt to explode beneath him, and was pleasantly surprised to feel it prick its ears and settle instead. Immediately behind, two hundred and fifty horsemen, that half of the wing Civilis trusted most highly, peeled away from either side of the column and rode forward, leaving the infantry behind. Moving at a trot, and, soon, at a canter, they steered their horses to the narrow strips of unpaved ground on either side of the trackway, where the turf was springy beneath the feet.

Valerius gave his colt its head and let it take the front, lengthening away from the rest. Longinus caught up with him, laughing. In Thracian, he said, 'The Roman message-boy loves you. Am I supplanted?'

At speed, the white-legged colt was being unexpectedly steady. Valerius sat lightly, waiting for that to end. He said, 'Only if you want to be, and not by him. I branded him last night in the presence of the god and he thinks that in doing so I called the god to speak to him. He has forgotten that the gods choose freely to whom they will appear and speak, and are not called by those of us who follow them, however carefully we learn the words of the rites.'

Longinus whistled. 'Was it wise to be filling the legions with pious fervour, when we may be fighting against them by the end of the day?'

'It was what the god required of me. I didn't take the time to ask if it was wise.'

Valerius clicked his tongue and urged his mount to a little more speed and the two gift-horses, both trained by Civilis, responded to the command, stretching out their necks and backs, and the pound of their hooves rolled lightly across the turf, as if on midsummer paddocks.

In the middle of the afternoon, two hundred and fifty Batavian cavalrymen rode at a gallop into the only defensible site suitable for a night camp in the forested part of the ancestors' Stone Way.

It lay in a natural dell, a broad, shallow scoop where the trackway dipped down to follow the lie of the land and veered at the same time inward, away from the marsh. The forest had been cut back on all sides by the men of the IXth at the time they had used it as an encampment on their first march north. Since then, passing legionaries had kept the area around the camp's margins clear, leaving chopped wood in piles for fires and for staves, but the ditches and latrines had long since been filled in, and the grass and moss allowed to grow over. The emperor's peace must be seen to reign in the east and the presence of an active marching camp on the biggest arterial trade route running north from the capital city of Camulodunum did not sit well with that.

The dell smothered the noise of the horses so that they entered into peace. Nearby, water trickled musically within the shelter of the nearer trees. Some time in the past two decades, an engineer with spare time and initiative had dug a ditch into the marsh and run a series of fire-baked clay pipes under the trackway so that they emptied into glazed troughs of differing sizes set to one side of the dell. Bog water trickled in at a steady rate, and out again from corner lips to drain into wide pebbled soak-aways below, so that horses could drink and men could bathe, albeit coldly, and the ground beneath would not be churned to quagmire by the second morning.

A legionary of rather less imagination than the engineer had carved crude stick images of either horse or man into the side of each trough, lest those who followed be confused by which vessels were for watering the horses and which for bathing.

The Batavians dismounted at the gallop and led their steaming beasts to drink. Valerius, arriving later and more slowly, got down and walked his horse in hand around the margins of the encampment.

The marsh fog was less here, as if it clung to the forest, or was held within the margins of the trees by an outside force. In the dell, a blizzard of snowdrops hung greenly white along the risen edges of the infill where the encircling trenches had once been. Layers of leaf litter drifted against the ridges, and a part-circle of mushrooms rotted near the centre, broken by the greying skeleton of a hind. Her rear hind leg was missing, and her jaw fractured raggedly with claw marks along its length, to show where a bear had struck it.

Longinus kicked at the broken edge of the mandible. 'The she-bears will be happy with that.'

Valerius said, 'The she-bears left it there. Look at the inner edge of the mandible; it has Cunomar's mark of the bear paw on it. The rites of the bear will weaken the legionaries, or so they believe.' He drove a short iron stave into the ground. 'Stand here and tell me if I step off the line.'

For ten years, they had done this together: marked out the outer walls of a marching camp. Valerius paced backwards, unwinding a thread of oiled wool from the marker stave. Longinus shut one eye and watched. 'You need to go half a pace left,' he said and then, a little later, 'Left again. It's that bloody mad horse; it doesn't ride straight. You're leaning right.'

They paced and marked. Near the end, Civilis came to watch. Valerius said, 'Have your men start digging. Standard camp, standard size, standard drill. I'll mark out the tent lines.'

Half a wing of Batavians, cursing amiably, fetched mattocks and shovels from their saddle baggage. Working in pairs, they began to break open the green earth. They were big men, used to war, and still the first of each pair took care to lift the turf with its mesh of snowdrops and set it to one side, to be replaced with equal care in the morning when the camp was taken down.

Elsewhere, grass and moss were turned over as sods to mark the trench lines. Spade load after spade load of friable, much-shovelled soil became, quite soon, ramps within the trenchwork. Following Valerius' direction, smaller trenches, little less than divots in the turf, were dug within the camp lines to show the incoming legionaries where to place their eight-man tents and the larger, more stately pavilions of their officers. Long before they had finished, the sound of marching rolled to them up the trackway and the gold and scarlet of the standards breasted the mist.

The officers were already dismounting. Behind them, the first four men of the infantry reached the dell and halted. The Batavians howled insults, cavalry greeting the infantry as they had always done, for being late to camp or battle. Grinning, the infantry hornsman in the front rank lifted his cornu and blew. The sound brayed down the marching column and was repeated back and farther back and on down the line to the last century of the last cohort, where tired men heard it and knew that rest lay safely ahead.

Valerius, who in his guise as engineer had begun the hardest part of the camp-making and thus saved them many hours' work, raised his skinning knife in salute and hailed the incomers derisively in Latin, Batavian, Thracian, and one of the native dialects, entirely foreign to the men of the IXth legion. They cheered and answered in kind, with friendly obscenities.

From the forest close by, almost lost beneath the sound of marching, and of halting, and of men thrusting their heads into clay-piped water, a lone owl called thrice in daylight.

BELLOS THE BLIND KEPT WATCH AGAINST THE LEGIONS OF ROME from the side of an unlit fire pit in the newly deserted great-house on Mona.

Cold kept him awake and his mind sharp when the too-familiar smells of hearth and peat and thatch and the jostling afterthoughts of the departed warriors and dreamers might have lulled him to inattention. So many men and women had lived in the great-house and the settlement around it, so many children had been born, so many of the old and the not-old had died where Bellos now sat. Each had carved something on the roof beams and each had left behind the imprint of thoughts and memories. They were not bad thoughts, nor ugly memories, but they made it harder to focus his attention.

He had trained three full years for this; it was not impossible, only hard. Sightless, he stared at where the fire had once been and stretched his mind past the boundaries of the settlement to the shores of the gods' island and then out across the treacherous water of the straits towards the mainland and the wall of iron and sweat and pained horses and bored, frightened, hopeful, angry, determined men who slept in tents in the mountains of the far shore.

Urgency gave him a confidence he had once lacked. In the early days of his blindness, three years before, Bellos had prayed to every god he knew that he might be allowed to see again. Lying or walking or, once, running high-legged to avoid another fall, under the ministrations of Luain mac Calma, Elder of all Mona, Bellos had believed that he would be healed. Mac Calma's skills had been legendary and the blow to the head that had stolen Bellos' sight had not been hard, barely enough to cause a headache; there had seemed little reason to fear that the light might be banished from his life for ever.

It was only later, looking back, that he could trace the moment when the taste of the infusions he had been given to drink had become less bitter and the stories mac Calma had sung over the fire had changed from tales of golden-haired Belgic youths riding to victory over their foes to ones of the blind dreamers of the ancestors who had suffered hardship for years in order to learn how to walk in the other-worlds and had thereby saved their people from destruction.

Then, in the days of the ancestors, children of great talent had been chosen young and shown all the wonders of all the worlds and then blinded by hot irons that the sealing of sight in this, the smallest of the worlds, might open them more fully to the visions of all the others.

Luain mac Calma, Bellos came to understand, would never deliberately blind anyone in his charge, however gifted in the dreaming, but if a youth came to him who had lost his sight by accident, and if he suspected that youth might be possessed of a talent that stretched far beyond anything yet explored, then he considered it his duty as Elder and as a healer to test that youth's limits.

Even that much had been said slowly, by careful degrees. The turning point had come on a day in the spring, nearly a year after Bellos' blindness had first struck. He had been sitting outside the small hut with the stream running at his feet and a fire somewhere behind when he felt the tall, lean Elder come to stand by the first stepping stone that crossed the brook. Mac Calma's dream was the heron and it was easier to think of him as such. In the empty dark of his mind Bellos pictured the angled legs and the stabbing beak and shielded himself against its probing. The Elder turned and walked away, his feet soft on spring turf and the cast leaves of winter. From some distance back, he said, 'Where am I?'

He had asked the same thing the past three days in a row, from almost the same spot.

'By the curve in the stream,' Bellos said, wearily, and then, because it was his task for that month to paint clear images in his mind of all the things he could not see, he filled in all that he could imagine of the stream and the canopy of oak and hazel and drooping willow with the furled spring leaves and the first hints of catkins.

He placed the rocks of the crossing place with the moss damp and fresh and the swirling water around and a chaffinch, because it seemed right to him, and then was surprised when his mind filled in the detail of mac Calma as a man, long and lean, standing with one foot up, holding an unsheathed sword in his left hand. In his mind, the Elder tilted his head to one side and raised a brow.

Piqued, Bellos said, 'You have your right foot on the first stepping stone and you carry a blade that was not made for you.'

'Really? Who was it made for?'

The thread of doubt in the Elder's voice stung Bellos to answer. 'Valerius made it for the sake of the making. He had no-one in mind to wield it, but then you came to his forge in Hibernia while he was hammering it with news that his sister was dead and it carries the fears and angers of that day.'

'How do you know that?'

'I heard you tap the iron with your finger. How else?'

'If you can tell me how you can hear by the tap of a finger what the smith felt when he made a blade, I will be most interested to learn of it.'

The voice was closer, suddenly. Something shifted in the air, a hush of a foot on stone and a hand moving away from its resting place. In the dark world of Bellos' blindness, the heron was now, vividly, a man, so that each of the lines on the Elder's face was clear. This close, it was hard to doubt that mac Calma had sired Valerius; there was too much that was the same in them.

Hurt, Bellos backed away. He felt his eyes prickle and the skin of his throat flush hot. 'I'm not a seer. If the future were open to me, do you think I would have taken a path that led to blindness? I can't be what you want of me. Why can we not just let it go? Even if I were Roman, you would not torture me like this.'

'Is it torture, Bellos, truly?' Mac Calma had followed him. Cool, callused hands held each side of his face, turning it until the tracking tears, which he might have hidden, were exposed. 'Are you in pain still?'

Six months of silence broke apart without warning. Weeping openly, Bellos sank to sit on the stone. 'Does pain have to be of the body to be real? I want to *see* again, to see the ocean and the trees and the great-house, even now that it's empty and a travesty of what it once was. I want to see the sun set and the moon rise and the storm clouds cover the stars. I want to see the small things: the scratch on the side of the beaker I drink from in the morning, the wren that feeds from my hand, a leaf fall from a tree on a day without wind. I want to see a hound at a distance and know its colour, to see the look in a horse's eye and know if Valerius trained it and, if so, whether it is safe to ride; I want to see the first look of a lamb when it stands after birthing. I feel as if someone has wrapped a bandage round my eyes as a bad joke and I want them to take it off. I want *you* to take it off.'

Bellos was in blackness again, and thought mac Calma had left him. He sat on the stone and turned his face into the wind and heard nothing, and wondered if he had gone deaf, too, which would have been the end of living. He jumped as lean fingers settled on his shoulder and mac Calma's voice, stripped of all taunting, said, 'Bellos, I'm so sorry. In all the planning, I forget what it is to be young and powerless and in pain . . .'

The fingers moved down Bellos' arm, firm healer's hands that knew what they were about. Unresisting, he let his right hand be smoothed out flat and felt the hilt of the sword that had been forged by Valerius press into his palm. Confused, he gripped it, feeling foolish for his lack of warrior's skill. Even so, the familiarity of it coursed through him, bright as a Hibernian morning.

He had never held that blade before, but he knew without effort its balance and weight and the ridges on the grip. As if they were his own, he could feel the fear and pain and anger that had coursed through Valerius as he had beaten the last part of it to shape on his anvil.

The anger took hold of him, matching his own pain and sending it on to its natural conclusion. Before he could arrest the thought, Bellos saw himself dead, in the Roman way, fallen forward onto the blade so that the length of it entered his chest in the front and came out again, wet, at the back.

Shocked, he dropped the thing and heard iron bite into turf. Imagined blood splashed out in rivers across the green grass and he could not make it disappear. He looked up and saw a heron take flight and yet knew that in the world of his blindness, mac Calma had not moved.

Something split apart in Bellos' head and he saw the heron circle in over the stream and felt mac Calma's half-smile and watched his own ghost greet Briga, who ruled death, and take the first steps to the lands beyond life before it faded into a future that would never happen.

He would not let it happen. If his first prophecy were proved false, it would be his last; no-one asks for visions from a failed seer. Bellos sat on the ground and breathed slowly and the knifing pain behind his temples became less. He said, 'I am not going to fall on that blade, now or ever. Whatever is happening is not the future. I really don't want to be a seer.'

'Which is fortunate because you would need to train for twenty years to come close, and even then it is not always easy to interpret which dreams show futures that may happen only if every condition is met and which are certain.'

'Are there any of those?'

'Very few, in my experience. And there are more that are purely born of unspoken anxieties. Your vision of yourself dying was a fear, not a future. The two are quite different.'

Mac Calma bent to pick up the blade. Bellos could feel its shine, not as the moving of air, but as a raw awareness that let him feel the essence of the blade and the man who had made it overlaid with the heron-soul of the Elder who held it out across his palms.

Mac Calma said, 'The blind dreamers of the ancestors rarely chose to become seers. Their skills were better used in other ways. As yours will be.'

'What other ways?'

They were facing each other now, with the stream alongside. The water chuckled and mumbled over smooth stones. The shapes of it made sculptures that formed and melted in Bellos' mind in a way that was quite different from his mind-made imaginings, as if a door had opened and the land beyond it were not clouded in blindness. He clasped his hands about his knees. 'I don't understand how seeing fear and anger could be useful.'

'Do you not? It will not only be fear or anger you can see, but all strong feeling. Even so, suppose an enemy army were to come to battle and you were to know the hopes and fears of the men who fought in it. Could you see how that might benefit our warriors? Or our dreamers? It is not a simple thing to send dreams into clouded minds. Easier to pick up the threads of those fears that already exist and weave them into something stronger. Men who fight afraid, die afraid. If we face overwhelming numbers, making more of their fears may be our best – our only – hope.'

There had been no army of legionaries camped at the straits then. War on Mona had seemed impossible; Rome had been a distant threat, with the legions enmired in an endless, apparently unwinnable battle against the tribes of western Britannia. In his naiveté, Bellos had said, 'The warriors of Mona number in the thousands. The dreamers are twice that number and twice as dangerous. How could any army outnumber us when they must cross the straits by boat, ten at a time, or try to swim it in columns, towed by their horses?'

A certain closing had happened in the worlds that had just opened. Sitting by the stream with his senses scraped clean, Bellos had experienced, also for the first time, what it was to have a mind shielded against his new way of seeing.

From the strange flatness that had come suddenly to obscure him, mac Calma had said, quite kindly, 'We must lure the legions to the west if Breaca is to have a chance to free the east. To do that, we may have to sacrifice Mona.'

'How?'

'You will see, if it happens. I will not destroy lives for the sake of it; as many as may be of those who live here will be sent west to Hibernia. Already we have the ships waiting.'

'But then Mona will be undefended.'

'Not entirely. We will not leave it empty and the gods have ways to protect their own, but even so it seems likely that there will be an assault by at least one legion, maybe two, on this island. When that day comes, we will need you as we have never needed one man before. If it would help us to destroy all that is Roman and push it from the land, would you learn what I can teach you of the ways to walk between the worlds?'

The day had fallen quiet. The skip of the stream and the chatter of children at the great-house and the sighing wind had all been hushed. Only the wren that fed daily from Bellos' hand sang clearly. The dreamers told that the wren was mightiest of the birds, beloved of the gods because it alone could fly higher than the eagle, and see farther. With nothing to obscure the purity of the sound, the spiralling notes stippled the sky, beautiful as leaves that fall without wind in autumn.

Bellos had said, 'If you think I can do it, I will do my best. I make no promises of success.'

The heron that was mac Calma had been more than usually gentle as he said, 'The gods never ask for the promise of success, only that we try.'

For three years, Bellos had tried his best to learn all that mac Calma could teach him.

With each successive year, he had watched the sacrifice of Mona brought closer with a ruthless single-mindedness that had shocked him more deeply at every step.

Valerius had played a part in it, leading the warriors to battle to allow the evacuation across the short sea to Hibernia of dreamers and children, livestock, breeding herds of horses and all that was sacred and could be moved.

The great-house could not be moved. The ancestors had built it to withstand storm and tempest and the tests of the dreamers, but the vast beams of its walls and the turf on the roof, which were old when the gods were young, were as much a part of Mona as the rocks of the foreshore and the forests of the interior; they could not be uprooted and shipped west to Hibernia, however welcome they might have been.

With its long lineage of dreaming, with the carvings along the roof beams showing the dream of each elder going back hundreds of generations, the great-house of Mona was the most profound of mac Calma's sacrifices, designed to draw the Roman governor to attack the island, and thus to commit his forces to a battle they could not win against an enemy who had already fled the field.

The plan had succeeded in proportion to the cost. With horrified admiration, Bellos had watched as a pacifist Roman governor had been slain and his successor, picked for his skills as a general, had been goaded into a progressively more savage war against the Silures and the Ordovices. These two tribes had successfully held the west for the twenty years since the invasion. Under mac Calma's guidance, they had gradually, and apparently unwillingly, been pushed into retreat, luring the legions westward by slow degrees as summer closed into autumn and the fighting season drew to an end.

Feeling victory close, the Roman governor had advanced hard at the onset of spring until he camped with two full legions and eight wings of cavalry in the mainland valleys less than half a day's ride from the vicious currents of the straits that guarded Mona. So large an army, to capture and subdue a scrap of an island that a warrior on a fit horse could ride round in a day.

The legions were afraid of Mona, and of the men and women who lived there under the gods' care. That much was obvious to anyone, whatever their vision and training. It was to learn the shape and size and texture of those fears that Bellos sat beside the cold fire and sent his mind beyond the confines of his body as he had been taught.

It was becoming easier with practice. The hardest part, always, was crossing the short stretch of sea that divided the mainland from the island. In the world of sight that other men inhabited, the gods' water flowed grey and wild and unpredictable, with shifting sandbars and hidden currents to drag into drowning all those who sought to conquer Mona. In the worlds through which Bellos the Blind alone could travel, the sea was a chasm of untold depth that sucked souls into the void of its heart and destroyed them.

Less than two days before, he had finally found a way across. Something mac Calma had said gave him the key. *Remember that this world is an illusion as much as the others. We who have sight see what we choose to see and so make it real.*

Understanding the truth of that made it possible for Bellos to view the chasm at least partly as a product of his own fear. For nine days, he had worked on focusing his will until he could make himself believe it nothing more than an illusion. On the same sharp spring morning when geese mourned a dead messenger in the lands of the Eceni, Bellos the Blind, sitting in the great-house on Mona half a month's ride to the west, and passing through a world in which he alone could see, crossed the gods' chasm as if it were dry rock and, for the first time in his life, stretched his mind to touch the mainland of Britannia.

His quiet satisfaction as he saw the rocks and seaweeds of the shore lasted less than a heartbeat. Even as he paused to look around, he was enveloped by a wall of blinding fog, product of the wine and fatigue and ill-considered dreams of the legionaries.

Bellos had become used to being able to see in the other-worlds. Suddenly blind, he stumbled across unseen boulders with his arms outstretched, feeling too close to the days of his youth as a whore in a harbour tavern in Gaul when Manannan of the waves had sent the sea haar to fill the town and made everyone white-blind.

Panic made him careless. He felt himself trip and began to fall forward as if his body had real weight and might be cut to ribbons on the sharp rocks of the shore. Mac Calma's voice held him: *. . . an illusion as much as the others . . .*

An illusion. Only that. Bellos breathed deep and made the rocks less sharp and gave himself the kind of balance Valerius had in battle. Steadier, he closed his mind to everything but the earth at his feet and stood still on flat ground of his own making. The fogs of his childhood had been harsh and wet and cold and had mirrored his life of the time, which was not his life of today. The understanding of these two things, and the difference between them, made his fear less. He laid aside past memories and remembered instead the warmth of the great-house in winter when the fires were fully lit, and the care that surrounded him now.

Thus enfolded, Bellos stretched his mind again towards the palpable textures of a thousand men's nightmares, and was not blinded.

He breathed in the hopes and fears of the legions. His head buzzed with the myths and rumours of defeated men who had fought too long in a land where they were not welcome. He listened to old conversations, recalled by sleepy minds, which laid the hell of the weather and the sucking insects and the bad food and the bogs and the quicksands and the routine mutilation of slain legionaries all at the feet of gods who supported the tribes and loathed the legions.

None of it was specific. None of it was enough to halt an invasion.

Bellos took in a breath and set about to find what he needed. First, he created clarity, hand's breadth by hand's breadth across the ground in front of him. His hands spun the fear-fog into cords that could be teased gently from their moorings without alerting those from whom they came. The men thus robbed would wake in the morning with thicker heads than their wine might have predicted, but, more important, the full colour and terror of their nightmares came to Bellos as he wove, so that he came gradually to see the common threads that ran through all of them.

He was working near the centre where the officers' pavilions were pitched, when he found the pinpoint of light that showed a wiser mind. He watched it sideways for a while, never looking directly in case his gaze was felt. From this one man, he took no threads of thought, only skirted him and left the thinning mist of his comrades as a cloak. Even so, there was a reaching out from the other and a kind of recognition, as if they shared more in common than they knew.

Surprise and a trace of his own fear loosened Bellos' hold on the place where he stood. A ripple of cold spread across his chest in warning; in the great-house, he was no longer alone.

Holding fast to the cords he had spun, he made the easier, lighter crossing back to the world of his heart and daily life and opened his eyes into blindness and the draught of a lit fire.

'Luain mac Calma.' Some men he knew simply by the way the air changed around them. He said, 'I thought you were on Hibernia overseeing the building of a new great-house to shelter those who have been evacuated from here.'

The Elder was sitting by the fire pit. The smell of new smoke came from between his feet. He said, 'I was. The great-house is done, or nearly so. They have less need of me than you do.'

'You think I have need of you?' Bellos felt himself stiffen. 'Have I risked more danger than I knew? Or failed in the tasks you set me?'

'I don't know. Have you?'

Bellos was learning how thoroughly mac Calma cloaked himself. In this man, alone of all the warriors and dreamers he had searched in his training, Bellos could see nothing that he was not shown. He saw humour now, and the archness of the heron, and watched, surprised, as both softened to something warmer.

'I'm sorry. That was disingenuous, and also dishonest. I have a need to be here that is separate from what you do.' The Elder rose and moved away from the fire. He sounded more like Valerius than he usually did. He said, 'For twenty years since the legions came, I have watched the tribes driven into servitude in spite of all that I and others can do. This may not be our last chance, but it is our best. If we can draw Suetonius Paullinus and his two legions fully to us, and destroy them – even if we can only weaken them – then Breaca and Valerius may prevail in the east. If they can take Camulodunum and restore the god to his seat, then we may finish what we have begun; we may wake one day in a land free of Rome. The whole of that action begins here, now, on Mona.'

The cold that had touched him before sat again in Bellos' chest. He said, 'You haven't answered my question. Am I failing in my part of this?'

'Not at all. But I may be. I have risked the sacrifice of Mona and all that is precious here. A hundred generations of elders have learned in this great-house and I will see it burn to preserve those things I believe are greater. I may be wrong. This may be the greatest hubris and the biggest mistake ever made by one man in the face of the gods. Only by being here as it happens will I know which it is.'

In the fire-warmed quiet that followed, Bellos saw something of how the Elder of Mona might look if he chose not to shield him-self to one who walked between the worlds. He said, 'The legions are terrified of the straits. They believe them filled with sea-serpents and spirit-women who will lure them in by song and drown them. They fear the threat of warriors who kill from the forest and the high lands and do not stand in lines and fight. More than all of that, they fear the dreamers; their commanders have told them that we sacrifice living men to the fire and read the future in their screaming. They have all seen the circus in Rome and been rendered weak in their guts for fear to see the same deaths enacted on the men of the legions. If we can bring any of these things to reality, they will come to us already beaten.'

'Or they will fight with the carelessness of men who know their lives forfeit and want only the clean death of battle. I have seen that, and not only in the legions; when the fear is greatest, some-times it turns to battle rage and is all the harder to contain. But it's good to know what they fear. We can work with it. Thank you.' Mac Calma tapped the tips of his fingers on Bellos' knee, as he had done once or twice in the days of their training. 'I have an idea of how hard that must have been. We may need you again. Will you be willing to do it?'

'It was effortless,' said Bellos, and believed himself. 'If it will defeat Rome, I will do it whenever and for as long as you ask.'

'But not tonight; you need to sleep. Thorn has lit a fire in your hut. She may still be there if you go.'

Thorn was there. Like mac Calma, she made no allowance for Bellos' blindness, for which he was daily grateful. She was warm and giving and glad to see him, and that, too, left him speechless with wonder and gratitude.

He had been a child whore in Gaul, used by men, not kindly, and beaten after by the tavernmaster if he baulked at their advances. He had resolved early in life never to inflict the pain of his desire on another human being. Then Valerius had come, with his guarded, over-careful kindness and the brittle touchiness born of need to show always that he was never going to ask anything unwanted of the child he had freed.

Bellos had not expected ever to feel rejected by a man, or to care if he were. The hurt of that, too, had taken some time to heal and it was only latterly, as he had come to understand the pain that drove Valerius, that he had begun to comprehend the fastidious care with which he had been treated. He had started to love then, and to yearn in his own right, and had needed time to set that aside before something approaching true friendship could grow. It had done; he believed that and kept the memories of it fresh in his heart.

Thorn had come to tend him after Valerius left for the east. She, too, had been careful in her affection, becoming a part of his life as surely as the wren that fed from his hand, never asking for more. He had been slow to understand her, too, and so the moves towards something deeper had been all hers, taken so slowly and carefully that she had been in his bed, winding her body around his, before he had truly understood what had overtaken him, and that it was allowed, and safe, and would not cause hurt to either of them, and that she wanted it of him and that he wanted it more than anything he had ever imagined, or could imagine, except possibly the return of his sight.

When mac Calma had returned sight of a kind, Bellos' one fear was that he might lose the want of Thorn. In the event, his need had been no less and his joy greater. He could envisage no greater gift than the greeting she gave when he returned, cold and worn, from the great-house and she was waiting for him with a fire lit and her hands chafing his to warm them and the smell of stewed hare in the pot and her voice weaving a magic that brought him back to this world, where he might be blind, but he could reach for her and hold her close and explore the contours of her being with the same wonder as the first day and each day since.

He put the bowls aside, carefully, not to spill what might be left. Thorn came to him, teasingly delicate. She smelled of the sea and of wood gathered from a forest floor and of the pepper-musk that flavoured every part of her. Her skin was smooth as polished stone and her hair spun wool under his fingers. He had no idea what colour it was.

He let her draw him to the pile of horse hides that was their bed and cradle him in her arms as if he were a child. Her breasts and her sex pressed on his back and the feel of both brought him back so that he understood how far into the other-worlds he had gone. He might have been afraid of that, but the urgency of his own need pushed the thought away so that he rolled over and took her face in his hands and kissed it, and waited until her breathing told him that her need was as great as his before he entered her.

Later, as her hound warmed his back and she warmed all that was still warm in him, he said, 'I thought you had gone to Hibernia with the rest of the dreamers?'

'I had.' Thorn smiled into the crook of his neck. 'I came back. Mac Calma's dreams showed me here when the legions come.'

Bellos felt the cold in his chest for the third time that night. His fingers halted their combing of her hair. 'Do his dreams show you still living when they leave?' he asked.

She bit the edge of his collar bone, reproving. 'The dreams don't yet show anything after the first battle. We have to make the future happen as we want it. That's why I'm here.'

X

CYGFA, ELDER DAUGHTER OF THE BOUDICA, MADE THE THREE-fold call of the owl at Valerius' signal. A relay of hidden warriors passed it on down through the mist and the fringes of the forest to the place at the farthest end of their line where her brother, Cunomar, lay on his belly under the winter-flayed roots of a fallen oak.

Cunomar lay on ground that juddered to the stamp of marching feet. The legionaries of the third cohort of the IXth legion who marched a spear's length from his face continued to sing the fifteenth stanza of the marching song they had begun when the first ranks passed him by. They did not hear the owl, and if they had, they would not have known what it meant. Cunomar heard it and knew exactly what it meant, and did nothing.

No part of him looked human, nor did he feel it. He was naked but for his knife belt and the king-band on his arm which had been his mother's last gift to him, in the winter before the procurator's destruction of their steading. Bear's grease coated him from the soles of his feet to the line of his brow, tinted with woad to render it densely grey. Bands of white lime ringed his eyes and made skull marks on his cheeks. His hair was stiffened with pig's fat and white lime, making a pale grey scythe that stood up from his scalp.

In the past day, since the burning of the watchtower, he had dis-carded even the feathers that marked the kills of his past. That act alone severed him from all that had gone before, setting him apart from his peers more than his bloodline or his missing ear could ever have done. Mist-given and woad-held, he was a warrior without any ties to the living, with nothing to fight for but the battle itself, nothing to sway him but the breath of the gods, nothing to care about but the next breath and the next and the next . . .

The elders of the Caledonii had taught him the ways of discipline that allowed him to hold his mind still and empty, that he might become a part of the earth. Since dawn, he had held to it, with only the occasional lapse, but the owl's cry brought with it a memory of the night's dreaming that would not be shaken off.

Even as he strove for emptiness, Cunomar smelled again the fetid breath of the bear and was back in the nightmare that had woken him the past three nights; this was not a dream of the she-bear, beast of all mystery and glory to whom he had given his soul, but a rank, injured male, which had been hunted into a blind-ended cave and had turned at bay in all its pain and fury, raking out with claws that stretched and stretched and reached past the warrior who came to kill it to the injured child, his sister, who had been sent to the cave for safety and was only now waking and standing, and reaching for her brother, not understanding the danger. In the dream, the bear turned, and rose on its hind legs and smashed a single long-clawed fist down and down and—

Graine! No! Cunomar did not speak the words aloud; his discipline held so much.

Doggedly, he set about controlling his breathing. Sweat rolled greasily from his armpits and buttocks. Presently, he was able to hear again the iron clash of the marching legionaries and the newest stanza of their song.

He worked as he had been taught to clear his mind and would not linger on the memory of Graine's face as the bear fist smashed down to break her, or on his own failure to save her. It was not the first time the dream had come and he did not believe it would be the last; he knew only that he would give his life to protect his sister, and that no bear, in the dream or out of it, would reach her while he lived.

He could not find the silence again, and stopped trying. Freed, his thoughts fell first on Ardacos, the mentor who had shown him what it was to be a ghost-warrior, giving him a mark to aim for that had seemed beyond all possibility to the child he had been.

Ardacos had long since discarded his own kill-feathers. The small Caledonian warrior marked only those kills where the combat had been single-handed against a worthy opponent; for those he bore a band of red ochre round his upper arm. There were three, and he could name all three warriors and the means of their dying, with each act of their life, as if they were heroes. Not one of them had been Roman, although he had slain as many legionaries as any other living warrior.

Cunomar was not certain whom he considered a worthy opponent now that the world had changed. Through all of his youth, he had dreamed of killing a certain decurion of the Thracian cavalry who rode a pied horse and was known as the scourge of the tribes from east coast to west.

For so many reasons, that man's death would have been worth an ochre stripe. Then Valerius had ridden his pied horse into the steading and crushed the life from the Roman procurator in an act of blinding savagery that had sealed his return to the Eceni. Only afterwards had he declared himself the Boudica's brother and by then it was already too late to kill him.

Thus, unwilling, Cunomar had set aside ten years of yearning, or at least had left it in abeyance. He had not yet said so aloud in the council circle, but it seemed to him obvious that a man who had changed sides twice in his life might easily choose to do so again. For that, if for no other reason, Valerius was not fit to lead the war host if the Boudica should not prove able. Cygfa, clearly, thought otherwise and she was not alone.

Few had spoken of it openly, but it was there to be read in their eyes: the fear that the Boudica had lost the wildfire and must soon be replaced. Many simply refused to believe it could happen, but, like Cygfa, Cunomar had seen his father broken by Rome and knew the signs.

He had no idea how long it would be before the rest came to see as he saw. He only knew that it was not enough to be the Boudica's only son; he had to prove to himself, to his sister, to those others who might doubt him, above all to the she-bear and the watching gods, that he was the obvious one – the only one – to whom they could turn in adversity. Then, when Valerius stood against him, he could fight, and he could kill, and the world would come to hear what kind of warrior was the Boudica's son.

It took a deal of self-control not to move at that thought. Cunomar held himself motionless and was rewarded for it. Ahead and a little to his right, in the damp mulch of the forest's floor where small things crept and a single leaf was large as a round-house, a shrew stalked a thready earthworm. Cunomar breathed out a long, controlled exhalation and the shrew did not stop. Since dawn it had skirted him, wary of the stench and the unexpected warmth of his body. Then the worm had surfaced, and was too good to ignore.

The elders of the Caledonii gave their approval sparingly, but they would have given it now. The ultimate test of their teachings was that the small things – or large – of the forest or heath would come close without fear.

Cunomar breathed more quietly still. His skin itched beneath the layers of grease. A ring of white lime round each eye had dried, pulling the skin into a frown. Small twigs dug into the flesh at his ankles, his hips, his ribs, his chin, all the places where his frame pressed hardest onto the forest floor. Perversely, his throat was dry and craved water at the same time as his bladder began to nag with the need to empty. The flesh of his back ached where the wounds of the flogging had not yet healed. His missing ear burned.

Ahead, the shrew finished its feed. Round-bellied and wet about the muzzle and breast with the life of the worm, it prodded its way under the leaves and curled to sleep. Cunomar catalogued in turn each of the demands of his body and then, setting them aside, gave a good part of his attention to the pattering heartbeat and small, vicious mouth of the shrew and strove to banish all thoughts of Valerius and everything he represented.

A change in the pounding rhythm of the earth drew his gaze back to the ancestors' trackway. His eyes were level with the high-est point of the road, on the apex of the curve that tipped down at either side to marsh and forest. Close enough for Cunomar to smell the sweat, the sandalled, studded feet of the last ranks of the IXth legion stamped by. Living flesh impacted resonantly on leather and armour. The lungs of a hundred men drew in the thickening fog and exhaled it, rasping. Ten thousand iron studs hammered the stone track and the sound echoed off the trees onto the marsh and was sucked to silence. Marching men became iron-clad, helmeted ghosts, passing out of the bog mist and back into it, visible only for a spear's throw either side of where the Boudica's son, at last, prepared himself to move.

Then they were gone; the last men of the last cohort passed by and the mist closed behind and there were no more. The silence ached more than the noise had done.

A night's waiting, and half of a morning, bore the fruit they had promised. Cunomar moved his hand a hair's breadth to the left. Leaves shivered where the shrew slept, and were still. Kneeling in the loam, with the night's dream banished, with his pulse clear and light in his head, and the breath of the she-bear warming his heart, Cunomar put his two thumbs to his lips and made the sound of a bittern, booming.

Ulla joined him, and Scerros, and his girl-cousin of the northern Eceni whose name Cunomar had never learned. They were barely recognizable, hidden behind the skull patterns of white lime on grey woad. Each smiled, a flash of white teeth that proved them not yet ghosts. Full of the she-bear, fired in breath and heartbeat, filled with the promise of honour and the need for vengeance, they stepped into the fog that shrouded the trackway, and were invisible.

After half a morning of lying still, to move at all was an act of will. To run silently across the last spear's length of forest, onto the trackway and up behind the last four marching legionaries was worthy of a winter's tale in its own right.

The stench of bear and pig grease warned the rear guard of the IXth that they were under attack, but not soon enough. Four hands caught four helmeted heads and drew them back; four blades cut through fog and skin and cartilage. Four men screamed pain and warnings and death through severed windpipes that transmitted no sound. Like culled cattle, they bellowed soundlessly, and died as fast. Their eyes rolled up in their heads to show the whites beneath and their limbs fell limp.

Blood flowed in blackening cataracts on the grey, cold pavings of the ancestors' Stone Way. Four ghosts stepped free and were guided fast away by Airmid and Gunovar and Lanis, who joined together to see that the dead of both sides were not left to wander lost in the cold mist; Valerius had asked for that and no-one had spoken against him.

Other warriors came forward from the trees and helped support the bodies and catch the dead men's shields and their packs so that nothing might clatter onto the stones and alert the legionaries marching ahead to the slaughter behind. With care, the dead were carried aside and propped by the trees and left to be stripped of their weapons by the children and grandmothers later, when it was safe.

Already the cycle had begun again. Four more ghosted warriors had stepped out from their places in the trees and, as greyly, as silently, caught the helmeted heads of the last four men and cut the breath from their throats before they knew they were dying.

The remaining men of the IXth marched on, caught in their own rhythms of flesh on leather and iron on stone. Far to the front, the horns of the first cohort beckoned, promising with each new refrain tents already pitched and cooking fires lit and wineskins broached; the reward offered to those who marched in the rear-guard of any column was to arrive in the evening to a camp already built.

Thus enticed, the men of the third cohort marched into a mist that opened three rows in front and closed behind. The forest to their right was as quiet as it had been since they started, and the bog to their left as improbably innocent, and neither was enough to make them break step and look behind.

The third row died, and the fourth. The warriors who had carried away the bodies of the first legionaries sped forward to make kills of their own, running barefooted on the paving slabs, slick with bear grease, protected from the curses of ghosts and the iron cuts of living men by woad and the power of the she-bear.

Twenty marching rows were taken in silence. Eighty men died, and there were still thousands marching. The entirety of the she-bear, all forty-seven warriors, were up and running on the road, pushing their luck with each footfall, taking greater risks with each cut of the knife.

Bloodily wet in his coating of woad grease Cunomar propped a body against a tree and ran forward between two dying men. Ulla was on his left, the girl-cousin on his right. Scerros, a little late lowering his man to the earth, caught up as they reached the next row of marching legionaries.

Breathless, a little flustered, not quite riding the power of the bear, Scerros fumbled his hold. His knife scored flesh and the edge of one pumping vessel, but not the ridged pipe of the trachea. The legionary screeched like a throttled hen and his death was neither neat nor fast.

The three men of his row were too late to profit from the warning, but the ones in front had time to call out an alarm and draw their short stabbing swords and shoulder their shields and turn at least halfway to face the mob of grey-slaked phantoms who came howling at them from the mist, all pretence at secrecy abandoned.

The rearmost four men died messily, inflicting wounds before they did so. The next four achieved a kill, cutting the number of the she-bear to forty-six. In the time between, Cunomar put his bloodied fingers to his lips, filled his lungs with bog air and let out a single, mind-numbing whistle that reached at least to the head of the cohort. Lest it be misconstrued, or unheard, he took from his belt a cow's horn lipped in copper, and brayed a note, harsh as a legionary mule, that rocked the mere and silenced the crows gathering on the margins of the forest. That done, he paused to wipe his knife blade free of the gobbets of flesh that had clung to it, and, howling the name of the newly dead she-bear as a fresh battle cry, hurled himself joyfully into battle.

The Boudica, and those waiting for her, heard a whistle and then an ox-horn pierce the fog. At that signal, four axes finished what they had begun before the legion's march. The oak that fell across the trackway as the last note sounded was broad as a man is long and thickly branched. It killed three of the four men passing under it and crushed the legs of the fourth, so that he was an easy target for a slingstone.

Breaca sent the stone, aiming for the soft part of his skull where the bones met above the ear. There had been a time when she could split a held hair at fifty paces. That time was not now, but half a morning's practice had restored enough of the old skill to hit a trapped man less than a spear's length away. Among a clatter of thrown spears and slung stones, hers hit close enough to where it was sent and she made her second kill in two days and heard it cheered by the youths around her as if it were a victory in itself.

Dubornos was at her side. He, too, had once been whole, until the ravages of Rome had reduced him to the sling and the knife.

She felt his hand on her shoulder. 'It'll come with time,' he said, quietly. 'For now, what we do doesn't have to be glorious or honourable, only enough to teach warriors who have held their first blade for less than a month how to fight.'

Valerius had said exactly that in the council meetings of the night and Breaca had repeated it to the war host: this battle is a training ground; don't expect heroism, only do your best to survive.

It was Longinus who had said: 'Even if you cut off the rear part of the legion, it won't be easy. The centurions of the Ninth have all seen action in the Germanies; they know how to fight. As soon as they realize they're on their own, they'll take command and try to hold order until help arrives. Don't expect them to give their lives away.'

Longinus had impressed Breaca more each time she met him. Her brother's soul-friend was quiet and thoughtful and when he spoke, which was rarely, it was to good effect.

With his warning in her ears, she had watched the glitter of mounted officers riding at the head of the column, and marked the harder, more knowing faces of the centurions as they passed. These were the men who had recognized the possibility of ambush long before it came, and might have seen the part-cut trees swaying at intervals along the margins of the trackway ready to fall with two more blows of the axe.

It was for these men that she had insisted the chippings be cleared as the axes created them and the ruined trunks wrapped about in moss and lichens. For these, too, the best slingers had been stationed, watching for the marks of rank and authority, with orders to target them soon and early.

They were not soon enough and Longinus was proved entirely right. Deprived of all contact with senior officers, the twelve centurions trapped on the wrong side of the fallen oak took rapid command of their men. Startlingly fast, they drew order out of chaos. A dozen of the legionaries nearest Breaca turned, raising their shields to form a roof against falling spears. It was an obvious move for men who had not served in the west and did not know that slingstones were aimed for the unshielded knees of those who lifted their shields to protect their faces and heads, crippling them as effectively as if they had been hamstrung.

Somebody knew it, further up the line. Breaca heard frantic orders bellowed down the ragged column. The exposed men were already falling, but one group, higher up, were making better use of their shields.

Leaving the new formation to Ardacos and those who fought with him, she ran between the trees towards the source of the shouting. Oak branches stabbed at her. Leafing hazel slapped her face. She came level with a group of eight men who had formed a ring, kneeling, with six shields held outwards and two above. She could see no place where a pebble could pass through between the shields, still less a spear. From the centre came the bull's bellow of a centurion, passing orders down the line. Already other eights were forming; spent spears glanced off the raised shields and skittered uselessly into the mere.

Dubornos was close to Breaca's right shoulder. He had not been flogged as she had, but Rome's inquisitors had ruined him long before that. For the past eight years, the only weapon he could bear with his right hand had been a sling. He had practised harder and for longer than anyone she knew, and was breathtakingly good.

Without turning, she said, 'If I part the shields, can you at least wound the centurion in the centre?'

'If I can see him, I can kill him.'

Anyone else would have grinned, saying that. Dubornos had never been light-hearted; he carried too much guilt and grief for that. He slid a stone into his sling, and circled his wrist fluidly. 'If you can do something to lower the shield with the black swans on it, it would give me the easiest target.'

The black swans faced each other on either side of crossed thunderbolts painted scarlet on black with the centurion's left-pointing chevron below. Breaca could see the wind-burned skin of the man whose mark they were. His eyes looked momentarily over the rim of his shield and were hidden again. She said, 'We should be mounted for this,' and ran out, holding her spear before her as if she were hunting boar.

The tip caught the left hand of the two swans, which was inmost on the shield, and drove through the bull's hide to lodge in the laminated wood behind. Breaca thrust her whole weight in and then wrenched it back, snagging the shield in its wake.

The spear twisted in her hands and cracked and broke. A sling-stone blurred at the edge of her vision. The wall of scarlet thunderbolts swayed and parted. Then her own private thunder-bolt punched her in the back, between the shoulder blades where the flesh was most damaged. A scream split the air and she knew it as hers in the infinite moment before she fell. Sometime before she hit the paved rock of the trackway, hands caught her and held her and carried her. Some of them remembered not to touch her back.

The pain in her shoulder was astonishing, like a new wound break-ing open. Someone whimpered, childlike. It seemed not to be her. When she was sure of that, Breaca opened her eyes. Dubornos' face loomed above hers. He was not whimpering, but swearing and weeping together. Tears made shining tracks on his cheeks. He looked ten years older than he had done when she ran past him to break the shield ring.

'Never,' he said, 'never, never, never did I think you would do that. Why couldn't you throw your god-cursed spear like anyone else who values life above stupid, stupid displays of heroics? We have to *survive*, that's all. You of all people have nothing to prove here.'

There were too many people too close to answer that, and a place on her shoulder that burned as if she had taken a sword thrust, which seemed unlikely. The whimpering continued and still she could not place the source.

She sat up and looked around. A young copper-haired youth knelt nearby with a bruise flaring crimson across his mouth and wild, white-rimmed eyes. The hair hung in furls by his left ear, as if the war-braids had been forcibly ripped out, and a livid welt at his right wrist showed where a sling had recently been stripped from him. He stared at Dubornos as if the singer were more dangerous than all the avenging armies of Rome. The whimpering was his.

To him, Breaca said, 'Was it your slingstone that hit me?'

His face was answer enough. He was too terrified to speak. She said, 'What's your name?'

Dubornos answered for him. 'Burannos. He was one of those who failed Cunomar's spear trials. He trained instead as a slinger. Not well enough.'

Breaca said, 'We could list for him the failures of our youth but it would take longer than we have.'

She tried to stand, and succeeded on the second attempt. She was deeper in the forest than she had been, shielded by trees from the track. Sounds of battle came clearly enough, but not the detail. She asked, 'Did we break the eight-ring?'

Dubornos looked down at his hands. His sling still hung from his wrist, cradling a pebble as if it were the easiest thing in the world to walk with the pebble held, not something youths practised for months without success.

'No. The centurion is dead and one other, but when you fell we brought you clear and the ring re-formed. I set a dozen slingers to keep them occupied. If we leave it too long, they'll remember that attack is better than defence and charge us instead.'

'Then we have to break them open again before they begin to think.' Someone offered Breaca a sling and she took it. 'Burannos can stand between us. Set anyone with a spear who knows how to throw it to aim at one of the shields. We can direct the stones through to the centre if they can make a big enough gap.'

Back on the track, with fighting on either side, the black-swan shield was central now in a ring of five, with one held as roof-shield above. Young warriors hidden in the tree line with slings took time for target practice. Pebbles rang on bull's hide and iron. The sound was lost in the other noises of battle.

A dozen youths with spears stepped past the shelter of the trees to take foot on the margins of the track. The legionaries trapped within the ring saw the danger. Momentarily, they pulled their shields tighter until the edges overlapped and there were no gaps at all, like a woodlouse, curling. Then one in the centre, seeing what might come, gave three words as an order and smoothly, beautifully, as if by an act of the gods, the entire ring unfolded and became a line.

For a heartbeat, perhaps two, the legionaries were not moving, each man looking sideways to see if he remained in line with his neighbours. The junior officer was in the centre, and had taken his centurion's helmet. The horsehair crest waved black in the wind. He looked along the line and drew breath to shout a fresh order.

Breaca was before him. 'Now!'

Dubornos' pebble was too small to see, only a whisper of marsh mist as it passed her. A legionary whose elbow had been carelessly shown screamed and pitched forward, the bones of his forearm shattered.

The men who flanked him were already running. They jumped their comrade's fallen body and when they landed they moved together, filling the gap where he had been. A spear angled low beneath the shield of one and he had to jump to avoid it. The second time, Breaca was waiting for the flash of flesh at his throat.

Burannos was ahead of her. She felt the swing of his throw and saw the legionary stagger. Her own stone was aimed lower and broke the man's kneecap. A spear jammed into the shield of his running-mate, thrust by a rust-haired girl who, if she was not Burannos' twin, was his close kin. A sword peeled skin off her forearm as she jumped back. Another warrior, careless of death, stepped in to jab a spear into the face of a legionary who died in the moment when he realized he faced a dozen warriors alone.

Breaca reached for her sword and swore violently as the first two strokes with it pulled at muscles that were still stiffened from her night's combat against Valerius. Then she warmed into the movement and, for a time, there was no room for doubt or the sluggishness of pain, only action and the need to survive, and with luck, to show an example that was not all bad.

In a lifetime of untidy skirmishes, it was the messiest. At the end, Breaca lowered her blade. There was blood on it, but only from cutting the throat of a man already down. She leaned back on a tree and the press of it down the length of her spine was almost welcome.

'Not glorious, but we lost no-one. It could have been worse.'

Dubornos spoke from his place at her shoulder. Together, he and Breaca watched the youth, Burannos, run forward to the rust-haired girl and embrace her in the middle of the trackway, as if they had fought a final battle, not a minor skirmish that cut the tail-tip of a serpent whose head still waited unawares and could smash them without thought.

Breaca said, 'It needs to be immeasurably better before we can take on a full legion.'

She wiped a slick of sweat from her face. On either side along the trackway, a dozen similarly disorganized skirmishes still raged, as warriors of all ages engaged legionaries in rings or lines. Plumed helmets in black and white reared at intervals above the lines of battle. She saw one in red that reached higher than the others, and watched it fall. Spears arced over and vanished into the mere.

Exhausted, Breaca sat on the turf and thought of Valerius and what he would say at the lack of discipline in the warriors of her war host. She thought of Ardacos, and how the she-bears he had led for ten years in the western war had not needed the discipline of rank and fear, but had followed the fire and heart of the bear with Ardacos as their leader in spirit more than in flesh.

She thought of the warriors of Mona and the years that went into the training of them, so that each took to the field in absolute trust of their own skill and those around them. She looked at the wavering line of untested, untrained warriors and considered what it would take to bring them to that. She felt the weight of her blade in the palm of her hand and the numbness that had been in her since the start of the day's fighting and she ached almost to weeping for the loss of the sharp, exciting pain that drew her into battle and sang inside of immortality and of stories by the fire.

XI

FAR FROM THE FIGHTING, THE LEGION'S NIGHT CAMP ROCKED TO the rhythm of marching. Row after row, column after column, centuries of men flowed in through the gap in the trenches that Valerius had left as a gateway, dropped their packs in the place their tent would stand – where it had stood in every marching camp they had ever raised – and began to help with the digging of trenches, and the raising of the earth rampart with the network of crossed staves on top, and the pitching of tents and, as evening came, the building of fires and the cooking of meals.

They were drawing lots for guard duty, and finding in their packs the strips of dried mutton and figs and hazel nuts that would enliven the evening meal, when the peace was shattered by the harsh, high squeal of a legionary cornu blaring the alarm. Three notes sounded three times, with a gap left between the second and third repetitions, and a minor flurry at the end.

'Gods, they've cut off the whole of the third cohort and two centuries of the second. Your sister's been busy.' Because his life and the actions of the next few moments depended on it, Longinus spoke in Thracian, quietly, and contrived to frown.

In Latin, loud enough for anyone to hear, Valerius said, 'The tail of the legion is under attack. Find Civilis. Be ready to ride.'

He was already turning. The legate's pavilion lay offset to one side of the centre point of the camp, where the direct and lateral pathways crossed. The pennants of the legion and Cerialis' personal mark of the dolphin in blued green on white hung still in the mist. Lucius, the message-youth newly branded for Mithras, stood outside with his head tipped up, like a hound startled into the scent.

Valerius called to him, 'Cerialis? Where is he?' and followed the jerk of the boy's head inside.

Finely cured goat hides scented with rosemary oil and rosewater made the roof and walls of the legate's pavilion. A brazier kept it warm. A clerk's desk was placed to one side.

Valerius caught the legate in the act of rising from his bath. He was damp and draped in linen about the thighs. His armour hung from the centre pole of the tent, slick with oil and polish.

'Your excellency?' Valerius let the tent flap crack closed behind him. 'You heard the alarm? The rear part of the second cohort is under attack and the third is in grave difficulty. The centurions have already sounded the recall-at-speed, but if the Eceni war host has command of the forest, even those who can run may not be able to reach us here without help. With your permission, I would take Civilis and his Batavians and make the rearward centuries secure.'

There was a risk in offering a tactical opinion to the man who considered himself the master tactician of all Britannia, more skilled than any previous governor and at least the equal of the one currently waging war in the west. Valerius, waiting, took time to pray.

Cerialis reached for his undershirt. Whoever his bath-attendant had been, he was no longer present. He said, 'How soon before they attack the camp?'

Valerius shook his head. 'I don't think they will. Even the Eceni are not mad enough to attack a fortified night camp, but the cornicen of the second cohort has signalled that his men are in combat against superior numbers and that he has lost connection with the ranks behind.'

Cerialis' body was knotted with scars in front and behind, testament to tactics of attack and retreat that had been less than wholly successful. He pulled on his shirt.

'You can't go,' he said. 'The Batavians are not reliable.'

'Civilis has been with the Ninth since they were stationed on the Rhine.'

'And he dreams of death in glory in circumstances just such as these. You would find yourself at the centre of a bloodbath, with discipline abandoned in the quest for a name sung in the winter halls.'

The smell from the brazier was not unlike the one sacred to Mithras. The red of it was the red of spilled blood and the mottling of a bull's hide. The governor's armour was ruddy in the heat, and made a mirror, disjointedly.

Valerius took a soft step to the side, and another, until he could see the legate's face clearly reflected alongside his own. Watching himself and the other man equally, he said, 'We need horsemen to reach the rear ranks in time, or they are lost. Better to risk Civilis than to lose the better half of the Batavians.'

Their eyes met, glancing off polished iron; a legate and a decurion turned messenger who offered tactics in a voice so dry, so clear, so lacking in emotion that it was hard to see past it.

Cerialis averted his gaze first. He reached for the beaker of wine that sat on the clerk's desk and drank, savouring the richness. He did not offer any to the dry-voiced decurion standing just inside his tent. Presently, he said, 'I need cavalry here; we can't be without horsemen when the forest may be full of rebel warriors. Take the half-wing you brought here with you under Civilis' command. Leave me the other half under his sister's son, Henghes, who is prefect and would lead them now if they were not so heart-sworn to the old man. Find Henghes and send him to me. And signal the second cohort to make more speed in their retreat. The men are to reach here with all expediency, only to fight if actively engaged.'

'Excellency.'

The tent flap let in a little cold as it opened and closed. Cerialis drained his wine to the dregs and let the clerk-boy refill it before he looked again at the armour in which the decurion's face had been reflected. It was hard to remember the shape of it, only the passion in the black eyes that was the opposite of the empty dryness of his voice.

Outside, Longinus held the white-legged colt for Valerius to mount. The beast stood well in the chaos of others' mounting. Through the commotion, men of the second cohort flooded in, running now, knowing themselves lucky not to be caught in the carnage, and grateful to their legate for ordering them in to the safety of the night camp with its ditches and stockade, not forcing them back to save men who were beyond saving.

Behind, half of the Batavians had mounted, half had not. Riding out, they took the track south, with Civilis at the head, and the horns of a full cohort sent them on their way. They kept to the centre of the paved trackway this time, pushing hard, and the legionaries of the second cohort ran sideways to let them past and then ran on again, in near-order, for the camp.

When there was no-one to overhear, Longinus said, 'You have exactly what you wanted: the half-cohort that is most loyal to Civilis rides with us and the rest are left behind. Did you bewitch the legate?'

'No. I told him the truth and he heard it. The gods support that above everything else, always. Tell the standard-bearer to blow five times on his horn.'

Down the length of the ancestors' stone trackway, the fivefold notes of a Batavian cavalry horn ripped apart the remains of the fog and let the sun in, blindingly.

Hearing it, knots of warriors and legionaries paused in their fighting. Blades and teeth and gouging fingers loosened their bite on flesh and skin and bone. Legionaries and warriors alike believed the sound signalled help for them alone, only that the warriors had been told to appear afraid, and did so, convincingly.

Without orders, or any coherent agreement, both sides stepped slowly back, relinquishing the narrow strip of green turf that had become their contested ground.

Early in the fighting, warriors who wanted to live had learned not to take on any groups of legionaries who formed a shield-wall and advanced on them. The legionaries, for their part, had found that stepping off the trackway into the forest was suicide; once past the first rank of trees, it was impossible to hold their shields together, and with the wall gone, they were easy pickings for spear and sling.

Quickly then, the narrow track of turf between forest and track had become the debatable territory, the no-man's land where neither legionaries nor warriors held sway. For no better reason than that it existed, and could be deemed a victory to take and hold, this band of green had become the focus of the fiercest fighting.

It lay open now, and quiet. Peace fell raggedly. Men and women on the brink of slaughter dared to breathe deeply and think of more than survival.

A hot afternoon sun burned away the last of the mist. Shafts of slanting light fell equally on the dead, the dying and those left standing who drank water from skins passed along each line and glared at those opposite. Behind them, the marsh lay innocent as a new day, spreading green-grey and flat but for rushes and tussocks of sphagnum moss. Damp scents spiked the air, delicate in the carnage.

Breaca stood in the shelter of a budding birch and counted the numbers left standing. For as far as she could see to either side, there were more warriors than legionaries amongst the living and more legionaries than warriors amongst the dead.

For these two facts, and for signs of battle sense emerging amongst pockets of previously untested warriors, she was grateful. For the lack of the passion within her, she was afraid and heart-sore and numb. She had killed efficiently enough, and given a lead to the youths who had followed her part of the battle, but the gap in her soul was vast as the eastern horizon and the wind blew through without cease. She spun the hilt of her blade over and over in her hand and ached to hear the music that was gone.

'There are not many who will see what's missing, and fewer who will know why.'

The voice spoke from just behind her left shoulder. Branches wavered and parted and Cygfa was there in a shine of blond hair laced with kill-feathers and a tight, taut smile and grey eyes sharp and hard as midwinter ice. Her face was freckled finely on one side with spots of dried blood, as if she had come too close to someone else's death. Her blade hung at her side, unused. She was breathing lightly and fast, like a horse at the end of a race.

Cygfa had always been beautiful; she was everything of Caradoc, her father, but made as woman and more graceful. Two years' imprisonment in Rome with the half-man her father had become had left her quieter and harder, less forgiving of others and startlingly savage in battle. Rape after rape by the procurator's men had driven her further down the same path; she was bright and brittle, like a blade that has been over-polished and must rust soon, or break.

There was nothing to be done, or said. Airmid had offered healing and been turned down after three days. Only Valerius, flawed and clearly damaged, had offered a kind of example. Alone of the warriors, Cygfa had accepted him without question, seeing in him the one man who could teach her how to destroy everything of Rome.

Breaca said, 'Have you run down the full length of the track?'

'Most of it.' Cygfa grinned, and accepted the waterskin. She rinsed her mouth and spat and the water was threaded red where her lungs had bled a little from the run. 'There was no reason to stay after I'd passed on Valerius' signal and I wanted to get here before him.'

'To see him fight?'

'Partly. I saw him in Gaul; he'll be different now and I would like to see it. But not only that.' Cygfa handed the skin back. Her gaze was sharp and cold as a flaying knife in winter and she made no effort to soften what it cut. 'If it comes to a battle between your brother and your son for leadership of your warriors, do you know who you would have as your successor?'

Except Valerius, no-one else had dared touch on this. There was relief in having it spoken so openly. Breaca said, 'You have already chosen. You showed it on the morning the messenger died. With your clear support, it should not come to a battle, only to words.'

'Possibly, but Valerius will need more than me on his side if the war host are to accept him. The youths only know what they see, but most of the spear-leaders are old enough to remember when he was burning their steadings and slaughtering their warriors. It is not only Cunomar who believes he will side with Rome again in the end.'

'He knows that. It's why he took the message from Camulodunum to Cerialis himself when he could as easily have sent Hawk or Longinus. He's brought the Ninth legion this far. We may only have trimmed the tail of the snake, but we wouldn't have done it without him.' Breaca watched Cygfa shrug. 'You think it's not enough?'

'It's a start. He needs to be seen in battle, not just by us, but by the legions. When it's obvious whose side he's on, the warriors will begin to see who he is and what he can do. Until then, they are waiting each moment for him to betray us, and they'll side with

Cunomar if there's any conflict in the meantime.'

'There will only be conflict if I am seen to be failing,' Breaca said. 'It won't happen before Valerius is ready.'

'Thank you.' Cygfa had always been the most straightforward of Caradoc's children. 'I had hoped for that. And first, Valerius is on his way with the Batavians. They may do all the fighting for us, but if we need to join them, would you let me hold your shield side against the last few legionaries?'

Breaca shifted her grip on her blade. For ten years in battle, Cygfa had taken her shield side, and never had to ask. She said, 'That place is always yours, until you don't want it.'

Under the hard and brittle mask was the daughter who had shared life and death too often to count. Cygfa said softly, 'That won't ever happen.' She blinked fiercely and forced a smile. 'Watch for the black horse with the white legs and the moon on its brow. Your brother has found himself a mount to match the Crow-horse. If it brings him through alive, I'll fight him for it before Cunomar ever gets the chance.'

For the first time that day, Breaca grinned. 'That would be something to watch.'

The day fell apart smoothly, in the way of a dance laid out by the gods.

Valerius rode with Civilis at the head of his cavalry. At his word, the Batavians reined their mounts to a walk and rode in single file down the green turf track. The black colt with the white legs and the moon between its eyes led the way, stepping delicately over the bodies of the slain as if they were sleeping and must not be disturbed.

The line of living legionaries greeted horse and rider as if both were old friends. All of them knew Civilis and the colt he had trained; most had heard overnight of the messenger-decurion who was a Lion of Mithras, hidden god of the legions, and had risked his life to bring word from stricken Camulodunum. If they did not recognize Valerius directly, they knew that he brought victory and rescue and that the fighting, for them at least, was almost over.

They stepped forward onto the green turf, crashing sword hilts to shield rims in greeting. The rhythm of their welcome-chant matched the beat of the horses' walk, solidly four-time. They barely took time to notice the wall of warriors waiting at the end of the line.

There were two hundred cavalrymen and a little over three hundred legionaries; not enough to match them evenly, but sufficient for each horse to shield each pair of men. Thus, as the last of the Batavians passed the first of the Romans, the rider halted and swung his mount inward so that he faced the shields and lowered blades of two men who knew him, at least by sight, and greeted him, smiling, in Latin.

Each of his fellows did likewise, so that, to Breaca and Cygfa, stationed at the fore of the massed Eceni warriors waiting at the distant end of the trackway, the line of approaching faces became instead a broad band of bay horseflesh with chain mail shimmering above.

The war host did not chant, or stamp, or greet, but waited in silence, as Valerius had asked that they do. As he had not asked, but was inevitable, the overwhelming majority slid their blades from their belts as he approached, and watched him with hate and suspicion naked on their faces.

Quietly, for no-one else's ears, Cygfa said, 'If he makes one wrong move, there is nothing you or I can do to save him.'

The white-legged colt walked on alone to the end of the line until it faced the warriors, close enough for them to feel the soft rush of its breath damp and hot on their faces. White-eyed, waiting, believing and unbelieving, each one of them was ready to kill the man who rode it if he betrayed them now to Rome.

Facing them all, unsmiling, Valerius raised his sword arm.

His blade was Roman, and the mail shirt he wore. The sun was almost gone, carved to thin strips by the trees, so that the evening was more green than gold, shading to grey. Stray shards of light sparked off the honed edge of his blade, and the chain mail and the silver at his harness mounts. The white-legged colt snorted and shook its head, spraying white frothing saliva equally onto Breaca and on the Roman centurion who held the end of the legionary line less than three spear-lengths away.

The centurion grinned up at the mounted man and pressed the heel of his hand to the centre of his sternum in the universal greeting that passed between all initiates of Mithras.

Breaca saw a wave of grief pass fleeting over her brother's features. He closed his eyes and touched the middle knuckle of his own thumb to the same place. His lips moved in prayer, and she felt the pressure grow around her as the waiting became too much and too uncertain and more than one of the warriors reached a decision to kill.

Without warning, too fast to be seen or to stop, her brother's raised blade came down, whistling, and severed the sword wrist of the centurion.

Two horses along, Civilis raised his voice in the battle cry of his forefathers. The hornsman of the Batavians blew three barking notes that covered the start of the shouting. Before the last sound died, the slow unreality of the dance had changed to the hammer of conflict.

Four centuries of legionaries, trained to respond to any attack, however unlikely, came to fighting stance in moments. Led by Civilis, reborn as the hero Arminius, the Batavians hurled themselves into battle against the men who had been their comrades, singing paeans to death.

At the end of the line, the mass of Eceni warriors, led by the Boudica, took on the nearest century of men. Breaca fought with Cygfa at one side and Dubornos at the other and did her best to let the rhythms of fighting pull her forward so that she might remember what it was to kill without thinking, without planning, just because the opening was there, and so mend the hole in her soul and let the wind blow through less coldly.

Valerius was never far away. He watched her as he had in the forest, when she tested herself with the blade, and, as it had then, the knowledge of that spurred her forward, and gave her a spark that was not truly hers, but was good none the less.

Towards the end, she felt his attention waver and saw him draw his horse upwards to kill someone. It was not as savage as the annihilation of the procurator, but neatly efficient and done without thought, part of a greater move that broke through the last remaining shield wall of the enemy.

She heard him shout orders in guttural Batavian and saw men answer who had never been under his command and yet followed him because he led them to victory. He drew them together, a fist of mail and flesh, and drove it into the small circle of legionaries, smashing it apart.

Breaca watched it, with her heart and soul laid bare to the beauty of it. Dubornos swore softly at her side. 'I had forgotten what it was to watch him fight. He is as born to it as you are, but he cares less about living. If he had been with us in the beginning, so much might have been different.'

Thoughtfully, Cygfa said, 'It's a pity Cunomar isn't here to see it.'

Which was when they found that the Boudica's son was nowhere to be seen, and that he should have been, and so set about finding why he was not.

XII

VERY SUDDENLY, THERE WAS NO-ONE LEFT TO FIGHT.
On the ancestors' trackway, with marsh in front and forest behind, Valerius sat his new mount and gave attention to breathing before his chest exploded and his heart leapt out from between his ribs for lack of air. His head swam with the aftermath of battle; more than usual, the swarming spirits of the dead clamoured for attention and an explanation of the betrayal that had killed them.

He fought to see past them, to where Breaca must be among the living. Like a lover felt from across a room, he had known exactly where she was throughout the fighting, and had only lost the sense of her towards the end. Still, he believed he would know if she were dead.

Longinus came to him, pushing through the throng. 'Your sister lives,' he said shortly. 'And Civilis.' Longinus, too, was breathing as hard. The last few legionaries, encircled, had faced outwards and fought with the ferocity of men who have nothing left to lose.

Civilis had hurled himself at them, spurning shield and helmet. He had fought as the Germanic tribes of his heritage fought: with a savagery that drove hardened soldiers to desperation. Desperate men make errors and all those who came against Civilis made mistakes that killed them, and thus denied him the death in glory that he craved.

'There you are!'

The old warrior rode up to Valerius and clapped him thunderously on the back. His face was scarlet and the wattles of his neck purple almost to black; his hair shone like frosted silver in contrast. His horse and his blade were both running wet with sweat and blood and the slime of men's guts. His eyes shone as those of a youth in first love, or first combat.

'Son of my soul, what a battle! And that only the first half. Gather your warriors now; we have a fast, hard ride to Cerialis' camp before nightfall.'

Valerius' breathing had calmed a little. His hair straggled across his brow, pasted in place by sweat and other men's blood. He ran his fingers through it, rearranging the gore. Somewhere, he found the energy to laugh.

'I don't think so, old man. We are training youths here in the hope that they may live to fight on, not sending them to death, however draped in glory.'

Civilis shook his head. 'Valerius, this is not a time for jest. We have to ride. Now.' He spun his horse. Valerius shifted the white-legged colt so that it blocked his way. The Boudica's brother was no longer smiling. He laid a hand on Civilis' reins.

'No.'

'I don't understand.' The old man frowned. 'Will you let Petillius Cerialis keep to his night camp in safety and ride on in the morning to attack your people? Is that what we have fought for through this afternoon?'

The old voice croaked high, like a crow. Inevitably, he had been heard, so that more ears than Civilis' were awaiting the answer.

Cursing inwardly, Valerius raised his voice to match it. 'We fought this afternoon to halve the ranks of the Ninth and we have nearly succeeded. One cohort at least of the three is gone. Tomorrow, we will wait until Cerialis has ridden on and do the same again. Perhaps better, now that we are half cavalry. What we will not do is attack in a fortified camp a man who has made his reputation in the conducting of sieges, from within and without. We don't have enough—'

'Valerius.' Longinus spoke, quietly urgent. Among the crowd, men and women parted to let a small knot of others through.

'. . . warriors to indulge in suicidal displays of valour. In any

127

case, I don't want to set one half of your Batavians against the other. Henghes is good and those who follow him might yet decide to join us if we give them half a chance. It will make our lives a lot easier if a full wing of Batavians could guard against the remaining cohorts of the Ninth should they find themselves able to muster—'

'Julius, it's your sister.'

He had to turn, then; Breaca was next to him, with Longinus at his other side, looking concerned, and there was no time to explain that he knew his sister was there, and had known it before the crowd parted, or that he knew she was angry and had no idea why, only that he was exhausted and not ready for confrontation in front of a thousand strangers, when the battle was so recently won and the plaintive whispers of the dead still filled the spaces between the land and the sky. He breathed in noisily and so missed the first of what she said to him.

'. . . thinks he can storm Cerialis' night camp with a handful of the she-bear.'

'What?' The words caught up with him late. 'Who?'

'Cunomar, who else?'

Breaca was angry with Cunomar, not with him. Ridiculously, the relief of that left him giddy.

She said, 'He hasn't been seen since the oak tree fell and trapped the legionaries. Ardacos believes he has taken his she-bears and run them along the side of the track to the night camp, to attack it when dark has fallen. It is something they sing about at the winter fires: the attack of the she-bear on the eagle under the kiss of Nemain's moon.'

Valerius found that his mouth had fallen open and closed it. Presently, when it was clear some answer was expected of him, he said, in wonder, 'He really is determined to prove he can outmatch me, isn't he? Do the songs say that any of the she-bear lives through to morning? If so they're lying.'

He thought Breaca might lose her temper, which might not, after all, have been a bad thing. He braced himself for it, and saw her smile and shake her head and realized how much of her he still had to learn.

'Of course they're lying, that's what songs do. But if we are to keep any of the she-bear alive, you'll have to gather the Batavians, and as much of the war host as can find horses, either to stop him, or to help him. Can you do that? Will you?'

He thought, *This has come too soon*, and saw from her face that she knew it. He said, 'I can help him, Breaca, I can't stop him. Only you can do that.'

She shrugged, and he saw that the anger was founded on grief and frustration turned inward on herself and the failings of her body.

'The survival of the war host matters more than one warrior's dreams and ambitions,' she said, and stepped back. Louder, for the listening ears, she said, 'Cygfa will go with you. Where she goes, I go in spirit, if not in fact. Ride to the aid of my son, knowing that I would be with you if I could.'

XIII

THE BRIGHTNESS OF THE STARS, THEIR SHARPNESS AND THE patterns they made in the void, told Bellos that he was dreaming.

He watched them for a while, until the pinpoint lights resolved into patterns that made sense: the Hunter gave the salute as he always did to the Hare, who was coursed for ever by the Hound; the Serpent surveyed a God and the three Swans who accompanied her. Lost in the wonder of them, Bellos did not immediately remember that neither Serpent, nor God, nor Swans were ever laid out in the stars in the world of his blindness, and it was some time before he understood that if the god came to him now in the dream time, whatever her form, it must have meaning.

He strove to gather his attention, not to be lost in the small things that might drag him back into the fog of unclear dreams, to recall instead the questions a dreamer might ask of the gods when he encountered them.

A wren flittered past and he was halfway to joining it, for the thrill of flying and the sense of freedom. His own voice said, 'Stop. Think,' and he stopped and thought and made himself remember that he was dreaming and should look up. Above, the shape of the god was closer and made of more stars and the swans that were with her had circled and become nine, thrice three. His feet tingled and his breath seared his throat.

Hoarsely, he said, 'What is it that you want of me?'

A voice he had known from before his own birth said, 'Bellos, whom do you love?'

The words sank into him, setting light to his blood, to his bone, to his flesh; the sound of the all-mother, who could have called him home to the lands beyond life at any moment if she had so chosen, and instead left him to live out his span on the earth with only the faintest of memories of her company to warm him.

He answered, 'You, above all else.'

She laughed with him and for him and through him and then, not laughing, said, 'And when you are on the earth and I am a memory carved in stone and wood, whom do you love then?'

He might have said Thorn, but did not; in the dream one does not tell the half-truths of daylight. He said, 'I love Valerius, but only as a son loves his father. He knows that.'

'Perhaps.' The god to whom his soul had long been given considered awhile. He feared he might lose her and strove to keep his attention fixed on the last wave of her voice as it swept over him, and over and over. Presently, she said, 'If there were one who needed help, and helping that one would help Valerius, would you do it, even if I tell you that it may cost more than you imagine?'

No god should need to ask that question. He spoke to the far side of death without fear. He could give his life in the morning and have no regret. He said, 'Of course.'

'Thank you. I am well served. Watch then, and do what you must.'

The wren that had caught his attention returned and it was impossible this time not to join it, not to fly for the freedom of it, for the stretching of spine and limbs, for the freshness of the day and the heightening of the scents, for the sight, from high above, of a small child with ox-blood hair sitting straight-backed and cross-legged before a fire and a weapon, with a finely made youth lying in the shadows behind her.

Bellos stopped and ceased to be a wren. For a long time, he did not know what form he took, only that he could watch and listen and learn. At the end of it, he had some idea of what was required of him, if not yet what it might cost. He had much less idea of whether he could do it, or how.

He made himself wake and drink water, that a full bladder might bring him back if he journeyed too far in the dream. Then, lying warm under the bed hides, he settled himself to sleep and held to the memory of Valerius, and all that he knew of him.

Her grandfather's blade lay on the far side of the fire pit, waiting.

Graine felt the pressure of it, like the threat of thunder, or of war, and could do nothing. The silence that held her was not unfriendly, but there was an ache behind her eyes that was different from the pain that kept her awake at nights, and a murmur in her ears that was not the chatter of her mother's war host in the clearing outside, and a knowing in her heart that her grandfather was there and had a need to speak to her and she should be able to hear him, and could not.

Sighing, she pressed her hands to her eyes and cursed the empty dark. Once, she had liked the dark; the grandmothers had come in the almost-dreaming at either end of sleep and shown her the ways of gods and the long-dead ancestors. The pathways between life and death had seemed open to an eight-year-old girl in ways the outer world was not, and if nothing had ever been certain, there had been a safety in the grandmothers' presence that kept the worst excesses of war at bay.

Then the men of Rome had come to collect their dues bringing every excess of war, and all safety had gone. Graine was alive, which was a miracle, and she was grateful for it, and had been since the moment of waking on the folded sheepskins in the bed beside her mother with the Romans gone and the war host gathering and the world made whole again.

Except that the world was not whole and could never be. With that same waking had come the slow understanding that the grandmothers had gone from her, and the dreaming with them. No ghost, it seemed, would deign to visit an eight-year-old child who had been raped by half a century of men and their absence left the world unmade with nothing the living could do to mend it.

Madness loomed close if Graine thought about that, or a despair so profound it was the same thing. For twelve days, she had hovered on the edge of insanity, until it was hard to remember how she had been before. Now, she made herself breathe in the smoke from the fire and the dampness of the air and dug her fingernails into the grooves on her palm where she had dug them each time before.

Nothing was left to distract her. The steading was quiet for the first time since the procurator's death. There had been some peace in the noise of war. Graine had lain alone in her hut until the chatter of the warriors wove into a blanket of wordless sound that could seem safe to a child who needed to hear it that way.

Smoke, too, wrapped her close; rain spattering on the thatch had damped the air and smoke from the fire pit seeped sideways to the walls before ever it rose to the roof. The thickness of it dulled the glow from the fire so that only the deepest red leached out to colour the sword lying opposite.

The sword: her grandfather's battle sword, with its blade of blued iron and the feeding she-bear in bronze as its pommel. It was three years since the Boudica had hidden the blade in a place no man could discover, and yet Valerius had found it and brought it back and hidden it beneath a stone that had been sacred to Briga since the time of the oldest ancestors.

If the grandmothers still spoke to Graine, they would have been able to tell her how such a thing could have happened. Or Eburovic, her grandfather, whose blade it had been and who had been last to die with it in his hand.

Nobody spoke, only the fire cast out its blood light and the blade was washed red as if newly used and the sense of waiting was more urgent than it had been and there was nothing Graine could do to change it.

She had always been a patient child and Rome had not taken that from her. She sat for a long time, quietly. Smoke seeped steadily sideways. Rain dribbled through gaps in the imperfect thatch. Beyond the walls, where such things did not matter, a man cursed. A woman laughed and another, intimately. A trio of hounds squabbled over a scrap from the midden. A hen in the hut's rafters clucked contentment and roused her feathers, dropping one down, so slowly down that it might have taken the whole of the night to touch the child watching its fall from—

'Graine?'

The fire was dead for lack of wood. The rain had stopped, and it was a day and a night since the warriors had left to attack the men of Rome. The soft voice in the doorway was Valerius' and should not have been. Graine realized all of these things before she knew that she was lying sideways, and so had fallen asleep, and that the feather might have been the beginning of a dream, her first that was free of the memories of the night that had broken her.

She clung to the drifting shape, wanting it to return.

'I'm sorry, I didn't mean to wake you.' Valerius was still there. 'Should I go away?'

'No.' She sat up. 'I'm awake.' She looked round. 'I thought you were with the Ninth legion, leading them into ambush?'

'I was. The first part of the ambush is done. I am riding now with your mother's war host to help Cunomar attack the Roman night camp.' He did not explain how he could be there and riding at the same time. She did not think to ask. He said, 'I can't stay. I need to be with the warriors. I've brought your grandfather to speak to you.'

She rubbed her eyes and stared into the dark by the door. 'Why can't I see him?'

'If you can see me, it's enough. What would you ask him?'

So many questions. Why can I not dream? What will it take to heal? Words danced in her head. For no better reason than because it was there, she said, 'What should become of his blade?'

She waited, watching the dark. From the shape that was Valerius, her grandfather spoke. *You are the holder, but may not hold. One who is bound to you by earth and sky may carry it in your stead and for your care.*

She said, 'Hawk? He's bound by the oath of earth and sky, but he's not Eceni.'

There was silence. Panicked, she said, 'Valerius?' and then called it, 'Valerius!'

His voice sounded a long way off. 'I'm sorry. I have to leave. There's someone else here who needs to meet you, someone still in the land of the living; a friend. May he come in?'

'If he's a true friend, yes.'

Valerius was too shadowed to see properly. He stepped back and someone new came in, who was not Hawk, or Dubornos or Ardacos or anyone else of the Boudica's inner council. He stepped forward and there was fire light, where there had been only dark.

He sat where Hawk usually sat and he was the opposite of the dark Coritani: blond as threshed corn with his hair a little wavy and pale brows that made silvering lines against a pale face. His eyes were those of a wildcat, greenly yellow at the rims and piercingly bright.

They skinned Graine and dissected her and put her back together again. She wanted to feel uncomfortable at that, and did not. She stared back and saw the glare of them reduced.

'I'm sorry, that was unnecessary.' The stranger pressed his palm to his forehead in deepest honour. His voice had a rolling lilt to it that she recognized sometimes in Valerius. He said, 'I am Bellos. You are Graine, who is of Nemain.'

'*Was* of Nemain. I'm not any longer.' It was becoming easier to say it. Bellos did not flinch in the way her mother had done. Graine said, 'I can't see the paths to the gods any more. I am only Graine, daughter of Breaca.'

'And also Graine daughter of Caradoc. Never forget who your father was. I met him when I was a child. He would have been proud of you, as you should be of him. Any child would be proud to have either of these for a parent, but still, you were more, and could be again. Do you want to heal?'

'Of course.' She snapped it without thinking and saw the cat's eyes widen. Softly, Bellos said, 'You know better than that. It isn't good to speak idly in the dream.'

'This isn't—' She stopped. Valerius had been a shadow and was gone, returned to his warriors, riding through the night, taking the shade of Eburovic with him. Bellos of the cat's eyes had lit her fire with a sweep of his hand, and yet there was no warmth, only light enough to see him by. Hawk was asleep; she could hear the rise and fall of his breathing. Graine said, 'It can't be. I've lost the dreaming.'

She felt him smile. 'This is my dreaming, the gift of Briga. I am on Mona. If you would heal, you must come to me here.'

'The legions are on the western coast, preparing to assault Mona and all who remain on her.'

'I know. The battles have not yet begun. Until they do, and are over, I will be here.'

'Hawk won't let me go.'

'Yes he will.' Hawk stood behind Bellos. His eyes were bright as the bird for which he was named, but nothing to the cat's eyes that still held her. He said, 'My mother was a dreamer of the Horned One. She would never let me stand in the way of another's dreaming. If you need to go to Mona, I'll help you to find a way.'

'Thank you.' The dream of Bellos put his palm to his forehead once more. 'You should leave with the dawn.'

'We can't. We have to tell mother.'

From far away, Valerius' voice said, 'Breaca is returning to you. She'll be at the steading before dawn. Dubornos is with her, and Gunovar. Both know the ways to Mona and could guide you. Tell them I said that, and remember the words of your grandfather. Hawk should carry the war blade of the ancestors. Hawk, not Dubornos. Eburovic has said it.'

'But how can we—'

The air became hollow and then full again. Graine opened her eyes. Bellos was gone. The fire was unlit. The feather was still falling from the ceiling. Hawk slept resonantly on his hides. Graine lay awake in the dark listening for the sound of horses that would tell of her mother's return.

XIV

CUNOMAR BALANCED HIS MOTHER'S GIFT-KNIFE ACROSS ONE
finger and watched reddening sparks reflect from the blade.
A southwesterly wind blew warmly, raising glowing
filaments of ash from fifty different fires in the Roman night camp.
It teased and blurred the murmur of Latin and Germanic voices
recounting the day and the occasional clash of sword to shield as
one guard met and challenged another in their ceaseless circuits
of the camp. The dark mass of the legate's pavilion was a shadow
in the sparking lights, blotting out the fires behind it.

The ditches Valerius had marked and the Batavians had dug
were invisible shadows with unclear edges. For those studying it
from the outer rim of the forest, crossed and sharpened stakes were
the most visible markers of the camp's limits, strung along the
inner edges to repel invaders foolish enough to brave the ditches
and the slops that had been dumped into them at nightfall.

The one song of the she-bear that told of an assault on a Roman
night camp spoke only in the loosest terms of how the Boudica,
aided by Airmid, dreamer of Nemain, and Ardacos, father of the
western she-bears, had entered such a camp and brought about by
their dreaming the death of the governor.

The event had taken place while Cunomar was a prisoner in
Rome and he had heard his mother speak of it only twice in the
years since his return. Her account bore very little resemblance to

the song, but by questioning Ardacos and Airmid through the years he believed he had come to a fuller understanding of what had been done. Whether he could replicate it was entirely another question, but the bear rewarded valour above all else and Cunomar had thirty-eight she-bear warriors left alive, far more than the eight who had accompanied his mother.

A fire was extinguished in the northwest part of the camp, and another beside it. From the dark to Cunomar's left, Ulla said, 'The fires are going out faster now. There are half as many as there were at nightfall.'

'When there are thirty, we can attack. Any more and we'll be seen. There are never any fewer. I've watched enough camps in the western mountains to know that much, whatever the songs say about the absolute dark of the Boudica's raid.'

Another fire flickered out. Patches of dark leaked through the night. Around Cunomar, the remaining she-bears drank water, and did not speak. The sweat and grease of their bodies warmed the night. A warm wind blew their smell ripely back into the forest, away from the camp.

Within the stockade, a string of six camp fires rippled to nothing one after the other, as if a god had blown them out. Cunomar spun his knife high and caught it. His guts fluttered liquidly and were still. His missing ear was painless. He braced his feet slightly apart and swung his shoulders a little to loosen them. The earth rocked to the rhythm of his feet, pleasantly. He swayed with it, back and forth, and came to a still point in the centre.

The earth continued to rock under his feet.

Ulla said, 'Horses. Two of them. Coming through the forest, not up the track.'

'Cavalry. Valerius has turned traitor.' There was no time to think, and no need. Cunomar spat. There was time for that. A flashing of eye whites and naked iron showed him where the thirty-eight blades of his honour guard waited for his command.

A small part of him considered storming the night camp and, with enormous regret, abandoned the thought. There was no hope, any longer, of secrecy, and the lives of those who followed him mattered too greatly to be cast away on a whim, however willingly they might have died on his behalf.

'Go.' He swept his hand back. 'Become part of the forest. Don't return without my call.'

He waited alone, with his feet braced and his mind empty as the elders had taught him.

The two incoming horsemen rode to the camp's gates. They gave a password, and were admitted. The dark mass of the legate's tent became suddenly less dark, lit from within by a brazier, and then torches. Shadows of men played on its wall. Cunomar hissed out an oath and dropped to a crouch. He edged a pace forward, and then stopped, as the shifting brightness of the legate's tent was blocked by a darker shadow.

'I don't think so,' said Valerius, softly. 'Two very good friends of mine are currently risking their lives in an effort to convince the legate that his night camp is not under threat. I would prefer it if you did not prove them wrong.'

The skin prickled on Cunomar's scalp. He would have believed Ardacos could approach so close in the dark without his knowledge, but no-one else. His knife came silent to his hand. He saw no metal glimmer near Valerius' star-lit shape.

He said, 'You have sent the Thracian into the camp?' Disbelief coloured Cunomar's voice, and contempt for a man who would send his soul-friend to danger and keep clear of it himself.

'Longinus has gone in, yes, and Civilis, who was the soul-father of my early days in the Roman cavalry. He's the Batavian who turned his cavalry against Rome in your mother's name today. Without him, the Eceni losses would have been much higher.'

In the camp, more fires were being lit. Valerius' outline became sharper. His face was still impossible to see. Only his voice could be read.

Thoughtfully, that voice said, 'If you kill me now, Civilis and his Batavians will be lost to the war host. I think they would be useful to protect our backs while we assault Camulodunum. Even if we wipe out every officer and serving man in the camp, there are still four cohorts of the Ninth left behind in winter quarters.'

It came late to Cunomar that Valerius had chosen the path of greater danger in coming to meet the Boudica's son unarmed and alone in the dark; or it could be made to seem so afterwards to those who might choose to use it.

Noiseless, he slid his knife back to its sheath. The firelight played across his face. The elders of the Caledonii had spent a winter teaching him how to school his thoughts so that nothing might show to an enemy, even one taught on Mona to read the minds of men laid bare in their eyes. Thus armoured, he said, 'The she-bear do not kill unarmed men, whoever they may be.'

'Thank you.' A thread of amusement came and went in the dry voice. 'Is there a reason why your sister Cygfa could not be the one to lead the war host if your mother proves unfit? She would seem to me admirable in every respect.'

Cunomar was not expecting that. He had never considered his sister a threat. It took him a moment to remember why. 'My mother was shown the final assault on Rome in a fever-dream. Cygfa was on the right wing, and Ardacos on the left. Dubornos is a dreamer who fights as a warrior and he was not seen anywhere else. It could have been him, but he's too damaged by Rome's inquisitors ever to lead the host.'

'I see. And so of all those close to your mother, you are the only one left to take that place if she can't. Apart from me.'

A fire flared on the edge of the camp, brightly. A small, deliberate movement brought Valerius' face from shadow so that, at last, he could be seen. He looked exhausted and ageless. Neither, or both, may have been true.

He said, 'We should be plain about this. I have no wish to lead the Eceni now or later. But I will not let one man's search for personal glory destroy the war host, or lead it to ruin. The future of our people and our land rests on this war. They matter more than your vanity, or mine.'

Thus were their private lines of battle drawn. Cunomar said softly, 'And I will not let one man's treachery destroy what my mother has given her soul to build. You forget, I was with you in Gaul when you betrayed the men you had fought for.'

His eyes fed on the other man's face. He believed – he was certain – that he saw a flicker of grief, or doubt, or fear, break through Valerius' mask of control. It was worth the comfortless night, just for that.

Raised voices in Latin broke the moment. Torches flared at the camp's margins. It became necessary to move quickly and silently into the shelter of the trees and there to wait, pressed to the cold earth, until a tent party of eight armed men had gone past, thrusting light and iron into the undergrowth.

A long silence passed after they had gone. Cunomar pushed himself up to a crouch and brushed the dead leaves from his face. Nothing moved around him. He had no idea if he was still in company, or alone. Into the dark, he said, 'It was not a search for personal renown that brought the she-bear here tonight.'

'What then?' Valerius was very close. His voice was distant, as if he had been sleeping, or dreaming.

Cunomar said, 'There are two thousand legionaries in there. To attack it with thirty-eight she-bears would be madness. We had intended to enter in secret, and kill only the legate, as the Boudica killed the governor in the days when my father was held captive in Rome.'

'Unless you had been caught, in which case you, too, might have been taken captive to Rome. You should consider some time that the Boudica's son might be worth more to Rome alive than dead. I don't think this emperor would find it in his heart to offer a pardon.'

Clouds broke apart then, and allowed the moon to reach them. By the sudden light, Valerius looked as much like his father as he had ever done, and he was, without question, exhausted. He said wearily, 'If we may consider tonight? We need to give the warriors another chance to fight in the morning. They need greater experience of battle before we assault Camulodunum. The veterans of the Twentieth who call it home won't be strung out in a line with a marsh at their backs, they'll be defending the land that was their prize for twenty-five years with the legions. They'll fight like bears turned at bay and even with a battle-hardened army we'd be hard pressed to defeat them.'

. . . like bears turned at bay . . .

It was inconceivable that Valerius could know of his nightmare. Stepping out of the moon's light, Cunomar said, 'We can't take on the column again as we did today. They'll be waiting for it.'

'Obviously. So we have to take them as they begin to break camp.' Valerius sank to a crouch. He drew a square in the soft loam with his finger.

'This is the camp,' he said. 'We are here, on the western edge. Longinus and Civilis are inside now, spreading lies to the legate.

Unless you can suggest something better, this is what we will do . . .'

A series of horn calls shaped the morning.

Cunomar waited within the shelter of the trees with the she-bear spread out on either side of him. In the night, when he had called them back to him and whispered what Valerius had asked of them, Ulla was the one who had said what the rest had not. 'I would rather we had done as you first planned, but there's no going back now. Valerius has given us the best part, and the rest of what he wants to do is sound if the men within the camp can do as he says.'

If. Everything hinged on that. Cunomar lay in the cold morning, watching legionaries light fires and cook barley cakes for breakfast. Around him, the whispers of the spear-leaders echoed Ulla's doubt and made it stronger.

More than the destruction of the IXth, Valerius' fragile standing with the war host depended on the success of his plan. If the she-bear fought well and made it happen, they would bolster his cause as much as their own. If they failed, they would damage their own reputation as much as Valerius'. The bitter irony of that did not make their morning any warmer.

Inside the Roman camp, the hum of activity was already sharp; the remaining men of the IXth legion had woken before dawn, if they had slept at all. The morning's activities, the striking of tents, their packing, the dismantling of the camp, progressed faster than usual, as they strove to make themselves ready for the road.

Cunomar had lain by an uncounted number of night camps in the western mountains, watching the same pattern unfold: always the centuries who had arrived first were first to pack their tents and leave, while those who had marched in last were left to fill the ditches and cover the fires.

Usually, the men talked, or sang, or whistled as they worked. In the clearing at the edge of the ancestors' trackway, they worked in a silence that pressed in from the edges so that every clatter of a shovel and flap of a falling tent echoed to the trees and back.

A single centurion stood near the western edge of the camp and prayed aloud to Mars Ultor, god of the legions, that the men of his century caught overnight in the forest were, even now, marching down the track to join their legion.

Ulla had no Latin. Cunomar, who had lived two years in Rome, put his mouth to her ear and translated for her, the words no louder than a breath.

The threefold notes of a cavalry horn shattered the silence, and the prayers, and the muttered translation. The noise rose and looped and rose again, exactly as Valerius had said it would: *Three notes rising, falling and rising again are the signal of a party under attack by overwhelming numbers, in urgent need of rescue. It's a long time since I last blew a horn but then even a cornicen under attack might make a mistake. If I can make it sound even halfway authentic, the camp should fold into chaos.*

It must have been more than halfway. With a sliding sense of urgency gripping his bowels, Cunomar watched the camp fold very rapidly into chaos.

The silence was abandoned: men shouted and ran and shouted again; horses were gathered; horns blew with no obvious coherence. *Wait for one long note blown on a rising scale. That's Civilis' call to the Batavians to mount and be ready to ride.*

The note came, soaring up to greet the dawn. Half of the Batavians were already mounted; theirs was the apparent failure, theirs the need to recover their honour. Civilis was amongst them, a white-haired fury, shouting orders that could be heard far into the forest.

Cunomar kept watch on Longinus, who was calmer, and stood with Cerialis. There was a moment when a decision hung in the air. Cunomar saw Valerius' soul-friend tilt his head in deference, and make a small gesture with his hand, taking in the cavalry and the ancestors' trackway. Very soon after that, the decision was made.

Cerialis is impulsive. All he needs is a moment's quiet encouragement to tip him into action. Longinus is there to give that word. If he can do what we need, the legate will lead the cavalry charging out and on up the trackway.

What if they turn round and come back? Cunomar had asked.

Civilis' men may block the trackway. If they fail, or decide they can't fight their own kind, we'll be stranded on foot against Batavian cavalry. I would suggest that we all run into the forest and don't look back. Valerius had grinned as he said it, so it was hard to tell if he were serious.

Cunomar, who had decided he was almost certainly very serious, nevertheless had no real intention of leading his warriors into the forest. Watching the sudden, clashing order that descended on the cavalry as their legate joined them, he allowed himself at least to consider the option.

Even by the standards of Rome, the exit of Petillius Cerialis, riding at the head of his cavalry to the rescue of his stricken cohorts, was impressive.

A flurry of trumpet calls announced his departure. The notes had barely died when the signal was given for men on the ground to clear the palisades that blocked the gates. As the last one was freed, the legate and two hundred and fifty horsemen of the Batavian cavalry burst from the gates in a hammer of furious vengeance.

They went from standing to racing, all on fit corn-fed horses who knew the sounds of the horns as well as any men, and strove to answer them; all but two, which went lame within the first five hundred paces and had to be pulled up. Just beyond the margins of the forest, Cunomar watched Civilis and Longinus, swearing roundly, drop back and away from the rest.

These men are my friends. They have risked a slow death for this plan. I would appreciate it if your warriors could refrain from killing them afterwards. Valerius had not smiled as he said that, and the edge to his voice had made it perfectly clear he was serious.

Nobody killed Longinus or Civilis. They stood at the side of the track and appeared to confer, then, with evident dejection, turned and began the slow, lame walk back towards the night camp.

Their comrades continued to race on down the track, and so did not see the half-wing of Civilis' Batavians, their former comrades, who stood silent in the tangled forest, their hands over the soft muzzles of their mounts lest one of them call a greeting and give them away.

The sound of the cavalry's passing faded to silence. The forest caught the hum of the camp and reflected it inwards so that the dell became an echo of men's voices, staccato shouts rendered musical in their repeats.

Cunomar eased himself to his feet and drew his knife. 'Not yet.' He said it to himself and then, in a whisper that passed down the line, 'Not yet.'

In the dell, a column of infantry formed within the ring of the palisades and prepared to march, even as the men of the rearmost cohort were filling in ditches and taking down the last of the staves. A lone horn sounded. A blade hilt clashed on a shield boss, sharply. The column of men started forward, heading north, following their legate in case he had need of them in the fight against the Eceni. The rescue of Camulodunum was abandoned, temporarily, for the greater need of the IXth legion.

Like ants on a trail they passed in fours, fresh and eager as the horses had been, and as ready to fight. Their nailed boots struck equally the dewy turf and sharp on the stones of the trackway. The marching song was the same as they had used the day before, with a new verse, made in the night, that praised Civilis and a lone Thracian cavalryman for their courage.

Cunomar watched them greet Civilis and Longinus as the two men led their lame horses back towards the camp.

'Not yet.'

The full count of men had marched into the forest when the first of them died.

The Batavian cavalry surged in from the trees, blaring false horn calls that left the marching men confused for the few heartbeats it took to annihilate their formation and prevent them from forming defensive rings. The Eceni war host surrounded the remains of the camp, with its ditches filled in and the palisades packed and the struck tents lying like stunned moths on the floor of the dell.

'Now!'

Cunomar's she-bears, as had been promised in the night, took the first, and so the greatest, part. At his word, they hurled themselves through the part-dismantled gates of the night camp, falling on the remaining century of legionaries who had not yet begun to pack, but stood with shovels and staves in their hands, and used them as weapons.

The fighting was bloody and brief and when it was over, the men of the first and second cohorts of the IXth legion lay dead and there were more of them than there were dead Eceni by five or six to one. None of the Batavians, and only two of the she-bear, had died.

The longer process of stripping the bodies of their armour and weapons, of emptying the packs of food and clothing and scraps of iron that might be melted for sword blades, extended far into the day.

Near midday, Cygfa came to sit beside Cunomar as he stripped the body of the last centurion to die. The man's blade had broken, so hard had he used it, and his shield boss was crushed beyond mending. A scatter of dead warriors lay round him, all with wounds to the head or chest. Blood leaked from beneath his armour, and from the killing gape in his throat where a blade had finally won under his helmet.

'He fought well.' Cygfa sat on an upturned shield and watched her brother unbuckle the man's greaves. She, too, was bleeding. A shallow cut on one thigh leaked dark blood; two on her sword arm more brightly.

Cunomar said, 'I saw you kill him.' He loved Cygfa. On the day they had been released from the procurator's execution, he had sworn in front of Ardacos that he would protect both of his sisters for the rest of their lives and his against the ravages of Rome. Cygfa had never needed his protection, but it had helped him believe she would recover. The needling pain in his chest was not worthy of her or of him. Graciously, he said, 'He would have killed a dozen more if you hadn't come in so fast.'

Cygfa shrugged. 'He was tiring, and Dubornos was keeping his attention. I didn't come to talk to you about that.'

The elders had taught him to face his pain directly. 'About Valerius, then? Did he give you the white-legged colt?'

Of all those on the battlefield that day, two had stood out: Valerius on his Crow-horse, the half-Roman who fought for the Eceni with the carelessness for his own life that marked the truly great and set them apart from the rest; and Cygfa, soul-daughter to the Boudica, bright-haired daughter of Caradoc, who fought at the other side of the field on a white-legged black colt that was clearly cut from the same stamp as Valerius' notorious pied mount.

It was not as savage as the Crow, but it answered Cygfa's thought more readily than any horse had ever done so that the two were welded to one, and drew eyes from all quarters, the bright flame of her hair rising high over the black-on-white of her new mount. Cunomar had seen it, and had tried not to see the horse as payment for her earlier actions; he did not wish to be a man who begrudged others their good fortune, least of all his sister.

Cygfa grinned, a sight so rare that in itself it gladdened Cunomar's heart. She said, 'Valerius heard a rumour that I was going to fight him for it and made me a gift of it before I could make the challenge.' She ran a hand through her hair, sobering. 'I didn't come to talk about that, either. It's Valerius. I—'

'You support him as leader of the war host. I know. Everyone knows. You made it plain at the gathering.' It had hurt at the time. Now, with the success of battle behind him, Cunomar was glad only that they were both alive to talk about it.

'Everyone else can know what they want.' Cygfa wiped grime from her face, replacing it with more. 'You can know that I support the man the gods have fashioned for us who is, just now, the best we have if Breaca cannot lead.'

Her eyes were on him. Cunomar laid the pair of greaves carefully on the pile. With similar care, he said, 'Just now?'

They knew each other well, these two children of Caradoc; they had faced death in Rome together, and two years in exile after their pardon by the emperor Claudius. They had shared the chaotic escape through Gaul and the stark, stripped moment on a beachhead when it became clear that their father was too broken to return. They had come back to Mona and made it their home and left it again to travel east with the Boudica. Only they two knew what these things had cost, or what it was to fight as the child of a warrior the whole world revered, to have to carve a name that was not always spoken in comparison to what had gone before.

Through the full weight of that, Cygfa said, 'Leadership is not only about courage. No-one doubts you have that, and these past two days you showed it to any who might not have seen. But a leader sees the greater picture and knows that lives matter more than glory. A leader would not have brought three dozen warriors to assault a night camp alone, leaving behind the three thousand who needed experience in battle. There is time yet. Breaca's still healing. She couldn't be here, but she'll lead us against Camulodunum. Sometime after that, we will see who leads beyond it. I will support you then if I can believe you will not lead us into heroic disaster.'

Cygfa was smiling as she said it, and gripped his arm. Her hair was a chaos of bright gold and battle filth, her face the same. She was his sister, which mattered above all else.

She stood and gave the salute of one warrior to another. 'The Ninth is gone. We have a clear path now to Camulodunum. Make best use of it, little brother, and you might yet lead the war host in the final assault on the legions.'

II
LATE SPRING AD 60

XV

THE IXTH LEGION IS DESTROYED. THE SERPENT-SPEAR IS awakened in the east. The Boudica battles Rome and the gods guide her hand. Freedom is there to be taken. Join us and be part of the taking . . .

Word spread fast as fire, carried by traders who pushed their dray horses hard to be first at each steading with the news, and by youthful warriors with red-quilled war feathers newly woven into their hair who ran barefoot for home with tales of their own successes and of the deaths in battle – always with honour – of their shield-mates, lovers, cousins and siblings.

The traders returned early from shorter journeys than they had planned, with goods in which they did not normally deal. They drove into the site of the horse fair with iron and salt and wool and hides and more iron, and took less than half their worth in gold or silver or all of it in promises of corn to be paid when the battles were over.

Not to be outdone, the youths returned in their hundreds with other siblings, lovers, cousins, parents and friends and promises of yet more to come when the spring planting was over, or perhaps before then; after all, who needed to plant corn when the granaries of Camulodunum, Caesaromagus, Canonium and Verulamium would soon be broken open and the grain they held returned to those who had worked to harvest it and yet starved for its lack through the cold winters under the heel of Rome?

Others began to gather who were not of the Eceni: Coritani and Votadini from the west and north, Silures and Ordovices from the west, Dumnonii and Durotriges from the far southwestern toe of the land.

Warriors came whose tribes had been enemies for generations, and learned in days not only to share each other's fires, but to share food and exercise and the teachings of war with a half-wing of Batavian cavalry.

A few shared all these things with the Boudica's half-Roman brother. Those who could not stomach it chose to train only with her bright-haired son. Efforts were made by those whose business it was to oversee such things to ensure that the war host did not become divided so early in the conflict. They were not wholly successful.

Other matters arose, of greater moment. Rumours began of a second assault by the IXth legion. Very quickly, those who were most competent were despatched to guard the trackways north and west. These killed eight messengers within two days, all of whom bore pleas for urgent help from Petillius Cerialis to the governor of all Britannia. After the head of the eighth man to die was returned in the saddle packs of his horse, no others were sent.

No avenging cohorts marched south, either. Once, it seemed as if a war party of Batavians was going to assault the war host, but the latter's luck held and there were Batavians guarding the road that day who recognized their former comrades and persuaded them to listen to their petition and so the host gained another one hundred cavalry, who preferred to fight for Civilis against Rome than for Henghes in the name of the emperor.

The rumours changed and said that Petillius Cerialis, legate of the IXth, had withdrawn to his winter quarters and sat watching the sea rise and fall with the tides. In time, they said that he had dismissed the Iberian stonemason, but not until the foundations of the baths had been thoroughly waterlogged.

Five or six days after the burning of the watchtowers, a trickle of incomers began to arrive from the south, from the city of Camulodunum. First in ones and twos and then in handfuls, poorly armed and nervous, men and women of the Trinovante walked and rode up to the site of the Eceni horse fair where the war host was massing.

They came first as refugees, fearing the attack that was so plainly coming, driving wagons, carrying sacks with live chickens, herding cattle. Only later did they dare to offer themselves in war. When they did, there were two thousand of them, and they took to battle training faster than those who had not lived as closely in the shadow of Rome.

Before the month's end, all those who had fallen had been replaced and the number of the war host was once more at five thousand. By the first quarter of the next moon, it had grown by half as much again. Not one of those who arrived bore any news of the Boudica's younger daughter, although all had heard of her journey to Mona. A child and three warriors, it seemed, had passed through the land unseen. The Coritani were ready to praise the scouting skills of Hawk, who could hide himself in a black cloak on a snowfield and could easily conceal three adults and a child. Others noted that Dubornos and Gunovar had both trained on Mona and that either was completely capable of remaining hidden if they did not choose to be seen. No-one spoke openly or in quiet of the other alternative, which is that all four were dead.

The war host was divided by those who had responsibility for their training. Two thousand of the most able warriors were left with Civilis and his Batavians to keep watch on the routes by which the IXth legion might yet decide to attack. The Boudica, mounted on a bay colt that was a gift from her daughter, led the remaining host south towards the place once named sacred to the war god Camul, later Cunobelin's dun and most lately Camulodunum, Rome's capital city in the province of Britannia.

Over five thousand warriors made camp in the valley of the Heron's Foot, at the place where three rivers joined to become one; where, in the days before Rome's invasion, the boundaries of Eceni, Trinovante and Catuvellauni lands had joined, leaving the valley owned equally by all three tribes and thus by none, which made it the province of the gods; where, nevertheless, a party of Eceni had been attacked on the valley's sacred soil and seen nearly half their number slain, including Eburovic, father to the Boudica, who was cut down defending his daughter, including also Bán, her younger brother, whose body was stolen from the battlefield so that she believed him dead and mourned him as such for nearly twenty years.

Where, for the first time since 'Tagos died, leaving the world open for rebellion, Breaca took time alone for herself and bathed.

The heron stood at a widening of the river where still waters gathered. An easterly breeze ruffled its reflection. Small fish kissed the surface around it and were ignored.

It blinked, slowly. Breaca lay on her back in the flowing cold and let her hair stream into the weed and watched her own reflection vanish and appear again in the arc of its eye.

A shadow slid up her body and blocked the weak spring sun from her face. Without moving, she said, 'Luain mac Calma always seemed to be more heron than man. Has he sent this one to us, do you think?'

'Possibly. I would prefer to think he would send a flesh and blood messenger if he needed to pass a message urgently to any of us, but I would never be sure.'

Airmid stood on the bank, a hand's reach from the bird, which did not move. She was tall as the Elder of Mona, and as lean, but there was nothing of the heron in her. Increasingly, since the procurator's attack, there was less of the frog that was her dream and more of Nemain, daughter to Briga, god of water and of the moon, of healing and dreams and all that had been lost to Graine.

When she thought of the god now, Breaca thought of Airmid; the two had become inseparable. That, amongst other things, accounted for the new distance between them.

The dreamer came closer and sat down on the soft earth. Pulling a stem of grass to chew, she said, 'If he needed to send a message about Graine, he would surely use something more certain, but he has no need of that yet. Word has come from Dubornos and Hawk, sent with a salt trader: Graine and those who went with her are safe.'

. . . Graine . . . safe . . .

The words met Breaca in a slide of cold water, seeping through her bones to her soul. The river washed her face and she wanted to weep and could not; as far as she could remember, she had not wept since the Roman procurator had first ridden into the steading with his veterans at his back.

From the distant place that was the land, Airmid said, 'The message was sent from among the southern Ordovices. They're taking Graine south, to where Gunovar's people, the Durotriges and the Dumnonii, have control of the land. The Second legion has a fortress there, but they're under permanent siege and dare not step far beyond its walls; it is as safe as anywhere in Britannia for the Boudica's daughter. Graine can take ship there for Mona, if there's any point, or for Hibernia if mac Calma has evacuated the island before she gets there.'

She was talking for the sound of her voice more than the words it contained, as Valerius had done through the days of the fever. Her voice was smoother than his, the quality of love quite different. Even so, it was not as it had been.

After a while, when Breaca floated and said nothing, Airmid fell silent. The river whispered between them. Early bees danced to the catkins hanging over the water. The heron ceased to blink and uncurled its neck. Its beak shattered the surface, fast as any sword thrust. The fish it speared was fat and brown and thrashed the water white before it died. The bird swallowed and became disfigured in the neck and then smooth again. It roused its feathers and blinked and rose from the water and was a spear against the clouds and then gone.

Breaca rolled over until she lay face down in the river and stayed there until the cold made her cheeks stiff. Surfacing, she swam to the edge and accepted Airmid's hand to lift her onto the bank. The air seemed hot after the chill water. She scrubbed herself dry with her tunic and slid it on. Her back was a mess of scabs. Some of them broke open as she moved, but the cold had taken away most of the pain and the warm wind had not yet brought it back again.

She sat against a tree and used the frayed end of a twig to clean the grime from beneath her fingernails. It was not possible to talk; too much time had passed with too little said for her to find the words.

Sometime later, into the cold quiet, Airmid said, 'Should I name your fears aloud for you? Would it make them any less?'

'No.' Breaca studied her hands. Resentment made her chest tight. She had not expected intrusion from Airmid, of all people.

She said, 'I am a warrior who has lost her taste for war. Naming it will not help, nor make it easier to bear.'

Her nails were clean. She laid the twig in a circle of sunlight, bounded by shadow, and turned so that, for the first time, she might see and be seen.

Airmid was close. She smelled of hawthorn smoke and lanolin and, beneath that, of herself. Side on, her face was strong in the river light, perfect, unscarred and beautiful; and her lashes were wet.

Breaca said, 'What is it?'

'Should I name my fears aloud for you?' Airmid smiled wryly. 'Everything. Nothing. War. Graine. You. You're gone and I don't know how to reach you. Naming that doesn't help it, either.'

Breaca's hand lay quiet by the cleaning stick. She moved it, just enough. After a moment, long, clever fingers intertwined with her own. A hand that knew every part of her better than she knew herself eased the muscles on her shoulder, avoiding the worst of the scars.

The voice that was the bedrock of her life was cracked, which was not something she had ever expected to hear.

Through faster tears, Airmid said, 'You are the Boudica. You do what you are born to do. The rest of us support you as we may, which is what we were born to do. And we have failed. You are not healed.'

She had not expected this, was not ready for it. Baldly, she said, 'You've done everything you can, you and Valerius both.'

'But it's not enough.'

With care, Breaca leaned back and put her shoulders to the tree. She untwined her fingers and used both hands to rub her face free of the anger that had moulded it. She was tired more than angry, and grief weighed at her, for the loss of Graine, for the loss of the self she had been.

'Perhaps it's as much as can be done. I'm alive; I can wield a blade. I can ride now, at the speed needed for battle. I can be present, and can perhaps not die, at least while the war host grows and until either it comes to recognize in Valerius the leader they need and want, or Cunomar grows into himself and shows the leadership he has within him. If one of these happens soon, it will be enough.'

'Enough to let you die?'

She had not expected that, either. A lone bee wove a random path through the catkins and came to settle near her knee. When it rose again, she said, 'I don't know. I want not to have to pretend to be what I was, and am no longer. Perhaps death is the way to do that.'

She reached blindly for Airmid's hand and traced the lines on the palm with her thumb. 'Do you think death is an ending? That's not what the elders of Mona teach. For them, the fish is gone but only in this life and this world. In other times and other lives, it will be the heron and the heron will be the fish, or both, or neither. You speak all the time with the elder grandmother, who died on the day I left childhood. Would she say that death was an ending?'

'She might say that there was a right time, and that leaving early for self-pity was not the act of the woman she delivered to adulthood.'

Breaca had not expected sharpness, when she had set aside her own anger. There was a moment when it would have been possible to fall back to that again, to find escape into fury.

She shook her head. 'Don't. I don't want to fight with you. We have little enough time together as it is.'

'We're not together. I can't reach you. I don't know how.'

'Then perhaps I should try to reach you.'

They were still too far apart. Breaca took hold of Airmid's fingers and, turning, found that she was neither as stiff nor as sore as she had thought. After a while, she turned again and lay down with her head cushioned on Airmid's knee, so that it was possible to look up at her without straining her neck.

She had forgotten what it was simply to lie together in peace, without need, or pressing urgencies. Airmid's fingers combed her hair dry. Airmid's pulse beat under her ear. Above, Airmid's necklace of silvered frog bones sparked against Airmid's skin. It had been broken in two places by the procurator's men. Someone with skill had mended it. Breaca traced the line with her finger, and then the skin beneath, and thought, but did not say, how much easier it was to heal silver than flesh and bone and the soul beneath, but then silver had no soul and was destined for ever to be silver when flesh and blood were long gone and the soul had moved to other things.

After a while, thoughtfully, she said, 'If we go into this war fearing death, death will come seeking us; that's always the way in battle. If we die early, the war will fail and generations after us will live under Roman rule, cursing our names. If we succeed, we'll die anyway, in time. I would rather go to Briga leaving the land free behind me, if I have the ability to choose. I'm not sure that I do, and I've never been unsure before. That's more terrifying than anything.'

She stopped then, because it was more than she had meant to say; more than she had thought since the moment of waking from the fever.

Airmid's hands lay loose in her lap. She looked down at them, at the broken, reddened skin with white engrained in the creases from making an ointment or a paste. She said, 'I think you are living now as everyone else has lived; knowing your own mortality. Can you fight like that and keep living?'

'I don't know. I can try.'

There was more peace in that uncertainty than there had been. The day was quiet and the spring sun shone for them and the world was not yet openly at war. It was not the same as it had once been, but they sat, and then lay, together at the river's edge and for a while each found solace, and some healing of grief, in the other.

Later, nearer to dusk, Breaca went in search of her brother.

She followed the drifting smoke and the scents of the cooking fires and the sound of almost-battle and found him in the centre of the horse fair's clearing, surrounded by youths in their dozens, possibly hundreds, armed with sword blades, shields and spears. There were fewer of them than there had been; each day more learned who he was and what he had been and left him to train with Cunomar, or Ardacos, or any of the other spear-leaders with experience of war.

Those who had not heard, or were able to see beyond the past, stood in rows, blade against blade, spear against blade, blade against spear, and clashed with muted enthusiasm while Valerius watched and encouraged and tried to keep them from injury. Seeing Breaca, he gave his place to Cygfa, and stepped to the side.

His eyes probed her much as Airmid's had done. He said, 'You have heard news of Graine?' and Breaca was not certain if she should be grateful that he could read her so well, or disappointed that she was so open to be read.

'Dubornos sent word with a salt trader. She's alive and safe.' Even now, the newness of that had not yet worn off. She looked past him to where a half-line of young warriors had stepped back on Cygfa's order and were resetting their shields on their arms. She said, 'Are they safe yet?'

He laughed, shortly, shaking his head. 'They might handle a siege, if we could persuade them to listen to us, but for a full-out attack against the veterans of the Twentieth, fighting through the streets of Camulodunum, no, they would be butchered where they stood. But they're better than yesterday and tomorrow will be better than today. It's the best we can hope for. Although we have a new problem.' He pulled a wry face. 'Most of them were born in the years after the invasion, and they all have the same name. I shout it once and half a hundred step forward.'

He was eyeing her sideways, in a way that she knew. Wearily, she asked, 'Breaca?'

'Indeed. And the boys, of course, are all Caradoc. Slightly under three dozen at the last count. But not only you two. There are thirteen Machas, upwards of a dozen Cygfas and at least five named after Ardacos, although they say it differently here which makes it marginally less confusing. It's still a nightmare if we hold a mock battle.'

'And will be fatal in the real thing. What are you going to do?'

'Cygfa has asked them all to pick a new name. They're going to hold a ceremony later, at the rise of the moon. Each of them has to choose something distinct, that sounds different.'

'We had better delay the assault, then – you could be here for days arguing. Do you need to be part of it?'

Valerius ran a hand through his hair. 'That would be unwise. Most of them still spit against the wind or make the sign to ward off evil when I pass. They listen to what I say if I give them a good enough reason, but it would be fair to say they are not yet given to me heart and soul as they would need to be to let me name them.'

He was hurt by that; she knew him well enough to see it. She said, 'They'll learn when they see who can best keep them alive,' and then, because there was no avoiding it and she had already delayed too long, 'When were you last inside Camulodunum?'

Valerius' face froze. His lips made a fine white line. A great many memories passed between them, few of them good.

Bleakly, he said, 'I was there about a month before Caradoc's capture. I imagine it will have been sometime around Graine's birth.'

'Eight years, then. Nearly nine.' It was not easy to meet his eye then, but necessary. She said, 'I've been there more recently, but things will have changed; wells will have been dug, walls built, the theatre and the temple completed. If we're to make a proper battle plan, somebody with an eye for strategy really should go in and look before we attack.'

'And? There needs to be a better reason than that. Men have been assaulting cities they half knew for a thousand years without the need to go into them first.'

'And I want to talk to Theophilus to see if he can be persuaded to leave before the fighting starts. His apprentices came with the last wagonload of refugees, but he's wedded to his hospital and thinks he can't leave. He sent us warning of the procurator's coming; without him we'd have lost the full war host. The Eceni have never abandoned their friends in times of war. I don't want to start now.'

He was beginning to read her as she could read him. The planes of his face softened. 'Could you tolerate company or must you go alone?'

'Why else am I here?' Unexpectedly, she found herself smiling. 'I would welcome your company if it were offered.'

XVI

BETWEEN ONE NIGHT AND THE NEXT, THE BLACKTHORN flowered.

White blossom scattered the landscape, sporadic as old snow in the brown melt of spring. Heather lay dormant, bracken not yet unfurled; the mountains of the west were barriers of mud and towering rock, left by a capricious child-god to keep the legions from Mona and all who took refuge there.

That was the easy way to see it, the way that did not feed into crippling nightmares and waking visions that were decimating the troops as effectively as had the zealots of the Republic, leaving one in ten men as useless as if they were dead.

In truth, more than one in ten was incapacitated. Quintus Valerius Corvus, prefect of the Fifth Gaulish cavalry wing, sat at his desk in the relative calm of his tent and listened to the wind hiss through the guy lines wishing he could hear in it words of comfort that would erase the detailed personnel listings being read to him by Ursus, the decurion of the second troop.

'. . . and Flavius has the runs so badly he can barely get up from the latrines to drink water before he has to sit back down and let it flood straight out again from the other end. Sabinius says it's all in their minds; there's nothing wrong with the food or the water or the weather, they're just shit scared of the dreamers and what they do to men they capture alive. Sabinius is fine.'

'He would be. He's lived in Britannia long enough to know the dreamers do nothing we don't do. And they've never yet crucified anyone, or even attempted to.'

Corvus spun a knife end-on between his hands. The tip scored a small reddening dent in his left index finger. A falcon's head in hollow bronze made the hilt. It rolled cool and smooth against his palm, a talisman against the jagged ache of the wind.

'What matters is how many are fit to fight. Out of five hundred men, we have at most three hundred and forty who could sit on a horse and at least thirty of those would be more of a danger to themselves than to the enemy in combat. It isn't enough.'

'It's enough if all we're going to do is sit here and watch the heather come into bloom on the mountainside while the governor counts his stocks of javelins and tries to tell the Batavians that their great-great-grandfathers once swam the Rhine in full armour so they'll have no problems at all with the straits.'

Ursus jutted his chin, aiming for defiance and falling, as ever, halfway short. The scabs of old flea bites showed in a crop where his helmet strap rested. He needed to shave, but then almost all of the men needed to shave and the only ones without fleas were those already dead. Ursus was simply more solidly earthen than the rest of his peers, less taken with the pretensions of office. On most days, that was a good thing.

Corvus sighed and placed his knife edgeways on to the writing tablet on which he had made his notes, then placed his stylus as a wedge beneath to stop it rolling off the table. Nothing here was on the flat except the governor's tent. One of the few advantages of rank was that his table was at least level enough to balance a half-full beaker on without slopping wine into the mud.

Ursus was still waiting for him, doing his best to appear at ease. Mildly, Corvus said, 'That's treason. I should have you flogged in front of the entire wing and you know it. Just because you've escaped the nightmares of the dreamers, there's no need to bring on a dose of those unique to Rome. What do you imagine—'

'It is the dreamers, then? You believe Sabinius that they're making it all happen?'

'Of course it is. I can feel them doing it. The only question is what else they have waiting for us when we begin to advance. Don't stare like that, man, it's unhealthy. Think; if you're dreaming peacefully of the olive groves you remember from childhood and suddenly the trees begin to walk and the bark shows human faces and they all speak with one voice of the doom that awaits the moment you wake up, and this happens four nights without a break, then you can be fairly sure it's coming from the outside. The trick is to learn to make friends with the speaking trees. Which is what we should have done with the dreamers and we wouldn't have half of our men out of action. Come on, we should be with the governor. Don't ask him when we're going to attack; he won't thank you for it.'

Corvus held open the tent flap. Outside, rain had begun to fall, turning almost to sleet. He reached his cloak from the bench and pulled it tight round his shoulders. Beside him, Ursus pulled on a balding, poorly cured wolfskin, bought for a silver coin ten years before from a Dacian trader. The thing stank and earned him no friends, but it had been his luck-charm for three years until a good day's battle had persuaded him that it was not necessary. The fact that he had unearthed it now did not bode well.

They walked together through mud and driving rain towards the governor's three-roomed pavilion. Halfway there, when they were as far from all tents as possible and least likely to be overheard, Corvus said, 'Is Flavius still sore about what happened with the procurator?'

To his credit, Ursus did not break stride. He sucked a breath in through tight teeth, shaking his head. 'I don't know why any of us tries to keep a secret from you. Yes, "sore" would be a small measure of what Flavius is feeling. And if he thought I'd told you, he'd see to it that I got a blade in the back at the next dusk skirmish when no-one could prove it wasn't the enemy. And if he thought I hadn't told you, but you'd guessed, he'd have you crucified for being a soothsayer, if he could find a way to make it happen. I don't plan to give him a chance to knife me. I suggest you don't give him an opening to talk to the governor about you.'

'He hasn't looked me in the eye or spoken a civil word since we rode out of the Eceni compound,' Corvus said. 'Before that, he was as unctuous as any man who thinks he can gain promotion by making himself indispensable. If I'm a soothsayer for noticing that, then we have an army of magicians and most of them are holding rank. Just at the moment, I think that would be rather useful.

Sadly, it's not true. Shall we go in and see how many braziers the governor has lit for our comfort, and if his hounds are taking the heat from all of them?'

Seven braziers warmed the outermost of the governor's three tent-rooms, eating the air so that it was hard to breathe. A dozen tallow torches stood about, blazing thick, indulgent light.

Eighty officers of varying ranks from the governor himself, through the legates, the senior and junior tribunes of two legions, the prefects of four cavalry wings and their subordinate centurions and aides, stepped diligently around a pair of smooth-pelted slate blue running hounds, which lay stretched across the floor where the heat was best and the rushes driest.

A native youth with, for those who could read such things, the clan marks of the Atrebates, longest loyal to Rome, on his fore-arms, sat on his own couch by the wall. Even those who knew nothing of the tribes and their affiliations were struck by his looks.

Word had passed that the hound-boy and his two beasts were a gift from grateful tribal leaders to their governor, known the world over for his love of hare coursing. Paullinus' other loves, clearly, had become known among the tribes, if not yet to his wife.

A map moulded of mud and stone ruled the centre of the tent's floor, taking up a quarter of the remaining standing room. Laid out inside pale oak borders in the likeness of the mountains and the sea, fragments of heather stood for forests, moss for turf, while a gravel of broken pottery made the straits across to Mona, with white chalk grit marking the sweep and curl of currents that were known to have killed.

The island itself was a single unbroken rock, chiselled flat and marked with scratches at the inlets along the coast. The whole edifice had dried long since in the heat of the room; the mud had cracked and stones that made mountains no longer stood vertical. The smell of moss and earth was less than it had been which was unfortunate; there had been a time when it had fought a winning battle against the strains of sweat and wine and old diarrhoea reek-ing from the officers who gathered, and the unique stench of Ursus' Dacian wolfskin.

The mountains were currently the focus of attention. A huddle of small tents lovingly constructed of scrap hide and stick had been recently placed in position on the lower slopes of the tallest mountain. The emblems of two legions and four wings of cavalry were laid out in rows together with counters marking the numbers of men.

Corvus and Ursus were last to enter. The governor's secretary was a balding, broken-nosed former legionary who had lost his right leg in battle and learned to write when he could no longer ride. He looked up at the draught from the tent flaps. 'How many?' he asked.

Corvus said, 'Three hundred and forty who can ride. Three hundred of them whom I would trust to be effective.'

'Officers?'

'All of them are fit to serve barring one standard-bearer and I could probably get him to move.'

'Really?' The word fell into the space and caused quiet. It came from a lone man on the far side of the mountain map. Suetonius Paullinus, by Nero's pleasure fifth governor of the emperor's province of Britannia, was so purely Roman that he could trace ancestors in the senate back to the time when there was no senate. Accordingly, he was a small man, neat and freshly barbered and fastidious in his cleanliness. His hair was oak-dark, peppered with a flinty grey at the temples and thinning a little on top. His eyes were brown and newly bloodshot and his nose complained of the cold winters and damp of Britannia.

He sat on a carved oak chair draped with scarlet and wore his parade breastplate in a tent where the air was thick as soup with men's breath and men's wind and the muggy heat of the braziers. Without rising, he raised a finger to Corvus, who stepped forward.

'Every other wing has at least half of its officers unfit to ride. The men say, although not in my hearing, that the ghosts of the dead are feasting on the souls of those who have been in the land longest, and those are always the centurions and decurions, the standard-bearers and the masters of horse. You don't believe it?'

'Your excellency, I don't. I've been in this province longer than anyone else in this army. If what they say were true, I would be languishing in my tent with my bowels running out of my backside. Which evidently I'm not.' Corvus smiled, neutrally. 'I am, as ever, ready to serve where I may best be of use.'

'Evidently.'

The governor's gaze passed in succession from Corvus to his secretary, to both of his senior legates and one of the juniors, to the Atrebatan hound-boy and, lovingly, to the hounds, and back to his secretary, who nodded. The man made a small addition to the mountain map on the floor; a small model of a horse was transferred from the site of the governor's gathering camp to the shores of the straits.

'I wish an advance party to seal off the landing grounds of the ferry; according to local spies and to three of the enemy questioned recently, the ferries from the god-cursed island only land in one of two places and both are close by. I wish you to go there and make secure the jetties at both sites: no-one is to reach the island, or leave it, without my express permission. When you have done that, report back to me and I will send you the men and the means to make the barges that will take us across. The Batavians will come to you soon after, to watch the water and see how the horses may be swum across; we cannot risk them in the small-craft we will build for the legionaries. We will join you soon after that, when the barges are built and the legions are back up to strength.'

'Did we want to be doing this?'

Ursus asked it, sitting on horseback at Corvus' left hand. Ahead of them, the savage sea swirled between the shore on which they stood and the mist-hung one, not so far distant, that marked the only part they could see of the gods' island of Mona. At the feet of their mounts, two jetties were manned by armed auxiliaries who already cursed the cold and the salt sea wind and the cries of the gulls that became, all too easily, the howling wails of the dead.

'Flavius is going to hate you as much for leaving him behind as anything else,' said Ursus, because he had got no answer.

'Flavius hates what he cannot own. It doesn't necessarily stop him being a good officer, only makes it unwise to trust him with anything important.'

Corvus' face was already reamed white with cold and blown salt. His mare was shuddering under him, having been ridden too hard and then made to stand still too long with the sweat still wet on its hide. It was bay and long-legged and had been the gift of the Eceni child the procurator had been going to crucify at the steading before Corvus had halted the proceedings with a lie. These things made sense to Ursus only in retrospect and then only vaguely.

Corvus turned his mount away from the sea and the island beyond, careful of the rocks beneath its feet. Ursus stayed where he was, watching the waves break grey on the black rock, studying barnacles and shreds of seaweed, because both calmed his mind.

He did not hear the horse stop, only felt a hand on his shoulder. His flesh jumped, and his soul with it, and he heard Corvus' calm, quiet, heartbreaking voice say, 'I do know what it feels like, for both you and him. I can't change the way of the world, or offer more than I am able; all I can do is promise honesty and my best efforts to keep us all alive. For what it's worth, I don't despise either of you. But I trust you, which is more than I do him.'

The hand left his shoulder. Ursus' flesh ached. Dryly, Corvus said, 'Don't stay at the sea's edge long if you want a quiet night; the dreamers know we're here. The closer we are, the easier it is for them to taste the fears we harbour.'

The bay mare walked on over rock to shingle and then to turf. Ursus stayed longer than cold or sanity said that he should. When he left, the patterns of the sea breaking on the rocks were no different from when he arrived, but he felt calmer than he had, and more at peace with his own world.

When he finally turned his own mount and walked it back to the noise and false bravado of the shore camp, it was to find that Flavius had risen from his sickbed in the tent beneath the mountains and ridden alone along poorly guarded paths to reach the men who had left him behind.

Ursus and he greeted each other as a decurion and his standard-bearer might be expected to do, but a balance had shifted between them, and both of them felt it. Ursus grinned and found that he went on grinning through a day of cold and sleet and vague shifting shadows that rose out of the sea and left men white and shaking. Adding to the miracle, he slept that night without nightmares for the first time since reaching the west. Flavius came late to the tent and was drunk.

Sometime in the following dawn, lying awake, listening to the unstable sleep of all those around him, Ursus came to realize how far he had gone towards making of his standard-bearer a lifelong enemy and how hard it would be to claw some sense of safety back. He should have been afraid. Staring at the roof hides of his tent, watching the certain place where the drips grew fat before they fell to join the puddle on the ground, he found that he would rather have the known enmity of Flavius than the unknown terrors of the dreamers and that if he put all his attention on the one, he could forget the other, and thus fall back into sleep.

XVII

THE MILITARY HOSPITAL THAT SERVED THE CITIZENS OF
Camulodunum was as quiet as it had ever been.

Three beds were occupied: two by women suffering milk-
fever after childbirth, in both cases exacerbated by fear and five
days of siege-hunger; the third by Peltrasius Maximus, a garrulous,
opinionated veteran of the XXth legion who was suffering from
gravel of the bladder.

Peltrasius had been ordered to drink a flagon of well water at
each watch – water being the only thing in plentiful supply – and
this had naturally increased both the frequency and the volume of
his urination. His howls of pain as each corn-sized piece of grit
passed down the length of his urethra could be heard as far abroad
as the theatre and the forum.

In happier times, men would have made jokes of Peltrasius' pain,
and built a mummery around it, so that the theatre would profit
from the man's misfortune. Now, with the smoke of a thousand
fires obscuring the horizon and the numbers of the Eceni war host
rumoured to be in the tens of thousands, the more gullible among
the population, veterans as well as natives, claimed to have
heard the ghost of Cunobelin arise from his grave mound and seen
it stalk the emptying streets of the city. They would not have it that
mortal pain could sound like the vengeful souls of the dead.

Peltrasius was not close to dying, only wished that he were.

Theophilus of Athens and Cos, once physician to emperors and reduced now to tending retired soldiers who suffered from an excess of their own indulgence, came as close as he had ever done to wishing that he could administer a dose of something permanently quieting to the man under his care. He would have had his apprentices tend Peltrasius and let them keep the payment, but he had ordered them to leave and, finally, on the third time of telling, they had done so.

More than he had ever imagined, he missed the fast wit of his clerk, the boy he had named Gaius, and the slower, more lugubrious care of Felix, the apprentice physician. Their absence left a gap in the life of his hospital that the healing of others did not fill.

He had not expected how much it would hurt when he had first asked them to go, standing with them at the open window of his second floor bedroom on the night the watchtower burned. Clothed in his nightrobe, his bare feet cool on the wooden floor, Theophilus had felt from them the awe and reverence of youths who think they know fire and war and are still young enough to worship both.

Theophilus was not inclined to worship anything, and would never stoop to advocating war; he had too many friends on both sides not to see the tragedy of it too clearly. He watched the ball of orange flame blossom into the night, and then the string of others as the watch-chain was needlessly lit, as if more fires were useful, or necessary to augment the message of the first.

Before the chain was complete, he had turned from the window, saying, 'The Eceni are rising. It can be no-one else. They won't attack here while the Ninth might come at their backs. We have some days to make ready. You should find your families and leave. Go north to the Eceni if you want to take part in their war. Go south to Caesaromagus or west to Verulamium if you would find sanctuary amongst the supporters of Rome.'

'And if we want to do neither? If we want to continue our studies with you? What should we do then?' Felix had asked it, the round, cheerful lad who had hands that could soothe a woman in childbirth as easily as they could support a man dying of flux or mend a youth crushed under falling masonry in the temple. His voice was softly resonant, and warm, like the flames that lit the horizon.

'He'll tell us to leave anyway. There will be a siege and then a battle and he thinks it's his duty to protect us from both, not the other way round.'

Gaius had answered before Theophilus had time. The clerk had grown in the last year and was tall as any of the other tribesmen, lean and stringy and long-faced with bright, sharp eyes that saw dust in corners and cleaned it even while he was revising in his head the rates charged for a night's keep and bandaging and the additional percentage levied on a bill for setting a broken wrist because the one who came to pay had made the mistake of opening his purse and showing the quantity and colour of his gold.

That same sharp intellect showed as he offered one of his rare smiles, saying, 'But we know it's our duty to protect him. He can't make us leave. If we choose to stay and face the Eceni at his side, there is nothing he can do to stop it.'

Which was true, and had remained true, and, for six days, they had resisted Theophilus' pleas and his orders and his attempts at reason and had continued to tend the dwindling numbers of sick and injured and increasing numbers of food-poisoned who presented themselves at the hospital's door and asked for help.

When Peltrasius began to scream and the rumours flew, they had washed their hands and donned their plain woollen robes without being asked and gone out in the evenings when the howls were at their height and done their best to persuade those who would listen that the man they could hear was very much alive and had no intention of becoming a ghost.

Sadly, as is the way of panic, the sight of them had fuelled more rumour so that soon there were reputed to be three ghosts of Cunobelin, or possibly the man and two of his sons, one who screamed and two others who moaned and murmured and touched passers-by with fingers of death. They gave up finally when a child they were treating for a broken finger swore in the names of two gods that his father had tried to attack one of the apparitions and his sword had passed straight through the ghost's body and out the other side; the risks of someone's trying to repeat that miracle in a population heading fast towards hysteria were too real.

Gaius and Felix had left, in the end, when the only ones who remained in Camulodunum were veterans and their families, or those who had given themselves so completely to Rome that they dared not leave. The two had come to Theophilus together on the seventh day after the burning began. Drawn and white, Gaius had said what was needed. 'There is no-one left but us who does not support Rome. If we stay, we are supporting something that is insupportable. The Boudica is calling warriors to the place of the Heron's Foot. If there's war, she will need physicians. Would you come with us?'

Theophilus had known what they would say. Half the night, he had listened to them talk in the dormitory room two storeys below his. He had watched the moon rise and set and watched the glow of night fires on the horizon that showed how close the war host gathered. Listening to their feet climbing the stairs to find him, he had brought to mind the speech he had spent the night preparing.

He did not know how lined he looked, or how old, when he said, 'I can't leave a hospital while there is still someone in it. If the women recover, if Peltrasius passes his last stone, or his last breath, if no-one else has come to take their places, I will give thought to what I should do.'

They had expected as much. They would have killed Peltrasius for him, and perhaps tried to cover it up, but not the women. Felix had smiled through tears and said, 'We brought you a gift, to remember us by.'

The thing was outside the door and they made him turn away while they brought it in between them. He thought it might be wine, or the smoked boar he had enjoyed before the fires began, or olives saved in a cold store from the last shipment in the autumn. For a moment, hearing a rasping breath, he thought it might be a hound whelp, and panicked, because he had never yet owned one and was not at all certain that he wanted to give his heart so completely and have it broken, as he had seen other men do.

It was not a hound, but a sword, and that was every bit as surprising. The blade was of middle length, a little shorter than was the fashion of the tribes, who fought alone from horseback, for the honour of it more than the killing, but longer than the legionary gladii that were fashioned to stab between the shields and so keep the integrity of the lines intact. The iron of the long-blade they gave him was burnished to mirror brightness and the hilt was of red copper and gold, in the shape of the Sun Hound, which had been the emblem of Cunobelin before his fall.

Theophilus felt his jaw hang slack. 'I don't . . .'

'You don't know how to use it. We know.' Felix patted his arm. 'But Peltrasius fought with the cavalry and he has spent his last ten years making a study of the ways the tribes fight. It's a hobby of his. Get him to show you whenever he's not howling. If you're here when the Eceni arrive, you'll need it, whichever side you decide to fight for.'

He had no intention of fighting for anyone. He had thought that obvious, not needing to be spoken aloud. He said, 'You should know by now that I—'

Gaius put a cautious finger to his lips. 'Don't say it. Not here. Not now when the gods are listening. We don't need to know.'

He had thought they had both abjured their gods, preferring the cool waters of rationality to the hot turbulence of faith. They were aching to go and it was not time to begin teaching all that he wanted to tell them.

Lost in the pain of the moment, Theophilus held out his hands and they gave him the blade, laying it across his palms as if he were a warrior among the natives. Felix was weeping openly, which was usual. Gaius was wet-eyed, which was not. In Alexandrian, a little rustily, he said, 'Father, whatever you have taught us, we will use well and for healing, not for harm.'

Theophilus bowed. 'Then if Peltrasius dies, I can rest knowing it will not have been your doing.' It sounded too formal. He did not trust himself to smile.

They backed out, palms on their foreheads. Later in the same watch, he saw them leave, riding along the near-empty streets on horses bought for a year's salary in gold from the quartermaster.

The hospital was too quiet with them gone, except when Peltrasius howled, when it was too loud. For the first time in his life, Theophilus the physician wished at least one of his patients dead and the other two mended without him.

At dusk, he made himself perform the tasks of both assistants, washed the women and fed them, saw to their water and the pots beneath their beds and gave them the infusions that had been standing half the day in his dispensary. He opened his stores, which had not yet been raided by desperate townsmen, and cooked a sparse meal for Peltrasius of field beans and barley with wild garlic to help the passing of the stones and carried the man a full ewer of tepid water in which to wash. He held him while he screamed and gave him poppy after, for the ease of them both.

He lit a small oil lamp and made the journey down to the cellars to draw more water from the well. The cold and the dark were as far removed from war and others' pain as he could imagine. He cursed them mildly and set the lamp on the platform above the well. The light sent his own shadow dancing along the rough-plastered wall to where the first spider to escape Gaius' care was building a web. He watched it and the flittering shadows that joined it, and listened to the small scuff on the stone floor that was not a rat or a mouse.

Without turning, he said, 'Greetings, Bán mac Eburovic, beloved of Mithras. I had expected you here by a more direct route, and sooner.'

The hair prickled on his scalp. He imagined a blade, drawn and advancing. When there was no more movement, nor any slicing cut to his back, he turned, slowly, keeping his hands in sight.

'My brother is outside,' said Breaca of the Eceni, from the far side of the well. 'He is beloved of Nemain, too, now, not only Mithras. In both of their names, he will make sure we are not disturbed.'

It had not been easy for a brother and sister, soberly clad, to enter Camulodunum at dusk on the ninth night of the city's siege, but equally, it had not been unduly hard.

The ditches and dykes that had protected Cunobelin's steading in the days of his power were easily passed and not close to the city. The trenches and walls that had served the fortress of the XXth in the early years of its existence had been pulled down and filled in when it became instead a veterans' colony. They were no barrier any longer, only a line of rubble with grass growing thinly through to show where it had been; an infant learning to walk could have stepped over to get into the city, or to leave it.

The streets had been less quiet than Breaca had imagined; looking down from the slope above the city, there had seemed few fires, and so few people out after dark, but she and Valerius had been stopped and challenged four times in the first hundred paces by groups of men who gathered by the dozen under the shaded light of tallow tapers and reed-bunched torches.

They were Roman for the most part: dark-haired, dark-skinned, dark-eyed veterans, closer to sixty than fifty, with flab at the belly where once-fitness had lapsed. Some talked animatedly, and only fell to silence when the newcomers were seen, but most had been building barricades or digging trenches against incoming horses and were more suspicious than their fellows. They stopped the strangers at blade point and demanded to know their business. Valerius answered shabbily, in Catuvellauni, and then stilted Latin, saying that he had come from the northern quarter of the town and was bringing his woman to see the physician. They let him go. Nobody asked him why.

There were women, too, under the tallow tapers, but fewer of those; young and underfed, with the smoky grey eyes and red-blond hair of the Trinovantes, they were pregnant or nursing or with silent children at foot, gawping and shadowed by a fear they did not fully understand.

None of these chose to stop the pair of natives, dressed in the brown stuff of merchants with clan markings worked at the hem. Only a child, looking at them, had removed its fingers from its mouth and said, 'Who's that? Have they come to help us?'

She had spoken Latin with a tribal accent. Her mother had hushed her, saying, 'They're Catuvellauni, friends to Rome.' It had been hard to tell if she considered that friendship a good thing, or despicable.

They had abandoned the main thoroughfare shortly after that and taken to smaller streets with deeper shadows. A lone veteran with a drawn sword had challenged them in the first of those, his voice rusty with fear. Breaca answered this time, saying that she was suffering from bloody flux and stinging water and was being taken to the hospital for urgent treatment. The veteran backed away, making the sign against evil with his left hand.

The mention of flux had been more than a lucky guess; the stench of rancid faeces had been with them for a while now, mingling with the thin, scouring stench of fear that robbed Camulodunum of its heart. Once, the streets had stunk of life and vibrant feeding; now they smelled chiefly of rats' urine and rotting vegetables. The smell stuck to the back of the throat and made slime on the tongue. Breaca put her hand to her nose and walked on. No-one else stopped them. Nearby, echoing, a man began shrilly to scream.

Valerius tapped her shoulder, making her jump. 'Left. Here.' His voice was light with half-suppressed laughter. She had heard him like that in Longinus' company once or twice; whatever the danger, he was enjoying himself – perhaps because of the danger. She followed him into a street even smaller than the one they were on, barely wide enough to walk down without shuffling sideways, and then into a solid brick-built house camped improbably in a row of wattle and daub huts. Stepping inside, she nearly tripped over Valerius, who crouched in the middle of the floor.

Looking up, he said, 'Help me lift this?' and she knelt, and did so.

There were two rings set into the floor, covered by an excess of dust and old straw. They took one each and pulled and a section of the floor came up smoothly on tallowed hinges so that it smelled meaty even while it hissed to vertical.

He said, 'There are steps down. You could have light but it's as easy to feel the way, and you're less likely to risk being seen. There will be light in the well room if anyone is there. I'll wait here and make sure you're not followed. Shout if you need me. Theophilus will be surprised, but not, I think, discomfited.'

He had been right, of course, which was why she had asked him to come. One of the reasons why she had asked him. She had felt her way blindly along a short tunnel of rammed earth and into a cellar of neatly fitted stones, as flat and smooth as any in the forum or other buildings of state. Further along, they were layered with plaster and white lime that flaked off under her fingers. Then a flame had flickered in the dense black ahead, and an old friend had trodden on the pavings, muttering and breaking wind, who had no reason to consider himself overheard.

She had scuffed her foot to let him know she was there, believing it necessary for his pride, and he had thought she was Valerius, which was probably reasonable. Unreasonably, she was angry that he had not known her better.

She answered him too sharply, and was sorry, and he saw both of these. She had forgotten his prescience; he could read her almost as clearly as Airmid, and perhaps in some places better because he was not so close, nor blinded by love.

'Breaca?' He reached out and drew her forward into the

lamplight. His hand was on her shoulder, and then he had turned her and was running long, lean fingers across the span of her back, which was not a good thing at all. Her flesh cringed from his touch as it had not done from Airmid's who knew her.

She made herself stand still, not to insult him. He was delicate and adroit in his investigating. He stopped quite soon and took his hands back to himself. If she kept her eyes closed, or her back turned, his voice was ageless and belied the weariness she had seen on his face under the probing light of his oil lamp.

Quite steadily, he said, 'Have you come to me in my role as physician? Airmid has done well by you, but a true healing of the soul takes longer than the healing of the body and even that is barely begun.'

She turned to face him, trying not to be angry again. 'Is it so obvious? Or did the veterans tell of all that they did over cups of wine when they came back?'

'Both.' He shrugged an apology. His face was long and lined and grey under the haphazard orange of the lamp's flame. 'The veterans sang of it over their wine for the few days before the siege began when they thought themselves safe and needed something to banish the disgrace they had suffered at Corvus' hands. They sang of a legionary flogging inflicted on a woman of the Eceni, and then, when the wine hit, they sang also of the irreparable damage done to your daughters, for which I cannot express enough sorrow. But of you, I would have known the most of it as soon as I saw you, from the keening and black wind in your soul which is there to be heard by someone who knows how to hear it. Your brother was much the same; that's why I mistook you. You must grant me that much in my craft: I can hear the mourning of what has been lost. Would you have me lie and pretend ignorance to my friends?'

He was her friend. He had sent warning of the procurator and so saved the war host at a time when discovery would have destroyed it. Before that, he had been friend to Airmid and Graine, to Cunomar and to Corvus, who had loved – who still loved – Valerius, and was loved by him. He had helped her in the killing of Eneit, when it had needed to be cleanly done. For all of these, and basic decency, she owed him honesty.

The rim of the well was of rough stone, with fish-tailed goats stamped head to tail into the mortar on the flat surface. Breaca sat beside one and traced the curled and scaled tail with her finger.

She said, 'Valerius has come into himself as a healer, as well as a dreamer. There are things he can do that Airmid cannot, and things she can do that he will never aspire to, but still—'

'But still, you are trying to fight a war when your soul is broken apart and your body does not yet answer the commands of your mind. And yet, however damaged, you are here and your warriors are camped within sight of the city and nightly Trinovantes who are loyal to you wreak havoc with what attempts are made at forming defences. The veterans dig trenches against your horses and the youths and children of this city fill them in; the Romans build barricades and they are torn down before dawn. Two nights ago, the statue to Victory was pulled from her plinth; a thing of marble, bigger than you and I together and yet nobody heard it fall. A man was hanged for that. The two veterans who hanged him are dead now. If you wait, Camulodunum will fall to mutiny and insurrection without a blade raised against your warriors. Is that what you plan?'

'Not entirely. We will wait a little longer, but not indefinitely; I would not have innocent men hanged on my account. And I have warriors who need to learn to fight. The scouts say you had re-inforcements sent from the west. Is it true?'

'Partly. We have two hundred mercenaries who marched up from the port at Vespasian's Bridge when the watchtowers first burned. They came on the pay of an Atrebatan glass merchant who keeps a villa here. A quarter of them have the bloody flux. Fifty more have counted the numbers of your warriors' watch fires and have handed back their pay to their employer. They'll leave in the morning if your warriors will let them out as they have let out everyone else who has attempted to leave. The rest will fight, I believe, as will the veterans. Then there are two or three thousand Trinovantes who swear they are loyal to Rome and will fight against your war host. I believe perhaps half of them may be telling the truth?'

He had better manners than to look at her for an answer. Breaca studied the workings of the well. The bucket was of waxed pigskin, held agape with a loop of iron at the mouth. The rope from it led up to a pulley and an assortment of wheels and it was not immediately obvious how it might be lowered and then raised again.

Examining it, she said, 'About half, yes. And those who will fight against us are known by those who will not. Many will be dead before— Is that one of your patients?'

The scream died away, echoing from floor to ceiling.

'Indeed.' Theophilus grinned, fleetingly. 'You will have to take my word for it that his health is improving. But if you were to listen on the streets, you would hear that the ghost of Cunobelin walks again and seeks vengeance for the desecration of his tomb. This, too, does not speak well for the defence of our city. If you will allow me—'

He reached past her to the well's mechanism. 'An Alexandrian friend made it when he was stranded here for the winter. It is designed to be effortless to use for an old man with limbs not as supple as they once were. I take it as a gift, grown out of a magnificent intellect, not an insult.'

The physician wound a handle and three sets of cogs turned. The bucket disappeared jerkily into the dark beyond the lamplight. A while passed, and they heard it hit water. Theophilus said, 'If you turn the handle beside you, it will rise again.'

She did, and felt the almost-weightlessness and thought, obscurely, that Cunomar would have enjoyed the mechanics of it. She thought, also, that Theophilus had given her more information than she would ever have asked for and ought not be pushed further on the weaknesses in Camulodunum's defence. She had not come, after all, to extract from him details of defences that could be seen in the streets. She had not come intending to ask him for healing, either, but he had spoken of it and Airmid before him and there had been time to think between.

Winding slowly, she said, 'When Dubornos came back from Rome, he told me of Xenophon, who was your teacher. Valerius has some tales of him also. He seemed ... a very learned physician.'

'He was. And I was, indeed, his pupil in my younger days. If you are asking whether I have his skills, then no, there are things he took to his grave that none of his pupils will ever know. If you're asking if I know some things he did not, then yes, I believe I do. The winter I spent as your guest in Airmid's company was worth years of learning. You need to stop winding now, and move the brake onto the handle. Then I swing this lever – so – and the bucket moves towards us. You see? Effortless.'

The bucket tilted a little and slopped water onto the floor. The smell of it rose chalky and cool. Theophilus stepped back into darkness and returned bearing two beakers in green glass with gems set round the rim.

Seeing her look, he grimaced. 'I took four of these in payment for a difficult childbirth. It's not generally considered wise for a physician to question the good taste of a first-time father. Particularly not if that man is the Atrebatan sub-chief who controls all the trade in glassware from here to the southern sea ports and has command of two hundred mercenaries. In those days, his men were young and well armed and did not have flux, nor were they queuing at the gates to go home. Would you drink water with me, in spite of the colour of the glass? I regret that I have no ale and would not insult you with Rome's wine.'

She accepted his water. Regarding her over the rim of his beaker, he said, 'And so I ask again, have you come to me for healing?'

'I came to ask if you would leave Camulodunum before we burn it to the ground; I would not see you dead by any act of mine. But now that I am here and you have made the offer, then yes, I would be glad of whatever healing is possible. Certainly, I am not fit to fight long as I am.'

His face was green behind the glass. She thought she read a sudden encompassing peace, as she saw sometimes in Airmid when her craft had been best used and gave most joy: at the end of a hard birthing, perhaps, or when a warrior had been brought back to health from battle wounds that had seemed fatal.

For that moment, she saw all of his soul, then a part of him withdrew and something else she could not reach came to the fore. That part explored her as his fingers had done, but more deeply, so that she felt flayed again and had to hold the edge of the well to stay upright.

She stood rigid, drinking water and looking down at the fish-tailed goats through green glass. After a while, when her beaker was empty and he had still not spoken, she looked up. Theophilus was weeping, silently, and holding the glass to hide it so that green tears rolled down green cheeks.

He was not a warrior and the glass was not a shield, nor need it be. Softly, she said, 'Speak to me. Whatever it is, I can hear it from you.'

He drew a long, unsteady breath. 'Breaca of the Eceni, it would be the culmination of a life's work to heal you.'

She wanted that. She had not known how badly she wanted it until she heard it said. Still, Theophilus was weeping.

She was a warrior, if no longer the best; she had never backed away from hurt. Through a cold dread that grew in her chest, she said, 'But you can't.'

'But it may take longer than you can give. The damage within you was not only done in one afternoon, however badly you were treated. Airmid knows this, and Valerius. To heal you now would mean undoing the hurts of a lifetime and that will not be easy or fast; the wounds are not only physical, and the ones to your heart and soul are deeper than anything done to your body. Have you spoken to Valerius, to ask how long his healing took? Does he even know it was done?'

Breaca had not considered that. Thinking back to her brother's long tales at her fever-side, she said, 'His father, Luain mac Calma, demanded a year of him, and he gave it.'

She knew herself gaunt and would not hide it behind the green glass. Carefully, she placed the beaker on the floor beside the well where it would not be knocked over and break. She felt oddly hollow, as if the gap in her soul had come to the front of her chest, and was wide open to the night.

'How long would you need?' she asked.

His face softened. He had no idea how like her father he looked. He said, 'Luain mac Calma is Elder of Mona. He has resources we can only begin to imagine, but then your brother's wounding ran deeper than yours, I think, and was different in its nature. If I say that I would need to be with you, waking and sleeping – particularly sleeping – in no other company from now until mid-summer and possibly beyond, would you give that much? *Could* you?'

He was not a strategist, but he had lived amongst military men all his adult life. He had seen the watchtowers burn and could count the fires of the war host as easily as any other man, and so estimate the size of her army. He knew the distance to Mona and the disposition of the legions. From all these things and more, he had known her answer before he asked the question. It was why he had wept.

Breaca stood in silence. After a moment, when the ache in her chest became leaden and too heavy to be borne, she sat down on the rim of the well.

Theophilus said, 'I'm sorry. Wait here,' and was gone. She listened as the scuff of his feet on the stone faded to nothing. The oil lamp guttered and went out while he was away.

He tutted when he returned, and left again and came back with new light, which was, by then, unwelcome.

'My dear, oh, my dear—'

Breaca could weep after all, it seemed, and having started the tears would not stop, even when she was no longer alone, but held in the care of a foreign man, before whom it should have been easier to show weakness, but was not.

She heard his knees crack and the echo off the walls, then he was kneeling and his hands were round her shoulders, taking proper care of her back so that she tilted forward and her head was in the crook of his neck, smelling the sweat and the man-smell which was father-smell and the smokes of strange fires, and she could weep there, muffled by the white linen of his robes, and her tears, running freely, could merge into racking, bucking sobs as they had not done since childhood, and perhaps not then.

Her body heaved and she thought she might be sick and tried to find some control again, breathing fast and hard through her teeth.

'Breaca, Breaca . . .'

His chin was on her head, so that his voice filtered in through her hair. He patted her cheek and stroked it with his finger and when his hand came away wet and slimed with mucus he did not wipe it on the cloth at his belt. Instead, he held a beaker to her lips, a simple one of clay, not bejewelled glass, and tilted the contents to her mouth.

She tasted and drank and it was not poppy or vervain or hound-wort or any of the others she feared. It hit her somewhere under her diaphragm and the sobbing started afresh. She held her breath, to try to stop it.

Theophilus shook her, like a father with his child. 'Will you not let yourself be weak, even for this? Let go, woman. Weep if you need to weep; scream if you need to. No-one but me will hear it and if they do, they will think it Peltrasius, or the ghost of Cunobelin, whichever takes their fancy. When did you last sleep?

182

A proper sleep, not drugged or fevered or beset by dreams of war?'

A new voice said, 'When she was twelve, I would think, before her mother died, although there might have been some nights on Mona with Caradoc, or more recently with Airmid, when she let herself forget.'

There was a silence, in which only the unsteady rise of her breathing could be heard.

Breaca said, 'Valerius?'

He was somewhere out of sight to her left. She heard him with the same disembodied clarity as she had done in the fevers, but she was not fevered now, only drowning in despair. The lamp was all wrong and her vision was blurred with tears.

Her brother took her hand; she would never mistake his touch for anyone else's. His fingers were cool and dry and steady.

He said, 'My father spent a year working day and night on my healing, even when I did not know he was doing it. As Theophilus will tell you, I am not fully healed, but better than I was. If you want it, we can make that time for you.'

Breaca had control of herself again. Her brother's presence had done that, or Theophilus' draught, or simply time to breathe and to step back from the brink of the void that threatened to consume her. She pushed herself clear of both men and leaned against the wall beneath the newly filled oil lamp.

Valerius sat with his back to the mechanism of the well, watching her with the same tact he had used in the battle against the IXth and before that, when he had fought her in the clearing by Briga's altar, as if too much scrutiny might break her.

He might have been right. As one who has run to the point of exhaustion, she said, 'Then who will lead the war host if I am gone for six months? Who will keep Cunomar in check and stop the she-bears from launching more assaults before we're ready? Who will keep Cygfa alive long enough for her to lead the right flank if it comes to a full battle, when all her instinct is to kill and keep killing, whatever the risk to herself? Who will talk in council with the war leaders of the Coritani, of the Dobunni, the Durotriges, the Dumnonii, the Silures, the Brigantes, the Ordovices, the Atrebates if they choose to side with us? Who has exchanged gifts with them these past twenty years, who has given them guest-place at council fires and sat at theirs, who has led their people into battle and won for them so that they will join now and fight together, whatever the old tribal frictions? If you can give me a name that I can believe in, I promise you, I will be gone.'

Valerius was her brother. He sustained her gaze for longer than most men, and when he looked down, it was to pick up and study the glass beaker with the gems set at its rim. With the green light warping his fingers, he said, 'No-one else can do all of that. I know of no-one else who would want to try.'

'Then why offer what you cannot give? Where is the kindness in that?'

'I didn't say we couldn't give it, I said it couldn't be done by one person alone. There are people who can do each part of it if they have to: Cunomar is learning self-control and leadership, Cygfa is finding reasons to live beyond each battle, Ardacos is devoted to the destruction of Rome, and he can talk to the tribal leaders. Each of these can play a part, but none of them is the Boudica, who can do them all and fire the warriors in battle to stretch beyond their limits.'

'Any one of you can do that.'

'No. I saw you fight against the Ninth and you were not as you should be, but still the warriors around you came alive. In your presence, they fight as one; without you, they are green youths, each fighting their own small battles. You don't see this because for you it has been like this for years, but those of us who watch can see it, and can fear the moment when you break, and it breaks with you. It's the Boudica that makes the war host what it is. We need you for that, Breaca, but we need you whole or we are broken with you. Not yet, perhaps, but soon, we will reach a time when having you with us in body, but not in soul, is worse than not having you at all.'

'Why has no-one said this before?'

'Arrogance?' He did not look arrogant. He looked like a man driven to the edges of his own being. 'We thought we could heal you. And then we thought that being in battle would heal you. And then we thought that Graine going to safety would heal you. Even as late as today, we thought that Airmid, in and of herself, might heal you. We were wrong. What else is there to say?'

Theophilus was there, with a hand on her arm. She felt him as if her body belonged to a stranger. Her voice was empty. 'Perhaps I needed to know this. If I were to take part in my own healing, could it be done faster? In a day? In two days? In ten? We could perhaps spare that long before we burn Camulodunum and all who are in it.'

Her brother pressed his thumb to a ruby. It came away with the imprint white in the flesh. He said, 'To heal at all, you need first to understand what is lost and why. I know of no fast way that might be done.' He balanced the beaker with care on the rim of the well and looked up. 'Theophilus? Do the physicians of Athens and Cos have an answer?'

'You could sleep for a night in the temple of Aesclepius, but that is half a year's journey from here and in any case I doubt if it would suffice. Beyond that . . . I'm sorry, there's nothing I can offer that will give the speed you require. I did not speak lightly: I will give six months of my life to your healing and think in that time I can do it. I know of no way it can be done in less.'

There was silence, and time to think, and to sift the possible from the impossible, and find a way to go on.

Theophilus was sitting still where she had left him with his knees drawn up and his elbows perched on them in a way that undid entirely the dignity of his white robes. Breaca came to stand, and then to sit, before him. She did not touch him, but was close enough to feel the quiet heat of his skin.

'That you can think of it, and are prepared to give it time, is a greater gift than I could have asked for. It is not your fault, or mine, that I can't accept. We will both know that the will was there, and perhaps return to it one day. Meanwhile, I came to ask a different gift, one that is not impossible. The morning will bring war, if not this morning, or the tenth from now, then soon. Would you come with us to safety? Nothing will be asked of you; it is only that we owe you everything and would not repay it with death.'

'That, too, is impossible.' Theophilus shook his head. 'I can't leave here now. The hospital has three patients. By tomorrow's dawn, it may have more. I made an oath, once, never to abandon them. I would not break that simply to save my own life. If they all leave, or if it's clear that by staying I can do them no good, then, yes, I will follow my apprentices to your camp, but that may not happen before you attack. We should be clear that the decision to stay is mine. I absolve you of all harm that may come of it, to me or my hospital.'

The screaming began again in the room above, rising in pitch and volume, as if the afflicted patient did not need to pause for breath.

Theophilus stood. 'You see? How could I leave a man in such pain? You should go. If I can, I will join you. If not, then your gods, perhaps, will guide the outcome.'

He gripped them both along the forearm, hand to elbow, as warriors did before battle. His face was smooth with age and exhaustion, his eyes infinitely wise. 'Whatever happens, I have lived well and my life has been richer for knowing you. I would not have it otherwise. Go, and build the war that you must and make sure that in winning it you each find a way to be whole, or all this is for nothing.'

XVIII

THE GODS' ISLAND OF MONA LAY LOW IN THE OCEAN. PALE waves creamed its flanks and the sea ran thick as liquid iron in the straits that separated it from the mainland.

Dawn had not yet come. Graine lay on her belly in the un-light amidst colourless sea pinks and harsh, rimed grasses looking out to the place where water met land. The tide was on the ebb. Waves riffled up the shingle, a little further away each time. Periodically, she measured the distance from the frothing wavelets to the high-tide mark a hand's span in front of her face where the storm of the last three days had rammed a broken crescent of bladderwrack and sea-aged oak and clear jellyfish with pale purple stars at their centres far above the rest of the shore's detritus.

Time was measured by waves. In between was timeless and held its own peace. The pungent scent of sea and rotting weed seeped into her skin and hair; it lay ripe on her tongue and swelled the space of her lungs, drawing out forgotten memories of the time *before*, when she had lived on Mona, when she had been whole and the world had seemed safe, when her mother had been the beloved of Briga, a warrior without match and invincible, when Rome had been a distant, faceless enemy to be defeated by the greater power of the Boudica and the gods, when the Boudica's daughter had been the promised of Nemain, and had not ached in every part of her body from the assaults of uncounted men.

The pain was less than it had been; the sea's healing had worked on the journey over, and that – the freedom and exhilaration of the ocean – had been the first surprise. Until she had boarded the ship sent by Luain mac Calma to fetch her, Graine had not known how much happier she was riding the prow of a bucking vessel than she had ever been, or was ever likely to be, riding the calmest horse. The journey from the far southwest toe of Britannia to the south-westerly tip of Mona had taken three days, the last two sailing hard into the teeth of a storm. Every slamming wave had been a challenge as great and as miraculous as the spear-trials of her brother and sister; they had made as nothing the bruises and tears of her body, showing how small were the assaults she had suffered when the vast, crushing power of the god was so great. At first, simply to face that force without terror, to stay still and accept what was thrown at her, had been challenge enough. Later, numbed and cold and exhilarated, she had learned to fight back, shouting and screaming into the power of the sea.

Caught in the need of it, she had spent each moment of daylight, and a good half of the torch-lit nights, on the foredeck of the *Cormorant*, clinging to the prow rails, howling into the maw of the gale that Manannan had roused to protect the gods' island from Rome, with the sea lashing her face and hands until the skin grew red and peeled from her flesh and her ox-blood hair lost its shine and became brittle and greyed with salt.

Hawk and Dubornos had wanted to bring her below deck to safety, but Segoventos, the elderly Gaul who had put his ship to sea on her account at least half a month earlier than anyone else would have dared to, had promised to care for her life with his own. Then Gunovar had made a harness that tied to the prow rail so that even if she lost her grip she would not be swept overboard and the two men had given up their persuadings, and only brought her meals and asked her to come below to sleep when the night was darkest. On the last night, seeing the storm about to blow itself out, they had not done even that.

The wind had been dying as they had put down the small-boat and rowed for Mona's shore, so that the white manes cresting the waves had shrunk and shrunk again until they became just more green water slopping lazily up to kiss the rocks of the headland.

The disappointment of that was a blessing of sorts; if Graine had come straight from that wild joy to the desolation of the abandoned great-house and the hollow emptiness of the evacuated steading, the loss of all that was Mona would have been much harder to bear.

As it was, the five hundred warriors who had been chosen to remain had made an honour guard for her, and it had been necessary to greet them and to learn their names and to hear their stories and see the place set apart from the rest where their dream marks had been carved on the roof beams of the great-house, so that it was almost dusk before she had time alone to look for Bellos of the corn-gold hair and the godlike eyes whose dream had called her back home. Unlike the others, he had neither remarked on her bruising, nor pretended not to see it; he had met her in the dream and knew what she was. The relief of his easy presence had held her with him through the remainder of the evening.

She had been sitting by the fire with him, sharing malted barley and ewe's milk cream from the first lambings, before she had found that he was blind. She had been lying in the dark, halfway to sleep, before she realized that Valerius must have known of the blindness, and had not thought to tell her, but had left her to find out on her own.

She had fallen asleep thinking of that, and wondering why, and had dreamed of something, but had lost the shape of the dream on waking. The frustration of the loss, and the aching emptiness of the once-vibrant steading, had been enough to rouse her from her bed and send her down the path to the jetty to find a place where she could lie unseen and find out for herself if everything she had been told about the coming invasion was true.

It was not yet light enough to see anything. Alone in a kind of peace, she lay on her belly in the coarse grass, listening to the soft out-breath of the waves and breathing in the ocean's leavings while the dawn leached colour back to the world.

Shapes grew from the greys. Presently, she was able to see the barnacled wood of the island's jetty, a spear's throw to her right. For a little longer, there was only mist and the iron sea beyond it and she could hold on to the memory of Mona as it had been through all of her childhood; not at peace, because the warriors who made it home had conducted a war against Rome without cease and she had never known true peace, but the island had always been a place of sanctuary, secure against any threat.

It was secure no longer.

The sea became an ocean of muted mirrors, catching the early light and spinning it high, again and again, to the sky. A pair of oystercatchers sliced across the wavetops towards her and then turned at an angle and fled north to open water, piping alarm. Beyond the line of their flight, it became possible to see that the jetty's opposite partner, which should have reached back to offer a landing place on the mainland, had gone. Where it had been, the rock was scorched black and fragments of charred wood still dabbled in the waves.

There was tranquillity of a kind in the burned remains, couched in mist and rock, but straight lines were already taking shape amongst the curving stones. Right angles grew at their ends and, too fast, the burgeoning light showed the outlines of gunwales and prows of boats and soon she could see what Bellos had described: that dozens of flat-bottomed barges were strung end to end, bobbing in the quiet water like beads on a string hung for a child to play with, and beyond those, spread thickly along the shore and back into the purpled heather and bracken of the lower slopes, were the tents and pavilions and mules and horses and latrine ditches and quartermaster's piles, set about with chained hounds to keep off rats, of two legions of the Roman army and their four wings of attendant cavalry. Closer than those, two smaller clusters of tents sat about the burned heel of the mainland jetty, with horses in two separate corrals and two different cavalry banners cracking in the breeze above them.

Graine had no need to count them; she had grown in a world where she knew the standards and banners of Rome, and the numbers of men they commanded, as well as she knew the dream marks of her own kin. Taken all together, there gathered on the mainland eight thousand men trained for war. A stretch of water was all that kept them from Mona and it was not enough.

'They have their boats ready. Why did they not attack yesterday, when the storm first died?'

Graine asked it aloud, into the silent morning. After a moment, Bellos God-eyes, whom everyone else knew as Bellos the Blind, said, 'Did I make a noise, that you knew I was here?' He sounded amused and exasperated and had not answered her question.

'No. The oystercatchers took fright at you and turned away. You might have been Hawk; he can walk as quietly, but your tunic smells of applewood smoke and his still smells of the sea.' Graine rolled on her side to look back at him over her shoulder. 'Does anyone know why the governor hasn't attacked yet?'

'We were lucky; or perhaps we could say that Manannan extended his grace one more day. The west side of the island, where you landed yesterday, was clear, but here, on this side, a sea mist held both sides of the straits all through the day, so that it was impossible to see your hand in front of your face. That might not be a handicap to me, or perhaps to you, but it was enough to halt the legions, for which we may be grateful.'

Bellos had not mentioned his blindness before. Graine searched for bitterness in his face and found none, but only a closing of something that had not been truly open, as if he felt her scrutiny and was not yet ready to bare himself to it.

She said, 'Would that not have been a good time for them to attack, while the mist hid their true numbers from us? They did not need to see much, only enough to know that they were not killing each other.'

'The officers might think so, I suspect the governor will have done, but the men are too afraid of the nightmare beasts and the walking dead that stalk Mona's shores. They won't attack in anything except perfect daylight.'

She was learning to read him; to hear the faint lilt in his voice that was satisfaction, and the barest shavings of pride, even while he kept them from his face. Guessing, she asked, 'Are the nightmares of your making?'

'No, but I made them greater than they might have been.' He did smile at that, cheerfully, and came to sit beside her, stretching his bare feet down the stones until his heels met the gelatinous weed.

He was slim, almost bony, and more of a youth than he had seemed in the dream, or even at the night fires; perhaps three or four years older than Hawk but no more. His hair was fine as combed wool and a lighter, more brilliant shade of gold than Cunomar's, or Cygfa's. His eyes were a startling, noon-sky blue and they stared out over the water at nothing. Even so, he had walked alone from the great-house to find her and made his way down the beach without any hesitation.

She said, 'How well do you know the island?'

'Well enough to know my way around.'

'Is that why you haven't left? Because Hibernia would be a new place and it would be hard to come to know it as well as you know here?' It was not a delicate question, but then it was not intended to be; on the day she had discovered how frustrating it was to have others step around her own wounding, Graine had stopped doing so for anyone else. Still, she held her breath, waiting to see if she had overstepped a mark that neither of them could see.

Bellos smiled, peacefully. Everything about him was peaceful. Reflectively, he said, 'I lived on Hibernia for two years with Valerius after he freed me from slavery in Gaul so it wouldn't be entirely new, but yes, there's a bit of that. Then again, every sighted warrior would have stayed behind to see to the defence of Mona if they had been allowed to. In the event, only five hundred were given leave; the rest are better used elsewhere. Luain mac Calma is Elder; he decides who comes and who leaves and if he is in conference with Nemain and others of the gods as to his decisions, we are not privy to that. He has asked me to stay. If he had asked me to be in Hibernia, I would have taken ship with the others a long time ago, however unwillingly.'

'Did he ask you to call us to Mona?'

'You. I only called you. The rest are here of their own accord, and may be sent away for their own safety. Don't tut at me like that; I'm going to answer your question. No, mac Calma didn't ask me to call you, but when it had happened he did not ask me to stop it either. He has no dreaming of you.'

He has no dreaming . . . Once, Airmid had dreamed of Graine's birth, and Luain mac Calma had dreamed a place for her amongst the elders. As close as last night, even in the quiet grief and release of the morning, there had still been hope that Mona might have reawakened the promise of that.

The oystercatchers piped a long way off. A seventh wave hushed closer to the tide-wrack than the rest. In the cavalry camp on the opposite shore, a lean, bare-chested man with black hair growing thin on his head and thick on his pectorals stooped out of his tent and, yawning, stretched both arms up to greet the grey morning.

It was no easier to look at him than at Bellos. Dropping her gaze to the shingle, Graine said, 'Perhaps that's because there is nothing any longer to dream?'

'Perhaps. Or perhaps it's because even the gods don't yet know what will become of you, what you may be or may not be. We have it in mind that you are the wild piece on the board of Warrior's Dance, the one that can move from one end to the other unhindered and unseen and so win the game. If we are right, then between us we may save Mona.'

The dawn wind was too cold, suddenly, and the sea spray on her face too painful. Graine sat up, hugging her knees. She felt sick. 'And if you are wrong?'

Bellos was still peaceful, still smiling, still staring out across water he could not see towards the growing activity in the Roman camp on the far side of the straits. He pursed his lips, considering. 'Then we have two thousand dreamers who can help to cloud their dreaming. If they, too, fail, then of course we'll have to fight them. Which is what the five hundred warriors are here for.'

'Against eight thousand legionaries and enough barges to circle the whole of Mona? That's madness.'

'Perhaps, but I prefer to think it's practical. We know the island and are not afraid of nightmares. Eight thousand frightened men could become lost here very easily, and even before that, boats have to find a place to land and be filled with men prepared to step off them.' He answered absently. He was no longer thinking of her. 'I suspect we shall find out soon, and if I am wrong you may have time to tell me so. Would you say they are getting ready to march to the barges?'

He was still staring blindly out across the water, only that the tilt of his head was different. Graine looked along the line of his no-sight, and found that the random movements of morning were becoming more ordered and linear in the legionary camp at the foot of the mountains. Even as she opened her mouth to speak, a trumpet brayed the call to muster. The sound drifted patchily across the straits.

Bellos pursed his lips and blew a small huff through his teeth. 'Mac Calma was right, then; it will be today.' He got to his feet and held out both hands towards her. His blue eyes smiled to somewhere just above her head. 'If I offer to help you stand up, will you offer to lead me back to the great-house? I could find my way alone, but it's far faster with help and today, I think, we don't have the luxury of time to spend feeling the lie of the birch bark and lichen on stones to find a sense of direction.'

As at the Roman camp, the five hundred warriors and as many dreamers who had slept in and around the great-house of Mona were rousing to a slow, grey dawn that might be their last. New fires scattered at intervals across the clearing flickered pale flame and blue smoke against the backdrop of new-leaved oaks.

Half-dressed men and women were washing or using the middens or standing quiet-eyed, speaking to the gods of their dreams. At the fringes, ewes were being milked and hens tracked down to their night roosts to find the eggs and corn was being ground and baked into bannocks for the morning meal.

Near the stream, a mare newly in season was being held to be served by Hawk's horse, a flashy blue roan with a white forehead, which had been the gift of a cavalry commander.

The horse was Thessalian and bred for chariot racing until it fought too much in the stables and was sent off to be trained for war. At loading time on Segoventos' ship, they had thought it was too hot-blooded to stand a voyage without destroying itself, the ship and everyone on board and would have to be left behind. In the event, it had taken to the sea crossing without demur and it had been Gunovar's solid black wagon horse that had panicked on the gangway so that a man had to be with it for most of the voyage to keep it from kicking the ship apart.

Gunovar was there now, making sure the mare did not damage the horse while he served her, or the other way round. Graine sat a little away, leaning against the stone hut that had been Airmid's before she followed Breaca east and was now, apparently, Bellos'. Gunovar had spent the night inside; the flavours of her wound's-ease and fescue and meadow garlic still hung around, as they did any place where the scarred Dumnonii dreamer had woken and made herself the infusions that helped her to manage the morning.

The horse served the mare boldly as horses were meant to do. It augured well for a strong, fast, sharp-minded foal and Hawk, it could be seen, put a great deal of effort into not looking too pleased so that nobody might think he saw his horse as himself and the mare as his lover. Graine made herself watch and let the nausea rise and was not sick, which was an achievement in its own right, the more so because no-one was watching and she did it for herself alone. She fixed her gaze on a certain branch in the woods beyond and breathed in deeply and did not move when a shadow slid over her, blocking out the faint warmth of the sun.

'Did you go down to the jetty at dawn?' Gunovar stepped back three more paces and sat down at her side.

Graine said, 'How did you know? Did you dream it?'

'No. I saw Bellos go out and asked him where he was going. He hadn't dreamed you either, he just has better hearing than anyone else. Losing one sense brings up the others. It's why they used to blind the best dreamers in the old days.'

Gunovar grinned, lopsidedly, as she always did. Because the morning was what it was, Graine took note of the scarring in the other woman's face and on her hands, of the rolling, un-comfortable way she walked, and realized how long it had been since she had last noticed any of these. Gunovar was not beautiful, and had not been before the Roman inquisitors had broken her – she was too big-boned and thick-set for beauty – but she carried herself with a dignity and self-possession and humour that stepped over such things, so that it was not only possible to see beyond the damage, but essential.

Graine said, 'The mist is clearing and the legions are getting ready to launch their boats. The cavalry are there. Before I left, Valerius said that if he were in command, he'd make the cavalry swim across first to take and hold a beachhead so the barges could land safely, but that the governor doesn't know how to order his cavalry and would probably set them to swim alongside the barges. Did you bring any skald-root with you from the east?'

'Yes. Why?'

'I have an idea. Sulla the ferry woman used to say that the currents of the straits were her friends and she could swim across from one side to the other and back without dying. We'd have to work quickly, before the mist is fully gone, or Sulla will be seen, but if we can do that, there is a thing that can be done that might help us.'

It was a morning to savour the small pleasures: the surprise on Gunovar's face, and the flash of uninhibited joy that lit her eyes as she understood what was proposed, so that it was possible to see she had been handsome once, and then the swiftness with which she moved and brought her herb sack from the hut and set about doing what was needed while Graine went to find Sulla and see if it was still possible for a ferry woman to swim the straits.

It was indeed possible, and Sulla took the idea and made it better and Dubornos set himself to help her into the straits and out again, which made him less likely to fret over Graine, and so, for a moment, on the brink of war, the island was at peace.

There was long enough, just, to savour it, before a bull's horn sounded a long, low, looping note that rattled the ribs and shook the air from the chests of all within its reach, signalling the Elder's call to meeting.

Across the clearing, the dreamers left their morning's preparations and began to file in pairs and silent handfuls into the great-house where Luain mac Calma waited to discuss with them the dreaming of the night and all previous nights and how they might make use of whatever they learned in defence of their island, and everything it stood for.

By the river, where the skald-root had been boiled, Gunovar stopped scouring out her cooking pot and straightened, frowning. 'Do you want to come? Whatever else has happened, you're still a dreamer by birth and right. You'd be made more than welcome.'

Graine was calf-deep in the stream, washing herself clean of the things she had made. Brown water coursed in furrows around her, turbid with peat. Vaguely, she could see pebbles and sand and the pale shapes of her feet. The right one was still purple-black from arch to ankle where she had tried to kick a man and he had grabbed her foot and crushed it in his hand, forcing it outwards.

She looked at the bruising and made herself speak and not feel. 'I haven't dreamed of anything since we came here. This morning, perhaps, but I don't remember it.'

She did not say, *Bellos and Luain mac Calma think I am the wild piece on the gaming board, and that's more frightening than having lost the dreaming, because I have no idea what to do or when or even if I can do it if all the rest becomes clear.*

Gunovar laid her pot upside down on the damp grass. Straightening with some effort, she said, baldly, 'Bellos may be wrong. And mac Calma. It is not unknown.' Her face was quite neutral, offering neither challenge nor support.

Graine stood very still in the water. Her legs were cold. She noticed that as if they were part of something else that should be cared for if she could muster the interest.

For most of her young life, she had been part of the world where a thought might be lifted from the air if it were strong enough; she had never understood why everyone could not do it and some were afraid when it happened. Now she understood both of these, and that this, too, was lost to her.

Something hard lodged in her throat and would not be swallowed away. She said, 'Do you dream me as the wild piece on the board?'

The old woman's face was soft with care. 'No. I dream you as a child who is wounded and may yet be healed. Mona has great healing, more than you have yet met. The heart of that is the great-house and if we fail in our defences, the great-house may not be standing after today. Will you not come with me and be present in the company of dreamers one last time?'

She went, because she could think of no reason not to. The cauldron lay upturned on the river bank with the remains of the skald-root beside it, and the cooling embers of a wormwood fire.

'What do you see?'

Bellos God-eyes asked it, who was blind and so, perhaps, had good reason. He set his question quietly, not to interrupt the Elder, Luain mac Calma, who was speaking.

Graine answered the same. 'I see a fire badly built of hawthorn and pine, with damp wood and too much smoke so that it has almost no heart.'

The fire trench took half the width of the great-house. They were at the northern end of it, near the folded black mare's skin where sat Luain mac Calma. The Elder had nodded to her as she came in but there was no greater acknowledgement; Mona's end was too near to speak to children, however wild their dreaming might be.

'But there is some light?' Bellos asked. 'I can feel the heat.'

'A little. It's red at the heart, yellow almost to white at the place where flames grow out of the wood.'

'People? What do you see of the people?'

'As much as the dark will let me. I see faces that I half remember. I could name some of them perhaps, if it mattered to you.'

He was leading her somewhere and Graine resented it. Gunovar was gone, called early into the press of the dreamers by one of the half-remembered names. Bellos rested his elbow on his knee and tilted his face towards her. The striking blue eyes were almost white in the poor firelight, like ice lit from behind by the sun. They carved their own path into her, which had nothing to do with ordinary seeing. He said, 'Sit with the flames then, and make them what you want. There will be time enough for that before the talking is done.'

He was treating her like a child, which was unfair, and it was impossible to make what she wanted: a place full of mystery and dreaming and the answer to the end of Rome. Instead, it was full only of weary, frightened dreamers, sweating in the dank dark, with the fire built badly and smoking and the horsehides on which she sat stiff with age and brine.

More than that, she wanted power and ideas from mac Calma, strategies that would defeat the thousands sent against them. Instead, she sat in the treacherous dark and heard him name exactly the disaster that faced them, and name after it his lack of any answers. He invited the dreamers to share whatever the gods had given overnight and they did so, wordily, lacking the precision and drive of other mornings and other sharings so that time passed and nothing of value was happening except that Sulla had swum to the mainland and back and Dubornos, who had gone to help her, slipped into the great-house and nodded to Graine to signal some measure of success.

Six dreamers had spoken by then; men and women made hoarse and uncertain by the proximity of danger. Their voices had been dull and lifeless, so that simply to stay awake while they spoke was a challenge. Six more spoke after them, as dully and to no more benefit, and others, and others.

Frustrated beyond all telling, Graine stared into the fire and wished she had stayed outside with Hawk, who had ideas that made sense and were not based on the shadow of a buzzard seen on water in a dream, or the flight of a spear that took three days to land and killed the Roman governor each day, resurrecting him overnight the better to kill him again on the morrow.

It was not for Bellos but for herself that she built the shapes in the fire. Hawk was first and easiest; it wasn't hard to take the flames and weave them into his form. She carved out the sharpness of his eyes and the way he rode and laughed, or was serious, according to her mood. She had not noticed, until then, how closely he mirrored her, giving whatever she needed. She sent his image out to do battle against the legions on the foreshore, and he went willingly, leaping over rocks like a deer with his black hair flying behind him and the lizard marks of his clan alive on his arms.

Hawk alone was not enough. Graine wished Valerius were there; however ambivalent she felt about him personally, there was no denying his strengths in fighting Rome; he would never have allowed the Elder's prevarication. Her mother, too, would have insisted on action rather than words. With flames encompassing all of her vision, Graine thought of black hair and copper, of black eyes and green, of the flash of a dry, ironic smile which could have come equally from one or the other, of the easiness with weapons and horses that should have been her birthright and so clearly was not.

She envied that; in the fire she could admit it and become what she sought. The fire showed her patterns of the warrior she could be, fighting as Cunomar did, or, better, Cygfa, because, even now, Cunomar was still too taken with proving himself and Cygfa was long past that, if she had ever known it.

In her mind and so in the flames, Cygfa came back to Mona, and waited on the foreshore while the Roman cavalry swam their horses across the straits. She sat tall on the white-legged colt who had the mettle of his grandsire; Valerius joined her on the Crow-horse itself and then Breaca, mounted on the bay that had been Cygfa's gift.

The enemy mounts neared the land. Their manes were white as the crests of Manannan's horses, which were built of water and waves. They were heading towards the place where Graine had watched the dawn rise. She had been there for a reason, and had not known it then. In the fire-fancy, it made sense; she had made her peace with the god in three days of a storm and again in the quiet of a turning tide. The vast bulk of the water knew her as well as she knew it.

Taking a quiet breath, she sent herself into it, spreading out and out until she had no margins, until all of her was all of the ocean. She felt the lap and rise of the waves and the far slower rhythm of the tide. Within it, she felt the enemy horses like hornets attacking her skin. She could feel a panic in them that was her doing, and was sorry, except that it meant they were more likely to flounder in the sea, which was good.

She did not feel sorry for the men at all; they were jagged iron, with souls that harboured desecration of all that she cherished. It did not feel good to have them there. They were scratching at the place where the tide turned, where the great mass of water that was her soul came to rest and then, answering Nemain's call, turned about and began to move the other way. There was a fold in it that she knew, that she had known for all eternity, a way of creasing the waves one on the other at the turning of the tide that would do for the men on horseback what they wanted to do for her.

Smiling now, Graine turned herself over in the ocean and felt the fold of the sea crease over and saw the horses flounder and pull away and saw men in armour, unable to keep afloat without the support of their mounts, tumble and sink and spin and become still on the sand that was her resting place and theirs.

They were not all dead. Perhaps a hundred still lived, of the thousand who had set out to swim the straits; such things can happen in a child's imaginings. These few surged out of the water onto the foreshore near where Graine lay.

She pulled her soul from the sea and fitted back in her body like an arm in a sleeve. She lay flat in the shingle and used the blade of her skinning knife to catch the sun and make flash-signals as Ardacos had taught her. Spears of light went out to dazzle the men, so that, fresh from near-death in the sea, they came to a land of fire and smoke.

The fog-smoke wreathing about them was hers. At some other time, she had placed pots of fire and plants around the headland, full of ash and wood and the poor, damp fire of the great-house and other things she knew of: the smoke of plants that Airmid had taught her about, and Theophilus, the Greek physician who had spent a winter in her company. The story of the skald-root was his, and of the other plants which, when burned, would confuse men and horses. All these, Graine had carried in pots from the great-house, because in the dream she was a warrior, the same as her mother or Valerius, but different.

The smoke they made was thick and vaporous and stole the minds of those who did not know how to protect against it. Even Graine, who had made it, felt that the roof of her mouth was rising to break through the top of her skull. It loosened her mind, making it easier to push the path of her thoughts out from her body into the land and the sea and the smoke.

She remembered Valerius' stories of what it took out of the men to swim in full armour, and how hard it was for them to fight on the other side. Into the smoke she wove the certainty that the swim had been the ultimate exertion and the men who reached land were too cold and tired to fight. They came out of the water slowly, dazzled and befuddled. Led by Valerius, the five hundred warriors of Mona met them and slew them where they stood, except for Corvus, who was a friend to them all and did not need to die. Graine asked the gods for his life but did not know if they heard her.

There was respite then, for a while, before more of the living came. In time, they paddled in a wide wave across the water. Hundreds of barges packed with men, each one tight with fear and resolution, not fully understanding what had happened on the island.

Graine whistled. Her mother was no longer there, but Valerius and Cygfa rode like the gods' hunt to the water's edge. Their horses were vast, with tags of lightning at their polls and crests and thunder rolling from their feet. They were three, against three hundred vessels and eight thousand men, but the fire was on their side, and the smoke, and the three thousand dreamers within it, who were well versed in the dream-fears of the men that Bellos had fostered. They wove a web between them of smoke and sea fog and fear and cast it like a net into the water, ensnaring the legionaries before ever they left their barges.

The five hundred warriors were ready to step into the spaces between and kill men as they stumbled ashore but they were barely needed. The dream-web confused the landing men and set them one against the other so that whole cohorts turned face on and set about each other with the ferocity of fear and fury.

Behind them, the five hundred warriors of Mona waited, to take on those left alive. Graine, only true blood-daughter to the Boudica, raised a hand and brought it down again, as she had seen her mother do, setting it all into action.

Somewhere in the background, a low, monotonous voice was still speaking. The contrast with the brilliant colour and action of the fire-dream was laughable.

Graine? Graine? 'Graine? . . .'

Her name came to her from a long way distant, from outside the great-house, perhaps, or even beyond the island. Cool fingers touched her wrist. Blue eyes the colour of the noon sky came into the line of her sight and Bellos' hair, framing them, was the dazzle of sheet lightning.

'Graine? It is enough for now. You can stop. Stop. It is enough.'

Her throat hurt. She was croaking like a gannet. Mid-word, she stopped, and there was silence.

They were silent, all the talking, droning dreamers, watching her and listening as they had been, it seemed, for a long time.

Luain mac Calma was at her side, white with a strain she did not fully understand, as if he had been holding the entire net of the fire-story and all the three thousand dreamers within it and the effort had cost him dearly.

He said, 'I'm sorry. We had no way to ask it of you, only to hope it might happen. Bellos is right, it is enough and more than enough. All we need now is to put what you have shown us into action as best we can. What was not clear is what plants you would use in the smoke to befuddle the horses and the riders, and how to know Corvus, that we may do what we can to spare him. If you can tell us those things, you can sleep, or you can go back to Hawk, who is angry with us for using you, and may have good reason.'

Graine stared at him, unable to speak. She felt hungry – ravenously, achingly hungry – and tired, and under those, as the meaning of what he said became apparent, she felt a blind, screaming panic that cut holes in her heart and threatened to choke her.

Someone passed her a waterskin and she drank, dribbling gouts of it down the front of her tunic. Still croaking, she said, 'It wasn't a dreaming. I have had those, and this was not that, only an imagining that anyone could have done.'

'Anyone who is the daughter of the Boudica, whose uncle is Valerius, who shares blood with Cygfa, who can build her fancies in a fire made of yarrow and oak when the rest of us are choking so we can barely speak and the tears are streaming from our eyes.

We have few enough of those on Mona.' Luain mac Calma was smiling sadly. 'I'm sorry. We should not have used you like that, but so much has already been sacrificed for this, and now is not a time to set care of a child above the welfare of Mona. You're right, it wasn't a dream. This is not your healing, nor even the beginning of it, but you have given us what we need. Can we be grateful for that now and do with it what we may? If you are angry, which you have every right to be, you can tell me of it later and I will make what amends I can. For now, we have an island in peril and must do what we can to protect it.'

XIX

'I CAN SEE MOVEMENT IN THE TREES OVER THERE.'
Corvus, prefect of the Fifth Gaulish cavalry unit, halted his bay mare carefully upwind of his second decurion and the poorly cured Dacian wolfskin that he wore slung about his shoulders. If nothing else could be said of Ursus, at least these days one knew always where he was.

Other things could be said of him, of course: he had burned the southernmost of the two jetties efficiently enough, or at least had given the orders to have it done and seen them promptly carried out; he had organized the supply chain that had kept the horses and men fed for the half-month while the barges were being built; he had had the forethought to mark out the place for the Batavian wing to make camp some distance from their own tents so that it had been ready when at last the huge Germanic horsemen had ridden in at dusk three nights late, still green from their vomiting and diarrhoea and wearing fetishes that reeked far more strongly than Ursus' wolfskin had ever done, even when it was newly bought. For such small grace as this, amidst the mist and the thankless cold, Corvus gave thanks to whatever god chose to look over him.

Now, following the line of Ursus' gaze across the water, he said, 'There has been movement over there since before dawn, but this is in a different place and there are more of them, and they've got smoke pots, which doesn't bode well. There's nothing we can do; they could hardly be expected not to notice that we're about to launch a flotilla against them.'

'We could delay, so it is less obvious that it's today. They're building fires over there. The smoke's already too thick to see through.'

'I know, but the Batavians are as ready as they have been or are ever likely to be. This is it. If we wait another half-day, a cloud of the wrong shape will slide over the sun or the moon will show a red halo, or a sparrowhawk will chase a cock redbreast across a rock of a certain hue and the entire Batavian cavalry wing will retreat to its tents and sacrifice another mare and make neckbands of her innards wound round with tail hair and the arm bones of a newborn infant girl. So if you could—'

He stopped. Ursus was staring at him, with nostrils so tightly flared they were white at the rims. He said, 'Tell me you made that up.'

It occurred to Corvus that Ursus' sense of humour was improving and that he could give thanks for that, too, when surrounded by Batavians with no humour at all. He grinned. 'All right, if you insist, I made it up – some of it. But that doesn't mean it isn't true. And the principle stands. We get them ready, as sober as may be and in the water before noon, or the crossing will never happen. If the governor gets here and the cavalry haven't forced and held a bridgehead so his precious boats can land in safety, we're all dead men.'

'I thought we were going to provide an escort for the barges as they sailed?'

'No, that's what I came to tell you. Paullinus has listened at last to the advice of his cavalry commanders. A messenger has just come with a change in the orders. They've seen the warriors and dreamers gathering on the island and they don't want to land the barges against opposition. The governor wants us to take and hold a bridgehead to give them safe landing. He wants us to go now. If we go fast, we'll make it across before the tide turns. It's time to muster the men.'

A pair of small black and white birds carved a path across the tops of the waves. They flew parallel with the headland for a wing-beat or two and then turned west, direct for Mona. Both men watched them go. Reflectively, Ursus said, 'You've lived amongst these people. Is it true that the dreamers can send their souls as birds to spy on their enemies?'

Corvus grimaced. 'I hope not. And if they can, I would prefer to believe that they can't understand Latin.'

'Hold that bloody horse or I'll kill you myself!'

Ursus shouted himself hoarse and he may as well have whispered. On the headland, horsemen who had been riding before they could walk were having trouble holding horses who had been schooled and drilled to instant obedience and had bits in their mouths severe enough to puncture their hard palates if they should forget their years of training and force their riders to be hard with their hands.

They had forgotten it, and the savagery of the bits made no difference.

'It's the dreamers! They're bewitching the horses!' A Batavian screamed it, from a horse that stood vertically on its hind legs and appeared to be trying to climb to the sky. Once, it had been grey. Now it was black with running sweat and its eyes bulged whitely. Its mouth ran with blood in the frothing saliva and it screamed with the need to escape. Around it, mounted and unmounted horses spun uncontrollably, fed by its fear.

From Ursus' left, Corvus said quietly, 'Archers, kill that man's mount.'

There was a hiss and a feathered whine and the dull slam of iron in flesh. The Batavian whose horse died under him had the presence of mind to throw himself clear as it fell. He rolled and came up against a rock where he sat for a moment, shocked, then bent his head to his knees and howled in anguish. More than the Gauls or the Thracians, the Batavians loved their horses.

Corvus did not have to raise his voice greatly to send it above the still air and the sudden, bruising quiet.

'Listen to me! I have lived among these people and I tell you now that they may enter the minds of men and send you nightmares; they may make mist to confound you on a battlefield; they will certainly take your bodies and mutilate them, even before you are dead – you know this and have seen it. But they would not, never have and never will, enter into the minds of beasts who have not made the choice to be here, nor have any power of their own to leave; their gods would not allow it.

'If your horses are panicked, there is a good reason for it, one we can find and change. Look at them! See the way they are all looking in the same direction, towards the barges? They have the scent of something they hate. Ursus, set your men to search the boats. Grannus, get your Batavians to back their horses off to the far end of the beach. I have a young black colt newly trained for war. It's in the second corral, with the Eye of Horus branded on its left shoulder, for luck. Give it to the man whose mount was shot.'

They had been going to kill him; Ursus felt it even as the first arrows were airborne: the flicker of shock and the anger that had followed it through the entire Batavian wing. He had thought Gauls were difficult and overly emotional until he met the Batavians with their bluster and thin-skinned arrogance and the waves of weeping that came whenever the wine was passed too freely, and the sore-headed fury that came afterwards and was only barely held in check by a semblance of military discipline.

In the officers' quarters at Camulodunum, it was said you could flog a Batavian and he would stand at the post in silence and grin at you afterwards, but for the rest of your life you had to make sure he was never near your back in battle. Not many of them were flogged and not ever by anyone but their own officers.

No-one, to the best of Ursus' knowledge, had ever ordered a Batavian's horse shot out from under its rider. He was surprised, therefore, to feel the anger recede at the gift of the black colt and, even as he was giving the orders to search the boats, prayed that there was something to find in them that would prove Corvus right. That was the one advantage to their astonishing superstition: if they thought a man lucky they would do whatever it took to keep him alive. Corvus badly needed to be seen to be lucky.

Ursus' men had heard the command and needed only to know how he wished them to split up. He sent them in tent parties along the shore to examine the lines of bobbing boats. It did not take long for Corvus to be proved very lucky indeed.

'Pigskin? They were scared of a pigskin? I thought Batavian horses rode into battle with the rotting flesh of their enemies' heads tied to the saddle posts?' Flavius snorted and spat. The bundle had been found in the closest of the boats, and tipped out onto the shore.

Ursus said, 'Horses hate pigs, and from the smell of things there is more here than only the rotting hide of a wild boar.'

He prodded the bundle with one foot and discovered that the stench outdid his wolfskin, which surprised him. Holding his breath, he bent and cut the thong that bound it. The bundle fell open, revealing the hair-side of a rotting boarhide, scoured almost smooth by the sea. As he tipped it over, a thick armful of herbs rolled out, held by their own thong. On the beach a good spear's throw away, horses jerked in panic.

'What's in there? It's the herbs the horses hate, not the boarskin.'

'Fescue, wild oats, battlewort. Nothing that a horse should be afraid of.' Corvus was beside them. He knelt upwind and stirred the contents with a piece of driftwood. 'Unless . . .' He poked the stick into the thicket of herbs. 'Cut this open, will you? Don't get close. You may have to ride later today if we can ever get this invasion started and I want you to be able to mount your horse without driving it mad.'

Ursus used his knife gingerly, at arm's length. The bundle of herbs spilled open. A small disc of fatty tissue rolled out.

'Burn that! *Now!*' Corvus jumped back. It was the single fastest move Ursus had ever seen him make off a battlefield. 'Make sure the fire's downwind of the horses and then find out where the rest of these are. Where there's one, there will be more.'

They built a fire beyond the burned-out jetty, well away from the barges and the leaving point for the crossing. The fat crackled and flared and the smoke was greasily black. A further search found five more of the bundles, spread out along the coast. The camp cur found the last two and was rewarded beyond anything it had previously known in its short, harsh life.

Later, when the chaos was stilled and the horses settled and the men were ready, almost, to mount, Ursus said, 'I don't understand. The thing that scared the horses most was the foaling plug from a mare; they pass one every time they foal. We used to collect them from my grandfather's paddocks and dry them over the fire and wear them in strings round our necks to count the number of foals in each herd. The good mares used to walk up and touch their muzzles to the one that was theirs. No horse I've ever seen has been afraid of one.'

'They're not usually.' Corvus signalled behind and one of the horseboys brought his mount and Ursus'. Leading them down to the sea's edge, he said, 'I've seen it done once before, in Alexandria, to set a chariot off course. The mare-plug is soaked in skald-root and the urine of a red-haired child and then charred over a fire made of wormwood. I don't understand why, but horses are terrified of it and whoever has placed these here knows it. If the governor hadn't changed his mind, we'd have been trying to swim the horses alongside the barges. I leave you to imagine the chaos that would have caused.'

'Thank you, I'd rather not.' Ursus rolled his eyes. 'And I'm not in a hurry to work out where it came from, either, if it means we have insurgents in the mountains behind who are bold enough to come down while we're asleep in our tents.'

'I think it's worse than that.' Corvus brushed his hands on his tunic. Ursus saw damp sweat marks where they had been. His commander smiled at him, weakly. 'The hide of each bundle was sodden and the boats they were hidden in were quite dry. We have been here on the shore all morning and seen nothing. I think someone from the island has found a safe route to swim across that we don't know about, which is not an encouraging thought. And we're going to miss the tide.'

Ursus felt the blood drain from his face. The route they were planning to take had been given by a Siluran who had lived all his life crossing from mainland to island. Two things had been clear; that theirs was the only safe route, and that it must be made before the turn of the tide. The inquisitors had sworn the information was reliable; that the man had not changed his story from the first, when he had tried to sell it for a very large sum of gold, to the end, when he had bought himself a much-wanted death with the same information. The inquisitors were not often wrong, but the times when they had been were numbered amongst the wing's worst catastrophes.

Faintly, Ursus said, 'We're going to die.'

'Possibly.' The men were lined up. The sobbing Batavian had dried his eyes and was leading a black colt better than anything he had ever ridden. Corvus raised his hand. Along the beachhead, from one jetty to the other, the Batavian and Gaulish cavalrymen mounted their horses in one smooth, armour-clashing movement. The sun blessed them, and the green waves spread smooth at their horses' feet.

Corvus turned to his second decurion and smiled. He no longer looked nervous, if he ever truly had. His grey eyes were clear and achingly alive. Meeting them, Ursus remembered, suddenly, that his commander had once been shipwrecked and nearly drowned. To live through that and still lead his troop across unknown water in full armour took more courage than any man should have to contemplate. Ursus flushed, hotly, for too many reasons to name.

Corvus eyed him askance. 'I think,' he said, 'that as we go into the water, you would find it wise not to ponder too closely on the question of what has been or may be and particularly not on what's waiting ahead. It's too late to do anything about it now anyway and fear in battle is better saved for what can be seen and known. Shall we ride?'

To his own astonishment, Ursus felt himself grin and nod and realized he had just been asked for, and had given, the order to begin the invasion of Mona. He opened his mouth to take it all back and thought better of it.

To his right, laughing, Corvus dropped his arm.

The sea devoured them.

Cold, green water ate at their horses' legs. Fronds of weed dragged them down. From the moment the horses began to swim, and the men slid from their backs to swim at their sides, the ocean felt them and knew them as the enemy.

Corvus was ahead of the rest. For the duration of the crossing, it was the safest place to be, clear of all the thrashing hooves but those of his own mount.

It did not feel safe. Waves which had seemed from the shore small things, barely a child's hillock in the mountains of what a sea could be, grew huge as houses and hurled themselves down, dousing him in cold, searing salt that filled his armour and his ears and his throat, that made him sneeze and then inhale and brought him, choking, to the verge of drowning so that if his mare had not stayed true to its training and swum bravely forward, if his arm had not been hooked into the loops plaited into her mane, if he had not trained to do this in daytime and night time for most of his life, he would have died.

He had trained, and his mare, which he loved with all of his heart, did swim brave to her teaching and the men behind him, coughing and cursing, followed his lead and the sea spat them out again, bobbing, one man beside each horse, and they made their way with excruciating slowness along the route they had been given, knowing now that it was not the only safe way across, and may not even be safe at all.

They were just over halfway to the island when Corvus felt the tide turn. The mass of the ocean beneath and around hesitated in its grinding of him, a great holding of breath and deciding and then a shift so that the power came from ahead instead of behind, as if the pull of the moon had become a push, holding him back from the island.

Because water and wind were cousins, the breeze that had fluttered astern backed round at the same time and blew harder in his face. The ocean, committed now, came at him with new power. A rolling wave lifted him up and dashed him down, and another, so that he choked and breathed in cold and salt and choked again, smashing the water with an armour-clad arm to keep afloat. His mare, blessed of all beasts, kept swimming through water suddenly twice as treacherous as before. He pulled on the mane-loops and lifted himself higher in the water and so he saw before the others the flat patch of water, smooth as poured iron, with small circles growing and receding in the centre that lay ahead of them.

'Go right!' Flailing, Corvus raised his arm. Sabinius, his standard-bearer, was behind and to his left with a shortened standard fixed to the pommel of his saddle. As the next wave bore him up and down again, he saw the tilt and flap of the wing's banner. A little after, with the sea draining from his ears, he heard Sabinius' voice, hoarse with inhaled brine, too faint to be heard by any but those closest. An echo came, in Ursus' voice, and he was glad of that, then Flavius and, surprisingly, he was glad of that, too, and then there was only time to survive, not to listen for who else might keep clear of the too-flat water.

The waves were too small now. Perversely, he wished them bigger, more robust, able to bear him aloft and smash him down again, to push him away from the plate of wide, green water that lay flat as quicksand just ahead of him.

He was too close. Already the suck and pull of the current drew him in faster than he could pull away. He was on the wrong side of his mare. It was swimming straight ahead, taking them closer to death. He pushed his shoulder against it and said, 'Right. Go right.' His voice was a high-pitched whine.

The mare had been a gift of the Boudica's daughter. The Eceni trained their horses to hair-fine reactions in battle, but not in water. Corvus had no idea whether his years of teaching would count now that they were in the real ocean.

Kicking with all his strength, talking in Eceni and Latin, leaning in with one arm across her withers, all he felt at first was a loss of pressure under his shoulder, then a tilt and a turn and then – beloved of all beasts – she was pulling him right, away from the sucking treachery of the current.

He could have wept for relief but had not the breath for it. He pushed and kicked and swam and time stretched so that lifetimes came and went between the crests of each wavelet and then suddenly he was in surf again, with the gods' horses about him, white-maned and beautiful, and his mare was scrabbling on some kind of footing and ahead water furled whitely between green weed on one side and brown weed on the other and Corvus knew that the Siluran who had tried to make himself rich and had gone on to buy his own death with all he had that was of value had not lied.

Then the sun glanced off something polished amidst the rocks and the flash of it dazzled him and he remembered that there were warriors on the land, waiting for him and his men, and knew without question that he had not the strength to fight now, or even to stand.

The dazzling came again and through the spearing brightness he saw shadows that moved with purpose down to the water. He heard Ursus' voice in his head, heavy with dread, say, *We're going to die*, and knew it very likely true, and not necessarily unwelcome, or unreasonable in the circumstances, except that he had a professional pride and did not wish to be seen to fail in his appointed task.

His mare's feet touched sand and churning shingle and there was a moment when the beast was land-borne and Corvus was still buoyed by the water, and then he pulled on the mane-loops and twisted himself over and up and into the saddle and shook himself free of the water and drew his sword, because twenty years of training had made it an automatic action, whatever the state of his body, and then he was riding forward to live or to die, to kill or to be killed, probably both. It was only as the mist closed in over him and he found he could see nothing that he thought to turn round and look for Ursus or Sabinius or any of those who should have come safely from the sea, at least, and by then it was too late, because the mist was not mist but a stinging, insidious smoke and it wrapped itself tight about his eyes so that his nose was running and his eyes were streaming and he really could see nothing at all.

'Corvus?' The voice was Valerius' which was impossible this side of death. 'Corvus, dismount. You are not safe on the rocks. The mare will break her leg and fall and you will die.'

'Am I not already dead?' He said it, and heard his voice thicken with the smoke so that the last of the words drew out longer and longer and spiralled round his head.

He dismounted, not to offend the gods. The rock swayed and lurched under his feet as if it were the deck of a ship. He remembered Segoventos, ship's master of the *Greylag*, and the solid stability of the man as he held the steering oar of a ship that was heading for destruction. He felt the lurch and slam of the sea and, for the first time in a lifetime of sea voyages, he felt sick. He was, in fact, going to be sick, quite soon. Now, in fact.

He knelt on the swaying rock and pressed his sweating forehead to the weed and vomited until his stomach threatened to invert itself in his throat.

'Corvus? That's enough. Drink this; it will help.'

He knelt on the hard rock and Valerius' arm was round his shoulder and his other hand was on his brow and the rock was still slewing as if in a mid-ocean storm and the boy was not puking, which meant that both of them were certainly dead and that here, in the lands beyond life, Corvus had found again the love that had driven almost all of his waking, breathing moments for over twenty years.

The pain in his heart, which he had ignored for years, became all-consuming. He made himself lift his head and look at the fine brow and high, aristocratic cheekbones, at the long, straight nose and long, straight, black hair, threaded through, now, with silver that had never been there before. He saw the things that were present and the other things that were absent and loved them afresh.

'You're older than I had thought you would be when life left us,'

213

he said. 'And you have lost the scar across your throat.' And then, because one thing struck him later than all the others, 'Why are you wearing the dreamers' browband? Did the Eceni take you back as one of their own?'

Deep black eyes met his and his worlds met in the heart of them. He saw the wry, dry irony that he had loved from the beginning, even in the youth who had not yet begun to use it as a defence, or even to understand the strength it gave him. He saw the compassion that had been so long missing and the care and the shadows of pain, and was sorry that death had not eased those.

The voice he knew better than any in the world, that he could have picked from a thousand others, said, 'Corvus, I'm sorry. I am not Bán, whom you knew as Valerius. I am his sire. But it may please you to know that you are alive still. If you trust me, you will return to the mainland alive, and if you are careful from here forward, you will meet my son at least once more in this life, perhaps enough to know your heart's ease before death claims you both.'

He would have seen it if he had not been sick, and heard the difference in a voice that had not known the pain of the legions. From the debris of his thoughts, he picked the shard that mattered most. 'It is not this life that matters now. Can you promise me we will meet after, in death? Will we have time together?' He had never asked such a thing of anyone, never so rawly, never so desperately wanted.

'In the place of no-time?' The black eyes were not as full of pity as he might have expected, only a sudden depth and a faint colouring of humour. 'All things are possible in death, as in the dream. If you can find him and are with him in your dreams, you will find him likewise in death. But I think there may be others seeking you, and whom you may wish also to meet. One other at least, is there not?'

A face flashed in the fog, with southern, Alexandrian features, and a hawk called and a gilded statue of Horus roused its plumage and settled again, one-eyed, to watch over him. He said, 'To meet, not necessarily now to love.' He thought the saying of it might finish him.

Luain mac Calma, Elder of Mona, gripped his wrist and helped him to stay upright. 'Don't be hasty to mark out your actions when life no longer holds you. All things are possible; all loves will be made whole and held so for lifetimes if you wish it. But if you would see him again in this life, you should go now. The battle for Mona is only just beginning and death stalks too close here for you safely to stay.'

'Go?' Corvus asked it like a child, dumbly. 'Where?'

'On your horse, swimming, back to the mainland. Or on a barge if you prefer to wait. There will be some empty soon, I believe, and the men in them who are left alive will need a commander with the authority to turn them back to safer shores.'

X X

THE BATTLE FOR THE CITY OF CAMULODUNUM BEGAN IN thunder, with god-spears of lightning dancing across the gilded roof tiles and rain falling in unbroken sheets from the ocean of the sky.

Cunomar's she-bears opened the assault, for the honour of it and because they fought on foot and could pass safely over treacherous ground in the pre-dawn dark when mounted warriors could not.

Naked, bearing no lights, drenched under continuous rain, they ran in a wave of silent destruction down the long slope to the city, across pasture land still muddied from the winter herds, past ploughed furrows ready for the spring sowing, under the Victory arch and past the empty plinth of Victory's statue with the fragments of its breaking still scattered on the pathway below, and on to the first of the trenches that had been dug across the trackways to cripple the incoming horses.

As they had for the past five nights, retired Roman veterans of the XXth legion stood guard over the trenches to protect them against the gangs of youths and children who came in the night to undo their labours of the previous day. Men in late middle age who had thought their night-guard days long behind them had drawn lots from a legionary helmet in the old ways of their service, and grumbled when they lost.

They had stood through the night and were tired and hungry and nervous of wandering ghosts and the more tangible threats of insurgent youths and the warriors whose fires had lit the hillsides through the night and then, very suddenly, had all been put out.

The night guards had been watching that, and shouting questions one to the other, when the rain had come and the crushing thunder. They were no longer young men, to stand out in the rain overnight; they had backed away into shelter, staring out into the blinding emptiness of the deserted city that became, just as suddenly, not at all deserted, but full of death, smiling, with sharp knives.

Wet and befuddled, they died without fuss. Their bodies helped to fill the trenches they had guarded, and were soon covered over with mud and rubble so that horses could pass over the places where they had been.

A small, unmanned barricade stood within the trench line, built of stone rubble and timber and parts of villas recently abandoned. With the trenches made safe, the she-bear ran on and began to dismantle it.

Dawn came slowly, clouded by the rain. Cunomar worked with his bare hands, hauling broken bricks and whole sections of plastered wattle to the side of the path. At some point, he realized that the dark was no longer complete, and that he could see the shape of Ulla nearby.

Her dark hair was plastered to her head so that the ends met underneath her chin and white lime paint that had swirled on her arms and shoulders instead puddled grittily in the creases of her elbows. A smear of it streaked her face across the bridge of her nose, highlighting the shape of her face. It would have been easy for Cunomar to imagine her a ghost if his fears had leaned that way. She grinned at him and they lifted a roof beam together and got splinters in their palms and stood for a moment, teasing them out with their teeth.

She was close enough for him to smell her sweat, to see the smear of her spit around her mouth and on her palm before the rain washed it off. Lightning flashed and she was silver suddenly, laughing. In the gap before the thunder, she put a hand to Cunomar's one ear and shouted over the drumming rain, 'We'll never light signal fires in this weather, the wood's too wet. You'll need to get the flag on a roof somewhere.'

'I know.'

The storm was moving away. There was a longer gap between the light and the sound. Cunomar had time to shout that much back into Ulla's ear and then the gods crashed the clouds together and the noise drowned out all talking. He tapped her arm and felt her follow where he led.

With the other she-bear around them, they ran north and a little east to a substantial, brick-built house that had clay tiles on the roof, not the gilded bronze of the villas around them. The outer wall was high enough to be useful, but not too high to climb. Cunomar had noted it from the hillside in the early part of three days' watching and was uncommonly pleased to find it not yet demolished, as so many of the outer buildings had been, to make a barrier to protect the inner city.

Ulla saw the possibility as he had done. She said, 'It will make a good place to raise the banner to the Boudica; and a better one to watch the battle for where we are most needed.'

'Yes.'

He was coming to expect her to think as he thought, even to depend on it. She had been the same when they lifted the roof beam from the barricade, and before that, filling the trench, and before that in endless small ways through the days of planning. Something had changed since the annihilation of the IXth; more than the flogging, or the winter in training, the act of having killed together in battle had brought them together as true shield-mates. The old songs spoke of it. Cunomar had seen it in his mother and her relationship with Caradoc and, later, with Cygfa.

As a child, watching, he had thought he understood. Now, in the heart of the storm with the ghosts of the dead walking openly towards the gods, with living men set to kill them a spear's throw away, with the war host on the slope awaiting his signal, it came to him that this was a door opening into a new world, that he was standing on the threshold looking in, and that it was somewhere he badly wanted to go. He thought of Eneit, who was dead, and knew that the same door had opened there, and that for all of his life a part of him would regret having closed it when he did.

'Ulla—'

'Later. We can talk on it later.' She was no longer grinning. Her eyes were obscured by the rain and poor light and too hard to see, but her face was still and open and it seemed that his thinking had carried her with him – or that hers had carried him, and she had reached this place first.

He said, 'Know that I care for you, and need you in battle.'

'I do.' A grin in the lightning. 'And you have to go up now, and set the banner, or we'll be too late.'

She braced her feet wide and set her shoulders to the wall and linked her hands to make a stirrup. Cunomar took a pace back then vaulted up, stepping lightly on her shoulder in passing. His toes smeared mud on her skin and the ball of his foot slipped sideways but he was already gone, grappling for the guttering and the tiles beyond, pressing his palms on wet clay, pushing up and up, thinking of the bear to find the power for the climb, swinging his legs up to catch a purchase, and then he really was up, standing on the sloping roof with the rain bouncing to knee height, hard as hail, and the wild wind lifting his hair in spite of the wet and the city spreading dark beneath the storm, with light only within the ring of the solid inner barricade that protected the heart of the city, where families kept night fires burning in the hearth for warmth and light and the illusion of safety.

The roof tiles were greased with moss. Water hissed past his feet, flowing over the guttering. Spreading his toes wide, he stood upright, feeling the tug of the wind and the power of the rain. The gods sent to Cunomar a distant roll of thunder and he shouted his own name, and then his mother's and then the first eight names of the she-bear into the retreating dark.

The wind caught the words and tore them apart, but the rain had lessened enough to let him untie the flag from his waist and tie it again to the stick Ulla passed up to him, so that when the last flicker of lightning came to scorch the sky and raise steam from the bronze tiles on a neighbouring roof, he knew without question that his mother and her warriors could see him and the serpent-spear in red on Eceni blue that he waved, and the bear's pawprint in white in the lower left hand corner, for the heart of the she-bear in whose light he lived.

The war host came in a storm of hooves and baying hounds. There was no need for secrecy now, if there had ever been. They blew horns and clashed their blades on their shields and some had thought to bring tinder in clay pots and lit brands of pitch and resin and tallow all bound about with sheep's wool so that they burned in spite of the rain and the tide of horses was sparked here and there with the fire they brought to Camulodunum.

They ringed the city and moved in slowly through the deserted streets. The horses churned wet mud to slurry and the trackways became trickling streams under the last of the rain. The height and breadth of the inner barricade halted them. Whole houses had been demolished to make it, and the bodies of hanged men lay in the foundations, to lend the strength of their bones to its holding.

The enemy gathered in growing numbers within the safety of its ring. Cunomar could see them from his vantage point on the rooftop: men in old armour scurrying from house to house, shouting in Latin and Trinovante, calling up the Atrebatan mercenaries, paid for with a merchant's gold, and the last remaining tribal residents of the city who had kept loyal to Rome.

Cunomar held his flag aloft until the first horses were within reach of the barrier. His mother rode past him with Cygfa riding as shield-mate on her left, as she had done so often on Mona after Caradoc was gone.

With newly opened eyes, Cunomar saw the shadow dragging at his mother's flame, but he saw, too, the tilt of Breaca's head, the beaten bronze of her hair, made dark by the rain, saw the shift in her weight as she lifted her sword and the stiffness that came from the unhealed wounds in her back – and he saw with a generous heart the matching movements from Cygfa as she kept cover on the Boudica.

For the first time in his life, Cunomar understood how his sister shifted her weight on her horse a fraction, to come in on the left so that her body made an extra shield for Breaca, and how this was done without thought on either part, but was simply the way that they rode into battle.

Something small and sweet pierced him, like the song of a lark on a moorland, and he knew that he had found by accident something unique, shared with only a few, and that if he had coveted it any sooner, the yearning alone would have killed him.

It was good to be adult and see these things. He looked around for others he knew in the seething tide of riders, and saw the pair-links or lack of them and the way that they fought. Valerius and his

Thracian cavalryman, blessedly, were out of sight: further back or coming in from the south, leaving the east to Ardacos who had led his own hand-picked warriors in from the eastern gate, closest to the Temple of Claudius, which was easily the most defensible building in the city and therefore the best guarded. There, the inner barricades were made of poured mortar and the streets had been scattered with iron spikes against the warriors' horses.

In the west, where Cunomar stood on his rooftop, the fighting began in earnest as the Boudica's warriors dismounted, leaving their horses to stand in the mud while they began to search out the weaknesses in the barrier. There were few places open to assault, but gateways had been left for the Roman veterans who had kept night guard on the trenches and they were hard to close effectively from the inside.

Cunomar watched a gaggle of young warriors group into a wedge opposite one of these openings. From his vantage point, he could see the Atrebatan mercenaries and Roman veterans gather on the inside. The Atrebatans carried hunting spears, broad-bladed and long with a cross piece at the neck that kept a boar from charging up the haft but could equally be used to hook a shield from the arm of an unwary, untested warrior.

A great many of the warriors with the Boudica were untested; those who had taken part in the annihilation of the IXth and so considered themselves battle-hardened were with Ardacos or Valerius coming in from other angles. The youths whom Cunomar watched forming their wedge had done so once in practice and never against a real opponent. The men waiting within the barrier sensed it and their line became visibly more solid.

Ulla was beneath the villa still, waiting. She looked up as Cunomar hissed her name and grinned at what he said. Five other she-bear were within reach: Scerros and his girl cousin and the three others knit most closely to the Boudica's son. They did not consider themselves battle-hardened – they had seen the Boudica fight before her wounding and seen Valerius afterwards and they knew exactly how much experience they lacked – but they had spent the winter training with Ardacos and Gunovar in the use of the knife and not one of them was unscarred or unsure of where lay the line between living and dying.

They were fit, too, and able to vault easily up on the stirrup of

Ulla's linked hands to the rooftop. She came last, pulled by Cunomar himself who lay on his belly with two of the others holding his ankles so that he could grasp her wrists and haul her bodily up.

They were armed only with knives, and the storm no longer hid them. Cunomar jammed the haft of his flagpole in a crack between two tiles and then, stooping low, led them at a run across the rooftops, jumping from green-mossed clay to the brilliant verdigris of bronze and then, more delicately and with prayers to the bear, onto a single-pitched thatch roof with a roof beam that was barely more than a stick and swayed as they ran across it.

Before he left the gilded roof, Cunomar had seen his mother reach the barricade and turn right, towards the south, where a greater opening had shown itself. Since then, she had been out of sight. For the first time in several years, he was very glad he could neither see her nor be seen in battle; very badly, he did not want the Boudica to rescue this particular group of untried youths at this particular breach in the barricade.

A midden gave an easy, if pungent, route from the rooftops down to the ground. Cunomar grabbed a handful of thatch as he left the roof and used it to clean the filth from his feet and calves as the others joined him.

They were in an alleyway, within the circle of the barricade. To their right, two groups of eight men stood with their square-sided Roman shields held edge to edge in two equal lines before the opening in the barricade. One on the right gave an order in Latin and they drew their swords. They were not Roman, but mercenaries, men of the Atrebates whose grand-elders had fought against Julius Caesar. In two generations, they had taken on the weapons and language of Rome.

Cunomar cursed them, softly, and with rising elation. Dawn was real now, and the weather easing. The air was no longer a single sheet of rain. He and his few she-bear were alone behind a wall that sheltered thousands of the enemy; death was a word or a breath away. Its promise was glorious, but life and victory were more glorious still.

Ulla tapped his forearm. 'We can't take them as we did in the forest; they'll see us.'

'There are spare javelins beyond where they're standing.' He had seen them from the rooftop. 'You and I need to go to the far side to get them, the other three stay on this side. Wait for the wedge to hit.'

They waited. The youths outside the barricade were chanting the name of the Boudica. At a certain point, when the noise had gathered their courage for them, they charged forward, all on foot.

Cunomar heard the barked Latin, and the names of Jupiter, Mars Ultor and the horned god spoken in Atrebatan, and saw the first line of mercenaries lean their shoulders against their shields and hold them secure while their comrades stabbed from behind with javelins, aiming for the faces and eyes of the youths who came at them, shouting war cries.

Screaming, the youths died, as it had been clear from the start that they would. At the height of it, Cunomar dodged left and then right, out of the alley. The javelins he sought lay loosed from their bundles, with the binding thongs ready cut so the men could reach for them cleanly.

Cunomar picked up two, one in each hand. He was at the far end of the mercenaries' row. The man nearest him was at full stretch, his javelin buried in the face of a young girl warrior. He saw the shadow coming for him and cursed and tried to pull free and, failing, jumped back and reached for his sword. The javelin took his throat, uncleanly, because he was still turning. Ulla struck past.

Because the man at whom she aimed was turning, because Cunomar was in the way and was unbalanced, because a man was thrashing his way to death near her feet, she missed and the force of her strike carried her, too, off balance.

Cunomar saw the lift of her shoulder and heard her short, stifled oath. He saw her brown skin, almost washed clean of the lime paint, and the rugged red-white lines of the scars on her back from the flogging – a thing he had almost forgotten and had contrived not to see in any of them for days now – and saw her stumble towards the man he had killed – who was not yet dead.

In the same slow, water-logged movement, he saw death come at her as the dying man raised his sword. He had no need to put strength into the thrust, only hold it still, at breast height, and let her fall onto it, as she was doing, slowly, liquidly, inexorably.

'*Ulla, no!*'

Cunomar had not known that he could scream so, nor that he cared as much. Death was beautiful and glorious and he had no intention of letting his newly discovered shield-mate find glory in the heart of the she-bear this soon.

He was off balance, but not as badly as she was, and, in the trapped time of too many futures, the god allowed him to move, allowed him to slew sideways and stretch out his arm and push her away in her headlong flight so that she came up against the man she had tried to kill, and the wicked, honed iron of the upheld blade scored instead along the inside of Cunomar's thigh and out again, missing his testes by the thickness of one night's sharpening.

They were in battle and could not stop. Cunomar's man had died, and Ulla's had not, until he was taken from behind by Scerros' girl cousin, whose name was Adedomara, or Mara when they were in battle and there was no time to shout anything that took longer than a breath.

'Mara! Right!' There was no time, and an Atrebatan on her right whose brother was dying because of her.

Scerros took him, striking low and angling up, to pierce the muscle of his thigh and, by luck although he would later claim it as skill, the great pumping vessel of the man's thigh that pulsed gouts of bright blood in time to his dying heartbeat. Two others struck and if none of them made clean kills their men went down and were no longer a danger.

They were still seven against twelve and those men shielded and armoured and ready now, turning away from the gap, but for three left to hold it, who had only to place their shields at the barricade's opening and lean on them and those outside could not reach past. The other nine made a wedge of their own, properly, and levelled their gladii and came forward at a half-run, aiming to split the straggling line of Cunomar's she-bears in half.

'Bears! Break on the wedge!'

They had practised this only once. Valerius had insisted on it when they looked down from the hillside and watched the retired veterans drilling with the Atrebatan mercenaries in the square before the forum. When Cunomar had resisted, Ardacos had taken Valerius' side. 'The veterans are old; they're not stupid. The time to find out how to act is now, not when they have drawn up in formation against you.'

The she-bears had done as was asked of them then and they did it again now, not smoothly, but well enough, so that the Atrebatans ran onto nothing but the side of a timber warehouse and those in the front had to swerve to one side and the greater bulk behind had to slow for fear of crushing them.

Valerius had said the legions could reverse a wedge and come back again in any direction at the shout of a single command, or the lifting note of a trumpet. These men were not Roman; they had not trained through a dozen winters in all weathers and all manoeuvres. That fact alone kept the she-bear alive.

It was hard to think clearly, to consider tactics when the blood was underfoot and the air sharp with fear-sweat. Cunomar sprinted left and felt Ulla and Mara with him. Scerros was on the other side of the wedge with three of their seven – their six; one was down, cut in the side by a passing blade. There was no time to see who it was, only that it was not Ulla or Mara and that Scerros, terrified, was running the wrong way.

The barricade made a safe wall to protect their backs. Cunomar reached it and raised his stolen javelin.

'On me!' His voice reached over the screams of the wounded. Ulla and Mara came to him and faced the mercenaries, who might not have been able to reverse a wedge, but were more than able to stand together in line and had done so and were waiting now, looking sideways along the street, holding their shields linked, unshaken, laughing, waiting . . .

'There are veterans coming down past the house where you left your flag.' Ulla said it, quietly. Cunomar could feel her heat, smell her sweat, and her unconcern with dying. She had nearly died. He had saved her. These things came to him separately, unconnected.

She glanced at him, fleetingly, without fear. 'We could make the line of the bear. If we're going to die, it should be to best effect.'

No-one who had stood in the line of the bear had ever survived to tell of it after. Each warrior marked a circle in the dirt or on the turf and was oath-sworn not to leave it, except to attack bodily the nearest of the enemy, with hands and teeth and knife, using flesh and bone as the foil to trap the enemy's blade, so that, in dying, at least one ghost would be their companion in the journey through the other-forests to the heart of the she-bear to whom their souls were given.

Scerros was nowhere to be seen. The other three were close enough to hear the idea. They were afraid and courageous together and were already looking at Ulla as if she had joined the bear and become part of the mystery. Cunomar felt a fierce, unexpected pride, for himself, for the others, most especially for Ulla. For the first time in his life, he knew that he had something to live for that mattered more than proving himself in the eyes of his mother and Ardacos.

Cygfa's voice rang distant in his head, separated by time and war: *A leader sees the greater picture and knows that lives matter more than glory.* He had known she was right when she said it; as with the shield-mates, understanding was different and ran far deeper. Urgently, he wanted to stop the battle, to find his sister and tell her that he had finally understood.

There was no time; as Ulla had said, a company of Roman veterans was coming and the three who held the breach in the barricade behind him had beaten back the youths of the wedge. For the she-bear trapped on the wrong side of the wall, there was nowhere to go – except up.

'Up!' Stepping back to set his shoulders to the wall, Cunomar slid his knife into his belt and looped his fingers. He shouted at them, over the howling of warriors. 'Over the barricade! On my shoulders, as we did with the flag.'

Ulla saw and understood; she was his shield-mate and soul-mate. She joined him and shouted at Mara. 'Go now, before they see!'

Already the mercenaries were moving, breaking the line to run forward, surprised as much as cheated; Eceni warriors never left the heart of battle – never.

The Boudica had done so, once, to save the children. The children were left now to save themselves – and were hesitating. Mara stood still, numb, not knowing what to do. Cunomar yelled, 'In the name of the bear, save yourselves! Ulla, go first.'

Mara was moving. Ulla would never leave him, he could see that. He had no power to order her, and no time. The mercenaries were within reach. He gave up, and took his knife and said so they could all hear, 'No, you're right. We'll make the line of the bear.'

He was going to die. There were things he should do, invocations he should speak, hidden names of the bear he should

226

hold in the forefront of his mind, where instead was the memory of Ulla, clad in lightning, laughing, and the first of the Atrebatan mercenaries coming in lazily, grinning, wall-eyed and flat-nosed with his blade held out in front of him, with no idea at all that he was about to kill the Boudica's son.

Cunomar spoke in his mind the ninth, secret, name of the she-bear, and felt his knife blade slip in the sweat of his hand and cursed, because there was only one chance to kill, and felt the mud warmly wet between his toes with another man's blood and remembered all the things that he loved in life, all at once, in a rush.

He stepped forward, bunching his muscles, and fixed his mind and his heart on the throat of the man who came at him so that it became the whole of his world, and a fitting target. At the end, he was amazed at the power of the terror he felt, and how it lifted him past everything else, soaring.

Soaring still, he made his leap.

The noise was extraordinary. In the middle of it, he heard someone shouting his name. He thought it was Cygfa and wished he had made amends with her and knew that he would have to wait in the lands beyond life, because he was dying and had not yet made his knife stroke, which was strange, because the wall-eyed mercenary was no longer grinning and there was more blood between Cunomar's toes when he landed on mud and not on the body of the man at whose throat he had aimed. He stumbled and put a hand out and felt iron slice across his fingers and swore.

A shadow passed over him. 'Here! Take it, damn you, there are forty of them coming. Take the blade and do something useful with it.'

It was Cygfa, looking just like their father, and beautiful. Dumbly, Cunomar took the blade she thrust at him. There was still no possible way to escape. He felt Ulla at his shoulder and did not know if he should be glad they would make the crossing and come to the bear together or sad that she had not survived to see more of the wonder of life.

Cygfa said, 'Move to the right; let the others through. We need even numbers.'

He did as he was told, because nothing made sense and the bear would be hunting for him. He waited to feel the pull of the forest and used the time to follow Ulla and Cygfa in a spider-scuttle to their right, so that more shadows could come out of the gateway behind him and make a line, and then another.

The incoming warriors were not of the she-bear. They did not fight naked and only with a knife, but clothed in leather and stolen chain armour with shields and long-swords and some of them with stolen legionary helmets.

He recognized warriors he had seen fight against the legions in the west. Braint was there, who had been Cygfa's lover in the days before their captivity in Rome, and was Warrior of Mona, with all the responsibilities of that rank; she had no reason, nor any means, to be here.

Others stepped into line alongside her, men and women who had fought in the invasion battles against the first influx of the legions and fled with the Boudica and Caradoc to Mona, to keep up the resistance there. They were as well drilled as the legionary veterans; more so because they had spent all their winters training and had not sunk into the wine vats of retirement in their twilight years.

They made a line, with Cunomar at the end of it. Ulla said, 'I would be your shield, as Cygfa is for your mother. Will you honour me and accept it?'

He said, 'It should be the other way round. You have the courage. I was slow and followed your lead.'

Ulla grinned. The crease it made in her cheeks was the last place where the white lime paint stayed. 'You brought us to this,' she said. 'If we die now, it will be in the best company. Half the warriors of Mona are here.'

It was too late to argue. The veterans slowed and steadied and made the same decision. The two lines stood for a moment apart in mutual recognition and then, surging equally forward, met in a cacophony of broken bone and buckled armour. Ulla became his shield. They fought together, with Cygfa always on the edge of their vision, bright-haired and brilliant, fighting with Braint for the first time since she was taken as prisoner to Rome.

Partway through, when the dead began visibly to rise, it came to Cunomar that he was not going to die and that this was a thing to celebrate, and that he could only do that fully when the line of veterans was gone and their city rested free under the Boudica's banner. The shock and numbness left him, and he soared instead on new fear, one that transmuted into true battle fever, and that was the third new thing that came to him on the first day of Camulodunum's battle.

He fought and killed and was hit and felt nothing and saved Ulla and was saved by her and saw the dead walk all around them and felt each breath in a gift from the gods and each breath out his gift to them of continued living, and of fighting, and of killing, and of friendship.

They came to rest near the timber warehouse, with the winnowed crop of veterans behind them, the fallen made surely dead by a knife-cut to the throat.

Exhaustion lay on them, so that it was impossible to imagine lifting a blade one more time, or raising a shield, or fending off a thrust. Speech was a thing to be imagined, for later. Shield-mates thanked those who had saved them with a nod and a croak. Wounded warriors bound the wounds of others hurt more deeply.

Someone passed round a goatskin of water. It was branded on one side with the serpent-spear and on the other with the heron of the Elder of Mona. Cunomar drank and passed it to his right, where Cygfa was leaning on her shield, laughing breathlessly at something someone else had said. She caught her brother's eye and sobered a little.

'That was good. We hadn't thought this would be the first breach. Breaca will be proud of you.'

He had forgotten his mother. There was a time when his own need to be seen would have kept her in his vision through any battle. He turned to look, and so found that the gap in the barricade which had been narrow enough for two men to defend easily had widened and was being made wider by youths from the war host who had organized themselves into teams and were dismantling the barriers far faster than the veterans had erected them.

Somewhere at the back of the milling crowds were horses and somewhere within them was his mother. Breaca had mud smeared across her face so that it looked like a darker version of the she-bear paint. She was gaunt-faced and hollow-eyed but she caught him looking and smiled back and when Cunomar had pushed his way through the gap to reach her, he read in her face the same kind of pride that he had felt for Ulla, and had never truly seen before.

The braids at her left temple had come loose, pulled by the

weight of the kill-feathers woven within them. She tugged one free and held it out. It was black, with a gold band about the quill for uncounted numbers of Romans slain.

'You should have this,' she said. 'I never tried to make a bear line with four warriors in the face of forty legionaries.'

Cunomar felt himself flush. 'You would never have been so foolish as to allow the warriors who followed you to be cornered with no alternative. A good leader sees ahead the dangers that will come.'

She eyed him a long time and smiled a little at the end of it. 'A good leader sees the way out of trouble and can make it happen. Perhaps my warriors would have listened to me and gone over the wall when I told them. That will come with time. It can't be forced. Even so, it was a good idea.'

That was true, and he knew it, and it had been his idea, not Ulla's. It was harder than he had ever imagined to accept the praise he had yearned for, freely given and deserved. He took the feather and did not try to hide the shake in his hands.

He had no hair at the sides of his temples in which to braid it; he had shaved off an arc above his missing ear, and then again on the other side, for balance. He wove his mother's feather into the queue that remained at the back. Around him, warriors he had known since childhood stopped to watch. He felt the weight of their experience and remembered what they had known of him in his youth, and regretted it.

'I don't understand,' he said to his mother. 'Why is Braint here, and the warriors of Mona?'

Breaca waited until the feather had been fixed and fell flat against the back of his head. When she spoke, it was wryly, so that she sounded like Valerius and it was hard to tell if the irony were tinged with humour or frustration.

'Because Luain mac Calma sent them to us having decided that the war here had more need of trained warriors than his own war in the west. He has the full body of dreamers there, all soaked in the power of the gods' island, and he has Graine, who has joined him. How could the legions possibly prevail against that?'

XXI

Smoke choked them all.

It rose yellow and grey, thick as sheep's wool and pungent from the smoke pots, and snaked out across the foreshore. Where it met the sea, it spread sideways into the troughs between the waves and was scooped into handfuls by the water. On land, it met the rock and the wind and rose between them, coming up to eye height and hanging there, forming a veil, easily torn, between this world and others, through which the unwary could readily fall.

Corvus' cavalry had fallen through it, those who had survived the fold in Manannan's sea. Of the thousand who had left the mainland, over half had drowned. The remainder sat shivering on their horses, staring blindly into smoke that swirled tight as bandages about their eyes. Corvus had not ordered their surrender, but neither had he led them into battle; it seemed unlikely that they could have gathered wit to obey him in either of these if he had.

Even so, the five hundred warriors of Mona had not set about them and there were, as yet, no Roman dead. There had been many dead in Graine's fire-weaving. Bellos the Blind, who alone of those at the foreshore was not newly blinded, felt the first faint line of a schism grow between the fire-fancy that Graine had woven and the reality that was building in the half-lands between sea and shore, and it worried him. He wanted to find Luain mac Calma to learn why the change had happened, but greater things were needed of him and the first of those was to fulfil his part in the future that the Boudica's daughter had built.

Three thousand dreamers stood shoulder to shoulder along the foreshore. Bellos walked in front of them, closer to the line of pots that he and Graine had filled and others had set out. Smoke rose from them in puffs and was denser in patches where the small fires smouldered. After a while, as he came to recognize the pattern of their placing, he held his breath when he was close to them and breathed more deeply of the clearer air in between.

Following his path of the morning, he walked down to the place where Graine had lain. He had noticed nothing special about it then and found nothing different now, but he had seen the place afresh in the fire and there had been an anchoring to it that had mattered and was not found elsewhere. Breathing in a chestful of thinning smoke, he lay down on his belly and tried to root himself against the first whispers of men's imaginings that came at him from the far side of the straits.

It was not easy now, when it mattered most. Other thoughts crowded where there should have been clarity; Thorn was at the far southerly end of the line, a long way out of reach. She had wanted to hold him, to talk and perhaps more, in the morning and Bellos had chosen to follow Graine instead. There had been no time to speak to her after, only a hand's touch in passing and a silence that he could not read.

Graine herself was not far behind the line, with her triad of warrior-dreamers to keep her safe, or to attempt it. Hawk, Dubornos and Gunovar; over the two days since their arrival, Bellos had come to know and respect each of them. He had felt their fears for the child and the degree to which they swamped any concern for their own safety. He had wanted to ease them, and had not known how.

He set them aside, his lover, the warriors, the child they protected, and sought instead the heart-swell of Mona and all that he loved of it. He sought, and found, the dreams of past elders, strong and durable as taproots, that grew down through the generations from the far ancestors who had first built the great-house to the latest, youngest, most vulnerable generation who might yet live to see its destruction, or die very soon before.

Among the leavings of the old and the very old, men and women, grandmothers and grandfathers, he found traces of Luain mac

Calma's passing, brighter and younger than the rest, looping across from one root to the next, building of them a network that formed the core of the gods' island. Beneath, deeply, lay the undercurrent that was the care of the gods and sustained them all.

Finding that, Bellos brought himself back to the shore, to seaweed and the mewing of gulls, to rich, heady smoke belching from Graine's fire pots, to the line of dreamers and the calm they held, to the distant, discordant maelstrom that was the oncoming legionaries. Breathing in all of it, Bellos opened his mind as he had once done by the fireside and sought out the fears of the men who came to kill him.

Fire. Flames. Heat. Death.

In the world of others' fears, he met a wall of ravening, insatiable flames that ate men for the joy of it. Heat devoured him, roasting his skin to flaking black, boiling his blood, reaching down into his lungs to suck his soul from his body. If he could have run, he would have done, but his limbs would not answer his call. He lay face down in the damp shingle and sweat streamed from his brow as it had once done in the heat of Valerius' forge. His face burned. He tried to breathe and every inhalation was painful. He choked, and felt blackness closing at the edges of his mind that was quite different from the dark of his un-sight.

Somewhere, mac Calma spoke, cool as a winter's kiss. *Remember that this world is an illusion.* He had forgotten. He drank in the words and remembered. Steam rose within his chest where they settled. Calm followed slowly and a separating of the flames so that he could begin to see the men behind them and the weave of their thinking.

'Why fire?' Mac Calma was there in person, kneeling at his side with a dry hand on his brow.

Bellos strained to find an answer. Thoughts slipped like eels through his grasp, too fast to be caught. He drew back and watched the patterns they made.

'The legions saw the smoke before they set out,' he said eventually. 'They believe that on Mona men are burned alive. They fear it above everything else.'

'But not enough to make them turn back?'

'No. It makes them angry. They want to kill everyone who might otherwise burn them.'

'Can you find more, beneath the fire, that will undermine the rage and weaken them? Or confuse them, so that one man fights his brothers; that would be best.'

'I can try.'

Bellos might have believed himself an apprentice again, learning his way, but that the wind was on his face and the smoke teased his mind from its moorings and Thorn faced men who would kill without compunction and all of Mona faced a ruin that was real.

Quietly, the Elder of Mona said, 'You were born for this. You can do what we need, Bellos of Briga.'

It was not meant to terrify him, but it did. Never before had he been named for a god and he had not known how much he wanted it – or that he had wanted this god above all of the others: the all-mother, bringer of life and keeper of death, guardian of the final river and all that lies in the lands beyond life.

He was offered a gift to surpass all gifts and was not certain he deserved it. The hopes and fears of a generation, of all the generations, balanced on his ability to see beyond his own blindness. For that moment, fear of his own failure swamped him so that he was a child again, lost without hope or future in the brothels of a Gaulish sea port. He thought of Valerius, and felt the confusion he always felt when he remembered the man who had bought him and why it was done and then, because of that, he remembered what it had been to see and that the god had taken sight from him, to bring other sight, and even that might not be enough. Four years of held anger cascaded over him.

Luain mac Calma said, 'Bellos. Think.'

It was enough. Confusion and anger and fear and doubt were a part of him, and would always be so, but he knew now how to set them aside, and did so.

He breathed in the last wisps of Graine's smoke and let it rise through the roof of his mouth and loosen his mind in its moorings. Clarity came, and the weavings of the elder-roots and the ancestors' dreams and the bright spark that was Luain mac Calma uniting them all and then the god was there, whom he had always felt and never named, and Bellos was a part of that weaving, and then rose over it, lifted up to skim over the web, freely.

Flames parted and let him through. Fear came at him split in two; half from the sea where men were afraid of the forthcoming battle, half from the mainland where they were afraid they would miss it. Aloud, Bellos said, 'Paullinus has not committed them all, only the Twentieth. The Fourteenth is held in reserve. This is not as it was in Graine's fire-making.'

'It's enough. The rest may come later. Today, we need only fight those who come against us now.'

It was more than enough. Five thousand men came at them in barges, paddling against the current. Bellos steadied himself, and cast the net of his mind wide to take them all in and then, one at a time, began to pick the leaping, writhing fear-fish from it, and bring them back for those who could best make use of them.

In the world of flesh and earth, he pushed his palms to the rock and stood up. Under his feet, stone became shingle, became sand. Around him, a line of three thousand dreamers faced twelve thousand legionaries and he could feel the sparks of each one, and name them and the colours that they brought to the world, and how the futures would change with their dying.

Time opened its own weave and he could see which were destined to die now and which later, and when. Thorn was there. He saw her cross the river into Briga's care and knew the time and the place and the manner of it. His own detachment surprised him.

On Mona's shore, he set off down the line, walking from one bright light to the next, delivering the images as he was shown them: 'You are the souls of all the slain grandmothers, come to take revenge on their killers. You are children, the walking dead. You are eyeless women, dressed in black, mad with grief and terror, and you cannot be killed.'

None of this was new; he had spoken of the legionaries' fears in the great-house as he moulded the dreaming through the spring, but now he matched the dreamers to the dreaming, spinning threads for each one, connecting them to the legionaries as fishers to their fish. For a few, were lesser evils, more readily created: 'Make the sounds of crow and eagle; mix them together if you can so that you are many of each, attacking in flocks. Throw sand in the air; make it form a snake. Send the grass to writhe amongst them. You are serpents, attacking by the hundreds.'

He reached the end. Thorn was there, alive and ready to meet him, tracing his lips with her finger, holding his palm to her cheek. He said, 'You are the gulls, feeding on men's eyes.' She clasped her hand in his and he felt the steadiness, as of long-rooted oak, and the un-fear of death. She sighed a little in concentration and he felt the pull of the sea and the sharp, clear sky and flocks upon flocks of white sea birds rising like the centre of a storm, growing to a tumulus of thunder.

Stooping, he kissed her brow. 'Thank you. I love you. Don't ever forget it.'

She pressed a smile into his neck, and he left her and a hole tore open in his heart.

The gaps in his web were all closed. There was nothing left to be said. Bellos turned slowly, spreading his feet wide on the shingle. A turning wind battered at his face, carrying the stinging spray from the wavetops. He could hear the lip and kiss of paddles in the water and the harsh breathing of many men.

Close. So very close.

Bellos reached for Graine with his mind, and found her, and basked in the brief joy-grief that flooded them both when she was touched so. Underneath that was a current of doubt, as strong in her as it was in him; they alone had seen the weavings in the fire. They alone knew the extent to which the preparation on the shore was not as she had seen it. Even if it had been, they had no idea at all if it would work.

Opening his mind to the god, Bellos turned the beacon of his attention on the dreamers around him, and the net they had woven that hung, waiting, above the incoming men.

A man's voice shouted in Latin, like and not-like Valerius. A flat-bottomed boat grounded on pebbles.

Bellos felt a pulse of undiluted terror. From the centre of it, praying, he said, '*Now!*'

XXII

CAMULODUNUM WAS BURNING.

The storm that had drenched the first moments of attack had passed westward. A freshening breeze had dried the timber of the merchants' houses and the wattle of the craftworkers' huts enough to feed the infant flames that lapped at the edges of the city, spewing smoke to the sky.

Valerius was in the south, leading the warriors who had chosen to train with him and fight with him. At their head, he faced a line of Roman veterans who had formed inside the brick and mortar barrier, all iron armour and leather with new-painted shields and quiet, waiting faces. He smelled the smoke growing in the west long before he could see it. The scent was welcome, but oddly out of place, as if the morning fires of a roundhouse had become bound up in all the iron-blood and sweat and opening bowels.

There were a great many opening bowels and most of them among the youths Valerius was shepherding into the attack lines. He had not yet found a way adequately to warn them how much the reality of war against the legions differed from the songs; that without the rites of the long-nights and tests of the spear-trials they had no basis for self-belief; that self-belief was what made the difference in the momentary crush and crisis of combat and the sum of those brutal moments was what won the day or lost it; that, even in the days before Rome's invasion, no-one had ever ridden or run into battle without gut-wrenching fear and that it never left, only lessened a little so that one could think clearly enough to fight.

Flames flickered on the edge of his vision. Turning away, he hailed a skinny, hook-nosed youth who had shown some initiative in training and sent him forward at the head of a half-troop – he still thought in Roman cavalry terms; he should cure himself of that – to swing round and come in at the far end of the veterans' line.

The youth was half his age and one of the many Caradocs. The ceremony to find new names for them and the several dozen Breacas had taken a night and half of the following day, but had been successful in the end.

Thus, Knife with the hooked nose ran forward at the head of his dozen warriors and formed them into an arc with surprising efficiency. A girl newly named Conna held the centre, with Longinus to help her, and Valerius himself was shadowed closely by a youth called Snail on a skewbald mare who held Valerius' standard and was, in fact, far more able than his choice of name might have suggested.

'Snail! Signal both wings to drive inward!'

Valerius shouted it over the din. The standard waved in a clock-wise loop and, blessedly, Knife and Conna were both looking and both remembered what to do. Their two half-troops came together, tightly, with shields overlapping at the edges and swords held between. At Longinus' command, spears were thrown from behind in a ragged volley.

None struck living flesh. Amongst the enemy, someone bellowed an order from near Valerius' end of the line and the veterans swung their shields back down, beginning the moves that would trans-form their line into a square as if they had been doing it all their lives, which they had, except for the past ten years.

They were smooth enough but not as fast as they could have been. Shields angled aside and back into place, rustily. Valerius saw the barest of openings between one man and the next and hurled the Crow-horse into it. Screaming, he slashed downwards with his blade, and felt the impact of iron on iron that moved the blood through his veins in a way nothing else could do.

Alive with the beginnings of battle fever, he shouted the names of both his gods and saw the youths who had followed him through the breach catch the feeling and grow with it, cutting harder and faster.

Even so, they were still young and untested. For every veteran who fell, a handful of warriors died, screaming. The smell of void faeces and spilled guts entirely swamped the smells of sweat and blood and smoke. To Valerius' left, the flames took better hold of the city and reached higher. He remembered lying on the hillside watching the veterans cut a fire break within the inner barrier, but could not map in his mind exactly where it was.

The fighting was too fierce to think that far beyond it and expect to live. Numbers told over experience and the veterans' square fell in on itself, broken by the Crow-horse and the mounted warriors who came after. Another command was barked down the line and former legionaries broke ranks and ran to their right, setting their backs to a masonry wall.

Wheeling left, Valerius sought out the man who was shouting the orders. The youth, Snail, was still in his shadow, still holding aloft the banner of the bull on Mona's grey that had been Valerius' through his time with the Roman cavalry. The boy held it with an awkward pride, as if he had not yet resolved the contradictions within it or within himself.

He was not alone; even as recently as the night before battle, the Boudica's war host had been quite clearly split in their feelings for Valerius and his leadership of them. The vast majority of the youths still hated the Boudica's brother for what he had been. A smaller number had damped their fireside songs and learned from him soberly and when the time came to apportion the war host it had been quite clear who would follow him willingly and who would not.

Snail had been one of those most clearly willing, and he had been more accurate than most with his spears. That was no guarantee that he could do in war what he had done in practice, but it was worth trying.

The fighting eased, as it always did; neither veterans nor youths had the stamina for long engagements. Two lines faced each other with the dead between, two sets of strangers locked in their own bubble of life and death while fire and sword and spear wreaked havoc in the other parts of the city.

In the quiet, Valerius pinched running sweat from his nose and said, 'Snail, the one with the ram's head in white on his shield. I want you to kill him with your spear.'

The lad was solemn and thought too much. His wheat-brown hair was thin and the aftermath of the rain still stuck to it so that he seemed all head and vast, shocked eyes. He closed them and the dreamer in Valerius saw the prayer that came and went, silently. The man in him saw the moments of self-examination and un-certainty, and mourned them for being out of place in the midst of battle. Snail said, 'You do it. You'll kill him. I might miss.'

'You won't.' Valerius reached over. 'Give me the standard so you can aim cleanly. Do it quickly, before he sees you.'

'And before I have time to think too deeply and spoil my aim?' Snail smiled, sadly. Saying nothing, Valerius twitched the Crow-horse away to give the lad a clear line. From his left, he heard Longinus murmur orders and saw that Conna's half-troop was making a diversion. Three spears sprang from their ranks, aiming for the left hand end of the veterans' line. The ex-centurion with the mark of his former unit painted fresh on his shield turned his head to shout a new order.

Snail's spear arced high, densely grey against the paler grey of the sky. For the briefest of moments, it hung in the air, seeming true. Then the spinning flight faltered and it fell to the right and struck, not the man, but his shield. What it lacked in accuracy, it made up for in strength. Iron bit deep into cowhide and laminated birch-wood. The haft wavered with the force of the throw and then sagged, dragging the whole shield with it.

A speared shield is worse than useless, a drag on a tired arm and a slow, unwieldy thing to lift and turn; any man who has survived more than one battle knows that. Before the haft had stilled, the centurion had thrown his scutum down and dashed forward to the clutter of dead men and discarded weapons ahead of him. A fraction later, without any command, four of his men followed, two to each side, as protection.

'Go!'

Longinus and Valerius shouted it as one. Long days of training bore fruit. The line of youths on foot dashed forward, keeping to their shield pairs, the one on the left protecting the one on the right so that the latter could strike with impunity.

Valerius was pushing the Crow-horse forward when he remembered Snail. He risked a glance back. The youth was an ugly, shocked green and showed no sign of moving. The too-vast eyes fixed on Valerius, asking questions he could not read.

'Come *on*!' Against all the rules of battle, Valerius turned his back on the enemy. Longinus was in the front of the action, closing with the centurion. Valerius could feel him as he used to feel Corvus; at once a safeness in the unsafe chaos of combat while yet a hidden flank, vulnerable to unseen attacks, to be protected at all costs.

'Snail! Get back or come forward. Don't take root!' He had shouted himself hoarse for half a month saying exactly the same: that the key to survival in battle was to keep moving. Breaca had taught him before either of them had ever been in battle, and then Corvus and Civilis and every other commander of any worth: *Watch the enemy; know who's behind and ahead and at the sides; never stand still unless you have a wall at your back and others hold shields at either hand.*

He might as well have been speaking Thracian. Snail was locked in a world apart. Staring blindly ahead, the youth said, 'Their shields. You told us to go for their shields if we weren't sure of a kill. I did that.'

'I did. You remembered. Well done.' The Crow-horse had begun to fight the bit, jogging and spinning; it, too, knew what was not safe in battle.

In the fighting lines, the centurion had picked up a new shield. The four men who supported him had turned back to back so that each was protected by the others. Like that, they sidled crabwise back to their lines. The remainder of the veterans advanced to meet them, fighting a way forward. Screams rose high and harsh, telling their own tales; three of the youths in the centre were wounded, possibly dying, and Longinus needed help.

Urgently, Valerius said, 'Snail, choose. I can't do it for you. Go back if you need to; there's no dishonour in it. You're no good to us with a sword in your throat.'

'Breaca's dead.'

'*What?*' Valerius spun, scanning the west whence the smoke came.

A hand grabbed his wrist. Small fingers clawed at the skin,

bird-like, dragging him back. Weeping, the boy said, 'Conna . . . I'm sorry. Her new name was Conna . . . The centurion killed her. It's my fault.'

Valerius prised the fingers loose from his arm. Conna. He tried to write the name on his mind, where he would not forget it afterwards.

He said, 'It is no-one's fault. I told you before, there's no blame in battle.' *Don't seek blame when you fight. Not before or after, especially not in the heat of battle. You do your best. If friends and lovers die, there is nothing you can do about it but make sure you live to mourn them.*

He had said that, too, too many times to count. The youths of the war host who followed him had listened, grimly silent each time, and had believed they understood. He had known as he was saying it that the breath was wasted; everyone found blame for themselves in their first battle. Hardness came later, when the numbers of the dead were so great they became impossible to count.

Unexpectedly, Valerius found it mattered to him that the shocked, shaking boy should never grow to the point where it was impossible to count his own dead.

They were not in the legions; he could not give orders, only ever advice, as of one equal to another, that might or might not be heeded. With what authority he could find, he said, 'Snail, go back beyond the barriers. I need you alive for other days.'

There was no time to make the boy listen. They were fighting against professional men who could read a battlefield as they read the roll of their dice. Valerius had been seen to give orders. Snail had been marked from the beginning as his standard-bearer – and the veterans knew that standard.

'Valerius!' His name was shouted in Latin, by a voice he did not know, and then a moment after, in Thracian, by Longinus.

'Valerius! Javelins!'

He was still holding the standard. Clutching it, he bent double, his face buried in black mane and scalding horse sweat. His free hand held Snail by the scruff, forcing the boy hard down onto the neck of his mount.

He felt a finger's touch of cold air and heard the breath of flying iron, marred in its purity by the ugliness of tearing flesh, and there was blood lacing the sweat that ran down by his face. The Crow-horse stood as if carved. Only the juddering of its neck under his hand gave away the presence of the wound midway down its crest.

Valerius had not lost so many horses that he had become hardened to the prospect of their dying; he knew exactly how much he loved this horse. A wave of panic loosened his bowels and another after it at the thought of what it would do to his reputation if he were to lose control on the field of battle. He sat up, cautiously, and released his hold on the youth.

'Snail, you have to go back. We can mourn— Get *down*!'

He dropped the standard in the mud. The blade missed them both, but only by luck. The gods had not warned him, neither Nemain's whisper nor the bellow of Mithras' bull. A part of Valerius railed at that, even as the rest wrenched his sword free and spun the Crow-horse and made space to swing a cut, to fight, to keep the centurion and the four men who protected him – how in Mithras' name were they all still alive? – away from Snail who was almost certainly about to die for nothing more than the crime of being young and grief-stricken and afraid.

All of that notwithstanding, for the next few moments there was no time to care about anything but staying mounted, and thus staying alive. Released at last into proper combat, the Crow-horse exploded in a frenzy of killing.

It was years since it had been wounded in battle; Valerius had forgotten what it was to sit the full heat of its battle rage. It was like riding the riptide of a mid-ocean storm, like bestriding lightning and the havoc of thunder. The beast reared and struck and slewed and bit and the veterans who had known it when it had fought on their side had no inclination to fight against it now.

A veteran lost his footing and slipped headlong in the bloodied mud and died for it. The centurion lifted a spent javelin and hurled it. Snail screamed, high-pitched like a wounded hind, and Valerius lost a heartbeat's attention in making himself not turn to look. A sword came at his shoulder and only the Crow-horse, swivelling without any command, kept it away. Valerius blocked the back-handed cut that followed and returned it. The force of that made his fingers numb.

Someone else killed the man he was fighting; he thought it was

Knife but could not be sure. The Crow-horse had already turned to face a new foe, the centurion, who was not, evidently, afraid of the horse.

He grinned and stepped past it and lanced up with a new javelin at Valerius' thigh. 'You should have stayed with us, twice-traitor. We might have kept you alive.'

Valerius and his mount were welded now; the thoughts of one were the actions of the other. They spun to face their enemy. The Crow-horse reared. The centurion stepped back out of range, raised his shield high and, stepping in, brought the edge slamming down on the beast's forelegs as it dropped back to the ground.

The hammer of wood on flesh was sickening. Valerius felt it as if his own arms had been crushed. The Crow-horse grunted and staggered but did not fall. It screamed rage and pain, spewing great gobbets of white spittle across them all. Valerius felt the red haze of true battle fury begin to mist his vision and fought for calm; too much rage killed men as easily as too little. The centurion laughed, and threw another javelin, goading him on.

There was no time for finesse. Valerius would have sent the Crow forward, trusting it to run the man down, but that the battlefield became suddenly overcrowded and the beast skittered sideways, shoved from behind. Horses milled about him, where there had been none before.

Longinus was there; still alive, still safe. He shouted, 'Slingers, here!' which made no sense because the slingers were all with Breaca on the other side of the city.

The impossible happened twice over. A slingstone whistled in front of Valerius' face and killed the centurion, striking clean at the bridge of his nose so that bone and cartilage pulped one into the other and his eyes were broken open. A second took the man who had held his left. Valerius did let the Crow-horse surge forward then and the third of the centurion's men died to a striking forefoot.

Longinus took the fourth man in the back, shaking his head at the shame of it, and then there was a rout: a swift pursuit of flee-ing men by seasoned warriors who killed efficiently with spear and sling and blade who had long since lost count of their dead and did not care if they saw a man face-on before they killed him.

Then it was over, with only a wounded boy to be tended if he was alive, and a horse, first to be brought back into some semblance of control, and then to have its wounds, too, tended, if it would allow.

Slowly, the Crow-horse began to settle. Valerius fitted his sword back into its sheath. His hands were shaking so that he fumbled and took longer than he should. He drew a steadying breath and dared to look around.

Longinus was with Snail, who must therefore be alive. Between him and them waited a short, wiry warrior with a broad, flat burn scar across his face that joined nose to ear and a single gold-banded kill-feather fluttering in his hair.

Catching Valerius' gaze, the newcomer cocked one eyebrow upwards. 'In the west, we still thank men for saving our lives,' he said, and then, 'Madb is here. If you remember who I am, I will show you where she waits.'

His voice was full of the music of the western tribes. He carried himself with the pride of kills unnumbered so that it was hard, but not impossible, to remember the boy he had been when, like Snail, he had carried a standard for a man he did not fully trust. Unlike Snail, he had fought with unimpeachable courage and had found a taste for battle. Which made it even more strange that he was here.

'You are Huw of the Silures. Fifth cousin on his mother's side to Caradoc. How could I forget the best slinger on Mona?' Valerius found his mouth dry and swallowed. 'Why are you here in the east when Suetonius Paullinus has two legions and four wings of cavalry bent on the destruction of Mona? Has the island fallen? Are we too late to stop its destruction?'

'We may be, but I doubt it. Luain mac Calma sent us. He said you would need some warriors who knew how to fight to balance the youth of the Boudica's war host.'

'And you'll have seen by now that he couldn't be more right. But what's happening on Mona? Is Paullinus' assault not going to happen?'

'The assault was all but started when we left. Mac Calma has the dreamers and the gods on his side. What need has he of warriors when we could be killing Romans to better effect in Camulodunum?' Huw looked to the scattered bodies and back. 'Although we were perhaps later than we could have been. Your mad horse is bleeding from its neck and the blow to its forelegs has crushed the flesh. I like my head in one piece so I'll not offer help, but Nydd is here and while he still hates you, he has always loved your horse. He has some skill with healing. If you ask, he may give it.'

'Thank you. I'll ask him if I need it.'

Valerius said it abstractedly, looking past him to where Longinus was helping Snail down from the skewbald mare and then right a little, to where a woman with slate grey hair and the bright eyes of a jackdaw leaned on the neck of a roan gelding, staring back.

Hoarsely, Valerius said, 'Madb?' and saw her nod.

The Crow-horse was calmer. It was as safe as it ever was to take it among other horses. Together, horse and man wove a path through the throng.

The jackdaw-woman had a strong face and broad, peg-like teeth. She bared them, grinning. 'It was good to see your beast fighting again. I thought he might be too old, that you might have retired him to the stud paddocks.'

'He would kill himself running at the hedges before he would let a war past and him not in it.'

Reaching over, Valerius grasped the woman forearm to forearm, as the Hibernians did. He felt uncommonly pleased. He said, 'Madb of Hibernia, it warms the strings of my heart to see you again, even if you are fighting again in a war that is mine and not yours. Are you here at Luain mac Calma's command, or do you follow your own path?'

She eyed him askance. 'I take commands from no man, as you well know. But I heard Braint was coming east and thought it would be good to see you again. It's a while since I saw a man fight and heard music in my head while he did it.'

'I'm glad it was music to you. I was hearing the voice of all the men I respect swearing at my care of a wounded boy. He seems to be alive, which is good.'

'The lad on the brown patched mare?' She looked beyond his left shoulder and nodded. 'He won't fight for a while, but that's maybe as well. He's not made for fighting, that one. Not like your Thracian cavalry friend. I hadn't thought to see him fit to ride yet, still less fight, but he, too, was good to watch.'

'Thank you.' Longinus had heard her as he was intended to. He was alive, unhurt, only dirty with the spillage of other men's guts and the blood of a wounded boy. He finished tying a sling of torn woollen cloak round Snail's neck and helped the boy to stand. His eyes roved the length of the Crow-horse and then Valerius. He said, 'We're both out of practice.'

'Of course. But better with each battle. We should move before the fires reach us. The wounded can go back beyond the outer ditch. The rest can come forward with us and our new cavalry troop.'

He used the Latin again, *turma*; he was never going to cure himself of it. Longinus grinned at him, rolling his eyes.

Madb spat to one side. She said, 'If Braint hears that, she'll have your skin for a horse blanket.'

'She may have it anyway. Does she still pray nightly to see me dead?'

'She might do, I don't ask of her nights, but she prays daily, aloud and in company, to be able to fight with the Boudica and Cygfa, the bright-haired daughter who fights as if the gods directed her blade. If the Elder of Mona had asked, she would have stayed to give her life for the gods' isle, but she is more than happy to be here. She joined your sister in the west side of the city, where the fire is strongest. She leads five hundred horse.'

'Five hundred?' Joy leaped like a summer fish in Valerius' breast. 'So then we have more than a wing and that equal to five of the enemy.'

It was almost true. The warriors who fought for Mona were the best that the tribes could garner, raised and trained on the island, where the legions had not yet set foot.

Valerius edged the Crow-horse sideways to make room for Longinus to mount and turned to look about him. Known faces, scarred and aged with battle, wise-eyed and steady, stared back. Not all of them smiled any kind of greeting – very few, in fact – but none made the sign to ward against evil or spat in the wind to avert his gaze.

Most of them looked west, to where the city was burning. Breaca's fire was vast now: a great long line of flame spewing smoke that veiled the entire western quarter of the city.

Raising his voice to reach the back of his troop, Valerius said, 'The veterans cut a fire break to protect the hospital, the theatre and the temple. Those that are left will be within the ring of it now, safe from the fire if not from us. The Boudica will meet us there, and Ardacos, who brought the she-bear to Mona and to the Eceni. Together, we will destroy what is left of Rome's capital.'

There was a murmur of something close to approval. Valerius sent the Crow-horse forward. It was sound, and no longer bleeding. Longinus rode to his left, laughing with Nydd as if the pair of them had not last met on opposing sides of a battlefield. To his right, Madb sang a battle song in rolling Hibernian, making her horse jog to the rhythm.

A little behind his left shoulder, Huw of the Silures, the best slinger on Mona, had retrieved the standard of the red bull from the mud and carried it as he had done once before, in the mountains, under a wilder wind than this. Knife of the Eceni, who had fought well and must be congratulated later, marshalled the foot warriors and brought them in good order behind.

They rode unopposed along the blooded street that led to the centre of Camulodunum. Leading them in the bleak morning sun, with Mithras' bull fluttering on Mona's grey above his head, Valerius found that a weight had been lifted from his shoulders that he had not known he carried. He felt lighter and – astonishingly – younger.

For the first time in as long as he could remember, he was genuinely happy.

III

EARLY SUMMER AD 60

XXIII

THE TEMPLE TO THE GOD CLAUDIUS, ONCE EMPEROR OF ROME
and all its provinces, sat vast and white in the sea of ash and
burned wattle that was Camulodunum.

Late afternoon light made the shadows less stark, and the
remaining fires more brilliant. The skyline was gap-toothed and
angular and dotted with red and orange blooms of flame that
flowed together in places to make walls of fire.

Smaller, more contained fires warmed warriors and cooked food
and heated water for the washing of wounds. Reed torches had
been scavenged from unburned houses to the east of the temple and
were strung along the streets so that rows of pinpoint light showed
where unburned houses arced out from the eastern margins of the
city.

The temple dominated everything. There was no elegance to it,
only an overwhelming size and a quantity of gold on the roof that
had not yet melted because the fire could not broach the great gap
of paved courtyard around.

If an emperor-made-god gauged the love of his former subjects
by the size of the building they erected in his honour, Claudius
would have been well pleased with the scale of the temple that had
been built on the site of his only victory. Ten tall warriors could
have stood one on the shoulders of the other, and the head of the
highest would not have topped the roof. Fifteen as tall could have

lain on the ground, heels to crown, and they would barely have stretched its length.

The flinted walls drank in the lights of many fires and juggled them, mixing in shadow, so that they seemed awash with battle-blood and gore, a shrine to the glory of dying. Across the front, a row of white fluted columns, thick as aged oaks, supported the roof. Behind them, great bronze doors, each as wide as a horse is long, stood shut against the warriors and the coming night. Above, the roof tiles were either gilded lead or, more likely, solid gold. They cast soft, buttery light onto the grey courtyard.

It was still breathtaking in its grandeur, however ugly. Standing in the glow of it, with Stone at her side, Breaca asked, 'Is it like this in Rome?'

Theophilus stood beside her. She had found him in the cellar of his hospital, safe when the rest of the city blazed around him. He was burned about the face and feet and down the length of one arm, but no worse than anyone else.

He said, 'A little. When all the roofs are made of gold, one notices them less and the minds behind them more. Your warriors wish you to share in their celebrations.'

Breaca wanted to talk to him about the well, or the burns on the feet of the war host, or anything else that was not war, but he was looking pointedly over her shoulder and so she turned, and tried not to look tired.

Cygfa was there, just out of spear's throw of the bronze doors, with Braint and a handful of others Breaca recognized from Mona together with several dozen she did not. They hailed her and she would have joined them and their enthusiasm but she saw Valerius on the fringes, sitting astride a low wall, leaning back to back with Longinus and talking animatedly to a lean youth with a burn scar angled across one cheek. He had tried to wash since she had last seen him, so that the old ash and dried blood had gone from his face and there was only a powdering of new ash, from the flakes that fell steadily from the sky.

He saw Breaca and his face became still, as it always did these days, studying her. He seemed content with what he saw and was about to speak, then he glanced past her and his eyes flew wide and she read astonishment and relief and an unfeigned joy and what was most surprising about all of those was that he made no attempt to hide them. Sometime in the last two days he had shed a skin and was emerging new and fresh in ways she had not yet fully grasped. He clapped the youth on the shoulder and said something to Longinus to bring him along and vaulted a second small wall to join them.

'Theophilus!' He embraced the old man gently, avoiding the more obvious hurts, and then held him away, the better to study him. 'Where did she find you? I thought nothing could live through that fire.'

'Like a mole, he took refuge in the well,' said Breaca acidly. 'And emerged alive to prove to us that Alexandrian engineering is the best in the world. What happened to your arm?'

Her brother had a cut to his forearm that needed attention. In the past, he would have hidden it; now it was open, oozing old blood at the edges.

'A man I thought already dead proved not to be.' Valerius had knelt to greet Stone. 'And another is standing in front of me. It has been a day for the dead being alive, only this time I am happy with it.' He was laughing and a little reckless with the relief of a battle over. To Theophilus, he said, 'Are you here to witness the fall of Claudius' temple? You've come too soon. Even without water, they'll hold out for a night and a day.'

'They have water,' said Theophilus. They've been storing barrels of it in the back of the *cella* since before you came to see me. And corn.'

'Have they, just? Someone was thinking clearly. So then Cygfa was right: we will have to break in through the roof.' Valerius caught the eye of the youth with the scarred face. 'Huw, they have water and food enough for a half-month. Will you find Madb and tell her? I'll find Ardacos, and bring him here to talk on it. Longinus, if you can call Cygfa we can meet at the base of Claudius' altar. Breaca, have you thought what can be done with—'

Theophilus put out a hand and caught him. 'Is it so urgent?' he asked. 'Or could you give me your sister for part of the night before you begin to plan your assault?'

It was the tone of his voice more than the words that caught them. Longinus had almost left them. He turned back and looked at the old physician with the quiet surmise he gave to most things that were serious.

Valerius caught Breaca's eye and asked a question, silently. When she answered the same way, he said, 'The warriors need rest and food. We won't begin again before dawn and there is not so much to plan that we can't do it without Breaca, although it would be good if she were back by dawn. What do you want of her?'

'I want her to come with me and see a place that will soon be gone.'

Breaca asked, 'Will it change what we do?'

'I don't know enough about siege warfare to be able to tell you that,' said Theophilus cautiously. 'But I believe it may change who you are.'

He led her through the eastern gates of the dying city and out across paddocks and open grassland. The ground was greenly undulant, untouched by the day's violence; a steady easterly breeze sent the ash and sound and smells of war the other way.

They walked slowly, because their feet were burned and because Stone was stiff from the fighting. Theophilus' ruined robes brushed the turf in time with his stride. The sound became the whisper of wind in the trees and joined with the freshening smell of the dusk to wash away the soil of war.

Away from the braziers and torches, the evening landscape settled into muted, overlapping greys. Breaca traced the lines of the distant slopes in her mind, and then again, and then, 'Are we going somewhere I should recognize?' she asked.

'I think you might.' Theophilus paused at the top of a small rise. 'You were here, I believe, when Cunobelin, the Sun Hound, was sent on his way to meet his gods?'

'That man had no gods,' Breaca said dryly, 'or only found them at the end of his life. But yes, I was here. Could we stop for a minute? He's not someone I would want to meet again unprepared, even if there's nothing of him left but a memory.'

She felt the touch of Theophilus' smile as he turned back to join her. 'Your brother was generous with his time,' he said. 'We have until dawn if you need it.'

They stood and then sat together on the peak of the hillock, a man, a woman and a crippled war hound, looking down towards the south and east to where a smaller, steeper-edged hillock lay nested in the landscape.

By feel, Breaca teased out the knots in Stone's pelt. Reflectively, she said, 'Cunobelin was the greatest diplomat of his day. Caradoc once said of his father that he could outmatch any man in the game of Warrior's Dance and that he never stopped playing. His manipulations hurt his family, but they kept his land safe. For five decades, he balanced the wishes of Rome against the needs of his people and kept the legions from our shores.'

'You didn't like him?' Theophilus read the tone rather than the words.

'He was father to Caradoc, whom I loved, and Caradoc is father in turn to all three of my children. No, I didn't like him. I learned to respect him and all that he tried to do, nothing more.'

'Then perhaps we should not go down to his grave mound,' Theophilus said. He balanced his chin on one fist, brooding. 'After you left, I had time to think before your war host descended on the city. It seemed to me then that there was something . . . different about the mound, that it could act for you as the temple of Aesclepius does for the Greeks.'

'You think I could dream my healing there?'

'At least the beginnings of it. Possibly. I make no guarantees.'

'No healer ever makes guarantees. No-one would believe them if they did.' Breaca rubbed a last clot of blood from Stone's mane and stood up. 'We should go on.'

Walking to the rhythm of Theophilus' robes, it was hard not to remember the clash and colour of the Sun Hound's funeral and all that had led from it. For all the brazen sun, the seeds of destruction had first sprouted there.

Breaca said, 'If it were not for this man's sons, I would have no children, but we would also not have war with Rome. It was Amminios, his second son, who first petitioned the emperor Gaius for help to regain lands he thought rightfully his, and so invited the legions to Britannia.'

'Which would you rather have, life as it is now, or no children and no invasion?'

'I don't know. I can't imagine life without either. Is this the mound? I had remembered something bigger.'

Theophilus said, 'We're coming at it from the back. The entrance faces east and it seems taller there. Once, there was a timber door, turfed over, but veterans took it away and chopped it for firewood. The children play games in it now.'

Memory and passing years had swelled the mound to the size of a roundhouse, bathed in dawn sunlight, made more brilliant by the layerings of gold. In the dusk of a battle-torn evening, it shrank again to a squat, low hillock, like a sleeping bear shouldered against the dark.

Set alongside the height and grandeur of Claudius' temple, it was nothing, a wrinkle in the flat paddocks only just high enough for a warrior to step into and perhaps twenty to stand inside, if they did not mind being packed close. It was oval, with the long sides facing east and west to the rising and setting sun. Breaca walked round the northern curve of it, and saw the gaping wound of the door and the stale darkness inside.

She was not given to open prayer, but she spoke aloud an oath to Nemain as the dark reached out for her. Children may have played in the mound in daylight, but it was hard to imagine anyone, child or adult, choosing to come to it as she did, in poor light at the end of day with broken wood and hide swaying in the breeze and the utter blackness of the tomb rustling with small beasts of the night.

Theophilus joined her, standing a little away. 'The place was untouched through all the time when the Twentieth maintained the garrison here. The order to break it open came from procurator Catus.'

Breaca turned and spat into the wind. 'I trust the Sun Hound has met him in the lands beyond life, and exacted payment for the desecration of his resting place.'

'Was it you who killed him?'

She had forgotten he would not know. 'No. I was barely alive, certainly not fit to raise a blade. Valerius did it, with his Crow-horse. The two are one when they're in battle. No man could survive them both.'

'I had hoped it might have been him.'

Theophilus came closer and ducked beneath the low lintel to stand just inside the grave. His robes became dimmer with the dark. From there, his voice echoed. 'This place is not a temple, but it has a feel to it that I have known only rarely and in the most sacred of places. I can stay with you if you'd like, or leave you alone with whatever may be here?'

It was night, then, no longer dusk. Stars grew sharp above, but did not give enough light to see by. Stone stood pressed against Breaca's leg and would not go forward. The grave's mouth yawned blackly open with fragments of broken wood at the margins. The air around it smelled dryly of old bones and leather.

She said, 'Could you wait on the other side? So that I can be alone, and yet not be left?'

'Of course.' Bony fingers gripped her shoulder, giving strength. 'Call if you need me.'

The soft slur of his robes whispered to the far side of the mound and fell silent.

The Greeks sleep in the temple of the dreamer-god, and dream of their healing.

So Maroc, the old Elder, had said in the halycon days on Mona when all that mattered was who might next become Warrior after the horn passed from Venutios.

The grave mound built for Cunobelin, Hound of the Sun, was not a temple to any god, nor, evidently, was it possible to sleep there.

At first, it was enough simply to step forward into the dark as Theophilus had done. The greying ends of the day were swallowed and made nothing. Breaca put a hand down and felt the hairs grow stiff on Stone's neck as he hung close to her heel. Goose-flight brushed her own spine.

'I was never an enemy,' she said aloud.

The dark waited, wanting more. For a while, she had no more to give; then, searching old, dry memories, she said, 'The Sun Hound gave me his ring and his oath. I am his daughter in spirit, promised his aid to the ends of the earth and the four winds.'

It was an old oath even when Cunobelin had made it, and had sounded archaic on the tongue of a man so evidently wedded to commerce and the mores of Rome. At the time, Breaca had thought the man glib and his oath prideful and had soon forgotten it.

It felt less so here, in the place of his resting. She waited in the grave's mouth. Her words were swallowed and did not come back, but the sense of enmity grew less, and she was able to step forwards, a pace at a time, and feel her way into the cavity.

Once, the mound's interior had been lined with new wood, ripe with resin and the scents of new-cooked food, placed there to send the dead soul to its rest in fine fettle. Only dry earth was left, which crumbled to dust under her fingertips, and spattered in her eyes.

She made herself feel round the whole perimeter before she lay down. The procurator's men had emptied it entirely. Nothing was left of the golden shield or the shining blades, nothing of the gilded chariot that Cartimandua had given, always too ostentatious, or the jars of wine and of olives, the platters and beakers of bread and meat and ale laid for three days and then broken, that they might pass to the lands beyond life and not feed the living. Nothing was left, either, of the bier on which the Sun Hound's body had lain, or the urn of ashes that was left after they burned him.

'They'll have taken those in daylight. No Roman would come here after dark.'

Breaca spoke to Stone, who lay down at her side with his head heavy on her leg and pressed his body tight to hers so she could feel his breathing and the fine tremor beneath it.

She lay a while, and thought of sleep, and of healing. When neither of these came, she let her mind drift to the mound as it had been, and the man for whom it had been built. She built a picture of him slowly, from poor memory, and filled it in with those things that had passed down the generations and so were nearer, and better loved: with Graine's eyes, with hair partway between Cunomar's and Cygfa's, with Caradoc's brow and the eagle's beak nose . . .

. . . And so thought of Caradoc, which she had not done since winter and Prasutagos' death, and so went back, and back, to the beginning, and day by day, year by year, began to build her life again, with all the hurts laid bare, as she had never dared to do.

She had reached Graine's birth, and the half-day of unsullied joy and all the chaos that followed it, when she heard the whisper of robes again, and the brush of feet on grass.

'Breaca?' Theophilus' voice was rusty with half-sleep. 'Would you like light? Or food? I have both.'

She sat up. 'How did you know I was awake?'

'I can hear you weeping. If you would rather have dark and solitude, I'll leave again.'

'No. I don't need dark to remember the light and I would welcome company.'

He brought a flaring torch dipped in pine resin and a brace that held it upright when he propped it on the floor. Light brought dancing shadows and pushed the past and the ghosts out into the night. They were in an earthen mound, with crumbling walls and the dried skeletons of mice on the floor.

Theophilus sat nearby, with Stone between them. From a satchel hung over one shoulder, he brought goat's cheese wrapped in nettle leaves, and a skin of water and a handful of hazelnuts.

From earliest childhood, her mother had saved for her goat's cheese wrapped in nettle leaves. Breaca said, 'Your city has burned to the ground. Where did you find these? Did Airmid give them to you?'

'Credit me with my own ingenuity.' Theophilus contrived to look affronted and gratified together. 'The hospital has a cellar which is made of stone and so has not burned. It was not an act of any particular genius to move the food to the earth closets there when the Boudica's war host so clearly came with fire and destruction in mind. I have an apple, too, if you'd like it? And a salve for the burns on your feet.'

In the midst of war, while others ate burned bannocks and chewed on strips of smoked meat, they feasted, and layered an ointment of crushed olives and comfrey on their feet.

Breaca said, 'I feel like a child who is sheltered from the realities of battle.'

'But only for this one night,' said Theophilus. He ate a hazelnut, delicately, like a field mouse. 'Tomorrow morning you'll fight as you did before. Or differently, maybe. Can you tell me why you were weeping?'

She thought a moment, and said, 'The past is too real in here.'

'Perhaps it needs to be.' He wiped his fingers on his robe. 'I would ask again, what makes you weep?'

It was a long tale, and there was not a great deal left of the night. The torch flared in a new draught and so, although it was not the beginning, she began with fire, and sunlight and the blistering gold of the Sun Hound's funeral.

Speaking aloud to a living ear, it was easier conjure the magic that Luain mac Calma had wrought on the first day of the funeral with his nuggets of gold set in the mound's green turf, to catch the first rays of the rising sun, and then the field of gold behind it that had roared to the dawn as the door hides were thrown back.

It was easier, too, to remember the man, to build his features in life and in death; to trace the lines of the waxen face on its bier, raised high to the skies, and then the fire and smoke afterwards when they had burned him, which smelled quite different from the fire and smoke of Camulodunum.

She spoke also of Caradoc, third son of Cunobelin, who was her second loss, after Valerius, and she reached Graine's birth more quickly, and the loss of Caradoc and the years of lone hunting that came after.

Theophilus knew already of her journey to the lands of the Eceni, but she told the parts she had told no-one, herself least: of the strained winters with 'Tagos who wanted to sire a child and could not, but tried all the same; of the loss of Cunomar and his return; of the death of 'Tagos, and the surprising grief of that; of the inexorable build to war, and the procurator, who had nearly destroyed it; of the grief of Graine, and Cygfa and Cunomar and the joy of Valerius, and back, as ever, to Graine again.

Morning was on them when the resin torch guttered to nothing and she came to rest. Breaca pressed a hand to her eyes. After a while, remembering she was in company, she said, 'I've kept you up all night. I'm sorry.'

'Don't be.' Theophilus came to sit in front of her. The late moon had risen, giving light enough to see. He tilted her face towards it and looked through her eyes to what lay inside. 'How do you feel?'

She felt the same; worse. Her head ached, thickly. Her tongue lay heavy from over-talking. The future hung as grey and featureless as it had done since the end of the fevers.

Striving for something, she said, 'I feel less afraid of this place and have more care for the man who was left here. As much as Eburovic, Cunobelin was grandsire to my children. These things matter.'

Theophilus caught her arm and turned her to the paler grey of dawn and searched her face with his eyes and her back with his probing fingers, and looked at her tongue and laid his fingers flat across her wrist and then her neck to hear the songs of her pulses. At the end, he let her arm drop. Grief and disappointment made him old.

Breaca stood abandoned at the grave's mouth. She said, 'You did tell me it would take six months.'

'But this place seemed different, as if it held so much of what was lost in you.' He stepped back. 'I'm sorry. Sometimes old wounds must be opened again, to let them heal cleanly, but I had not thought to wreak such destruction in you.'

'If there's destruction, I made it.' Breaca reached to embrace him, and found him as stiff as she was with cold. 'You did what you could. If there's no healing, it's not your fault.' She smiled then, because he needed it, and, with brittle cheer, said, 'We should go and warm ourselves at the fires of Camulodunum. Today, we have a temple to assault.'

XXIV

THE DEAD MAN LAY FACE DOWN IN THE WATER. HIS HAIR WAS spread out round his head like the fronds of a sea anemone, pulsing a little with the rock of the waves. It was a dirty yellow, the colour of old straw, which was no help at all in identifying him; he could as easily have been Siluran, a friend whose body should be retrieved and given cleanly to Briga, or one of the Batavian cavalrymen who should perhaps be taken care of with more respect for Corvus' sake if nothing else, as one of the straw-headed Romans who littered the XXth legion, a product of their time in northern lands. If he were that, then there was no reason he could not be left slowly to sink and feed Manannan's creatures in thanks for help in the battle.

Graine sat on the end of Mona's jetty with her feet dangling just above the lap of the water and watched him bump gently against the oak pillar. He wore no armour, but that said nothing; half the legionaries had abandoned their armour on the outward crossing when they saw the anger of the gods' sea. For men who lived and died by the sword, death by drowning was something to be feared almost as much as death by fire; better to face warriors unarmoured than fall into the hungry water and sink while still living.

An upturned barge nudged at the dead man, as a cow herds her calf, pushing him farther out to sea. The body spun a little, limbs outspread like a starfish. The right arm was missing from the elbow down. Blood leaked out in lazy threads to stain the barnacles and the green-grey weed. There was a tattoo that curled up towards his armpit. It tugged at old memories but not clearly. Nothing came clearly; the horror of battle had brought the workings of her mind to a halt and she had not found a way to start them again. She stared at the water and tried at least to pray. She failed at that, too.

'He's Batavian. I heard him fall.' Bellos came to sit beside her. He had a staff, which was a new thing; long and twisted and painted. She thought it might be hawthorn but could not be sure. It looked like Luain mac Calma's work: a gift from before the battle, perhaps. She borrowed it and reached down into the water and used the ram's horn handle at the end of it to hook the man's shoulder and turn him over so that his face could be seen. His mouth fell open. His teeth were white and very even. He could still have been Siluran.

Graine said, 'How do you know who he was when you can't see him?'

There was a small gap, time enough for her to realize she had been rude, and that he did not mind, but was concerned about how he should answer. At length, he said, 'His ghost is still near.'

She should have known that. The battlefield was crowded with the ghosts of the dead and she knew them only by the deadness blanketing her mind. She said, 'I think perhaps I know now what it is to be blind in the land of the sighted.'

Bellos was gentle and easy and tolerant. His day had been better than he could have prayed for; she had watched him stride along the beachhead, directing the dreamers as if he was as sighted as any of them. Only once did she see him stumble and that was because a horse had gone down and its thrashing hooves came too close to his head.

He said, 'No, you don't. But you are perhaps deaf when others can hear. It's not the same, but it's not easy. Did you want to know more of him?' He took back his stick and dried the handle on his cloak. Without waiting for an answer, he said, 'He was a cavalry-man. His horse was killed earlier in the day and Corvus gave him another. He stayed close to the decurion because of it and so lived when the sea came to eat them. One of the legionaries attacked him

263

when Corvus brought his troop across to escort them back to the mainland. He was too far into the dream to know friend from foe.'

'The legionary or the cavalryman?'

'Both. But the cavalry were recovering by the time this one died; they could see enough through the smoke to know land from sea and they were not all caught in the havoc of the nightmares as the legionaries were. Corvus understood what was happening. It was good that your vision in the fire said to leave him alive.'

That was what was wrong. Graine's stomach twisted in on itself so that she felt sick. She said, 'This wasn't what I saw in the fire. In the fire, the cavalry and all of the legionaries killed each other, to the last one. Not one of them was left alive except Corvus.'

She looked out across the straits. Far away, near the shores of the mainland, the first of the Roman barges was backing water with the leeward oars, turning broadside to bring wounded and exhausted men as close to the shore as they could safely go so they would not have to disembark in deep water. Corvus had marshalled them and they had left under his command, in something approaching good order. It was nothing like the ending she had woven in the fire.

She said, 'The governor only sent half of his men to attack us and half of those have gone back again. In the fire, two legions died on Mona. We should have killed them all.'

This time, Bellos took far longer to answer. Long enough for the nudging barge to herd the Batavian cavalryman out to the wide water of the straits where the currents caught him and began slowly to spin him, and then faster, drawing him down with each revolution until the spiral of straw that was his hair was gone too far beneath the water to see.

She felt a sudden tug in her midriff and a hollowness as of a room made suddenly empty. Because she was angry, she said, 'Thorn lived. I saw you say goodbye to her, as if you thought she might not.'

'That was for later.' Bellos was being remarkably patient with her. 'No-one lives for ever and there is no harm, ever, in catching the joy of a day while it lasts.'

He leaned over and trailed the tip of his staff in the water, carving a furrow. More seriously, he said, 'If we had not spared Corvus, then very likely the legionaries would have killed each other to the last man as they did in your vision. Certainly they were still held in the dream when he got them in the barges and made them leave. He's a good man with an understanding of the gods, so I'm not sorry that he was left alive, but it may be that we have altered something that will change the futures beyond what you saw.'

She had already thought about that. She said, 'I didn't see Corvus being killed when I looked in the fire. And I did see two legions attack Mona. Today, the governor only sent the Twentieth. He did not hold back the Fourteenth because of us.'

'No. And you saw Valerius and Cygfa lead the charge on the foreshore, but not the Boudica. It seems to me that perhaps you saw two things at once, that part of it was for today and that the rest is to come at some other time. Even if not, we can do nothing to change what has happened, only live with what is given us.'

Bellos stood. His staff came to the top of his head. The ram's horn was carved in the shape of a crow's head, with amber for the eyes. Small points of fire, they sparked in the sun. Snakes twisted below, rising and falling along its length.

Graine said, 'Mac Calma has marked you for Briga.'

He smiled, gently. 'I think the marking was done a long time ago. The Elder has simply made it clear for even me to see. Shall we go before it gets too dark? The legions won't be back today. Possibly not even tomorrow, and by the day after perhaps we will know why things happened as they did. Or we won't, and we'll fight again, but it will be against men beaten once, which is to our advantage, not theirs.'

He extended his hand; an apology for slights that were not his fault, an offering of help, a promise of support.

Graine took it and let him raise her up to her feet and they walked back towards the great-house along paths that he could feel and she could see, where plantain was beginning to spread and the cow parsley to scatter white flowers like frost now that the hawthorn was past, and a curlew rose, piping, from the higher reach of the beach and soared back over the salted grass of the paddocks to the new-growth greens of the heather and birch beyond.

Along the way, she saw a sword on the shoreline and ran back for it, so that, for the first time in her life, she walked in dusk towards the dreamers' place with a blade in her hand.

Corvus had dropped his sword, and so was unable to fall on it, which was unfortunate, when he had just pledged his life as a sacrifice to the sea.

He waded out of the water and watched his mare sink to her knees and then her side on the hard rock of the mainland. He sank to his own knees beside her and kept a hand on her heart. The beat rose faint to his touch and unsteady, but it was there. That mattered above everything; above Ursus and Sabinius and Flavius and how they had fared on the long, desperate swim back, above the men of the XXth legion who had heeded him through the fog of their nightmares and had brought themselves home across the mile of hungry ocean to safety. Most assuredly above the towering presence of the governor, Suetonius Paullinus, by the emperor's pleasure, and courtesy of the emperor's waning patience, governor of all Britannia, charged with the task of subduing the west or dying in the attempt.

The governor had not died in the attempt. Three thousand men had done so, to very little effect. Something close to two thousand others had returned from the battle alive but beaten. The governor, evidently, did not consider this to be any kind of victory and it was well known that he did not tolerate defeat.

He stood on the strand at the margins of the heather and the rock with his hands clasped tightly before him and his face was set as if already carved in monumental marble. Without looking down to where Corvus knelt, he said, 'Prefect, you will present yourself.'

Corvus pushed himself to standing. His teeth were chattering and would not stop. His flesh shook like a man with palsy. His hand dropped out of habit to the place where his sword hilt should have hung. With some effort, he remembered that he had un-buckled it and dropped it on the shores of Mona just before he set his mare back into the waves in a place where the currents were clearly lethal and already two barges had overturned.

In a world and at a time when he was certain of nothing from the solidity of the ground beneath his feet to the identities of the men at his side who had begun to take on the shapes of ravens, he had thought dropping the mass of iron bound to his waist a remarkable act of sanity. A part of him thought so still.

'Have you ever seen a decimation?'

The governor's face was very close. The bloodshot eyes were watering in the wind. Rage, or that same wind, had turned his nose red as a cock's comb and set it streaming with mucus. He looked like a mummer in a Greek farce.

As it happened, Corvus had indeed seen a decimation. The memory was carefully buried in the far reaches of his mind where it was not likely to emerge without warning and unman him. He was very careful not to think of it now. He said, 'No.'

The sea still washed through his ears and throat and sinuses. It juddered in his eyes so that he had trouble focusing, or perhaps that was the aftermath of the dreamers' smoke; he had not been able to focus clearly on Mona, either.

It was the sea, not the island, that had crippled his senses; his nose and throat had been scoured by the brine leaving only deadness behind. Ursus was close by and Corvus could not smell the Dacian wolfskin. There was a time, less than a day before, when he would have thought that a miracle. Now, it seemed yet one more waystone on the path to disaster. He considered the strangeness of a world without scent and, for a moment, it mattered more than the governor's threat.

'Corvus . . .'

Corvus sighed, and took no trouble to hide it. On the lee shore of Mona, he had stared into the eyes and hearts of things worse than death. Luain mac Calma had promised life, not sanity, and his protection had not extended to saving the integrity of Corvus' mind.

Wearily, he said, 'The second governor, Scapula, threatened decimation of the Twentieth at Camulodunum when the Eceni were in revolt. He decided then that he did not have sufficient authority. These men are in the grip of the water and the dreamers. They are too exhausted to walk; most of them can barely stand. Even if they could hear you, I doubt if they are physically capable of drawing lots, and if they did, I don't think you could find any nine of them fit to lift a club to the tenth. In any case, none of those who have lived through the hell on the shores of Mona is willingly going to slaughter a friend who stood at his side. The Fourteenth could do it, but if you set the men of one legion to kill those of another, you will cause a rift that will last beyond our lifetimes, however long we may live.'

The governor's gaze darted round the bay and came back to Corvus. He inhaled and clearly regretted it; doubtless Ursus' wolf-skin was close, and wet from the sea, which would not enhance its odour. He said, 'I do not consider myself likely to see the luxury of a long old age, and less so after today. We must take this island and wipe out all those who live there, or we die. We may die in the taking, but it will be better than what will happen at Caesar's hand if we return defeated. Have you no stronger reason why I should not visit the wrath of Rome on the men who have failed me?'

And so Corvus said the rest of what he had understood as he had dragged himself out of the water and realized that bringing half a legion of men back alive from the teeth of Hades was not going to be enough.

Quietly, distinctly, knowing what he did, he said, 'You have not earned the right. You were not there to face the enemy with them.'

He saw the blow coming and did nothing to dodge it. The hilt of the governor's knife took him on the left temple where his helmet might have protected him had he not thrown that, too, onto the shingle of Mona.

He felt the shock and sudden anger that always came when he was hit and then a long, long fall that lasted an aeon and was time enough to see the faces of those he would want to meet when eventually he was allowed to die. He did not think that would be soon, given the depth of the governor's temper. He saw Ursus, looking concerned, and was not sure if that was in his mind or not. Then he saw Valerius, riding his mad horse and knew he had fainted and so felt free after Valerius had gone to embrace the dark-haired Alexandrian who had given him the falcon of Horus as a parting gift and never come back. Last, he saw his mother, which surprised him, and then not: he had landed as an enemy on Briga's land; it was right that a mother should come to see his ending.

The Batavians were celebrating, and somebody had killed a pig.

The sound of drunken singing came and went in a rocking rhythm, more sonorous than the sea. It matched the throbbing pain in his head, focused on the left temple. The smell of gutted swine waxed and waned to the same tempo, and failed entirely to cover the stench of wet wolfskin that lined his nose and his head and his lungs, thick and pungent as month-old fish. Corvus lay still, savouring the ugly mix of flavours, and was grateful that he was not going to have to die without the power of smell to remember the world by.

He lay under cover, which surprised him. An uncertain rain stammered on a tent hide above his head, slurring the Batavians' choruses. Beneath the rankness of the wolfhide, the air smelled pleasantly damp. He lay on linen and was no longer in his armour. Someone had undressed and washed him; his face felt clear and clean and he no longer tasted brine when he licked his lips. He could not bring himself to open his eyes, but the crisp bite of the air spoke of night.

He was not in pain, that was the second surprise, except for his head, which had been broken open like an egg and was leaking his thoughts out onto the floor in a tumbling mess. That had happened before and Theophilus had treated the headaches that ground him down. He spent some time thinking of Theophilus and how he would take the news that his friend the prefect had been executed for failing in his duty.

Corvus wanted to reach him, to explain the nature of the sacrifice, willingly given, and the nature of obligation. He wanted it known, more widely than only by Theophilus, that the gods accepted such things in the spirit with which they were offered and that there was no dishonour, however it might seem in the eyes of Rome. The needs of his own pride surprised him; through all the years of battle, with death never farther than the thickness of his skin and the blade that might sever it, he had thought that what mattered was life and the manner of its living, not the nature and time of his death. Luain mac Calma, for whom he had an abiding respect, had said something similar: *Take the life that is offered and live it well, by your own heart's truth.*

It occurred to him that Luain mac Calma could see things that he, Corvus, could not and that the dreamer had not meant him to give his life to Manannan of the wild seas, for no better reason than to assuage the anger of another man.

In the never-ending dark, he heard the Elder's voice, with the god's sea behind it: *If you are careful from here forward, you will meet my son at least once more in this life.*

He thought he had been careful. He fell asleep, reaching for Theophilus and for the dreamer, to ask them where the carelessness had been. In the place of no-time, he dreamed of a decimation, and what it was to watch an entire legion in which nine out of every ten men clubbed to death the tenth with whom they had until that moment shared life and bread and battle and, in some cases, a bed and passion and love. In his dream, he was able to stop it, which he had not been in life.

When he woke next, someone who knew how clear air helped his headaches had lifted the tent flap behind his head and left it open to the sky. The breeze stroking his face was a kind one, not the cutting wind of Mona, which had carried the wailing of long-dead men and old women and the insidious smoke. The smell of swine and fresh blood had changed to one of roasting pork, which meant, now he came to think of it, that in his absence someone else had ordered the slaughter of the Quinta Gallorum's only hog.

A rough, tired voice said, 'That took you long enough. He didn't hit you that hard. I was beginning to think the dreamers had stolen your soul and I'd have to send Flavius swimming back to Mona to find it. He'd go, you know, for you. After today's work, I think he would follow you to Hades and back and not speak against it.'

'Ursus.' Corvus said it flatly, which was unkind, and smiled to take the sting from it. He had blocked a sword blow that otherwise would have decapitated Flavius. It had not been an act of any particular merit and he had not thought anyone else had seen it. Possibly, none had, and Flavius had spoken of it, which was telling of something, if he could only work out what.

He considered sitting up and thought better of it and stared up instead at the tent hide and then sideways to the small flickering soapstone lamp that cast odd-shaped shadows across his chest. He watched them awhile and saw that the rancid wolfskin lay on him as a covering. Never, in the five years he had known Ursus, had he seen the man allow another so much as a finger's touch of his talisman.

He said, 'I am more grateful than I can say, but you shouldn't be here. After today, I'm not safe to be with.'

Ursus sat by his head. He grinned, and was upside down so that when he winked he became for a moment the monsters of Mona's beach and Corvus had to close his eyes to be free of them. Against the black of his lids, he heard Ursus say, 'Safe enough until Paullinus is finished talking to the messengers, which could be morning, by all accounts. He doesn't often get sent word for his own ear by royalty.'

'Royalty?' Corvus sat up too quickly and the world became a deep, unpleasant red. He bent his brow to his knees and breathed through his mouth. Muffled, he said, 'Which royalty? Have the Eceni sent a messenger to the governor?'

'Hardly. If Sabinius is correct – and he's been spending an untoward amount of time fixing the haft back on his standard very close to the back of the governor's tent – then the message comes from Cartimandua, by the emperor's very great pleasure queen of the Brigantes. But then there's also the legate, two tribunes and the first two cohorts of the Second come up from the far southwest on their own initiative. They're bringing the same message, which means it is probably true.'

Corvus cupped his palms over his eyes and wished he could think more clearly. The pattern of his dreams pressed in on the sides of the tent, so that he could hear men screaming, and then the sudden quiet when it all stopped.

He said, 'What was the message? What is it that brings the fighting arm of the Second this far north and a messenger from Cartimandua south before the trade routes are fully open?'

There was no subtlety to Ursus. The news was bubbling out of him before he spoke, washing him with its greatness, and the implications, both personal and political. As a man offering a gift of great value, he said, 'The east is in revolt. The Eceni have risen again and are storming Camulodunum. It will be in ashes by now, and after it Canonium, Londinium, Verulamium. Without any legions to stop them, they have a clear run through all the towns south of the river down into the Berikos' lands that border the sea.'

It was impossible. It was inevitable. These two raced together into his mind and clashed agonizingly in his left temple. 'What happened to the Ninth? They hold the east. They could stop any revolt before it began.'

'Not any more. The Ninth is broken. The Eceni used Arminius' tactic from the Rhine and cut them to ribbons. What's left, which is not much, is under siege in the fortress on the eastern coast. Petillius Cerialis is alive, but I don't imagine he will be for long. If he has any sense at all, he'll fall on his sword.'

Ursus dismissed it, as if the loss of a legion were a small thing, to ruin only one man, not an event to bring down emperors and the men who served them. Striking back to the track of his heart, he said, 'Flavius thinks the woman we freed was the Boudica. It's lucky you saved his life today, he'd be reporting by now to the governor else, with you and me and Sabinius dead men on the back of it. Paullinus might forgive you for calling him a coward when there was nobody about to hear it. He won't forgive you for freeing a rebel who has lit the tinder in the pitch pot of the eastern tribes and— Are you listening?'

The Ninth is broken. The Eceni used Arminius' tactic . . . Not the Eceni: Valerius. No-one else could have betrayed Rome in the way Arminius did. Seeing him on his insane horse in the Eceni steading, with the procurator at his feet, Corvus had understood that Valerius was going to join his sister, if she lived, if the rest of the Eceni nation would have him and not stone him from their thresholds.

Viewed from a distance, with hindsight and the understanding of the tribes, it was possible to see that Valerius' whole life had been shaped by the gods just for this, if one wished to believe in the gods and their shaping of men. At that moment, Corvus very badly wanted to believe in something that shaped a life and all that came after it. *All things are possible in death, as in the dream* . . . He wanted to believe that, too.

Through the blackness of a sudden, knifing loss, he heard his own voice say, 'Of course. I always listen to you. If you had any sense, you'd turn me in yourself.'

He waited for an answer in kind and was met by silence. He took his palms from his face. The flame from the small soapstone lamp was too bright.

Ursus was staring at him, shaking his head. 'You're not listening. Flavius is unstable. He loves you and now he owes you his life and so he resents you as well. He'll talk because his mouth will run away with him and think of the reasons afterwards. I thought you were going to deal with it, but you didn't. You could have let him die there on the foreshore with no harm done. No-one else would have known.'

'Perhaps.' The smell of roast pork reached Corvus' belly and his head at the same time. Hunger and nausea gnawed at him equally, making him salivate. Sometimes eating helped. He considered it and regretted the thought.

Through a rising gorge he said, 'I'm a condemned man. The governor can have me hanged in the morning for leading the retreat on Mona, or for freeing Breaca of the Eceni from the procurator's crucifixion. Either way, or both, I can only die once. You and Sabinius have life still ahead of you. I prefer to think Flavius is his own worst enemy and will kill himself before he kills anyone else, but if you two think he's a problem, you can decide what to do about him tomorrow, or whenever it is that he forgets I saved his life. In the meantime, if you don't want me to be sick all over your wolfskin, do you think you could twist some favours out of the Batavians and get me some pork?'

A voice from beyond the door flap said, 'I have it. And I may be my own worst enemy, but I won't forget what you did.'

The air in the tent grew suddenly sour. The smell of the pork was overpoweringly rich and still did not come close to obscuring the stench of wet wolfskin. Corvus shut his eyes and opened them. He said, 'I'm sorry,' and the word dropped into the open abyss at his feet. It was not – could never be – enough.

Flavius stood by the door flap to the tent, not quite inside. He shook his head, flatly. 'You said what you believed, and he said what he believed before it. It may be he was right. If I had not seen you block the centurion's sword today, I might be talking to the governor now. And I might tomorrow, whether I remember it or not. But then, I may be too late, and may die with you. I am not the only one who knows what you did; there were twenty of us rode with you into the Eceni steading to face down the procurator and I can't be the only one who has worked out whom we saved. If you think I am alone in wanting to buy my own life with information, you are more of a fool than I took you for.'

Flavius' gaze raked the length of Corvus' body from the scars at his ankles taken on shipboard past the knotted spear-thrust beneath his ribs to the new throbbing bruise on the side of his face. Something flickered in his eyes that could have been grief or spite or contempt or the promise of retribution, saved for later.

He said, 'The governor wishes to speak to you in his tent. He has called a tribunal. You should dress first.'

He had brought a board, with three slices of hot meat laid on it and a cluster of olives at the side. The meat was perfect, running a little to pink at the middle. The crackling was brown-edged and fine. The olives had been stoned and were arranged all in a ring, pointing outward. He laid his gift down at the tent's threshold and stepped back into the unclouded night. He turned to leave and went three paces and turned back and the grief on his face was plain working from his throat to his mouth.

Thick-voiced, Flavius said, 'I had thought better of you.'

It had been the risk from the start. From the moment Corvus had ridden into the Eceni steading with the twenty men of his personal retinue at his back and seen a woman he knew on the ground beneath a whipping post; from before that, when he had seen a hawk-scout of the Coritani with a knife wound to his lip and recognized something of the wildness in his eye; from before that, when he had seen a youth of the Eceni in a horse fair in Gaul and recognized more than simply the wildness of him . . .

Tracing back the lines of intent was pointless. Boundaries had been crossed and trust breached and at each step Corvus had created justifications for himself: that he was not betraying his emperor or his standard or his oath to his general; that he understood the complexities of tribal life and was well placed – possibly best placed – to judge how things might be rescued from the calamities of others' actions; that he could act out of honour, and that it enhanced the honour of his race and his office.

Walking the short distance across heather and the beginnings of mud to the governor's tent, he considered saying as much to the tribunal waiting inside but the words warped in his mouth and he abandoned them, unspoken. He was not going to lie, to taint the life that was left. He had learned that much.

He thought of what he could say: *I did it because a woman once offered me her blade, when I needed it, and I did not understand, then, the depth of what she gave me.* Or, *A child gave me her horse, as from a sister to a brother, and in my ignorance I thought then that I did understand what she gave, and did not until I rode it today in the straits and found the greatness of it.* Or simply, *It seemed only honourable.*

The last sounded hollow. It was also the only one any of those inside might hope to understand. On the whole, he considered it might be easier to remain silent; he did not imagine it would make any difference to the outcome.

He reached the tent. The glow of braziers made reddened patches on the hide. He could feel the warmth and damp and sweat and fug of burning charcoal from beyond the door, and then smell them. He himself still smelled of wet wolfhide, which was unfortunate and could not be changed.

He breathed in the air and savoured the heather and the sea and the sharpness of a spring night's cold and then scratched on the door flap and heard the clerk inside step up to open it, and announce him to those who would judge all that he had been.

It was not a tribunal, but something greater. The legate and tribunes of the IInd legion were there, and the same of the XIVth. Two of the three senior officers of the XXth had died in the day, leaving only a junior tribune to lead his legion.

Eight officers, therefore, sat at the desk made for four, shoulder to shoulder, crowded, with lamps lit in front of them, so that the lines of dark and flame made bands up their faces. A ninth man, bulkier than the others and with white-blond hair, sat at the table's end, with room to breathe and move and stretch to wrap his thick fingers about his goblet of wine. Thrice three, the number of Jupiter; a full military court.

The rushes on the floor had been cut wet, and had begun to rot. Corvus felt them slip away from his feet as he walked. Time yawned for him, so that the distance from the door to the standing place, where the lamps all shed light, was as long as the swim out to Mona had been. He knew all of the officers who faced him, some better than others. Galenius, legate of the XIVth, had been a friend in his teens; Agricola, tribune of the XXth, shared the governor's tent. Clemens, senior tribune of the IInd, had quartered in Camulodunum for a winter, and shared baths, wine and dinner too often to count.

None of these men met his eye, or showed any sign that they knew him. It was left to the white-blond Briton to turn and study him, from head to feet and back again, and then to say, 'So this is the man you would see dead? He does not have the look of one who would face the gods and live long, in the sea or out of it.'

He spoke Latin, with the accent of the north. No-one chose to respond; in a military court, by consent and order of the emperor, those present deferred to the officer of highest rank, who was the governor. A man of the tribes, even a messenger sent by a loyal queen, was a barbarian, and so excused his ignorance of protocol.

Corvus finally reached, and halted before, the governor. The man at whose favour he might or might not be allowed to live looked up eventually from the two slate-blue running hounds who had held all of his attention. Paullinus was composed again; the rage of earlier had gone, replaced by the familiar dry, acerbic curiosity.

Corvus had seen him condemn men while in exactly that frame of mind. He met the open, brown gaze as evenly as his throbbing head allowed, and waited. It was possible to believe that the men who would judge him could not hear the beat of his heart in his chest. It was less possible that they could not see the shudder it sent through his frame with each spasm. He pressed the tips of his fingers lightly at his sides, to steady his hands.

Eventually, 'You have rested and eaten?' the governor asked.

'Yes.' It was a lie; one small untruth of little moment compared to the great well of deceit that Flavius, or one of the others, might choose to open. Of the twenty who had ridden with him into the Eceni steading, eight had died to the sea or the dreamers. He had trusted the others with his life, and they him. He tried not to think who else might betray him; these things showed too clearly on a man's face.

'Good.'

The governor shoved his chair back from the desk, stood, and rested his hands on the oak table. The clerk, whom Corvus despised, sat in dimness behind, poised to take note of the verdicts.

The governor lifted one of the lamps from the desk in front of him and moved it to a stand at the side, so that the shadows lengthened and the clerk became invisible. Paullinus returned to stand behind his seat and the only sound was the slip of his feet on the slimed rushes of the floor.

Rigid now under a brighter light, it came to Corvus that he did not know this man well enough; that of all the governors he had served, Suetonius Paullinus was the only one he had not taken the time or made the effort to understand.

The governor's loves were well known: beyond the easy pleasures of the hounds and their boy, Agricola had shared his tent since they first came west. So too were his hates – disorder and inefficiency ruled their lives – and his old campaigns in the Atlas mountains, roof of all the world. The details of these things were common currency in the legions who served under him, but they did not reveal the things that had shaped his childhood and his youth, the men he had admired, those he had scorned, those who still fired his mind, whose approval meant something, whose disapproval would wound.

Too late, the lack of this knowledge became obvious, and that the sharing of it might have saved Corvus' life. The pressure in his head became quite astonishing. He wondered if he might faint, and if it would change anything if he did.

The governor looked down at his own clasped hands. His fingers were fine as an artist's, the nails neatly cut and very clean. It took a great deal of effort to achieve that on campaign. Alone of all the officers present, Corvus' fingernails were similarly clean, but only because he had spent the better part of the day in the sea. It was not a useful thing to remember.

The governor said, 'I have described the failure of your assault on Mona to our guest, Velocatos. He is of the opinion that you should not be alive.'

There was relief in having the waiting over. Corvus said, 'You have it in your power to make that true.'

'Of course. And I may yet do so. Certainly there are those amongst your peers who would support it.' Paullinus ran his gaze along the line of heads beneath him. Clemens of the IInd coloured. The rest remained commendably silent and still. 'My guest, however, would consider that rash. He believes you possessed of extraordinary courage and fortitude, and swears that you must lie under the protection of this island's gods. The first, of course, is expected of any officer in Rome's legions. The second is . . . fortunate in the current circumstances.'

If you are careful, you will meet my son once more in this life . . .

Corvus felt the air crack and shift. Because he was being exceptionally careful, he did not ask what they knew, or smile, or take in the breath that he needed, but raised a brow and turned to study the blond tribesman, who sat in the only place of any comfort at the end of the table.

He was a broader man than any of those present, built like the Batavians, with a bull neck so that his head seemed set directly onto his shoulders. He had oddly effeminate hair that might have been a true silver-white in daylight, but the lamps had turned the burnished yellow of coltsfoot. It lay loose to his shoulders, falling heavily over a tunic in sharp green with a yellow knotwork at the hem and short sleeves. The gold band coiled above his elbow was richer than any of the southern tribes could afford. The long shape of a mare was laid into it in white gold, with a triangle above.

Velocatos. His name began to mean something; he was not simply a messenger. His placing at the head of the table made more sense than it had. Corvus said, 'It is a long time since we were honoured by a messenger of the Brigantes, still less the consort of Cartimandua, their queen.'

The man's eyes were pale in the lamplight. 'It is a long time since the Eceni rebelled. You were a prefect even then, I think, when the governor's son won his oak leaf at the battle of the Broken Tribes?'

The governor knew the truth of that battle, and he had never encouraged servility in his officers. With faultless courtesy Corvus said, 'Is that how it is known in the north? The Eceni call it the battle of the Salmon Trap and celebrate it as a victory. I would not argue with them, except that the reprisals afterwards on their people were savage and they could be said to have lost because of it.'

The younger tribune of the IInd gasped audibly while his peers kept better control. Galenius, legate of the XIVth, who had once been a friend, allowed his gaze to drift right a little, and drooped the lid of one eye.

At the opposite end of the table, the blond tribesman stared, and then stopped staring and reached for his wine. He swirled it in the goblet until his fingers ran red. At length, he said, 'There is luck and there is brazen foolishness. It is hard, sometimes, to distinguish the one from the other. Perhaps your actions on the gods' island today were less courageous than they seemed, and more a failure fully to comprehend the dangers. Do you think reprisals against the Eceni steadings will be enough to recompense the destruction of Camulodunum? Will it stop them from burning everything south of the city, to the far southern ports, where your ships land and your merchants trade?'

Corvus said, 'The Eceni alone are not numerous enough for that, nor, I think, would their ambitions drive them so far from their homelands.'

The blond giant smiled. His teeth were thick as pegs, with gaps between. 'Then it is unfortunate that they are not alone. The Trinovantes have joined them; how could they not when Camulodunum is under assault? The Catuvellauni may still be loyal to Rome, but the Coritani and Cornovii in the middle lands have sworn allegiance to the Boudica's standard and half a wing of Batavian cavalry has defected and holds the remains of the Ninth legion penned in its winter strongholds. The combined spears of the Brigantes have not yet joined in the host. My lady keeps those who might do so under a tight rein. If she were to falter, then without question the east is lost to you.' There was pride in his voice, behind the false sorrow.

Galenius of the XIVth was of next highest rank to the governor. He pressed his hands flat on the table so that the fingertips blanched. Speaking for the first time, he said, 'And our guests from the Second legion report that the Durotriges and Dumnonii of the southwest are less controlled than they were. They too, it seems, have joined the rebellion.'

There was a chair to Corvus' side. At a nod from Paullinus, Corvus sat down. The governor signalled the clerk who drew the sand box from the side. The surface was already swept flat. The clerk used a stylus to etch the outline of Britannia, with the toe in the west and the backbone curved to the east and the islands of Mona and its greater cousin, Hibernia, off the wild westerly coast. Fastidious in his every move, he laid down the stylus and placed a small coppered eagle on the coastline, opposite Mona.

The governor placed a larger thumbprint in the east, in one movement erasing the memory of Camulodunum. He swept his thumbnail down and angled inwards. 'Here,' he said, 'along the Thamesis that the natives call the Great River. Clemens believes otherwise, but I say that when they finish burning Camulodunum – which will be in the next three days unless a miracle happens and the veterans can withstand a longer siege – then they will come south to the site of their first defeat, to burn the trading ports along the river to the bridge that Vespasian built. He built it low, that big ships might not pass under it. The port he founded is the biggest on the river and the most likely to hold out against attack. If we can reach the bridge, take it for Rome and organize the local magistrates to hold it, then we have a route by which to reach the southern tribes that have been longest loyal to Rome.'

'Berikos' Atrebates,' Corvus said.

'Indeed. If we are cut off from all routes to the coast and the sea, we are lost. The bridge is our lifeline and attack is the best defence. The legions move too slowly; it can only be done with cavalry. I need a troop, led by an officer who knows the shores and the tides and the shipmasters who will accompany me. For the price of your life, you will come.'

Corvus stared at him. 'To face the entirety of the Eceni? Two of us and one wing of cavalry?' He had not thought the governor the kind to embrace death so willingly.

'Less than one wing – we will not fit that many on the boats. So we must arrive before the Eceni, in the company of riders who can return with orders. A legion can only go as fast as the slowest mule. Two dozen – perhaps only a dozen – horsemen can take ship from the port here to here . . .' He drew the stylus south and planted it as a flag on the coast, due west of the sea port on the river. 'The magistrates will know the nature of the danger, and how close they are to destruction. If we have time to call the legions down, we will do so. If not, we will know what it is we face. In my absence, the legate of the Fourteenth will lead the continued assault on Mona.'

'When do we leave?'

'With the dawn tide. The Eceni won't wait, or their allies. If we are to live, we must retake Britannia. To do that, we must ride.'

XXV

ON MONA, HAWK SAID, 'I'M GOING TO TEACH YOU TO FIGHT.'
'No,' Graine said. She sat on a stone by the river, where
the wagtails hunted. A birch trailed new leaves in the
water. Larks chirred over the hill. There was no wind. The blue
smoke from the great-house fire spread horizontally, as a layer of
cloud beneath the blue of the opening sky. War was a day and a
night away, a distant memory, and she did not wish to bring it
closer.

Hawk laid down the bundle he was carrying and leaned
against the trunk of a birch on the opposite bank, peering at her
through the drooping leaves. His hair was damp from swimming
in the pool further down. It lay sleek and black down his head like
an otter pelt, with the hawk's feather dangling from the topknot.
His skin was already brown from the spring sun, unblemished
except for the lizard clan mark winding up his arm and the green-
ing bruise on his lower lip that had come from Valerius' knife.

That was almost gone now; he could smile without his face dis-
torting. He did so now, disarmingly. 'Your grandfather gave his
blade into my care to keep near you, and then yesterday you came
back from the shore with another,' he said. 'I thought perhaps it
was time you learned how to use at least one of them.'

'They're both too big for me.' She eyed Hawk up and down.
'You could wield Eburovic's ancestor-blade; you're tall enough and

there's no geas against it. And the one I picked up would suit you on horseback if you chose to fight like that.'

Graine offered these not because she expected him to accept them, but in the hope that he might see the heart behind the gift and go away. She wanted him to go away, this lean, ardent, bright-eyed youth who had pledged his life to her without her asking; this man-boy who had followed her across land and sea with her grandfather's great war blade strapped across his back so that it seemed to grow from his shoulders.

She had wanted him to go and fight the day before, not for her or because he was needed, but because it was better than sitting beside him, feeling the tremors running through his body as he watched dreamers battle against legionaries on the foreshore.

He was a hound kept unfairly back from the hunt, a horse stalled at the start of a race when generations of breeding had made him only for that, and there was no point; she had not asked for the pledge of his life and his care, and did not need it. As he, evidently, did not need her gift of another man's blade.

'I don't think so,' Hawk said, mildly. 'The blades of your line are for your family, not a stranger from another tribe. In any case, I have my own blade. It was a gift from my father.'

He sat down cross-legged on the moss. Her mother had killed his father. They had never spoken of that. She did not want to now and neither, she thought, did he; she was coming to recognize the stillness that settled on him when he had gone inside beyond reach. He looked politely attentive, which was not a comfortable thing to endure.

The morning was too good to be spoiled. She sat opposite him and withdrew into herself and waited.

In a while, when all they had heard was the river and the distant larks, Hawk leaned over and unfolded the two ends of the sheep-skin so that it lay flat on the river bank with the skin side down and the wool up. The tanner had left the two ears on it, and the beginnings of the tail, so that the pattern of white and mud-brown mottles could be imagined as they had been on the back of the she-lamb that had run in the paddocks by the great-house through the last summer when it was alive.

Across the mottles and within them, lying part buried in the wool so that little could be seen but the matt sheen of blued iron, lay a sword and a knife of a size to suit a nine-year-old girl.

Graine said again, 'I don't want to learn to fight.'

Hawk lifted the sword. A running hare in bronze made the hilt, with its head as the pommel and the curve of its body set to fit a small hand. The hind legs stretched out and wound round themselves and flowed into the blade so that the join was a fluid thing, as if the hare emerged from water, or the moon. Down the length of the iron, sigils were inlaid in copper and silver. They swam before Graine's eyes, whispering words she could not hear. She looked away.

Hawk said, 'Valerius made these for you. Your mother gave them to me before we left. She asked me not to give them to you until you were ready to use them.'

There were tadpoles in the river. Someone had thrown the end of a jugged hare's haunch into the shallows at the side and it was fringed with small, bulbous eel-shapes, like a voracious black-petalled flower.

Graine dabbed her toe in the water, making rings, and watched the writhing blackness scatter into fragments and come together again. Not looking up, she said, 'Give them to someone who wants them. There are plenty of half-grown youths in Hibernia who would give their souls for the battle blade of an Eceni smith. If you don't tell them who made it, they won't disdain to use it.'

'Do you? I thought you liked Valerius.'

'I do.' Minnows came, between the tadpoles. A water boatman skimmed across the surface where her toe had been. She said, 'That is, I don't dislike him. My mother loves him; he matters for that. I don't disdain his blade, I just don't want to be a warrior.'

Hawk laughed, so that she looked up in surprise. Shaking his head, he uncrossed his legs and stood up and leaned his shoulder again on the tree.

With the mirth still dancing in his eyes, he said, 'Graine, dreamer-of-miracles, if I wanted to make you a warrior, you and I would spend the rest of our lives in the teaching and end in old age with both of us frustrated. I couldn't make you a warrior if I wanted, and I don't want to. I just want to make you safe.'

'I am safe. I have you and Dubornos and Gunovar. I can't move a step without one or all of you being there. You are among the best warriors in the war host, everyone knows that. If you three are killed, my having a blade will make no difference.'

'Yes, Graine. Yes, it will.' He was suddenly serious, not closed as he had been, but with the life in his eyes that she had seen once or twice before, when things mattered. He opened his mouth to speak and thought better of it and sank instead to a crouch and hugged his knees and tucked his chin on his folded forearms and studied her, thinking. Fronds of birch trailed about his face, framing the width of his eyes.

When he had arranged the right words in his head, he said, 'In battle, men kill those who threaten them. If we three are dead, then Mona is lost and you are lost with it. I think all of us would rather you died then, and crossed the river to Briga in our company, than were left alive for the legions to ... do other things.'

He pursed his lips, watching her to see if the words had done damage. Less tensely, he said, 'I am not going to teach you to kill legionaries, Graine of the grey eyes, I am going to teach you to look dangerous, so that death will come faster and you will never have to live through what you did before. Will you allow that much of me, with the blades your uncle has made?'

For no-one else would she have done it. For Hawk, for the stark-ness of his honesty and for the solemnity in his face and the humour that could be brought back again, and because she did not always want him to go away, she took the hand he offered across the river and took the two blades he gave her, the long one for the left, because she worked better with that hand, and the knife for the right.

She felt the balance of each, and how different it was from carrying Corvus' blade, or her mother's. The writing on the blade danced through the hare and into her arm and she felt a whisper in her bones that made her want to weep and throw them down. She gritted her teeth and grimaced and saw that Hawk had seen it, and the pity that came after, which was not what she wanted at all.

She made herself smile and when he asked it of her, she took up the stance she had seen every day since her birth and never thought to emulate, and began the first slow movements of the warrior's dance, knowing that she would never have to kill with it, only learn to look dangerous.

XXVI

I N THE BURNED CITY OF CAMULODUNUM, NOTHING WAS LEFT
living but the rats and the crows and the warriors who waited
in silent, layered rings about the temple to Claudius, once-
emperor, protector of his people, and the five hundred who waited
equally silently inside, praying for the protection of a god in whom
they had never truly believed.

Breaca wiped her palm on the front of her tunic and then the hilt
of her sword in the sleeve at the crook of her elbow. A thousand
warriors stood to either side with her behind the small stone wall
to the temple's courtyard and none of them was any easier with the
waiting. Along the length of their line, in the depths of their ranks,
was a silence greater and more tense than the one that had awaited
the men of the IXth legion as they marched down the ancestors'
way to oblivion.

She passed Valerius the waterskin and he drank and the small
scrape as he set the leather flask back on the stone wall ahead of
them was the loudest sound along the length of the wall. They
stood awhile, watching the dawn. A cloud lay over the sun and
would not move, so that, in a clearly blue sky, there was no rising
brightness.

Watching it, Valerius asked, 'Did you find what you needed with
Theophilus last night?'

'Perhaps the beginnings of it,' Breaca said. She was sick with lack of sleep and the smell of burning flesh turned her stomach.

He looked at her as Theophilus had, as Airmid had after, when she returned. As they had each done, he said, 'You don't have to be here. We can take the temple without you.'

'And after that?'

'After that, it might be that Cunomar is ready to lead the war host.'

That, too, had been said in the morning, although with less conviction. The line of battle was not the time nor the place to argue. At length, Breaca said only, 'That's not necessary yet.'

They fell to silence and watched the sky. Presently, the sun moved up above the trees, still locked behind its following cloud. When it was so high that the shadows should have reached halfway across the empty courtyard, Valerius said, 'If they don't come out soon, we'll have to—' and stopped, because the first part of the waiting, at least, was over.

Something brazen rang to the dawn, as of a shield struck to greet the gods. A grating came, of metal on stone, and the bronze door to the temple edged open slowly, as if it weighed a great deal and those behind were afraid to open it quickly.

For a breath's pause the silence returned, then a child wept, reedily. There was more waiting, and then four girl-children in stained tunics with dirty blond hair emerged on unsteady feet, blinking in the dull cloud-light. They stood on the white stone steps, half naked and filthy, clutching rags and wooden toys in their arms for comfort, staring out at the ring of warriors round them. They were crying, silently, uninhibitedly, with running noses and red, wide eyes.

Four girls, none of them older than Graine. Only four, no more.

The bronze door closed, shuddering.

Cygfa said, 'There must be more.'

'There aren't,' said Valerius.

Breaca said, 'They need help.'

Airmid had already stepped across the low wall towards the temple. She walked out alone, straight-backed under the late moon and the mist and the clouded sun. The limed stone of the temple made all the light white, so that it glanced off her hair and she was silver, marked for Nemain. She walked up the long courtyard, past the roughly hewn block of the altar stone, yet to be consecrated, to the foot of the steps. Seeing her, the girls shrieked and turned back to the doors and would have run, perhaps, to the unsafety of the interior, but she stopped and crouched and tipped her head to one side and said something too low to be heard where the warriors waited; only the murmur of it carried to them, and the sudden softening of the children, so that they walked to her, and were held.

Lanis joined her, who was a dreamer of the Trinovantes and known to them. They lifted one each and led the others. Four girls, when an amnesty and safe passage without harm had been offered to all the women and children inside.

Only four.

The clouded sun moved up, and the contours of the temple walls began to acquire a semblance of shadow and texture. Along the stone parapet that surrounded the compound, the tension eased. Men and women rested their shields and drank water and ate smoked meat and handfuls of soaked barley and spoke to each other so that the rock and rhythms of speech filled the silence. The warriors were not waiting, now, for anything, except some sign to show how one moment differed from the one before it and the final assault could begin.

Breaca backed away from her stance and went to see Airmid and the children in the safe place they had found in the broken arc of the theatre, close to the place where Eneit had died. It was hard to see it and not remember that; Breaca walked round the edge to avoid stepping on the sand in the middle, that had been the flight path of her spear.

The girls were at the edge, on the first row of seats. Theophilus sat with them, whom they knew well. He had one on his knee and two crushed against his hips, and was wiping their hands and legs with sheep's wool dipped in water and rosemary oil. They had been locked in airless, sunless stone for two days and nights, sharing food with five hundred, and water, and latrines that were the corners, with nothing to keep themselves clean.

Three of them welcomed his touch and relief patterned their faces. The fourth sat apart, clutching the wooden hound she had been sent out with, and stared ahead and would not speak. Her hair was rust-red when the others were dirty straw, her eyes were more green than their blue-grey and her nose was more strongly aquiline than theirs. Of the four, she smelled most strongly of faeces and stale men's urine.

Airmid had been gone and returned. 'I found this for them to eat. It's not much, but better than they have had.'

It was better than any of them had had, of the besieging army, or the besieged. She opened a willow basket and inside was malted barley and warmed oatcakes, a little crumbly for too little milk, and honey. In a burned city, inhabited by a war host that carried barely as much as it needed, Airmid had found honey. Even Theophilus had not had that.

For all the fear and tension and loathing of what the day held, Breaca had to swallow and resist an overwhelming temptation to reach for the basket. The three girls who leaned on Theophilus' knees had no such inhibitions; two days on corn uncooked alone had left them open to the bribery of honey and malted barley. They grabbed what they were offered and crammed more than they could swallow in their mouths.

The fourth girl, the one with the darker, rusty hair who hugged her hound and stared at nothing, looked past the food as if she could see neither it nor the woman who offered it. Her eyes were the colour of the straits that kept Mona safe, but red and thick from weeping.

To Breaca, in Eceni, Airmid said, 'Where's Stone?'

He was with Valerius, to whom he had given some of his heart when Graine left. Breaca whistled and the old hound trotted to her and smelled the oatcake she held out to him from a distance away so that his stride lifted and his ears flagged high. She broke it in half and gave him half of one and sat on the dusty earth and teased him until he lay down and rolled over and she could scratch his belly, away from the pink flesh and skin of the healing wound at his ribs.

The rust-haired girl watched sideways, without turning her head. Breaca studied her the same way, weighing the signs of care – her tunic, which had torn and then been mended awkwardly in poor light; her hair, which had been cut recently, so the ends were still level – against the signs of uncare that were more manifest. She was thinner than only two days' reduced rations might have created, and her hair was matted at the back, with straw and dung in parts of it. Her feet were filthy up to the ankles, as if she had stood in a pigsty, which was not entirely impossible; closer, with the wind from behind her, she stank of pig as much as of men.

Stone rolled onto his side and grunted as his wound stretched. Breaca ran her fingers round the edge of it, feeling for heat. To the girl, not looking directly, she said, 'His name is Stone. His sire was Hail who died to protect Graine and her father Caradoc. The Roman procurator tried to kill him. It has taken all of Airmid's skill to keep him alive. Are there hounds inside the temple? If they can be sent out, you could care for them. We would not have them harmed.'

There was no answer. The girl turned to look the other way. Breaca stopped speaking and sat up. Stone flagged his tail on the earth, raising dust and old, settled ash. She rubbed him with her toe and he mouthed at her leg and she forgot the girl for a while, until a thin voice, surprisingly deep, said, 'They killed the hounds to eat them and so they wouldn't eat the food.'

There was nothing to be said, nothing to be done. Breaca took her foot from Stone. He got up, puzzled, and went to nose the child, who pushed him away. Breaca called him and led him back to the warriors, leaving the children with Airmid and Theophilus, who did not make war and did not cause hounds to be killed for food in a temple to a man who had been made into a god.

In a sky of clear blue, the one cloud still covered the sun. The warriors still waited outside the parapet. The day was dust and death and nothing could be done to change it.

The cloud drifted sideways by slow degrees, freeing the sun. On the bronze door of the temple, a band of light grew at the hinge and widened. A knife blade of brilliance became a finger's breadth, became a handspan, became an arm's length of undiluted fire. The tiles above glowed softly gold, then dazzled, more brightly than the bronze beneath.

For those watching, the temple was consumed by the gods' fire, sent not by Claudius, but by the gods of the tribes, who had been petitioned since dawn, since the days of their first lost battle and all that had come since.

A murmur ran round, and rose to a shout and then stilled again, in awe and the shock of faith tested and found to have sure foundations. They had asked for a sign, the combined warriors of the Eceni, of Mona, of the Trinovantes, of the Coritani and the Votadini and the Brigantes; through the vehicle of Valerius, who spoke to both moon and sun, they had asked that something tangible be given and the evidence lay before them in the streaming, dazzling brilliance of the gods' furnace that opened before them.

Valerius stood very still, not wishing his eyes to tire of it. He had asked for help as the sun rose, going out beyond the eastern margins of the city to a place where he could see both the first arc of the new day and the old moon that pushed above the horizon ahead of it and so could open equally to the two gods he served. In grey-silver light with a thin spatter of frost crisp on the ground, with the air clear as river water and free from the taint of burning, he had felt the doorway open in the caved silence of his mind and had stepped forward to the threshold with a question framed on his lips.

He had not expected anything more than the release of asking. Then the dawn had come and the sky had grown to an aching, transparent blue, clear from one horizon to the other except for the one cloud that had sat doggedly over the sun, so that half of the morning had passed in its shade and the warriors had become progressively more restless, even after the children had been sent out.

Valerius had been about to talk to Breaca, to organize a withdrawal. They were together when the cover of the cloud was taken away by Mithras' hand, or Nemain's or Briga's or all of these acting together to send the gods' fire in the sky to meet the man-hardened fire of the earth and make the meeting of them radiant, so that the watchers basked in liquid sunlight and were blinded and god-touched and grateful.

It was necessary to move, to begin, to set the day in motion and all that might follow. Valerius did not sink to his knees in a weakness of relief, although the moment was there to do it. He flexed his fingers and forced some movement from them and said, 'Huw?' and heard Mona's best slinger move up to his side and the chuck of a stone falling into leather and the whispered whine of the flick as it was sent on its course.

The stone sent was a flint the size of a hen's egg that they had found together in the dusk-dew of the previous evening. One side of it was broken open, to show the black at the heart within the white skin. Briga, wrapped within Nemain; it had seemed a good choice to begin the ending.

The hammer of it against the bronze door was of a giant's war shield, struck by a god. It rang to the slope ten spear-throws behind, and echoed back on itself like ripples on water.

For two more heartbeats after, the quiet remained. Then, under the blaze of the gods' light, with all the noise and effort they could muster, Valerius and his warriors hurled themselves at the bronze door.

The noise was astonishing, greater even than the usual deafening clamour of war. It lacked the screams of wounded or dying, or the usual dullness of iron on flesh, but in their place was a constant rain of iron on bronze, and wood on bronze, and stone on bronze as swords and spear hafts and slingstones crashed endlessly into the solid metal of the doors. They made no dents, nor moved them on their hinges. They did not expect to.

Some time later, when he thought he had gone deaf, Valerius heard a whistle, high above the clamour.

He stepped back, slapping sweat from his face. His throat hurt, and his chest. His eyes were stinging as if he had been in real battle. His right arm ached.

'Here!'

He looked up. Cygfa was sixty feet above him on the temple's roof. Caught in the full sun, her hair was a blazing nimbus, her features fine as carved marble. She looked like the young Alexander on a fresco in a Gaulish villa. Valerius felt his past intrude unwanted on his present and shook his head to clear it.

Cygfa shouted, to be heard over the noise. 'It's done! Send up the fire baskets.' She mimed a throw and saw that he was ready and spun a weight down to him that, when caught, proved to be a gilded lead roof tile, cheap and easily folded.

He felt someone at his side. Breaca was there, from nowhere; she had not taken part in the attack on the door. He gave her the tile and she folded it in half, and then quarters, as the old men in Rome folded their curse tablets. Her face was unreadable; he was not used to that.

Behind her, the fire baskets were passing from warrior to warrior, smouldering, not yet fully alight, belching fine, dusty smoke and the smell of oak bark and pitch. Valerius looked out into the heart of the throng still assaulting the door.

'Huw!' The lad was not so far away, and he had seen Cygfa. He grinned and his sling flashed one more time.

Valerius signalled him and shouted to back it up. 'Pull back!'

The warriors did not have Roman discipline and the noise carried its own power, so that it was hard to stop and risk again the threatened silence of before. Still, they slowed in time, as more were needed to relay the fire baskets and others walked backwards, to stand on the parapets to watch Cygfa and the dozen of her honour guard gather basket after basket on the roof of the temple, sending smoke to stain the clear blue of the sky.

Those inside the temple discovered what had befallen later than those in the assaulting horde. The noise at the doors had been unpleasant outside; in the echoing stone chamber of the temple it had been truly deafening, so that the sound of the roof tiles being levered up and away was lost in the clamour of it. Wet hides had covered the growing gap that was made, letting in no light to betray early what was being done.

Eight warriors stood on the sloping roof, each holding a basket from the pile at their side. Four others held the edges of the wet hides. Cygfa held aloft a pitch pine torch, that out-blazed the sun.

Valerius gave the order, because the mix in the baskets had been his idea, and it was good that he be seen to be a part of the final battle.

He shouted up and raised his hand and Cygfa grinned and tipped her fire torch in a warrior's salute and then said something that could not be heard from the ground. The four warriors holding the goatskins pulled them aside. Cygfa spun in a slow circle and eight fire baskets took light, belching flames and dark, tarry smoke. The sound of a man's panicked shout, and then a cacophony of others, came up through the gap in the roof tiles as the first of the torches was hurled in.

XXVII

THE DEFENDERS BROKE OUT BEFORE THE LAST OF THE BASKETS
had been thrown down from the roof.

No-one expected otherwise; given an open choice, few
warriors, or even merchants, tanners, harness makers and
magistrates who might become warriors if given a blade to wield,
would choose death by burning over death in battle, or the chance
of life, if they could fight better than they had ever imagined.

The gods had spoken. There was no chance of life for those who
broke out, but they had been locked in the dark and did not know
that the sun's fire had already melted the bronze doors and that
they ran onto the waiting blades of warriors who walked with their
gods beside them and could not lose, even in death.

Breaca stood apart from the rest, with Stone at her side. She had
not intended to be alone; in the beginning Cygfa had been at her
shield arm and Valerius at her sword hand and both would have
died to protect her. When they were sent away, Cygfa to break in
through the roof, Valerius to assault the doors, there were others:
Braint of Mona; Madb of Hibernia who was honour-bound to
Valerius; and Cunomar, who alone of all those fighting was not yet
sick of the slaughter and led his she-bears with a fervour that
bordered on battle madness.

One by one, she had sent them where they were needed: Braint
to help Cygfa, Madb to support Valerius when smoke began to

thread through an opening crack between the doors; Cunomar to rally the few dozen Trinovantes who kept watch on the hidden exit from the temple, because if anyone was going to break from it, they would do it soon.

Thus, when the doors were flung back, suddenly, by men still able to think and fight, she was alone at the edge of the temple's courtyard with her crippled war hound and a blade hilt slick with sweat.

Breaca hefted her shield, testing her strength. The night's talking weighed on her, not only for lack of sleep. The shield felt heavier than it had done in the days before and then it had seemed heavier than ever in her youth; it did not seem likely that she would be able to hold it at battle readiness for the duration of a long skirmish.

She sought the song of her blade and could not hear it, or feel the stabbing ripple in her palm that was the foretaste of the wildfire that had always before sustained her in battle. There had been something of it in the forests of the northern wash, fighting the IXth legion, and she had thought it paltry and insufficient. Now, even that much would have been welcome.

She had seen others fight purely on their wits and skill, and never had to do it herself. Stone pushed against her leg, shuddering; it was impossible to tell if he was aching to fight or to run. She pressed back against him with her knee, having no hand free to ruffle his mane, and they leaned one against the other, watching the rush of the veterans from the doors down the steps and the ringing clash as they met the waiting warriors. Ordered lines disintegrated soon into the chaos of the battle and neither Breaca nor her hound had any great urge to join it.

Valerius was near the front, with Cygfa to one side and Madb, the Hibernian woman with the jackdaw eyes, on the other. Longinus, as ever, covered his back, loyal as any hound. Huw the slinger was somewhere just beyond his left shoulder, with Knife and others who had begun to follow him to the forefront of battle.

Her brother had his own honour guard, and would have denied that they existed, as they would have denied being so, and still have died for him. Breaca watched him kill a veteran and use his shield to shelter Cygfa while she swept backhanded at another. Her daughter's hair was a dancing flame in the newly unleashed sun, a flicker of almost-white against the bronze door and the smoke that billowed from it. She was the spearhead that held the top of the steps and stopped the flood tide of two hundred veterans and those who sheltered behind them from cascading down the white marble to the courtyard below.

Even Cygfa, who was Caradoc remade as woman, could not hold five hundred alone. Veterans forced past and were met by Madb or Valerius, and then others and others so that very few reached the foot of the steps alive. Then the cluster of bodies underfoot made the fighting more difficult, and because no-one was prepared to fight in towards the temple the warriors began naturally to back away, to make more room, and so more could flood past them.

The woman with the rust-red hair and grey-green eyes came at Breaca from the farthest edge of the steps. She was not a warrior; she did not dance with the song of her spear, or hear the soul-keen of her blade, but she was swift and clear-headed and filled with the rage of the she-boar roused to violence in defence of her young. With the power only of that, she killed the young Coritani who stepped up to meet her and crippled the Eceni girl who came after him.

There were no children running at her heels; Breaca checked that before she stepped forward to block her onward rush. They were caught in a corner of the courtyard with a low wall at one side, which was an insane place for either of them to fight. Stone circled out as the rust-woman came in, harrying her from the side, so that she was pushed against the wall and her shield hampered by it.

Breaca's blade was hampered also. She stepped out away from the wall to give herself more room. The rust-woman tried to push through the gap, leaving herself open to an angled strike from the side that swept her own blade from her hand and tossed it high over the wall to land in the ash-strewn mud beyond.

Killing was too easy, and there were questions that mattered. Breaca swung her blade in and held it level, at chest height, as a barrier. The woman stopped and stood still, breathing fast and hard. She hissed and spat like a wildcat, but did not make any move that would have made it necessary to kill her.

'Why were you standing in a pigsty?' Breaca asked.

The woman looked down. Her feet were brown to the ankle bone with old, dried ordure. Over the stink of battle, she smelled roundly of pig muck.

Something of that shocked her into moving. She snarled and swung her shield as a weapon so that it was necessary for a moment to block and step back and let Stone come in, but not so close that he might be hurt, and then to corner her again with the low stone wall at her back.

Breaca swung in and, for the second time, her blade ended at the woman's throat, and did not strike through skin and flesh and bone. She said, 'I could kill you now. Or I could tell you that your daughter is alive first. In your place, I would want to know that.'

Only the truly lost can face death without care and no mother who knows her child is alive is ever truly lost. The rust-haired woman stopped trying to fight. She dropped her shield and covered her face with one white-knuckled hand and stood, shaking, as Stone had been shaking, but without the urgency to it, only despair and terror and the grief of untold loss.

'How do you know?' she asked.

'That she is your daughter? She has your hair and eyes.'

There was the barest of nods. Breaca said, 'Is that why you had to hide in the sty? Did the mobs come for you? Had you betrayed them to Rome?'

'They said so.' The words came thickly, through muffling fingers.

Breaca moved her blade away and sat on the stone wall. On the steps to the temple, men and women, warriors and Romans died and were injured, or lived and grew bold in their own success. She was left in a bubble of quiet, with Stone standing guard and a broken woman in front of her. She said, 'Because your daughter's father was Roman? Or was it worse than that? Was he one of those who let Claudius into the city?'

The covering hand fell away from the woman's face. She had been pale before, now she was yellow and shaken by more than only the fear of death. She began the sign to ward off evil and saw herself and stopped, letting her hand fall useless at her side. 'Is it written in me?' she asked. 'Am I tainted to death and beyond by one mistake?'

'Not you. Your daughter carries his nose, and something of his cast of countenance, but she will live to be more than her father ever was. Was it Heffydd himself? Or one of his sons?'

296

'Him. He has no living sons. He wanted one. That's why he . . . why I . . .'

There were no words. They could have been alone. Heffydd had been past his prime in Cunobelin's time. On a day when the world was havoc, the thought that the false dreamer of the Trinovantes, the man who had betrayed his people and his training to Rome, could bring himself to sire a girl now eight was uniquely unpleasant.

Breaca said, 'Did he pay you?'

She said it without due thought. In the midst of battle, with death walking through the throng, it was an insult as bad as anything her blade could have inflicted.

The woman stared at her with fixed, wide-open eyes and her head held stiffly high. 'And so I am the kind who would sell herself, and to *that*.'

Her voice was more strained than it had been. Stone moved up to her, and pressed against her leg as he had done Breaca's. The woman reached down and gripped his mane at the base of his neck where the hair was thickest. When she took her hand away, clots of winter hair came away in her fingers. Absently, she rolled them into a wad, as if she might polish something with it later.

She said, 'Heffydd caught me marking my son for Nemain, under the old moon. Rome would kill us for that, me and Gwn and his father if he had not already died in the battle of the Salmon Trap. Heffydd saw something he liked in Gwn, that he was strong and could fight, even at ten years old. He offered us life, and patronage under his care with the best Rome could offer if I would give him a son equally strong.'

'What happened when you gave him a daughter instead?'

'He was dead long before she was born. Briga came for him two days after he set his seed inside me.' The woman bared her teeth, ferally. The canine on one side was broken. 'I killed him. They did not thank me for that, those who came in the night with their clubs and their knives and their slow death for those who favoured Rome. They would have killed a seven-year-old girl for the crime of having the wrong father.'

'But the veterans let you send her out to a new beginning, not knowing who she was? I am trying not to think what you threatened her with, to make her come out.'

'I said I would put down the sword they gave me and refuse to fight if she didn't go, that we would both burn together. I said if she went, I would fight, and promised I would kill before I died, so she would know me already avenged.'

'And you did that; I saw it. What about your son? Where is he?'

'I don't know. He left three years ago, to go to Mona. I have heard nothing since.'

It could have been lies, but Stone trusted her, and Breaca was inclined to trust him before a mob armed with clubs and knives and a slow death. A decision was necessary, one way or the other; the fighting on the steps and the upper courtyard had become ragged and fallen into knots and too many on either side were spreading out towards them.

Breaca said, 'If I leave you alive, will you fight against us, or help those who would?'

'No. You can read every part of me – can you not see that?'

'I would like to believe so. Go to Airmid and Lanis at the theatre. They have the girls there. Tell them I sent you.'

'Who are you?'

'Breaca, mother to Graine, who was raped by Rome. If I could have hidden her in a pigsty, I would have done. I will live the rest of my life regretting that there was not the opportunity to do so. Go over the wall and run. I will do what I can to stop others following you.'

Breaca watched the woman go and only had to stop Knife from jumping the wall to follow her, and then a veteran, who had perhaps understood better what was happening. They fought and the veteran died, because he had eaten badly for two days and had already fought five people before her, and both of them knew that if it had been even, he would have won; in battle, these things are clear, and only the foolhardy ignore them.

At the end, when the temple was empty and burning and the dead were piled inside, Breaca went to the theatre to find Airmid and Theophilus and discovered that both were working with the wounded at a covered area outside the city boundaries where the stench and the threat of spreading sickness was less.

The three girl-children Theophilus had washed and Airmid had fed were in the same place, playing half-hearted knucklebones in the ash and dust, listening to tales told them by a lean Eceni warrior with her forearm bound to her chest and splints along the long bones. She was one of the hundreds now who followed Cunomar, not yet a she-bear, but fighting on the periphery and hoping to be made so. Like the others with whom she fought, she had shaved her head in an arc above each ear, leaving a long scalp lock in rich copper reds which she had whitened with lime and goose fat so that it made a crest, like the keel of a boat.

The three straw-haired girl-children were fascinated by the result, or awed. They sat at her feet forgetting the knucklebones and she fed them stories of battles won against Rome that stopped only when the Boudica came, who had been the hero of the tales, second only to her son.

Breaca stood a little away from the group. The girls were more settled and no longer stank. Still, they stared at her great-eyed and stuffed the backs of their hands in their mouths. One of them squeaked and was stilled by the others. Breaca looked down and saw fresh blood on her tunic and was too tired to try to cover it on their account.

She said, 'What happened to the fourth girl? The one with the rust hair and the nose of Cunobelin's dreamer?'

The young warrior stared at her. Slowly, she said, 'Her mother came for her. You sent her, with hair from your hound as proof. She said you had promised her safety and that they could go without harm. We knew it must be true. How else could she have come out of the temple alive?' The girl frowned, confused now. 'Were we wrong?'

'No, you weren't wrong. Only my misunderstanding. I had expected her to stay, but there was no reason she should.'

Except that there was nowhere to go in a city burned to ashes and rubble. Breaca smiled for the warrior and said something right to the children so that they were no longer afraid of the fresh blood on her tunic and the sweat and gore on her face.

When she left them, it was to go once again to search out Airmid and Theophilus, to see to the wounded and find out the cost of the day and to speak, finally, of what could be done to bring leadership back to the leaderless.

By chance, on her way across the short grass eastwards, towards the horse training ring where the wounded were laid, she turned back, to look at the temple.

Noon had passed. Even as she watched, the last sliver of sun passed over the doors and the god fire dulled, leaving the vast plates of bronze featureless in the quieter light.

There was a memory in that, so small that Breaca almost missed it. She stood for a long time watching the dullness until she found it and could name it and bring it clearly to mind.

She did not go, then, to the tents that held the wounded, but skirted the pitched awnings of the horse grounds, and passed south instead along an old track, so that alone, without a Greek physician to offer company, she could return to the past and the company of the dead.

XXVIII

CUNOMAR LAY BELLY DOWN ON A MOSAIC OF PINK AND GREY marble, resting his chin on his fist the better to watch the black oak door that was the hidden exit to Claudius' temple.

Around him was an ornate walled garden that backed onto the slave's quarters of a centurion's house. Already the place was overgrown with ivy and a strangling of early bindweed scattered through with white unopened flowers, curled tight as ropes.

The wall was solid and not meant to be climbed; the flints and cob stones that formed it had been bedded too deep to make handholds and it was capped with rounded mortar with sharpened flints along the spine. Nine strikes with a log-splitting axe had broken the lock to the outer gate, letting the she-bear flood in and arrange themselves in battle order amongst the unthrifty olive trees and grape vines and the twinned green marble fountains, on which boy-youths rode dolphins across an endlessly dry sea.

Cunomar lay in the shade of the second of these. On either side, his warriors passed waterskins newly filled from the well in the ruined hospital. All of them were burned or wounded somehow. Cunomar's groin still ached from the missed thrust of the blade that had nearly cost him his manhood. Ulla, who lay nearest, was burned along the length of one forearm, but otherwise whole.

She passed him a waterskin and he drank and handed it back.

The door to the temple remained stubbornly shut. High as a man and five times as wide, it was made of seasoned oak with leather hinges studded with iron to make them less easily cut, designed for function as an escape route, or a secret entry, as if half of Camulodunum had not known it was there from the day it was first built.

The sun moved higher, and the patches of shade grew smaller. Presently, when the flies became too bothersome, those warriors who were not yet of the she-bear, and so knew less of discipline, began to take bets on who could first pull over one of the green marble fountains.

After a while, they forgot to whisper, and the bets became more serious. Three squared up to the fountain and spat on their hands. Each had shaved the hair on his head in an arc above both ears and set the centre line with lime paint. One had cut off his own ear, or had it done for him. Cunomar did not know the names of any of them. The largest set himself at the marble, hauling so that the veins bulged on muscles that knotted like an ox at the plough. Others shouted encouragement. The marble did not move.

Under cover of the noise, Ulla said, 'Your mother left the temple battle early. I saw her let a woman go when she could have killed her.'

'Everyone saw that,' Cunomar said.

'Did she do it so we would see? So that there would be no doubt that she no longer wants to lead us?'

In the midst of the battle, Cunomar's fear had been exactly that, tainted with the shame of it, and the panic that without his mother the war host would falter. He had missed a clean kill because of it, and had to finish the man later, when the battle had passed over and there was time to come back. Lying now in the shade of an olive tree, he saw it in a better light.

'I think that's exactly why she did it. By leaving when victory was certain, she made sure no-one would suffer for her loss. And she's left the way open for her successor to take over in the final parts of the war. The balance in the host is even between Valerius and me. I think she truly does not know which of us to support. She has left us the freedom to prove ourselves in front of the full host.'

Ulla said, 'It must be hard for a woman to choose between her brother and her son.'

'And for Cygfa the same. She admires Valerius for his Crow-horse and how he can fight with it. Both of them need a reason to choose one way or the other. We can give it.' Since the defeat of the Ninth, Cunomar had tried to see it like that. Here, now, with the prospect of a quite spectacular victory at hand, it was easiest.

The wiriest of the three youths succeeded in pulling over the marble fountain, by dint of tipping it a little and kicking a stone under the base, to hold it off balance while he swung all his weight on the scalloped green lip of the bowl – which hit the larger grey slabs around it and shattered into shards sharp as knife blades that sprayed out in a wide arc.

Cursing softly, Cunomar leaned to his right, to a lanky Trinovante youth who had known the way to the garden. 'Tell them to keep well clear of the broken marble if they don't want to cut their feet when the door opens. Pass it along the line.'

He watched the flow of the message as head nodded to darker or fairer head and away again. To Ulla, he said, testily, 'Valerius would have stopped them pulling the fountain over in the first place.'

'And they would have learned nothing, except to resent him for spoiling their wager. Your way is not necessarily the lesser.'

The message had reached the last of those in range of the scattered razor-stone when a lock was turned in the dark oak door and a bolt jerked back and a beam thrown aside and a hand's breadth of solid oak, as high as a man and five times as wide, slammed back onto the cob and flint of the garden wall.

Cunomar had time to shout, 'Hold the line!' and feel Ulla at his shoulder before havoc flew at him, in the shape of the fiercest battle he had ever imagined.

The veterans who charged from the room behind the door were lean to the point of emaciation, unshaven and filthy with burn marks florid on their faces and forearms, but their leather armour was supple and their blades honed and they had the tight, dense set of men who have known each other for decades, and can trust the surety of each other's presence.

Like the Spartan heroes of Thermopylae, or the Sacred Band of Thebes, these were men who dedicated themselves to war and never let themselves go. For days, Cunomar had lain on the drying turf above Camulodunum and watched a full century of veterans practise their daily manoeuvres.

When the Trinovante informant had come with news that a certain group met nightly in a hidden shrine at the back of the temple, he had known without question who they were, and how many. All he had needed from her was the location, and the extent to which they had stored their armour in advance.

This he had been given, explicitly: 'They will have everything they could want or need. I clean the room for them, and every part of it is hung with racks of armour, except for the length of one wall, which is lined with gravestones, carved to mark their honoured dead.'

The veterans came out in a wedge, aimed at the thickest part of Cunomar's line. They killed three of the younger Eceni before the door crashed back against the wall. A part-shaved head fell and cracked, severed cleanly by the speed of the men's passing and the ferocity of the leader's stroke. A dozen other youths fell back, their war howls croaking to nothing.

The true she-bear had faced a wedge at the watchtower and knew how to deal with it. They had Valerius to thank for that; he had made them practise through the winter. Remembering, those who knew found each other in the throng and made pairs or threes or fives and pressed their shoulders together so they could act as one.

They stepped sideways, beyond the sweep of the wedge, and threw spears and then fragments of broken marble the size of fists at the legs of the leading men. A handful tripped and were killed as their shields sagged. One ran straight into Cunomar's spear, swung horizontally, like a staff, so that the haft broke his neck.

The Romans had been a century; a full eighty men. In that first charge, they were reduced by less than a dozen. The remainder abandoned their fallen and split into their tent parties as readily as if they still slept each night in marching camp, not in their gilt-roofed villas.

They made squares, two to a side, facing outward, with shields held as impenetrable barriers and swords poking through. Unlike the men of the IXth, they did not stand still inviting attack, but came on, holding their squares, killing more of Cunomar's warriors as they did so.

'We need slingers!' Ulla shouted it, running from the path of the oncoming death. She paused to hurl a fist-sized piece of marble. It bounced uselessly off a shield.

They had no slingers, who were all with Valerius, paired with the better slingers of Mona, picking off defenders inside the vast space of the temple.

Cunomar shouted, 'Don't let them get to the gate!' He had said that before, as they lay planning in the grey dusk. 'If they get out of the garden, they'll come at the temple from behind. We'll lose hundreds before they're stopped.'

His followers had listened to him then. Faced with the ferocity of the veterans' onslaught, very few heard him now.

Ulla was close, and Scerros and a scattering of others who had fought with them at the barriers on the first day of the city's assault. Cunomar raised his knife and howled his mother's name. More struggled to join him, perhaps twenty in all.

'The gate!'

He ran without waiting to see if they followed. By the skip of their shadows ahead of him he knew that they had, and that two, at least, had been too slow and had fallen.

Fifteen lived to reach the gate.

'Spread out! Make two lines!'

Cunomar swept his arms wide. His warriors were slow, white-eyed and panting. Those who had fought at the barriers without fear found themselves undone now by the veterans and their methodical brutality.

Still, the days of drilling above the city worked. Fifteen made two lines, and blocked the gate.

Cunomar shouted, 'Ulla! Scerros! Go out through the gate. Close it and wedge it. Find Valerius, bring him back to help.'

They turned to leave. A part of him exulted that his leadership at last carried sway and the need to obey him overrode the need to stay. A greater part of him broke apart at the loss. He wanted to say something and there was no time: three tent parties of veterans had already formed an opposite line and were advancing at a shuffling run. He could smell the sourness of ill-fed breath, and the unwash of their bodies and the sleek, new oil on their leather armour.

Shadows came and went as the gate opened and shut behind

him. Something close to gratitude let Cunomar focus his intent on the veterans' leader, who advanced in the centre, opposite him.

The man's teeth were foul, and he had shaved with something rough, so that the skin was blotchily red on his chin and cheeks. Between, patches of black hair sprouted through. He could not have eaten a proper meal in three days at least, but he danced on the balls of his feet and when he raised his blade it was with a certainty of killing that Cunomar had never met before, except perhaps in Valerius, and then it had not been directed at him.

The man coming at him grinned. The air became fetid with old and new sweat. Cunomar spoke the ninth name of the she-bear and set his intent entirely on his enemy. Free of fear, he raised his shield and rammed it onto the incoming blade, twisting, to make a gap in the shield wall opposite. His own knife curved in an arc that should have ended in the other man's bowels—

And did not, because Ulla was there with her spear and had stabbed at a white flash of face beneath the helmet. Her scream or his split the air.

'Ulla!' Cunomar's howl soared louder. 'Get out! Find Valerius!'

'Don't . . . need to.' Ulla was still alive. She danced back, leaving her spear. '. . . already here.'

He had no time to look up, or around. The fighting was as fierce as he had ever seen or imagined. The twenty-four men of the veteran line fought on for the gate as if their honour and lives depended on it. They failed to reach it, but each took at least one of the war host with him as he died.

Slowly, amidst the miracle of his own continued survival, Cunomar came to notice that there were far more warriors in the garden than had come with him, and that a smaller proportion of them had shaved their heads in an arc above the ears, or pasted white lime in their hair.

When a slingstone passed him, and killed the man who most immediately threatened his life, his battle-slowed mind realized why. As he fought forward, away from the gate, and heard it opened, and tasted clean air in the stifling heat, and felt bodies slide past him on into the garden, and then caught a glimpse of the black oak door and saw yet more warriors pouring through that, he knew both relief and frustration, equally, which was not a new feeling, and far less welcome than the sweet, unhampered clarity of battle.

The fighting slowed, and it became clear to Cunomar that he was no longer needed; fresher arms than his took on the last two dozen Romans and forced them back against the wall and began the slow, dangerous task of killing.

He was leaning against the second of the two marble fountains when a cool voice he knew and loathed said, loudly enough for others to hear, 'That was well done, son of the Boudica. It would have gone hard for all of us if they had broken out and come into the temple at our backs.'

'Valerius.' Cunomar turned slowly. His whole body shuddered with exertion and the aftershocks of combat. 'Has my mother returned to the field of battle?'

'Would I be here if she had?' Valerius, too, was grey and slow. A wound on his forearm bled freely and he had a shining blood-bruise the size of a fist on the opposite elbow with the flesh already swelling on either side of it.

Cunomar said, 'So we need to talk.' They had always known it would come to this, or to more than this.

'Evidently.' Valerius smiled, crookedly. 'I would suggest we had better go elsewhere, where fewer ears are listening. Shall we see what the veterans kept on the other side of their black oak door?'

XXIX

IN DAYLIGHT, WITH THE SUN SLANTING FROM THE WEST, Cunobelin's grave mound was a peaceful place.

Breaca stood inside, facing the back wall with her knife in her hand. Experimentally, she stabbed the dry earth, and then again, a handspan to the right.

Go more to the left. The opening was aligned for the sun's angle on the day of my death.

She knew him by his voice; not the texture of it, dry as the dead earth, but the round curves of the vowels that had been Caradoc's after him and she heard still daily in Cygfa, who was most like her father, and so most closely mirrored her grandfather.

She turned, slowly. Had it not been daylight, she might not have seen him. He was not as distinct as her father had been and far less than the newly dead of the burning city, bright with the shock of their slaughter.

Cunobelin, Hound of the Sun, war leader of two tribes, was a twist in the evening light, no more substantial than that. As she had done in the night, Breaca patched him with Graine's eyes and Cygfa's hair that he might seem more readily human. He smiled for her then, and she saw that more easily than the rest; his smile had always been the warmest part of him.

She set her knife on the floor. 'I thought the westerly sun might warm you more than the chill light of dawn,' she said.

'If you would rather I not disturb your mound, I'll leave it now.'

Why did you come again? Like all the ancient dead, his voice was the rustle of wind in winter leaves.

'I saw the sun slide off the bronze doors and it reminded me of what Luain mac Calma did for you on the day we first brought you here.'

Mac Calma did it better.

'Yes. The engineer who built the temple to honour Claudius knew how to celebrate the full light of the noon sun, but Luain mac Calma built this mound so that the sun honoured you in its setting as well as its rising.'

Breaca lifted her knife and pricked the tip along the wall to the left and found the rectangle, as long as her arm and half as wide, where the earth was packed less hard. She began to dig there, using the back edge of the blade.

Clots of earth fell out over her. Brushing them away, she said, 'I met Caradoc in here on the third day of your funeral. We fought; he had just fathered Cygfa by another woman, and I had not known; these things mattered then. I was going to put your ring on the bier as my honouring of you. He stopped me, saying that you would not want that gift returned.'

As with so many things, my third son knew me best. It is to my eternal regret that I did not care for him better.

'He would have been a different man if you had, and perhaps not as great.' The truth of that sat newly between them. Breaca hacked with greater energy at the walls. 'Remembering Caradoc, I remembered also the last time I saw you in life. You called me daughter, and made an oath.' She gave more power to the words, sending them to echo off the curving walls. ' "The gods have not seen fit to grant me a daughter. Now, perhaps, I have the beginnings of one. If you need help in the name of the Sun Hound, it will be given, even to the ends of the earth and the four winds." '

. . . even to the ends of the earth and the four winds.

Two voices spoke the binding of the oath. The dead man's was the stronger.

'Is it binding beyond the grave?' she asked.

Always. As you will find in your turn. Humour warmed his voice, and something deeper, that might have been regret. *What would you ask of one who is bound to give aid? Would you have*

*healing from a dead man you did not trust in life? Would you trust
in my care for you – daughter of my spirit?*

The quality of his voice reached her, where his smile and his
presence had not. Truthfully, she said, 'You are grandsire to my
children. If you were to offer me healing, I would welcome it and
trust its giving.'

The earthen wall was crumbling faster under her knife. She
stabbed through living turf to the clear air beyond. A strand of
evening sunlight threaded in through the gap and cast amber light
on the floor at the Sun Hound's feet.

He became easier to see; a strong man with a pelt of tawny hair
and the cloud-grey eyes she had loved in his son. He regarded her
thoughtfully, no longer smiling.

*In all your rememberings, do you recall the prophecy of the
ancestor-dreamer?*

Caution pricked up the length of her spine. She remembered,
then, to whom she was speaking: the man who could outmatch any
other at the game of Warrior's Dance, and who never stopped playing. She turned, and laid down the knife for a second time. For the
first time, she gave him her undivided attention.

'It would be a hard thing to forget,' she said. 'I brought my
children east on the strength of it, knowing I might lose them. My
daughter has gone west unhealed because of it. My son moulds his
life around it, striving to be something he does not understand.'

The twist in the sun sharpened. The air at its margins became
less blurred. *You were given three tasks to complete*, he said. *Name
them for me.* The soft edges of his vowels were as iron.

It was not hard to take herself back along the path of her life, to
find again the cave in the mountains and the taunting presence
of the ancestor-dreamer; only something Breaca would not have
chosen to do.

From clear memory, she said, 'For the first task, I was to find a
way to give back to the people the heart and courage they had lost.
For the second, I was to find a way to call forth the warriors and
to arm them, to find the warrior with the eyes and heart of a
dreamer to lead them. At the last, I was to find the mark that is
ours – the ancestor's and mine – and seek its place in my soul.'

She was breathing fast when she finished, as if they had matched
swords in challenge. In her own defence, she said, 'The Eceni have

been given heart to rise in revolt. The war host is gathered and armed. The mark of the ancestor-dreamer has been revealed as Briga's. If it rests in my soul, it is up to the god to show it. I have done what I can.'

No, you have not. Who is the warrior with the eyes and heart of a dreamer who can lead your people, and give them back the heart and courage they have lost? His eyes burned her, studs of molten flint that pierced her soul.

She had no answer for that.

Think. He was leaving. The threat and promise of his presence became less tangible. What was left of him came closer, so that she could feel the place where the air moved around him. *Find the answer and it is all answers. Think.*

He laid a hand on her head and she was cold and hot together. A depth of care swept her so profound as to leave her shuddering, and a passion for life that she had known once, and forgotten.

Cunobelin said, *It has given me great pleasure to see you again, daughter of my soul. If you feel so moved, it would be good to have the window open, to let Luain mac Calma's dream live again.*

His parting voice fell about her lightly, like autumn rain. *In the asking is the healing, and the answer. Remember, too, my other gift. Neither was it given lightly.*

Feet brushed on grass. A cloak whispered, not Theophilus' robes. A living voice said, 'Breaca? Do you want to be alone?'

Airmid paused at the open grave mouth, a little back so that she had to shield her eyes from the low-set western sun. Her gaze took in the new light cast on the floor and the clods of hacked earth heaped at the back wall and the unsheathed knife laid on top. 'You've cut a window in the back wall,' she said.

Breaca said, 'It was here before, when the mound was first built. Luain mac Calma made it so that the light came in from the west to fall on the urn that held Cunobelin's ashes.'

'He bathed the dead with two suns. I'd forgotten.' Airmid hesitated, as if she might leave. 'Did you come to find peace? Or to talk with the dead?'

'Both. Come in.'

Airmid smelled of river water and Theophilus' rosemary oil

more than flesh-smoke and the blood and terror and pain of the healing fields. She did not bring much of war to disturb the quiet of the grave. She came to sit opposite, in the darker shadows. Tentatively, she said, 'The battle for the temple is almost over. I saw what you did to free Illenna's mother. It was an honourable thing.'

Breaca frowned. 'The woman with the rust-coloured hair? I'd forgotten her. I didn't do it for the honour. She was a mother who had lost her daughter. In all the killing, there was no need to make more pain.'

'Breaca?' Airmid reached for her hand. 'Do you need me to tell you not to fight any more if it sickens you?'

'No, it's obvious. I was coming to find you, to tell you that I was going to give my shield and blade to Cunomar because Valerius does not yet command enough support amongst the war host. Then I saw the sun pass off the temple doors and remembered a promise.'

She opened her hand. Cunobelin's ring lay on it, which had been his first gift. The gold did not spark with any particular life, but lay still and quiet on her palm in the evening light. It was heavy with a man's weight. On the flat surface was a hound, raising its muzzle to greet the sun. Breaca pressed it into the calloused flesh of her thumb and watched the hound mark grow white and then red.

Watching the colours fade, she said, 'Cunomar has spent years yearning to be the warrior with the eyes and heart of a dreamer, trying to build himself to be that. I am his mother. I wanted him to succeed. Until today, I believed it possible.'

Gently Airmid said, 'Your son is exceptional, and an honour to both of his parents, but no follower of the she-bear has the mind and heart of a dreamer, nor will they ever. Their hearts are given in oath to the bear, which is a great thing, and enough. Cunomar will learn to celebrate that and it will make him the stronger.'

There was such calm in the knowing of that, in having a half-met thought confirmed. Breaca tried the ring on her fingers. It was too big for any except her thumb. She let it hang there, loosely, a spark of honeyed warmth in the light, and wondered why it was so difficult to speak.

She waited for Airmid to fill the silence, which lengthened, unfilled.

In time, when waiting was harder than speaking, Breaca said,

'Valerius, then. It has always been him; he began as a warrior, but the dreamer is as strong in him now, if not stronger. I knew it when he came back to us, only that I did not know how to disappoint Cunomar.'

A small stifled cough, or a laugh, or perhaps the beginnings of weeping reached her across the short space.

Breaca raised her eyes at last from the ring. Airmid was staring at her, blinking. A wide wash of feeling crossed her face that was surprise and laughter and exasperation all together. The dreamer made a tent of her fingers, pressing the tips together, and brought herself by some effort to quiet.

'Breaca, I loved your brother when he was Bán; he was an exceptional child. I grieved for his loss and grieved more when we found he was alive and had lost his soul to the legions. I celebrated and could love him again now that he is Valerius but rides amongst us, but know this: your brother is a dreamer and has been from the day of his birth. If he had remained as Bán and had never been taken, he would be Elder of Mona when his father is gone. It was for this he was conceived and raised and he showed all the promise of its fulfilment as a child.'

Breaca said, 'But he's a warrior. You've seen him fight. He shines in the way Caradoc did, in the way Cygfa still does; or brighter than either.'

'He shines as you do, in fact, and for that we must be grateful that the gods see further than the plans of the elders. Bán would have been an exceptional dreamer, but he would not have known enough to destroy the Ninth, or perhaps to help us destroy the remainder of Paullinus' legions. The gods have shaped him for the need of his time. Very few men could have taken up the burdens he has done and come through them with heart and soul intact. He is a remarkable man and he fights as a remarkable warrior, but he is a dreamer first and a warrior second, and he will never lead the greater mass of the Eceni into battle.'

There was relief in that, too, if only for Valerius' sake.

'Who then?' Breaca said. 'Who else is left? Cygfa has never shown any facility for dreaming, and Dubornos is too damaged. Ardacos is of the she-bear, but if you are right about them, then he can never be—'

'Breaca . . .' Airmid was not smiling now, nor close to laughter.

She leaned forward and put both palms flat on the ground on either side of the sunlight. Her face was luminous in the old light.

'Listen to me. Think. Who was made Warrior of Mona younger than any yet? Who did the elder grandmother lead through the long-nights after the old woman was dead? Who carries the wild-fire that can weld together green youths with no battle experience and carry them so that they come through the fight alive? Who has this morning spoken with the dead in a grave mound, and before that in the caves of the western mountains, and before that on her long-nights? Who has been pushed beyond endurance and should be left to live in peace, but that we need you to lead us, and we need you healed?'

Think.

The Sun Hound had said the same and Breaca had not thought. She could not think now.

The ring dazzled her. She covered it with her hand and looked up. Airmid's gaze was a slant of sun across her face. Breaca looked away, at the earth of the wall.

Airmid said, 'If it's too much, if you can't do it, we can still ask your brother.'

'No. It's not that. I can do it. I want to do it, I just need time to think.'

Not only to think; she needed time simply to listen to the thronging ghosts that came to her then.

The elder grandmother was first, saying again, more gently, her words of the long-nights. *The blood of the ancestors runs in your line, else you would not dream as you do,* and there again, decades later, standing in the corner of Breaca's workshop, directing her in the making of heron-spears that only a dreamer-smith should make; and here now, in the shifting space of the grave mound, saying, *If we had named you dreamer early, would you have made of yourself the warrior that you are?*

The ancestor-dreamer followed and made the same offer as before, redolent now with other meaning: *I promise you nothing, only that I will be with you.* The air crackled with dry, caustic laughter.

Then her father was there, Eburovic, solid in the bulwark of his smithy, making her a blade with the serpent-spear on the pommel, and matching against her in play-fight with the ancestor-blade of his lineage, which bore the feeding she-bear. He was real to her now, in Cunobelin's grave mound, as he had not been when his blade had been lifted to moonlight from the dark of Briga's altar.

She felt the touch of his smile. 'We sent your blade to Mona with a warrior of the Coritani,' she said. 'I'm sorry.'

Don't be. I asked for it. There are things yet to be done with it. For now, enough that you know who you are. He was everything the Sun Hound was not: an open, clear, straightforward man, shining in his honesty; she loved him, and he was dead.

The dead came less distinctly after Eburovic, or she was less able to see them; Macha came to her and Gunovic and Maroc and a dozen other elder dreamers of Mona, each one less tangible than the last.

In time, there was only sunlight, and Airmid, living dreamer to the Boudica, who was solid and real and sat very still, as if breathing might break something too fragile to risk with a breath.

Breaca said, 'Why did you not tell me before?'

'In the beginning, I thought you knew. How could you not when all of your life has pointed to this? Later, when it was clear that you didn't . . .' Airmid looked away for the first time, and back again. 'I love you. I would not burden you with more than you can bear.'

'And now?'

'Now you know who you are; and the choice is still yours. You don't have to take this if you don't want it. The Boudica leads to victory because she *is* that victory, not because she has been cajoled into leadership, however benignly.'

'Benignly?' Breaca pressed her palms to her face. The ancestor had been last of the ancient dead to leave. In the after-shine of her parting, a war spear cracked twice over and became crooked. The two-headed serpents of its haft writhed out and wove over it, staring to past and to future: Briga's sign, before it was ever hers; god of war, bringer of life and death, hope and loss, holder of past and present, and all that stands outside time.

A single unchallenged god-voice said, *Boudica.*

'Airmid?' Breaca reached out, blindly. Long, lean fingers caught her own and held them, offering strength and an anchor in the present. Breaca leaned back and, as they had done in childhood, they lifted each other to standing. The patch of sunlight lay between them. They came together awkwardly, as strangers, afraid of what they might find. Breaca tilted her head to the shoulder that was offered. Airmid kissed the place on her crown where the Sun Hound had placed his hand. The feeling now was all of heat, passing down into the earth beneath their feet.

'You're back,' Airmid said. 'Welcome.' Her voice was something to revel in, to enter and never leave.

'I am back. And I do want to lead the war host. I always did. It was only that I thought I wasn't fit.'

'You are fit now. The warriors will see it, I promise you, down to the greenest of untested youths.'

Breaca eased herself free. She stooped to pick up her knife. 'It still may be too late. I left the field of battle early. If the warriors of the war host think I'm lost and have already accepted Valerius or Cunomar, we can't undo what's done. Would you come down with me to see?'

XXX

FIRE HAD NOT YET REACHED THE ANTECHAMBER TO THE TEMPLE, only a drifting of smoke that covered the smell of anticipation and battle fever that the veterans had left behind.

Beneath that, more dryly, was the scent of incense and old, spilled wine. Cunomar felt the hairs rise up on the back of his neck. Like a hound, he stepped stiff-legged into the space and turned round in a circle studying all of it.

It was a place that had been much inhabited without anyone's ever having lived in it until the veterans had need. The stone pavings of the floor were tracked by many feet, worn in places where the traffic had been highest. The walls, too, were of faced stone, and the roof of bare tiles with no lining. Torch holders stood out with black planes of soot behind from countless nights of burning, but there were no chests for storage, nor beds, nor signs of a workshop.

Instead, chain mail and scale armour hung from wall brackets alongside pieces of horse harness and old battle-worn weapons fixed on polished wood, preserved as they were when last used with bloodstains on hilt and blade.

Between and among them were the standards of the legions made in miniature; small gilded eagles clutching crossed lightning bolts stared from each wall to the door, a wild boar in red ran across a blue pennant that stretched half the width of one wall, a goat stood carved in time and wood, a horse, a three-headed dog, a ram with curled horns such as was never seen in Britannia; all of them were more than their shape alone, and the living wood knew it; the sense of being watched, then, was perhaps explained.

Cunomar said, 'This feels like a shrine to the might of the legions. We should be gone from here, and burn it like the rest.'

'This is only the antechamber. The true shrine is in the cellar beneath.' Valerius leaned against the far wall, one arm crooked up to pillow his head. He was grey with exhaustion, or pain, or both.

'The first temple to Mithras ever built in Britannia is in the cellar that can be reached from this room and the centurion's house beyond the garden. I was brought first to the god here.'

'Would you have us preserve it?'

'In the midst of a city that is burning to nothing? No. In any case, the god is in the stones and the earth, not in the places men build for him. He won't mind the touch of fire from here.' Valerius let his legs fold and sank to sit on the floor with his back to the grey wall.

They were alone, but for Longinus who stood quietly by the door, lest too many of the wearily celebrating war host unwittingly disturb the Boudica's brother and son in their conversation.

The necessary people waited close by outside: Ulla and Scerros and a handful of others who gave support without question to Cunomar; Longinus for Valerius, obviously, and Knife and the boy Snail who had found a role tending the wounded, and a wild Hibernian woman with jackdaw eyes, and Huw, the slinger with the scarred face, both of whom fought for Mona.

There were a surprising number of Mona's warriors who supported Valerius and did not appear to notice the existence of the Boudica's son. Cunomar had intended that to change with the battle for the rear gate to the temple. He was not certain that it had.

'We should talk,' Cunomar said, to the man sitting on the floor opposite. 'And then tend to the wounded. My mother withdrew from the battle at its height. She has done what she can and that is momentous; Rome's capital in this province is ours and we can burn every part of it. But we have three more legions and other towns to take before we can call ourselves free. To succeed further, the war host must be led from strength, not weakness. You said once that you would not let one man's search for personal glory destroy the war host. I would ask you now if you still think—'

'The leadership is yours.'

'—that my conduct in the taking of the city . . . What?' Cunomar rubbed his one ear, and felt foolish that he had done so.

Valerius' head had fallen back against the wall so that he looked up at the ceiling, as if he might find inspiration there, or support.

He said, 'The leadership of your mother's war host is yours. Those who follow me will continue to do so, and I will follow your leadership. You have only to say what you intend and we will do it.' His voice was entirely flat.

Something had disturbed the warriors outside the door. Raised voices twittered, sharp as morning birdsong. Very suddenly, Cunomar wanted to be in the fresh air, with only the stench of the newly dead thickening the air.

He stood, pressing his hands to the wood of the table. 'Let me be clear. You are saying that you concede all leadership of the full war host to me and that—'

'Julius?' Longinus spoke from the doorway. There was fondness in the word that went deeper than the careless intimacy of the battlefield or the bed, and a depth of care that took notice of the other man's exhaustion and forgave a decision badly made, and spoke of something else, that brought hope in a hopeless world.

All of these Cunomar heard, and misplaced, because he did not at first understand that the Thracian was talking to Valerius, who evidently had another name.

Thus he turned too late, only after Valerius had risen, and Longinus, quite gently, had said again, 'Julius, your sister is here.'

Valerius had thought perhaps he might sleep leaning against the wall, and eat there when he woke and then sleep again, and only after that begin to deal with the aftermath of the decision he had made as he watched his sister leave the battlefield.

Seeing her return, he rose on limbs that resisted, so that he came up stiffly, and more slowly than he wanted, and leaned back on the wall because simply standing was enough.

Breaca leaned against the doorpost, matching him. She wore a cloak in Eceni blue for the first time since the start of the war, pinned with a brooch in the shape of a serpent-spear with tags of old wool hanging down. Stone was with her, less lame than he had been, and Airmid was smiling which was something Valerius thought she had forgotten how to do.

'Have you come to a decision?' The Boudica's voice filled the room, as it would not have done before.

'No,' said Cunomar.

Valerius said, 'Yes.'

Breaca looked from one to the other and back again. The sharp edge of her smile was one that Valerius had seen on a boat, newly come from Gaul, and before that, not since his childhood. He could have wept. It seemed possible that he was actually weeping. He did not put his hand to his face to check.

Amused, his sister said, 'Should I go away again, until at least you find common ground on that?'

'What?' asked Valerius.

'I have just been seen to leave the field of battle. If one or other of you wishes to claim leadership of the war host, I have no right to deny it.'

Valerius had not been weeping, only tired. He laughed, rustily. 'Look behind you,' he said, and nodded past Breaca to the gardens, where the she-bear and the warriors of Mona had joined with the others of the war host and were no longer stripping the dead or lifting the wounded, but gathered in a solid mass of waiting, expectant humanity. 'If you want to turn round and tell them that you're leaving again, you're welcome. I'm not at all certain they'll let you.'

He found the energy to join her at the doorway. Cunomar had the sense to come to stand at her other side. Together, the Boudica, her brother and her son faced the mass of men and women who had just followed them to the edge of death and back; each one had been driven to the edges of resilience, each one made that small step beyond where he or she could have gone alone.

Between them, they had taken by force the first and only Roman city in their land. To do so, they had fought for two days almost without break in a way none had ever experienced or imagined; fighting through streets and in brick-built villas, against armed Romans and unarmed Trinovantes. They had killed at times with honour and courage and at other times without either of these, and the taint of that, and the euphoria of victory, lay equally on them.

They were greater than they had been, perhaps greater than they had ever imagined, and could be greater still, but they needed to be told so, and to be given a reason to find the paths to victory in themselves.

Out of habit, and two decades' training, Valerius opened his mouth to speak. Breaca was there before him.

'Warriors of the Boudica . . .' Her voice carried better than it had done when she first addressed them at the marsh edge, but not far enough; the garden was full and more were pressing in at the gate, or climbing the unclimbable walls. The hum and the press of a spreading rumour drowned out the first words, even when they were shouted down by others, who thus made more noise.

A plinth stood to one side of the door, that had until recently borne an urn. Breaca vaulted onto it, and stood framed by the white wall of the temple. Like all of them, she was burned and stained with ash and smoke and the debris of battle. Unlike them, she had been visited by a god, and it showed. She stood tall against the white stone of the temple and the late afternoon sun cast gold over the burnished red of her hair and polished to shining jewels the iron and bronze of her belt buckle, of her sword hilt, of her serpent-spear brooch.

Other gods came to add their touch: the wind lifted her hair and made of it a widening copper helmet. Her cloak bellied back, so that she was late sky blue against the white, with the cast of sun all around; a crow danced on the gilded tiles of the rooftops and cawed three times. The last call fell into a profound and waiting silence.

There was no question, then, of the leadership. If the Boudica's brother or son had tried to take it, their own supporters would have killed them; if the Boudica had tried to walk away, they would have blocked the gates until she gave her whole heart to staying.

Seeing that, knowing it, Breaca cast her voice out to its farthest reach, and began again.

'Warriors of the Boudica. You have won a city, and the first part of a war. Not one of you is without injury. Each one of you has lost friends, lovers, brothers, sisters, fathers and mothers in this battle and all that has led to it. But still, we have faced the army of Rome, which has fashioned an empire by virtue of its own might, and we have won. This was the legions' capital, their first fortress, their pride in the province of Britannia. When we leave, it will be ash, to be blown on the wind and taken back to the earth. Never again will an army sink its foundations into the clean ground of Camul's dun.

'This is only the beginning: Rome's other towns must be laid flat, Rome's legions must be destroyed. Our land must be made free. With your help, with your blood and your courage and the help of the gods, we will make it so. Our children and our children's children will live in a land in which Rome is a distant threat, long forgotten, and we will be the cause of that. Never forget. We are the war host that will vanquish the legions.'

She spoke the last into a silence as thick and crisp as when she had started. It softened, slowly, as five thousand battle-weary minds understood the full measure of what they had done and what they were asked to do.

They needed a response and were all too tired to think until, far at the back, someone unnamed shouted, *'Boudica!'* and gave them their answer.

'Boudica! Boudica! Boudica!'

The sound rebounded off the walls and would have raised the golden tiles on the temple's roof, had they not already been melted.

Breaca stepped down from her plinth. They swept apart to let her in, and came together again behind her. Very slowly, she walked through the middle of her host to the back gate of the garden. As geese follow the leader, they followed her out, and through the city to the green space beyond where they could rest, and eat and retell the stories of Camulodunum's burning, and plan all that was yet to come.

It was evening before Breaca was alone.

The full five thousand had not come each to speak to her personally, it only felt like it. Then there was the time of planning with those who had taken responsibility for strategy while she had not. Then Cunomar left, and the she-bear and the warriors of Mona. Cygfa, Dubornos and Ardacos finished their quiet thanks and the brief, understated eulogies of battle.

In the end, even Longinus, Theophilus and Airmid had stepped away, to find the evening cooking fires and the smoke that kept the dusk insects at bay. Only Valerius was left. Breaca sat with her brother on the turf by a smouldering heap of ash on the western edge of the encampment. One or other of them should have scraped the embers into the centre and laid on more wood from the small, neat pile left in the morning, when the world was a different place. Neither had yet found the energy.

Valerius began to shed his chain mail. He stood, bent double from the waist, while the slither of linked iron inverted itself and, chiming softly, oozed over his head.

He shook himself free and straightened up. His hair was vertical. His woollen undershirt was marked with sweat and rust and blood. The mail had left a reddened lattice of prints on his upper arms.

He attended to none of these, but sat down and said, 'They would not have agreed to that so readily if it was me or Cunomar who had suggested it.'

Breaca reached at last for a piece of cut wood and laid it across the fire. Through the new smoke, she said, 'I'm sorry there was no time to talk to you before. Are you happy to go south to take Canonium and the other towns? They're farther and harder to reach than Verulamium.'

'Verulamium is the easier battle, and by far the more glorious. Cunomar will do well with it. Yes, I'm happy to go south.'

It was Breaca's plan, conceived in the moment when she stood on the plinth in the garden and saw her war host so clearly divided. Even when they came together again, united in the roar of unison, it had seemed good to split them in two; fewer mouths to feed in each travelling host, fewer causes for conflict, twice the fighting power.

She had offered it, and it had been taken: Valerius had agreed to lead his followers south and then west to assault the Roman towns and ports along the banks of the Great River, ending at the place where the legions had crossed in their first invasion, which the Romans called Vespasian's Bridge; Cunomar had leaped at the chance to take his faction due west to annihilate Rome's second city, Verulamium. They already had scouts who knew each other; it had not been difficult to arrange the means by which a relay of riders could keep the leaders of the two smaller hosts in touch with each other.

Valerius leaned his back against his saddle packs and peered through the growing cloud of midges at his sister. He looked thoughtful, as Cunobelin had done, but weighed with the weariness of life.

'You didn't say what you were going to do while we are clearing Rome from the southern towns and ports. Cunomar thinks you will be with him, but is afraid that you may join me, which is why he didn't ask. The rest think his fears are right. I don't need you and you know it. So where will you be?'

Breaca watched a crow gather its courage to approach one of the unmoved dead from the temple's front courtyard. She said, 'Airmid has asked that I not fight for nine days. I'm going north to find Venutios of the Brigantes, to see if he will bring his warriors to join the host. He has at least two thousand spears with battle experience who will answer his call, and they hate Rome as much as any. We'll do better against the legions if we have them with us.'

'We still shouldn't face the legions in a line fight,' Valerius said. 'Nothing has changed that. Even Cunomar would agree, I think, after facing the veterans in the garden. If one century was hard, imagine a legion of a full five thousand.' The evening light lay on his face. He shuffled sideways a little and, taking out his belt knife, began to clean the grime of battle from beneath his fingernails.

'It won't come to that. We don't have to let it. The scouts can carry messages between all three of us. Mid-summer is five days from now. If your warriors and Cunomar's can be done by four or five days after that, you can meet at a place west of Verulamium. I will bring Venutios' warriors south and we can join the host again and you can tell us how to find victory against three legions.'

'If Venutios agrees to send his warriors,' Valerius said. 'He may not.'

'He may not,' Breaca agreed equably. The crow flapped from the wall and dropped raggedly to the body below. Bird of Briga, it called to its fellows to join it. Two others flew in, so that three fed together.

A last threshold waited, beyond which was a land she had never entered and from which she could not return. As three crows fed, Breaca said to her brother, 'I heard you had made me a spear, like the heron-spears of the Caledonii but with iron instead of silver for the blade, and that Airmid had carved the haft with serpents, so that it was a true serpent-spear, with no feathers to tip the balance, that might be used in battle. Is it true?'

Valerius stopped cleaning his fingernails. He laid his knife neatly on the front of his saddle. 'We told no-one. How did you know?'

'Nemain told me. At the end of the fever. She said you believed it would hold me more strongly to life.'

The moon had not risen yet. He looked west, to the setting sun. His face was Macha's made harder by battle. 'I was arrogant in my despair,' he said at last. 'You don't have to take it.'

'I want to, but not yet. When I come back from the north, and am whole, I would like it then.'

She rose and took his arm and he was Bán again and she Breaca and they were going to the roundhouse for an evening meal and life was as it had always been before the nightmare of the legions, or could be allowed to seem so for a night at least before they parted.

XXXI

CORVUS, PREFECT OF THE QUINTA GALLORUM, TEMPORARILY assigned to the governor's personal guard, celebrated mid-summer's dawn becalmed on the deck of a wide-waisted cargo sloop with a single bellied sail that waddled through the waves as a duck through a farm pond and left all but the most sea-hardened men vomiting in their bunks.

Corvus had not thought of himself as particularly sea-hardened, but clearly was more so than those who travelled with him. He stood wide-legged on the aft deck with the steersman and the ship's master and lifted a goblet of well-watered wine to the bleeding edge of the sun.

He had never been a priest or functionary in any of Rome's cults, but he spoke a few words to Jupiter, who seemed the most reason-able of the gods, and then spilled some of the wine into the green-grey sea for Neptune, that they might perhaps see some wind shortly, and come safely back to shore at a place where neither tides, nor currents, nor hidden rocks, might kill them. Last, in Alexandrian, which neither the master nor the steersman under-stood, he spoke aloud the care of his heart to the listening spirits of those who were closest to him, as he had done at every winter and summer solstice since he first came into the legions.

The ritual calmed him, as it had always done, and made the insanity of what they were doing seem less. Taken in the right light, the venture could seem to be heroic and doubtless would be made to seem so afterwards in the senate and baths of Rome, by men who enjoyed listening to the deaths of others and considered the search for glory and displays of courage to be entirely admirable in anyone other than themselves.

Corvus gave a last sluice of wine to the water and offered the goblet, two-handed, to the steersman who drank and passed it to the master, who drank and handed it back in like manner to Corvus, so that they each shared the mid-year bounty with the gods. The wine was mellow and smelled of autumn and ripe fruit. Corvus let it rest a while on his tongue and swallowed it with the next heave of the deck.

'Land today?' He spoke the words with exaggerated clarity.

'Nightfall.' The ship's master was from the northlands, a giant of a man with yellow hair and a ring of blue dots tattooed in the weather-red skin round his neck. His Latin was as rudimentary as his Gaulish and both were greater than his grasp of Britannic tongues. His understanding of light craft and the seas between Hibernia, Gaul and Britannia was exceptional. He was paid a retainer that amounted to more than the annual salary for an entire tent party of legionaries and their centurion, and was worth twice as much for his ability to bring craft to land safely.

The choice of ship had not been his; unaccountably, among tribes who were notionally entirely well disposed towards Rome, there had been no ships free when the governor had needed them. If the Nordic master had not used some of his own gold to keep the crew that he wanted, they would have had no mariners either. The cargo sloop had been bought, at breathtaking expense, from the son of a man whose life Corvus had once saved. Even then, they had been begged to take it after dark so that he could say it had been stolen. Besides its crew, it carried exactly sixteen additional men, with one horse each. Corvus chose not to imagine how they were going to ride safely across country to Londinium if no-one in the pacified territories was prepared even to sell them a ship.

The blond northman nodded forward, to where the ship's one small-boat rested in a sling. 'Tonight,' he said. 'Row. Dark. Horses swim behind. Not seen.' He rolled his eyes graphically. 'Birds keep dry.'

The pigeons were Flavius' special care; there were six, all homed to the flight in the fortress of the XXth whence a man on a fast horse might ride in less than half a morning to the coast. He cared for them as if they were his children and had told the northman, who seemed to consider them valid rations, that if he ate them, he would eat his testicles immediately after. At the time, it had seemed a strangely credible threat.

Corvus said, 'Tonight?' and tried to think what it might take to get the governor and his men upright by nightfall and able to walk and possibly – please all the gods that every one of the horses had come through the voyage safely – to ride.

'Tonight.' The giant grinned. 'Wind come soon. Boat go fast. Waves small. Governor less sick.'

They rowed at night, in the dark before the moon rose, with the oars and the breasting horses making phosphorescent fire in the sea, so that they left a fading trail that marked where they had been.

The governor was pale and smelled overly of peppermint oil, which did not entirely cover the smell of vomit. Even so, he was first to step ashore, and stood creditably straight with his blade ready while the others turned the boat round and sent it back with the ship's steersman rowing, to wait offshore for their signal, and Corvus and the two men he had brought with him led the horses ashore, and worked by feel in the almost-dark to find grass with which to dry them off and gave them handfuls of corn to bring the life back to their eyes and make up for the cold and the dark and the sea. They checked their legs and their flanks and found no cuts or swellings or heat and Corvus thanked Neptune openly for his gift of horses from the sea.

The quarter-moon rose in a veiled sky. By its light, fifteen men gathered in the dark on the sloping sand around their governor and general, wet to the thighs from the final wade ashore, wrapped tight in winter cloaks against a summer night's cold.

Eleven of them were of the XIVth and XXth legions. They were volunteers, but only in so far as the order had been couched as a request; none of them would have considered refusing. Not all were officers. Like Alexander of Macedon, Suetonius Paullinus had made the effort to know the names and achievements of the men who served under him, and so each was of middle age, a little younger than the governor himself, and each had proved himself outstanding in valour or wit or resource either in Britannia or in Paullinus' Mauretanian campaigns.

Only the two cavalry men were not of the governor's direct choosing: Ursus and Flavius came at Corvus' invitation, the one to offer support, the other because it was no longer safe to leave him behind where he could not be watched, and for his precious pigeons, which had kept dry on the row over and might yet save their lives.

Last and least of the fifteen was a local guide named Gaius who had lived so long at the fortress of the XXth legion that he had acquired an accent traceable directly to the gutters of three streets that passed between the Mons Avertina and the Tiber in Rome. It had been rumoured on board ship that the governor had promised him citizenship if the war against the tribes was won. More plausible rumour said that the man had three sons of whom he was exceeding proud and that he wanted citizenship for them more than he wanted life itself.

Suetonius Paullinus, governor of all Britannia, stood on the weed and sand of a native shore that should have been friendly, or at least not hostile. He wore leather armour, because he had no intention of dying if the small-boat sank, and his sword was built for use, not for the parade ground. The hilt was covered in boarhide, and the cross-piece, so that no part of it would catch sun or moon and reveal him. His helmet was matt with age and could have been any legionary's. They were all the same: grim, hard men who understood exactly what it was they were required to do, and how great were the risks.

His gaze read them, and was content. He said, 'From here until we reach and take Vespasian's Bridge, we will act as if the natives are the enemy. We will ride fast, we will ride hard. We will avoid confrontation or even meeting with the tribes, but whom we meet, we kill.'

They travelled hard, but not fast.

It was said that the emperor Tiberius, in the days when he was a general in the Germanies and not yet an emperor, had once ridden two hundred and twenty miles in a single day. If it were true, he could have ridden the full breadth of Britannia in that same day, except that the roads did not exist and it would have required him to change horses at the post stations every twenty miles.

Suetonius Paullinus and his fifteen men did not have his resources. They rode on trackways and goat paths and were dependent for their directions on the lead of Gaius, who was of the northern Silures and did not know the routes well, and each man had to nurse his horse, knowing that if it foundered, he would have to find another one immediately or be left at the wayside.

They met very few natives, and all of them warriors in paint, with kill-feathers woven into their hair. None of them came close enough to engage and the risk of ambush, or of destroying the horses, was too great to follow them. A boy was killed, who did not run fast enough and did not know that Flavius, like another before him, was skilled in the use of a throwing knife.

Beyond that one inglorious kill, there was nothing but hard days in the saddle, frequent turns back on themselves when a track proved impassable, and only the growing breadth of the river to tell them they were making any progress at all.

They came to the first of the deserted trading posts around noon on the fourth day of their travel. It was not an imposing place, a wharf no bigger than the jetty on Mona, lagged about with river weed and the debris of a skirmish; a length of rope swayed in the brown water, caught on the wharf's upstream footing, a tattered piece of woven wool showing green beneath it, the remnant of a child's cloak shed in haste or by accident in flight.

Eight merchant's huts were lined along the river up- and downstream of the wharf. The nearest was largest, paid for by the river tolls of those wishing to cross to the smaller jetty on the far bank, and the greater trading taxes of those who had bypassed the lower ports and sailed from the open seas through the mouth of the river and up this far.

Only one man could be spared at a time for reconnaissance. Corvus drew the white pebble from the helmet and rode down alone to look. He walked his black colt along the water's edge. The horse was not strictly his remount, but he had come through the swim to Mona better than the mare had done and the Batavian who had ridden him was dead: Corvus did not want to come back and find the man's soul-brother had taken his horse as were-geld.

The beast shied at a flapping door-hide and again more violently at a sow that had been left in a sty without food or water and screamed when it saw Corvus coming. He opened the gateway and let her out and she charged, ears flapping, for the river bank. A scatter of ducks rose in panic, honking so that for a moment there was screaming pandemonium and Ursus brought half of Paullinus' troop at the gallop with swords drawn thinking that Corvus was under attack.

'There's no-one here,' Corvus said. He had already checked each hut. The hearts of the fires were cold and damp, but, on a day when it was warm enough to ride in shirtsleeves, there was no mould yet on the fire stones. He said, 'They've been gone more than two days, less than five.'

Ursus said, 'Have they gone across the river, or east? They can't have gone west; we'd have met them.'

Gaius, the Siluran guide, arrived after the first flurry of action. He had some facility as a tracker. He walked the length of the eight huts and came back to lean on the pigsty. He was taller than any of them, as the northman had been. He stooped a little, not to seem so. 'The boats have gone,' he said. 'Some of them likely went across, but at least three wagons travelled east along the trackway.'

'How far are we from Vespasian's Bridge?'

'Half a day's ride. They will be there long ahead of us.'

'And any others who have gone there.' Corvus swung himself into the saddle. 'I hope the magistrates of the port are prepared for a thousand extra mouths to feed.'

The magistrates of the settlement that straggled along the northern bank of the Thamesis on either side of Vespasian's Bridge were not well prepared. The pandemonium in the circle of huts and trading booths and the central corn exchange matched the chaos of the sow and ducks for noise and was spread over a far wider area.

It was a trading port based on a bridge, and the bridge itself was by far the most imposing piece of architecture within it. The place was barely a town: it had a tax room built of oak timbers with weighing scales and a clerk's desk and another room built in stone for keeping records. It had two rows of stables for guest-horses and mounts for messengers who might have need to travel to Camulodunum where the centre of government lay. It had eight taverns, of varying reputation, and two brothels, one that supplied women and one that supplied everything else that might command money.

Of the hundred or so dwellings, the best were merchants' houses, and even those were little more than huts built of wattle with thatched roofs. Cattle and sheep and pigs and goats and five-toed chickens strutted on the rooftops and pecked in the barnyards. It had hay stores and feed stores and a granary and a string of wells for when the river became swollen with spring floodwater and turned too brown to eat. It had small muddy lanes linking house to house and passage to passage and slightly wider ones linking all of these to the great northern roads that swept northwest to Verulamium and up towards Mona and northeast to Camulodunum. It had a ship, wallowing at the dock, that was being loaded with all that was precious of those who commanded it, ready to flee.

It did not have a wall.

Paullinus pulled up his group on a wooded slope set well back from the chaos. They had been seen, but not yet approached. They sat for a while, watching wagon after wagon, family after family, roll inward from the two broad trackways, and none roll outward again. There were more children than adults and more women than men. They were unarmed, unless one considered their eating knives to be armament, which only an optimist, or a desperate man, might do. Like herded sheep, they converged in increasing numbers on Vespasian's Bridge. It arced across the river, broad enough for a wagon and a horse side by side, high enough for a sea-going vessel to pass underneath, handsome as any sculpture, a testament to the engineers of the legions who could create beauty and utility together. A man could weep for the beauty of it, and the inevitability of its loss.

Tired of the bridge and its township before the others, Corvus watched instead a haze of smoke on the eastern horizon and so was first to see the Eceni scouts.

'Enemy,' he said quietly. 'East of here and north of the scrub oak with the anvil-shaped cloud behind. Fifteen that I can see and I will bet there is at least one more. Youths on foot. Knives only. War braids and kill-feathers. They are equal in numbers to us, and most are women. That won't be an accident.'

They were seasoned men and they had fought in the west, where for every one of the enemy seen, there were a dozen unseen in the rocks and crannies of the mountains. They did not spin their horses, or shout, or stare, but talked and bantered amongst themselves and shifted their mounts a little to lessen their boredom and eased their blades in their sheaths for the practice of it until, as if by coincidence and certainly by chance, they were all facing a little more eastward and could look without seeming to at the place Corvus had described.

The scouts rose from their hiding, one by one. They stood half naked among the scrub elder and seeding thistles, wide-legged, with their knives in their belts, not deigning to unsheathe them in the presence of Rome. They were sixteen, of whom eight were women.

Once, the governors of Britannia had flogged men for suggesting that women fought in the native armies. Now, Suetonius Paullinus, fifth of the governing line, said, 'They send us the flower of their youth.'

'They send them to look down on Vespasian's Bridge, to show that the attack will come with the dawn,' said Corvus. 'Their gods do not support a battle of which fair warning has not been given.'

'They don't fear that the magistrates and people will rally a defence?'

'Do you see one happening?'

They did not. Fighting men know the sounds of panic and they were issuing now from the port at Vespasian's Bridge. Where before had been chaos was now clear panic.

On the bridge, the bottleneck became a logjam and carts broke their axles rather than back up or give way. Figures climbed over them and round them and fell into the water and were ignored by the others who thought that safety lay south.

On the river, the ship loading at the wharf was flooded, suddenly, with men and their families who abandoned the need to preserve their family silver and fought each other instead for room on the gangplank and then on the deck. The whistle of the master shrieked loud enough to be heard on the hillside. The men it summoned were armed.

Paullinus leaned on the front arch of his saddle. He ran his tongue round his upper teeth, thoughtfully, and the fifteen men around him found other things to watch, rather than catch his eye and so his attention. Twice in his past, once in Mauretania and before that in Parthia, Paullinus had faced a decision and had given the men with him the opportunity to vote on their action. Those who chose wrongly were allowed to fall on their swords before the rest moved on. The ones who hesitated had been staked out and left to die at their leisure.

The governor drew his horse to one side. 'Plebius?'

From the beginning, Plebius had ridden at his general's right hand. A one-eyed duplicarius of the Second cohort of the XIVth, he had a natural head for numbers and was obsessively conscientious. By default, he had become the quartermaster of their small troop, and carried the coins and gold they needed for bribes and payment. Wooden-faced, he pushed his horse beyond the hearing of his peers and listened while the governor explained what he wanted.

Given his orders, Plebius nodded and searched his packs and emptied what he found into the bowl of his helmet. Metal chimed heavily on metal.

Suetonius Paullinus swung his horse on its quarters and faced the semi-circle of men he had chosen to accompany him and whose opinions he professed to respect. His face was never expressive, but his eyes, for the most part, on most days, spoke from his soul. Now, in the cold wind that soughed up from the river, they were flat and watchful.

He said, 'You will each take one denarius and one as from the helmet.'

The helmet passed round. Corvus was last. The as was a copper teardrop against the dull iron. He resisted the temptation to bite it and feel the texture of the metal. The denarius was silver and too obviously foiled to be worth the biting. A young, thin Augustus stared moodily east from its one surface. On the other side, a younger, thinner bull stood haltered and garlanded, awaiting the sacrifice. Corvus closed his hand over it; the bull god had never been his.

The governor said, 'Two choices: we can stay and rally a defence in the township in an effort to preserve the bridge which is our best route to the south coast; or we can leave now, and ride hard for the coast and take ship and return in due course with the legions to face the Eceni war host en masse. Each of these has points to recommend it; I will not labour them. You will hold out your right hand containing a coin. When I request it, you will open your hand to reveal what is hidden. The silver coin votes to stay and defend the bridge. The copper votes to return to the ship and meet the legions wherever we may. Is anyone unclear as to which coin denotes which choice?'

They were not. A man may die cleanly who falls on his sword; every one of them had faced a worse death daily in battle. Each made his choice alone, as a soldier, as an officer of the legions, as a veteran with twenty years of fighting experience, as a man prepared to live and die by the quality of his tactical judgement.

Corvus had made his decision before he saw the scouts; the volume of smoke on the wind told him as much as he needed to know of the size of the advancing war host and the speed with which the port of Vespasian's Bridge would be crushed. He placed his two hands together and when he drew them apart the lighter, smaller, brighter, younger coin was in the right, so light as to barely be there.

He looked around. The rest sat easy on their horses and held out their closed fists so that the governor was ringed by brown skin laced with battle scars.

Only Gaius, the scout, looked uncertain. He could not have missed out on the story of Suetonius Paullinus and the doomed officers of Parthia, but he did not have the years of service to tell him that the only possible answer he could give was the one that military sense dictated. To survive, he had to make the decision as if he led a legion, or a full army; only then would he command Paullinus' respect. What killed men, what caused them to forfeit their honour and their lives in the governor's eyes was sycophancy, or an attempt to buy an ovation from the senate at the expense of winning the war.

They waited, because Gaius could not decide. The veins on his temples beat blue and matt with sweat. His skin was as yellow as his hair. He made a decision and unmade it and for that alone he faced death, and knew it. A watery sun shone on them, making the day hot. In the flowering elder behind, a thrush called. The scouts of the Eceni sat in the long grass and seeded nettles through which they had crawled forward and watched with interest.

In silence thick as curdled whey, Gaius thrust his right arm forward into the ring.

'Reveal yourselves.'

Corvus felt his arm turn of its own accord, and his fingers uncoil. Ursus was on his right. He saw the spark of copper on the grubby palm of the man's hand before he saw his own. The wolfskin had been left behind. He wondered, idly, if that might make them both unlucky.

Flavius, on his left, opened his palm a fraction later. He, too, held copper.

Around, fourteen men held copper tears on their palms. The fifteenth, bearing silver, was Gaius.

The governor's head turned slowly, as an owl's does, without blinking. 'You think Vespasian's Bridge can be fortified?' he asked.

Gaius was not a coward. 'I think the people can be rallied.' His voice was commendably strong.

'Get off your horse.'

He did so.

'Kneel.'

He did so.

'I promised you citizenship and now I grant it. You are Gaius Fortunatus, citizen of Rome and auxiliary officer of the legions in the rank of decurion. Your pay is one sestertius per day. You have been paid in advance. You will earn it.'

The man blinked in the poor light. 'How?'

'By rallying a defence amongst the people of Vespasian's Bridge. How else? You will go there now and hold it or die in its defence. If I hear you have fled, I will have you named traitor throughout the empire and your family will pay for it. Am I clear?'

'You are.'

There are worse ways to die and citizenship passed through the male line unless it was revoked. Gaius turned to look down at the place in which he would die and it seemed to Corvus that the smile that flowered on his face was genuine. He saluted up to the sun and across the river's water and spoke to them in a tongue that had not the least trace of the Tiber in its accent.

They watched him ride down. The Eceni stood at his passing, as if they had some idea of what had taken place.

The governor turned first, and sought out Flavius, who had care of the pigeons, and the centurion of the XXth who acted as his scribe and dictated a brief message to be sent to Agricola, and Galenius of the XIVth who commanded at Mona.

Flavius' care of the birds was of a man with a new horse. He held them gently between careful palms and made sure the message carriers on their legs were firm and would not chafe. He spoke to them in words no-one else could hear so that they bobbed at him, bright-eyed and ready.

He threw them up high, and they were waiting for the lift he gave them and spread their wings and cracked the air and rose and flew straight, one after the other, until four of the six were gone.

The governor saluted them, as he would have done a legate leading a legion to a distant battle. 'If the dreamers set falcons on them, I will have them all crucified.'

They rode west, fast. No-one felt the need to point out that their guide had just been sent to his death; they were all good trackers in their way, and could retrace any path they had taken once. The Eceni scouts put up a war cry as they left, a long ululating howl that echoed from one to the other to the other and lasted long after they were out of sight.

Later, as the sun reached over their heads and sank towards the west and the sea that they were seeking, Paullinus pulled his horse back alongside Corvus' black colt.

'You understand the native tongues better than most. What was it he said to the sun and the river before he rode down to Vespasian's Bridge?'

'Gaius? He was speaking in the tongue of their ancestors. He commended his life and that of his three sons to Lugh of the Shining Spear, god of the sun. In the days when the gods were young, Lugh felt the thirst of eternal fire and came to earth to quench it. He drank the Great River dry and then laid his head down to sleep. Nemain and Manannan together sent rain and the river swelled to flooding, but would not touch the god. It curved round, to leave him sleeping and dry.'

'And so the river is sacred? And the place where it bends, where Vespasian built his bridge, especially so?'

'It is. They would never have built a bridge there. And they do not name it after a Roman general. In the native tongue it is named after the god who first made it sacred. In the tongue of the ancestors, it is Lugdunum.'

The single standing elder by the jetty on Mona was in full flower. A cascade of creamy white frothed and bobbed on the breeze that rose from the sea.

Graine picked a half-head and teased out single flowers and ate them, dusting the pollen on her tunic so that green became green-gold in smudges. Shuffling forward, she dangled her legs over the edge of the oak and felt the biggest of the waves slide up to kiss the soles of her feet. The tide was at its highest, covering what was left of the debris of battle. A warrior walked with a hound whelp at heel along the tideline. Watching them, Graine found she missed Stone for the first time since she had left him to take care of her mother.

She watched a shadow lengthen and slide across the rocks at the base of the jetty and made a bet with herself as to which of three people it might belong to, which meant she could not turn round early to look.

'May I join you?'

She lost the bet. 'Of course.' She edged sideways just enough to be polite and Luain mac Calma, Elder dreamer of Mona, hitched up his tunic and came to sit beside her, dangling his long, lean legs over the edge and into the water.

'Who did you think I was?'

'Hawk. Or maybe Bellos, except you were not quite as quiet as either of them. So then I thought maybe Efnís had come back from Hibernia. If I had been asked, I would have said him.'

'He is back. I could get him for you if you want.'

'Not especially. Have you come to watch the legions leave? They have been striking camp since the tide turned. Maybe Manannan sent the big tide to scare them off.'

'I think it has more to do with the governor's messenger pigeon that evaded the cliff falcons and returned to its roost at mid-morning.' Mac Calma made a hammock of his fingers and hooked it over the back of his head, stretching his arms. His shoulder joints cracked, scaring some wading birds out on the strand. 'Your mother's war host has set alight to the east and south,' he said. 'I think the destruction of Mona is no longer the governor's first care.'

The day became suddenly cold. Graine pulled her knees to her chest and her tunic to her toes. Wrapping her arms round her shins, she said, 'Is mother . . . ?'

'Healed? Her healing has begun, yes.'

He left room for her to ask a question. Graine discovered a wedge of dirt between her toes and rubbed at it with her forefinger. 'Did you make the falcons leave the pigeons?' she asked.

'No. We couldn't do that. But we offered them two of the laying pullets to feed their young and they did not hunt on the day it came through. The gods may grant what we ask, but sometimes we must act as our wisdom dictates and hope that is enough.' Mac Calma's voice had not changed that Graine could notice, but they were no longer talking of falcons and Roman pigeons. He said, 'Bellos tells me you have been dreaming.'

Graine said, 'Not proper dreams. There was no purpose to them. I didn't know I was dreaming. I couldn't ask anything except of the hares.' There had been two hares in her dream. They had each given an opposite answer. She had not told Bellos that, or the nature of her question.

'Thank you.' Mac Calma lay back and hooked his hands behind his head.

Graine said, 'Will the people come back here to Mona now the legions have gone?'

'I think so. We might see what happens in the south first.'

'Will there be another battle?'

'I hope not. The legions will win if there is.' Mac Calma turned his head to look at her. Graine realized, with shock, that he was exhausted, as if he had fought the battle already, and alone. She had never seen him less than resilient, and always good-humoured.

He saw her look and smiled, wryly, in the way Valerius did when he was uncomfortable. He took a breath to say something and changed his mind and said instead, 'Graine, will you go to your mother? I think it will make a difference to what happens when they come to fight the legions.'

'Because I am the wild piece on the board of the Warrior's Dance?' She hated that. She had no idea what to do about it.

'I'm afraid so, yes. But only in part. The rest is because the Boudica needs you to be whole. And because you need her to be whole and each of you needs the other to find that wholeness.

Mona has done all it can for you: you can dream a little and you can reach into the fire; it's as much as anyone might have asked for when you came.'

It was not what Graine wanted to hear. Her eyes burned. Because anger was better than yet more grief, particularly in this company, she said caustically, 'And I can fight. Hawk has taught me. Don't forget that.'

He had taught her every morning for nine mornings while they watched the legions gather and plan their final assault, and plan, and plan, and never yet launch it. She was better than she had been, but she would never be more than a liability on a battlefield.

She watched Luain mac Calma make very certain that there was no condescension on his face or in his voice when he said, 'Yes, and you can fight.'

He reached into his belt pouch and brought out a small silver brooch, shaped like a hare. The design was not new; the lines were carved on beams in the great-house and stretched back for thirteen generations: she had counted them once. She thought the brooch itself might be new, or at least had not yet been worn by anyone.

He said, 'If I gave you this, and promised that it would join you to Mona as long as there is a Mona to which you may be joined, would you leave here and take it with you and go to your mother, wherever she is? Your honour guard will go with you, and Bellos, too, I think, and perhaps Efnís, if he feels he is not needed here— Why are you smiling?'

Graine stood, shaking her head. The thought of Hawk and Dubornos and Gunovar as her honour guard was either hilarious, or very sad. She did not wish to think too closely which.

She would have gone anyway, without the silver or the two wounded dreamers, but she took the hare as he offered it, and pinned it to her tunic high on her left shoulder. It ran there, as the hares had done in her dream, and still did not give her an answer.

IV

MID–LATE SUMMER AD 60

XXXII

THUNDER FOLLOWED THE LIGHTNING, BUT NOT AS CLOSELY AS IT had done. Valerius stood under an awning of bull's hide with his fingers laid on his wrist and counted the beats between the flash of the gods' fire and the blow of hammer on anvil that had created it.

When he could be heard over the noise and its echo, he said, 'Ten. It's moving away.'

'Could we petition one of your gods to make it move faster?' Theophilus stood with him under the awning, sharing in the fiction that by this they might be kept more dry than if they had, say, taken a step forward to stand outside in the everlasting rain, or gone to stand fully clothed in the storm-swell of a river that had brimmed over its banks and swept through the burned remains of the port at Vespasian's Bridge.

'It'll be gone by noon. Once they start to move, they don't stay long.'

Valerius did step out from under the awning then, and stood naked in the rain. He had stripped to the waist three days before when the storm began. On the second day, along with everyone but Theophilus, he had discarded the remains of his clothing as worse than useless and gone naked among the mud and fire-ash.

The rain ran over his body, pooling in the scoop of his collar bones, falling over in sheets that snagged on the knotted scars.

A man with the right knowledge could read his life's history there, if not the reasoning behind it.

Theophilus who could, and did, read new things daily in the mapped bodies of those around him, hesitated in the pretend-dry of the shelter. For reasons that were no longer clear even to himself but had to do with modesty and dignity and the habits of his youth, he had shed all footwear but continued to wear his tunic and cloak. Both had been saturated for three days. Cold, wet wool chafed him in the armpits and crotch and left him with a noticeably foreshortened temper.

Valerius stepped round him with amused caution, which did nothing to improve his mood. Eyeing him sideways now, the Boudica's brother said, 'We need to destroy the bridge before we leave. I know how you feel about it. If you would rather not be witness, you could begin the journey north now and we will catch you up.'

'Could I? Do you think the north road is safe for a man who has lived on both sides of this war? Myself, I doubt it.' Theophilus wiped the beak of his nose with thumb and forefinger and flicked a skinful of rain from them both. He regarded Valerius morosely. 'Sometimes I think you are almost as Roman as the men you are fighting. Then you look at a wonder of engineering such as that bridge and think to wreck it and I am certain you are worse than that; for all his bluster, Paullinus has a heart beating somewhere underneath his armour. You, by contrast, are more like Vespasian, or Caesar, who came here to plunder your corn and silver the better to feed his own armies.'

He waited a moment to see the other man's smile grow deeper, then, with a sour eye to the tilt of water streaming over the lip of the awning, Theophilus of Athens and Cos, both of which were eternally blessed with dry weather, braced himself and stepped out into the ocean of mud that had been a grazing paddock for the horses of Lugdunum, and later for the port at Vespasian's Bridge.

The rain cascaded down, sliding off his hair into his neck and onto his shoulders to soak further into the stuff of his cloak. For a moment, he did give serious thought to shedding his clothes and the indignity they had come to inflict on him, then he looked past Valerius and the sea of other, equally futile, awnings, past the miserable horses with their tails turned to the worst of the wet, past the naked warriors hunched in their shelter eating cold boiled mutton taken from the storehouses of the burned port, to the storm-swollen river where the bridge arced over the torrent.

The bridge commanded them all, now that the port at its feet had gone. Stark and black and proud against the mud and grey skies, it hung suspended in a lacework of geometric precision above all the chaos of rain and war.

Over the three days of the storm, Theophilus had come to identify with the bridge and its ability to endure all that had been thrown at it. It was the reason he was still clothed, and would remain so. It mattered to him that he keep faith with all that it held. Standing in the rain contemplating its destruction, he thought he might weep and then that he already was.

He caught up with Valerius. 'It *is* beautiful, far more so than the forum at Camulodunum, or the theatre, or the grotesque monstrosity of Claudius' temple. It's perfect – a testament to the powers of men over the gods. Why must you destroy it?'

'For that reason, if no other; we are trying to restore the gods to the land that men have taken, that we may hold it in trust for them.'

Valerius was himself again, alive and buoyant as if the rain fed the core of his soul, or the battles did. He was not like Julius Caesar, catamite to kings, but he was very much like Vespasian, who saw layers of cause and event beyond and beneath the wars.

He was, quite clearly, a man who had grown very close to being all he could be. If Theophilus had been asked to put a finger on what was missing, he would have found it hard, only that there was a piece still required to make the mosaic whole, and that when it came, and was fitted, the result would be exceptional.

The result already was far from mundane. The assault on Lugdunum had been a model of intelligent use of resources, so that there had been almost no loss of life on the attacking side. Through it, Valerius had used Theophilus as a sounding board, when he had things to discuss that needed a more classical insight than could be offered by Madb of Hibernia, or Huw, or the boy Knife, who was proving an adept scout.

He used him as such now, walking across the paddocks with the rain cascading off his shoulders and the swept lines of his torso.

'There are strategic reasons for removing it too: as long as Cunomar has wiped out Verulamium, then all of the land north of the river is with us as far as the Brigantes. The southwest has always been for us and against Rome. Down there . . .' he pointed across the river, 'every tribe south of the river is loyal to Rome and will remain so. If Paullinus decides to run his army south, I would rather he were not able to cross the river into Atrebatan territory. We can harry a marching legion to destruction; we've proved that with the Ninth. We'll be much harder pushed to attack them if they're in allied territory.'

'Paullinus wouldn't dare run now.' They had reached the north road, which had been made by the legions to speed the passage of men and provisions north to the war in the northwest. It had been paved and laid high on limestone rubble so that it was only awash with water, not thigh-deep in mud. Here, they could walk side by side and pretend to be civilized. Theophilus said, 'The governor was sent here to succeed or die. Even if he didn't have Nero behind him threatening death, he's not the kind of man to walk away from a battle, still less to run.'

'But he may choose discretion over valour. If he marches the legions south across the bridge, he could over-winter in safety with Berikos of the Atrebates, or Cogidumnos of the Regni; both men are given heart and soul to Rome.'

They reached the paddock's end. Valerius stepped over a fallen roof beam that had come, by accident, to mark the outer margins of the port. Rain flattened the stench of death, but not the sight of it. On either side, naked warriors and older children were still sorting through the debris of burned huts and merchants' booths, taking metal that might be usefully made into weapons, or leather for armour, or food that had not been spoiled by the fire or proximity to carrion.

There was more of that than there had been in Camulodunum: the storm had stopped the fires before they could cleanly burn everything, and there had been no final siege in a stone-built temple; Vespasian's Bridge had nothing sufficiently substantial to be worthy of a siege and no veterans ready to organize a defence. The slaughter here had been fast and most of it by sword and spear, with the fire intended to clear everything after.

Seeing the storm coming, Valerius had ordered his warriors to form a three-quarters ring about the port, with a gap only at the river, and only at first, and had them close in on signalled commands so that there had been no unexpected break in the wall of iron. The fighting had been swift and disciplined. Near the centre, the last cram of defenders had died of breathing smoke. They lay there still, exactly as they had fallen, bloating now, with the gas of warmth and death.

The road was completely clear of bodies and burned wood; Valerius had ordered that as a first priority. They walked down it, towards the bridge.

Valerius asked, 'In my place, what would you do?'

The rain eased a little. Theophilus' mood lightened in proportion. He said, 'Exactly what you are doing, only I would be more worried that Paullinus might order his client kings in the south to raise their sworn spears and send a war host north across the river to help him. And I agree with you: to prevent that alone, I would destroy the bridge. What will you do now that it's too wet to burn?'

'I have Madb of Hibernia as my engineer. She understands wood the way a smith understands iron. If you stay, you can see how the tribes take apart what Rome has made.'

The scout brought the news to Ulla who brought it to Cunomar who was with half a dozen others in a byre near the senior magistrate's house in Verulamium trying to round up three blue roan cattle and their two heifer calves.

'Vespasian's Bridge is down.'

Ulla stood in the doorway and shouted it, the better to be heard over the laughter and the lowing.

The laughter stopped. The lowing did not but grew less. Panting, Cunomar leaned on a tether post and swept a dank hand through his hair. The grin faded last from his face, after the rest of him had sobered, as if that part was least willing to let go of the game. He spat straw from his teeth and stared at the floor and made himself a leader of spears again.

'When did it fall?' he asked.

'Last night, just before dusk.' The morning's drizzle had dried. Ulla stood in watery sunshine, shading her eyes. 'Valerius made it a ceremony as it came down and gave half of the bridge as an offering to Nemain. The other half was burned at sunfall as a gift to Lugh of the shining spear, sun god of the ancestors. All of the warriors and refugees watched it. They say that the part of the war host that travels and fights with the Boudica's brother is blessed by the old ones and has formed a shining army in its own right.'

Cunomar's eyes grew tight at the margins. 'Valerius says that?'

'Of course not. But the warriors of Mona who fight with him say it, and they are of the gods' isle so everyone listens. He has more spears now than anyone: the Silures have come from the west to join him and warriors of the Durotriges and Dumnonii loyal to Gunovar. They were looking for the Boudica but couldn't find her and so have joined with her brother instead.' Cunomar was looking increasingly strained. Ulla said, 'They're with Valerius because they met him first. When they reach us here this evening, they may yet choose to join you.'

All traces of the boy who had enjoyed the morning's game vanished. 'Valerius and his host are coming north to meet us? Here? *Today?*'

The cattle fell silent at last. The youths of the she-bear glanced guardedly one to the other and began to ease themselves from the strawed slurry of the byre. They were brown to the ankles and stank of fresh manure. It had not mattered before; it mattered a great deal now if they were to rescue any honour at all from the task they had been set.

Unlike the battle for Lugdunum, the battle for Verulamium had not been glorious: there had been no ceremonial ending of a bridge, nor – yet – the burning of a city. The Boudica had given one-third of her war host to her son with a remit to crack open Rome's second city in the province, in order that he might prove himself as a tactician and a leader of spears in a safe theatre, before any greater battles. To his enduring shame and that of his warriors, he had thus far proved nothing of the sort.

The entire affair had been a wallowing anticlimax. It had not occurred to any of them that the town against whom they marched might not wish to be cracked open, but might instead greet the warriors with barely a fight.

In the event, the rising smoke of Camulodunum had told its own story and the inhabitants of Verulamium who had sold themselves most assiduously to Rome for the prize of citizenship were gone or dead by the time the Boudica's son and his warriors had arrived.

Several thousand old men, women and children had been left in the undefended town. At the sight of Cunomar's front runners, they had changed into un-Roman dress, or as near as they could find, and had swung open the gates, inviting the Boudica's son to enter with fulsome protestations of gratitude and great joy at his arrival.

Against a desperate wish to kill without cease, Cunomar had given orders that none of them must be slain and that instead they be given food and wagons with which they might leave if they wished before the municipium was burned.

Surprisingly few had departed, and so overnight Cunomar had found himself organizing the feeding of the extra thousands, which meant that the town had to be emptied of all possible food before it could be burned, which was why he was in the cow byre, chasing a skinny roan heifer with a group of friends, as if there were no war to be won and the worst that could happen was that they be covered in filth to the ankles and have to jump in the river to be clean.

The warriors in the byre were calmer now, and serious, awaiting his order. Cunomar surveyed them, making sure that his gaze met each and they could see that his gratitude was sincere.

'Thank you all. We should perhaps forget about trying to halter these and herd them out to the rest. They can be milked later, when we have more time. If you three' – he swung his arm and they swayed apart from it, dividing into two groups – 'could take care of that and the rest of you come with me? It seems we have a city to burn and not long in which to do it.'

The elders of the she-bear had warned against the intoxication of leadership. Taking care not to revel in the strength of their devotion, Cunomar watched the first half of his group move with commendable purpose to herd the cattle and then led the rest out to the alleyways of the town where the thin sun took the chill off the wind and dried out the building for burning.

Wagons stood outside the gates, surrounded by relays of other, similar youths who filled them with bushels of corn from the city's tax granaries and staves of straw and smoked meats and fish and jars of olives and figs in wine that were the gift of a grateful emperor to those among the natives who had given him the closest and most unequivocal support. Even more than Camulodunum, Verulamium had worked to make itself and so the province fully Roman.

Cunomar found work for those who followed him, and for

himself, and sent out more scouts to assess Valerius' progress and made sure that he was in a place where they could find him first when they came to report.

It was not a scout who sought him out when he was holding the corner of a laden cart that the split axle might be repaired, but Braint, Warrior of Mona.

Her hair was black, streaked with grey and a little mud. Her eyebrows were incised black lines above raven-hard eyes that pierced friend and enemy equally, with little warmth for either. She loomed over Cunomar, lean and angry and fired by something beyond the necessities of the day, even this day.

The axle was mended. The wheel was put back on and the pin hammered into place. He let go of the corner and flexed his fingers and led the Warrior of Mona out to the horse paddocks where there were fewer listening ears.

A wall-eyed chestnut mare stood in the far corner watching him warily. Cunomar had been trying intermittently to catch her for three days. He walked towards her now, with Braint at his side.

'I thought you were with Valerius?' he said.

'I was.' Her eyes were bright and cold as she said it. Cygfa might have placed her trust in Valerius, but it was widely known that her lover, the Warrior of Mona, hated the Boudica's brother almost as much as she hated the legions.

The fine margin between the greater hate and the smaller had let Braint carry Valerius' message. 'He sent me back with half of my warriors, bringing news to cheer your day: Suetonius Paullinus is coming south towards you, bringing whatever is left of his legions after the gods of Mona spat them out of the straits.'

Cunomar's guts lurched alarmingly. 'How does he know?' he asked. 'Our scouts have been out for half a day's ride in all directions and have seen nothing of the enemy.'

Braint said, 'Valerius saw Corvus and the governor with a group of other officers in the hills above Lugdunum. He thinks they had come to arrange a defence, but saw it was indefensible and left it for him to burn.'

'Which he has done.'

'Indeed. The Roman officers rode west towards the coast. Valerius thinks they'll summon the legions down from Mona to join them and that, together, they'll march south down the new road they have built, which is wide enough for eight men and stretches all the way to the Great River.

'Your mother's brother has ten thousand refugees from Canonium and Caesaromagus and Lugdunum. If the legions meet them, it will be carnage. He has sent me to ask, therefore, if you will harry the legions as you did in the forests of the east against the Ninth, until he is able to join you. The place named by the Boudica for her meeting with you both is just north of here. He wishes to wait there for her, unless she's already joined you here?'

There was a warning in the words, more than the casual question allowed. For a moment, the threat and promise of the legions was a small thing. 'She's not here,' Cunomar said. 'It's twelve days since she left and we've heard nothing since the third day after we parted. Has she not sent word to Valerius?'

'None.' Braint's eyes were less cold: Cygfa, who was soul-friend to Braint, had been chosen to ride with the Boudica. If Breaca was lost, then her daughter was lost with her.

Cunomar said, 'I had thought she was with you, or at least had sent word. We could send out scouts to search—'

'When she rides with Ardacos and Cygfa?' Braint grinned, sharply. 'We have no scouts who could find those two. If she wants to be found, she will be found. If she does not, or cannot, scouts will find nothing. They would be better put to seeking out the legions.'

Cunomar's mouth had dried so that he had to swallow to speak, and then again to loosen his jaw. 'How many are they?' he asked. 'And how close?'

'Almost all of the Fourteenth with a third of the Twentieth, plus two wings of cavalry. Perhaps six thousand legionaries and a thousand horse. As to how close, Valerius thinks that they will have reached the lands of the Coritani, who worship the horned god. There are places there which lend themselves to ambush. We should be able easily to attack the tail as before.'

Braint ran her tongue round her teeth. 'Valerius could have sent the warriors of Mona alone,' she said, 'but he has sent me to join you. If you were a hound, I would imagine he was throwing you a bone. Are you willing to take such a thing? Have you the warriors to ambush the legions?'

Cunomar sought the bear again, and was empty. He heard his mother, a long time ago, before they came east. *When the gods most fill you, you feel most empty. Then is the time to ride the wind and let it guide you.*

The wind came from the south and east. It blew north and west, towards Mona and the marching legions. Cunomar looked up. A scattering of crows came together from three directions, flung rags cawing in the fast air. They made the sky black with their circling, then turned and flew with one mind, north and west.

He felt hot breath on his neck. He let his eyes turn, but not his body. The wall-eyed chestnut mare was behind him, lipping at his shoulder, ready to be caught. For no particular reason, she reminded him of red-haired Corra, one of the would-be she-bears, who had broken her arm and could not fight, but was good at organizing; she had a wealth of good sense and could be trusted to complete the evacuation and burning of Verulamium, and grateful to be asked.

Others came to mind, in fast sequence. Quite soon, Cunomar said, 'I have fifty of the she-bear who could run alongside your horses into the land of the Coritani and then fight effectively at the end of it. If they combine with your warriors, I think we could give the legions a reason to slow down, as Valerius asks of us. If that's a bone to a hound, then I accept it.'

Braint made the warrior's salute, in the old way, that they still used on Mona. 'You are the Boudica's son, her Hound of the Sea. If it's a bone, then you have earned it, and will prove yourself worth more after.'

XXXIII

G RAINE RODE DOWN FROM THE WEST AND NORTH, A CAREFUL
day behind the marching legions.

The road hugged the coast; the sea was to their left and
mountains to their right. As if a god had stepped on it, the land
between was crushed where the marching men had been; heather
and grass were laid flat where tents had been pitched and men had
slept; circles of black ash showed where the cooking fires had fed
the seven thousand; latrines hastily dug and more hastily filled
again hummed with flies.

A child could have tracked them. For most of the first day after
they left Mona, Hawk was sulkily redundant, then he discovered
what it was to ride with a blind man who could see into the worlds
beyond and he grew buoyant again and rode alongside Bellos with
his eyes shut, trying to learn what could be seen without sight.

As had become habit amongst them, Dubornos rode a spear's
cast ahead, and Gunovar behind to guard their tail, which left
Graine to ride with Efnís, of the northern Eceni, about whom she
knew very little, except that he was the named successor to Luain
mac Calma as Elder of Mona and had been a friend to her mother
since childhood, and had cared for Valerius when he was still Bán.
What he thought of him now was unknown, and she did not have
the nerve to ask.

'What do you feel for Hawk?'

He asked it on the second day, peacefully, in the same tone as he had asked if she had seen the falcon stoop on the pigeon, or the three herons standing in the river. The sea was behind them, and the flat, boggy land that lay east of the mountains. They were riding through the broad, fertile flood plain of two rivers, crossing bridges made by Rome. The horses walked gingerly, hearing hollowness beneath them, and the rush of summer water.

Graine looked round to the road behind. Hawk was no longer playing games with Bellos. This last day, he had become a tracker again, or a hunter, leaving his horse in Dubornos' care and running ahead or to the sides on foot. She thought he was gone when she first looked, then found him off to the right, jogging through scrub hawthorn and blackthorn on the far side of the valley. He saw her looking and waved. She waved back.

To Efnís, she said, 'He cares for me.'

Mac Calma would have pushed for more. Efnís nodded a little and looked into her and through her and past her to the distant ridge and the small hill that rose near it and said, 'Your father fought there once, in the spring before you were born. Already they call it Caer Caradoc. There are three others with the same name within two days' ride of here.'

She was finding in Efnís a very different man from Luain mac Calma, who had sired Valerius in Hibernia and come to see him on the heels of a storm in the lands of the Eceni, and watched over him, it seemed likely, ever since.

Efnís, to the best of her knowledge, had sired no-one and did not seem overly inclined to start. He had shared a bed with one of the younger warriors and when she travelled east with Braint to fight Rome on Eceni soil, he had grieved openly and fully for the day of her departing, and then had thrown himself back into the evacuation to Hibernia. When next Graine saw him, he was himself again, open and clear where mac Calma was opaque and unreachable.

There were disadvantages to his transparency, she was finding; in many ways it had been easier to ignore mac Calma's oblique probing.

They rode on for a while, leaving the small hill and the ridges behind them, following the Roman road into broad, wooded land, that rose and fell gently and put no strain on the horses. Hawk took himself further off, so she could not see him. There was an urgency to his moving now, and an attentiveness she had never seen before. Because Efnís' question so clearly was not fully answered, she said, 'I feel safe in his company, as I do in yours.'

He stopped watching a pair of magpies that squabbled over something discarded by the legions and turned his attention back to her. 'I was not part of what happened to injure you. Hawk was a scout in Roman pay. He helped them to do what they did.'

'My mother killed his father.'

She wanted that to be enough. It was not. She said, 'He went for help. He brought Valerius and then Corvus who was able to stop the procurator and send the veterans away. Without him, we would have died.'

She had not seen that, but everyone except Hawk and Cunomar had told her of it, and of how Hawk came by the cut on his lip that had disfigured his face and still left a coloured bruise over three months on. She said, 'He has apologized so often his throat is worn out. I can't hate him for it.'

'Do you care enough to grieve if he were to die in battle?'

'Hawk won't die.'

She said it too fast, without thinking, and was surprised at the power of it; she would not have said the same about her mother, or Cunomar, or Cygfa or any of the others whose names and easy mortality tumbled through her mind. She would not have said the same about herself.

Efnís pursed his lips and she saw a shading of grief in his eyes, that mac Calma would have hidden and he could not. He said, 'I'm sorry. I should not have pushed you to that,' and was silent.

Some time later, after they had crossed a second bridge and the river had wound west again, and they had climbed a ridge and meandered down the other side, he said, 'We are coming into the lands of the Cornovii, who worship the horned god. They live a different life from ours, but still honour Mona, and I believe they honour the Boudica as strongly as anyone; certainly they will know you are her daughter and respect you for it, but they are sworn enemies of the Coritani and will know Hawk as one of them. If you would see him live, you should make clear to them your care for him.'

She had not thought to ask why Hawk had left his horse and taken to scouting again. Now, it seemed a fatal oversight. She made herself sit straight and not look aside to where she thought he might be. Her head spun. 'Why are we here? Why not go a different way?'

'Luain mac Calma was clear; if we miss the battle that is coming, we are all as good as dead. The only way to be sure we can be in the right place at the right time is to keep close on the heels of Rome. Hawk knows that.'

'But did he know the road came through the lands of the Cornovii?'

'He has fought these people since his childhood, exactly as he fought the Eceni. I can't imagine he would not.'

Breaca met alone with Venutios of the Brigantes after dusk in a wild place, near the edge of a rocky escarpment, with, on the one hand, brown, gritty rock that fell dizzyingly to scrub below and on the other heather, not quite in full purple, and crows somersaulting on the updraughts and a pair of courting buzzard mewling in circles above.

She had come fast, leaving Airmid with the bulk of her warriors. Only Cygfa was with her; speed lay in small numbers. Ardacos was already there with Venutios. Only he could have tracked a single man who took refuge from Rome and was wary of being seen, and only Ardacos was known by Venutios for himself first and as the Boudica's shield in all things second, so that his words were her words and carried the same power. A man wanted by the legions for the crime of treason against Cartimandua, his queen, would have come for no-one less.

The meeting place was high and flat, with a clear view all round so that no-one could come at them unexpectedly. The two war leaders sat on dry rock beside a fire rich with heather roots and old birch, circled by standing boulders that had been carved when the gods were young, so that the lichens were knotted into the carvings and even the edge marks that gave the numbers of dreamers and warriors were barely clear.

'We need you,' Breaca said. Stone lay behind hunting hares in his sleep so that the tremors of it shivered through her.

Venutios had been Warrior of Mona and had returned to his

people to hold the balance against his queen. He had aged since their last meeting, more than the passing years would have warranted, and it showed most in the depth and detail of his caution. He offered no answer, but chewed on dried venison and let that fill the gap.

Presently, he said, 'I came to you here because Ardacos reminded me of the she-bear dancing as it was done by him on Mona, and all that led from it. For that, and all that you have been, I owe you the honour of a hearing, even if my heart did not demand it. For what Cartimandua did to Caradoc, and I failed to prevent, I owe you life itself. But I cannot give it now. The Brigantes are evenly split. Half follow me and will fight against Rome. Half follow Cartimandua and will fall on our backs and kill us if we show any signs of joining you. If we come, we bring more trouble than help. Do you really want that?'

'If we drive the legions into the sea, or into the earth, if they are broken and will never return, if the emperor abandons Britannia and all that is in it, what of Cartimandua then?'

He grinned with unexpected savagery; she had never known him a bitter man. 'Then she is dead. We will kill her in the Roman fashion, nailed to wood and left to the skies. But even then, the blood of my Brigantes, and their flesh, would feed the crows for days after the battle that will lead to that. Just now, while Rome is still here and still commands power, it is impossible; we are too few and she is too great. We would lose, and you would have eight thousand hostile spears at your backs as you try to battle Rome. If you win – *when* you win – enough who currently favour her will side with us and she will be defeated. Until then, we must work quietly and win over a few warriors each day in secret by the power of our arguments, not thousands by the power of our spears.'

It was summer and the night was warm. Venutios wore no cloak and only a light tunic without sleeves. His arms were bare of ornament or clan marks, as they had always been; the once-Warrior of Mona eschewed the glitter that others enjoyed. It gave him an austerity that others lacked, and set him apart from the greater mass of his people.

He leaned back on the rock. Stars pointed the moonless sky; the Hunter raised his spear to the Hare as brightly as he had ever done

357

on Mona, when Venutios was Warrior. He studied Breaca a long while by the light of the fire, and then said, 'I'm sorry. I could have told that to Ardacos and saved you a journey.'

'You could, but I'm not sorry. Why did you not?'

'I thought you would have wanted to hear it from me. And I wanted to see what you had become. We hear things at third hand, or fourth, and rumours come in pairs, one part set against the other. I needed to know if it were true that the Boudica had lost her heart after the rape of her daughters, as some said, or if, as we preferred to believe, she had instead grown with it to be greater than she ever was on Mona and in the western wars.'

They were alone; his honour guard had taken themselves off to lie in the lee of the boulders, rolled in their cloaks, on beds of springing heather. Cygfa was hunting somewhere by herself. Ardacos was nearby and still awake, but no longer sharing the fire. He sat against a rock with birches on either side, not quite out of earshot; she could see the shine of his eyes and then presently the darkness as he closed them. She did not think he was asleep.

Venutios sat with his hands looped over one knee, watching her. The firelight danced across his face, exploring the new hollows that a year on the run had given him. He had taught her what it was to be Warrior of Mona, and had given the horn to her as she had given it to Gwyddhien. No-one else living knew what it took to do that. Because she could ask it of him and expect a clear answer, she said, 'What do you find, between the rumours and the fact?'

'That you are changed far more than I had expected. That parts of you are broken and parts are greater than they were, very much greater. I see you clearly now and there's a light that shines from within, as if a cloak has fallen that was a necessary concealment, to protect you from the brightness as much as us. I am thinking that it cannot be easy to live with what you have become, but I think also that you have found something to fight for that you did not know before?'

'I have, yes.'

It was late; they should have slept, and neither could. They put more heather on the fire and sat closer and then lay down, head to head, and for the first time since it had happened Breaca told of the ancestor's prophecy and the question it posed and the healing she had found in its answer.

Later, when Ardacos' eyes had been shut for a very long time and Venutios was, in any case, lying with his head so close to hers that the words passed from breath to breath between them, she showed him the ring that had been Cunobelin's gift and tried to put into words how it was to hold the lineage of the Sun Hound and its promise; how he was with her and yet not part of her as the ancestor-dreamer had become; how it had changed her understanding of death even though she had lived on the borderline between the worlds for all of her adult life.

Venutios was wise, and had been Warrior and knew what it was to fight for something greater than life and blood. He listened until she had run out of words, and at the end he asked a single question, and did not press when she was unable to answer.

Later, when he had taken himself to another fire to sleep, she settled down in the lee of a boulder with her head on her saddle pad and Stone hard at her side for warmth and lay staring at the stars, asking herself the same thing. She fell asleep without finding an answer.

She woke at dawn, and was no wiser.

The fire was a mound of red ash, only warm if she put her hands close enough to burn the skin. She fed it the thinnest of heather roots and dead leaves and nursed the flames until they leapt to bite her fingers and were safe to leave.

At her back, the sun made its own fire. It was larger here than in the south, hanging just off the lip of the crag so that it seemed she could step off the rock into its heart. She stood on the cold stone and watched the gods stoke their own furnace and asked them Venutios' question.

Red fire became gold, became white gold, and there was no answer. Around, laced frost melted from the rock. A long, lean pine tree became suddenly bare of crows. The sky became raucously black. A shadow slid to her side, and past it, and Ardacos said softly, 'So which would you choose to save: your land or your lineage?'

'I don't know.'

It had been a vain hope that he might not have been listening. She sat on the crag's edge and hugged her feet and looked over. Below, small shadows of men crossed the land as Venutios' hunters worked a deer trail. Ardacos came to sit on a boulder. He was naked and smelled of bear fat and his hair was wild as it was when he had been hunting. She said, 'What did you kill?'

'Nothing. I went to meet the bear, not to hunt.'

'Did you find her?'

'No. We're too far south and the legions have hunted too hard.'

Ardacos pressed the heels of his hands to his eyes. He was haggard and tired. Like Venutios, he had aged since the winter and Breaca had not taken time to see it. It was easier to remember him younger, more vital, dancing with a she-bear and her cubs on Mona, than to remember the man who was flogged by Rome and then made himself well enough to fight again less than a month later.

It was easier to remember either of these than the warrior who had nurtured her son for sixteen years and brought him body and soul to the she-bear, because only by that could he grow from the shadow of the Boudica to be all that he needed to be.

Because both Ardacos and the question needed more of an answer, Breaca said, 'It's not a choice to make now on a bare rock with nothing to give it shape.'

'No. But you are hoping you may never have to make it at all.' Ardacos rose to leave. 'You are stronger than that, if I am not. When the time comes, don't step aside because you are wishing the question would pass you by.'

Venutios was waiting for them by the fire. He was dressed more formally, with a good wool cloak dyed black for Briga and a brooch pin at his shoulder in the shape of the Brigantian horse. A youth stood nearby holding his horse for him. It was Roman bred, with a brand on the left shoulder.

He said, 'I must leave, but I have a gift for you, in parting.'

'Your question was its own gift.'

'I know. But that is for later. For now, there are things more pressing. My scouts have been following Paullinus and his legions as they pass down through the lands neighbouring ours. This night, they camped on the borders of the Cornovii and the Coritani. They are being followed, a day behind, by a small party from Mona: a red-haired girl-child and a woman dreamer of the Durotriges, with four other men, one of them a hawk-scout of the Coritani.'

'Your trackers are good.'

'The best.' He smiled diffidently. 'Excepting only Ardacos who is exceptional and found us before we found him. What do you know of the elder Cornovii and their worship of the horned god?'

'Very little; the Cornovan dreamers who came to Mona said that they no longer worshipped in the old ways. There were rumours that some of their elders still followed the ancestors' path, that they gave living men to be the Horned One and to run with the Hunter in the stars, to bring good fortune for the year after.'

'We have the same rumours. We believe them to be true.' Signals were passing among the Brigantes, of increasing urgency. Venutios' horse was brought forward. He accepted a hand into the saddle and sent the youth who had held it away.

Leaning down, he said, 'Rome has killed all of their younger dreamers who trained on Mona. The elders who have always followed the old ways are in the ascent and they are as desperate as anyone to be rid of the legions; they will do whatever they believe necessary to achieve that. Tonight is the first horned moon since the summer solstice. If they are going to sacrifice anyone, it will be now.'

Breaca took a step back from his horse. Pity showed clear on his face; she had never seen that from him, nor expected it. He said, 'I had not thought that the threat to your family would come from the tribes. I'm sorry.'

'Thank you.' The urge to turn and walk away left her rigid. She made herself stand and think and ask the necessary question. 'But they won't take Graine. She's a child and a woman. She can't be the god.'

'Not her, no. And some of her party will be safe. They won't touch the blind dreamer, or the woman dreamer of the Durotriges, although they may wish her to stand as Briga for them, at least for the night; they will see her presence as a gift of the mother. They will never risk the wrath of Mona, so the soon-Elder is safe, but there are two others in the party and either one might suit them. My scouts have not been close enough to find their identities or how the Cornovii might choose between them.'

'Dubornos and Hawk.' She stared past him to his warriors and their impatience to be gone. She said, 'Dubornos you know. He came to Mona in the year after me. He was taken captive with Caradoc and came back with Cunomar. The other is a young warrior of the Coritani. He—' A half-thought shifted and took shape. 'Hawk. They'll take Hawk. The Cornovii have been at war with the Coritani as long as we have. They have not yet learned that the tribes must fight together to defeat Rome.'

'The followers of the Horned One think themselves uniquely placed to defeat Rome without help.' Venutios moved his horse back so that they could see past him down the track. Two of his runners were waiting near where it led down from the crag. He said, 'Nothing will happen before moonrise. If you will follow my pathmakers, you can reach them by then. It would be good if you had Airmid with you – they hold Nemain as the daughter of their god and would listen to one so closely wedded to her – but there is not time for that. You are the Boudica, given to Briga. They will listen to you. It may be that they will also take heed of what you say.'

XXXIV

'HAWK?'
　　　　Hawk was nowhere. In his place were a dozen warriors, all of middle age, who ringed the road, where there had been nothing but morning mist and boulders and nettles and the signs of the legions' marching.

There were no women among them, only men, powerfully built and naked but for their knife belts and painted with red clay in straight lines from ankle to brow and armpit to wrist. Their kill-feathers were from a red hen and banded in black down the quills. Their hair was stiff with red ochre and smoothed back in two lines so that they were horned. Their knife belts were of red deerhide, and the knives that hung on them were hilted with antler.

Graine had not seen a naked man since the night of the assault; only now, through panic and nausea, did she realize the constant, quiet effort that had been made to ensure that she did not. Even now, with danger encircling, Dubornos pushed his horse across so that she might not have to look.

He was too late, but he had tried and she loved him for it. She looked down at her horse's mane and breathed hard through her mouth and felt Bellos' hand on her back between her shoulder blades, and the urgency in it, and the need not to make a scene.

Newly, Gunovar was near, sitting tall, with her cloak pushed back so that her scars were more readily seen, and the dreamer's thong from Mona. Throwing her voice out as if she were addressing the elders in the great-house, she said, 'We escort the Boudica's daughter. She has been to Mona for healing after her rape by Rome. She is needed now for her part in the war against the legions. Would you harm her?'

The men swayed back and forth, like birch in a breeze. One to the left, the northern side, said, 'Never harm the child of the Boudica.' His voice was thick with the accent of the ancestors, as if he had not lived through the nightmare of Rome, or even the wars between the tribes that came before it.

Gunovar said, 'So then we may pass?'

Hawk was there, a long way back, in the trees. Graine saw him, and Dubornos. They turned their heads to look elsewhere.

The red-painted men swayed once more and came back upright again. The north one said, 'Daughter to the Boudica may pass. Alone. Or she may wait with you and your men.'

It had never occurred to any of the party from Mona that Efnís, Dubornos or Bellos might be considered to be Gunovar's men. The strangeness of it echoed amongst them. The deer-elder saw it. He stepped up to Gunovar and raised his hand and set the heel of his palm on her forehead, and then his first two fingers, so that she was left with a smudged bar and two vertical lines of red clay paint above the dreamer's thong.

He said, 'Given of the god. Given to the god. Marked by Rome and by Mona. Now marked by greater than that. We honour you, if they do not.'

His eyes were deer eyes, wide and brown, but not afraid as deer's were. He regarded Graine thoughtfully a moment, and then set a small vertical line between her brows. She felt the press of his touch and then a tingling that lasted a long time afterwards where he had left the clay. 'Given to the hare-daughter,' he said. 'Young, but older inside. Not too young to dance. Better if you come with us and wait with the others.'

He stepped back and looked round at the scrub woods and heather moors beyond. So that his voice carried, he said, 'The Coritani will follow.'

Hawk was gone, a shadow somewhere in the trees. Still, there was no doubt that he would follow where Graine went, or that Graine would go where the others were taken.

Gunovar asked, 'For what do we wait?'
'Attendance on the god.'

They rode west, hard and fast through the day, and attended the god near dusk in a wooded valley, at the foot of a high limestone crag that fell vertically down. A grave mound of the ancestors sat squat and silent on the western lip and the red-painted deer-warriors would not look at it as they reined in their mounts on the crag head.

The sun was an egg yolk, broken open on the horizon. Rich light spread flatly out, to skim the tops of the trees in the valley below. The white rock was the colour of sulphur, falling away as if the gods' axe had split it down to the earth. Graine looked over the edge and felt the dream of herself tumble out into oblivion. She froze, clinging to the saddle, and could not move.

'We can't go down there.' Bellos said it, who could not see. The nearest deer-men glanced at him sideways with white-rimmed eyes. The leader, who was marked from the others by a single additional red strip that ran upwards from his chin, dismounted and wove a way between the warriors and the sparse young pine that studded the crag's head.

He alone was able to look Bellos full in the face. He did so for an age and then nodded and said, 'You can.'

'How? Can you carry us? I cannot see and the child cannot move.'

The deer-chief shrugged. His face showed a bored contempt. 'You go or you die.'

Gunovar raised her hand and he flinched. She said, 'You swore you would not harm the daughter of the Boudica.'

'We will not. But we cannot protect her if she is here. She is only safe in the valley with us. No man who stays at the crag head when the god comes can live.' He considered, and amended that, nodding to Gunovar. 'Nor any woman.' Speaking towards the trees, he said, 'If the Coritani wishes to meet his death cleanly, he, too, will come down with us. He cannot be concealed in the land of the Horned One.'

. . . to meet his death cleanly . . .
Hawk will not die.

Loudly, in Greek, because they had spoken it a little together on Mona and the deer-men were least likely to know it, Graine said, 'Hawk, leave. Find the Boudica. Tell her what has happened.'

The deer-elder grinned, and seemed less human. He nodded, as if she had played her part right in a ritual of his making. He waited, watching the darkening sun, and the smile faded from his face long after his eyes had taken the red heart of the gods' fire and drunk it in and made of it something older and less benign. At a certain point, when the sun's light was almost gone, he lifted his head and barked, deep and low, like a stag at rut.

The trees moved, and there were three dozen deer-men where there had been nothing, and Hawk was in the centre of them, backed by unsheathed knives. Blood oozed from a line down one side of his face where they had cut him, so that he was red-striped as they were, in parody, or as a beginning.

Graine saw it and would not believe. A part of her stepped away, to become separate and so safe, as it had done when the rape began. She heard Bellos' voice, clear as a wren's. 'Don't go. He will need you to think and care for him. Keep safe and ask Nemain for help.' She did not know if he had spoken aloud or in her mind but it worked and she came back and felt sick which was better than feeling nothing.

The deer-elder saluted Hawk, and then Graine, linking them. He spoke to his own men in a tongue that was still the grunting of deer and then once more stepped to the edge of the crag. 'We go down,' he said, thickly. 'Those who need help will be given it.'

No-one, this time, spoke against him.

The descent was a nightmare, better not remembered; a precipitous climb in which white, crumbling stone kept Graine alive, and a man who was not one of those she had learned to trust pressed his body to hers, holding her into the rock at the times when her foot slipped or a handhold proved insecure and she began to peel backwards away from the cliff's face.

Her head swam and her guts rebelled, but Bellos' words remained clear in her head so that she held the sight of Hawk in her mind with the single red knife-cut down his face and the power of that kept her moving and putting her feet where she was told and her hands gripped the rock and she did not become paralysed with fear as she might have done and there was an end to it after eternity, when she stood on flat ground, between two drooping birch trees, and clung to the deer-man and let him hold her until the shaking stopped.

By comparison, the climb up to the cave a short while later was easy. Bellos was helped by the deer-elder because the other deer-warriors would no longer go near him; he saw too much. Following these two, Graine scrambled over white rock and then up a small path that became a series of handholds carved into the rock and then a flat ledge wide enough to walk on that bent round a corner.

They came to the cave suddenly, as if it had moved out of hiding to reach them, not they it. The mouth gaped wide as a hunting bear's, easily big enough to swallow them. Fronds of fern drooped over the arch, fringing it with green teeth. Bellos stopped, and then Graine. 'The ancestors used this,' he said. 'It's older than the great-house on Mona.'

The deer-elder touched a hand to the rock, as if it were a thing of his own making, and he justly proud. 'It's older than even the grave mounds of the ancestors. There are bones of deer in this cave on which the year-marks have counted fifty generations and they were old before the marking began.'

It was impossible to imagine so much time. Graine said, 'That's older than Rome.'

The deer-elder looked at her and into her and seemed surprised at what he saw. He considered a moment and then stepped back and brushed a fern sideways so that they could see paintings on the wall of men with red-striped bodies and antlered heads.

'There were dreamers of deer here in the days before Rome was a village with three hens and a starving cow,' he said. His accent was less thick than it had been, as if he no longer needed to set himself apart. He spoke with the same quiet intensity as Luain mac Calma, or Valerius, or, less often, Breaca. 'We intend that they shall be here, free to dream, when Rome is reduced to that again. You who fight with us are welcome. The cave will keep you safe in the dark part of the night before the moon rises.'

They were different as they entered the cave; less prisoners moving under duress, more participants in a rite that had not yet begun. Graine felt an itch in the clay-marked line on her brow as if it were newly made, still hot from the boiling pans. She followed Efnís through a limestone cleft smaller than the big caves of the west, and whiter, but still with room for a fire and the dozens who grouped round it.

The cavern opened out at the back, to make a wide, circular chamber. Two stag's skulls adorned the entrance to this, one on either side, and on the arched limestone walls were paintings of stags and horses and hares and men who had become deer and danced to a painted fire.

A real fire was lit in the centre, far back so that its light barely reached the entrance and could not be seen from outside. Smoke filled the air, lightly: pine and green oak and the singed hair of an animal. Already other deer-men sat in rings about it, too many to count.

Like deer, Graine and those with her were herded into the farthest corner and left. She sat on the floor, and leaned back on the wall and tried to bring her breathing back to normal. A youth came and offered them oat bannocks, seared to blackness on the fire.

Dubornos said, 'They feast us. We should be honoured.' He sounded like Valerius; his voice had the same dry irony. She had not seen it before so clearly as a defence against fear.

Gunovar said, 'This is god-food, to mark us for the Horned One. They will have killed a stag. We will all be expected to eat of it before moonset in the morning. I suspect it will not be cooked.'

'The fire is for other things?' asked Bellos, and was not answered.

Hawk came in last and did not sit. He stood with his back to the ragged limestone and stared out to the night beyond the cave's mouth where a sudden, sharp storm had passed over and left the night cool and damp. Sometime in the descent, all their weapons had been removed. Hawk alone had been stripped. The knife wound ran the length of his body, from his hip to his shoulder to his brow. It bled as if newly done.

Graine shuffled across to sit closer to him. 'Do you know what they'll do?'

'To you? Nothing. They wouldn't dare. Even here, the Boudica's name is set next to the gods'.'

He had rested his shoulders on the wall. There was blood on it, from an equivalent line down his back. He was slick all over with a light sheen of sweat and there was gooseflesh on his arms.

Graine said, 'I wasn't asking about me. What will they do to you?'

'I don't know.' Hawk looked down for the first time, away from the cave mouth and the night beyond it. 'Our mothers tell us things when we are small, to make us squeal and grow big eyes and stay in the roundhouse until dawn. I believed them, of course, because all children believe their mothers, but then they told us similar things about the Eceni and I have not yet seen any of them to be true.'

He would not look her in the eyes. The bruise on his lip that came from Valerius' knife was gone to a faint green so that Graine could not have seen it if she had not known where to look. It mattered less now than it had done.

He had been the best hawk-scout of his generation and Valerius had treated him as an arrogant hound whelp in need of training. The men of the horned god saw him the same. She thought that Valerius might have been right, but that the journey to Mona and all that had happened there had changed him so that now the deer-men were making a mistake. She was not certain that they would treat him any differently if they could be made to understand that.

Gunovar finished her bannock and wiped her fingers on her tunic. She said, 'They will make him the Horned One, with paint and antlers, and have him dance with me, and mate at the end of it. If he will not dance, or refuses the mating, they will flay him and use his skin to cover one of their own who will do it instead. If he does as they ask, and dances well, they will kill him differently, and keep it short, so that his death fills only the time just after dawn when the sun and the horned moon share the sky.' She splayed her fingers, so that they could see the scars where they had been broken. 'It helps to know,' she said. 'If I were you, I would dance when they ask it, and everything else. I will not hold it against you.'

Hawk's head turned on his shoulders, smoothly, like an owl's. 'How?' he asked. 'How differently will they kill me if I do as they want?'

'As they have started, with knives. Or with the fire. I believe you will be allowed to choose.'

'That's what our mothers told us,' said Hawk. He sounded surprised, almost relieved. 'You were right. It is easier to know.' He hesitated a moment, then sat down to join them, and accepted one of the burnt bannocks and let Efnís and Dubornos draw him into conversation about the cave and the way it had been painted and the talk drifted into other things and he did not go back to looking out at the darkness.

After a while, when nothing had yet happened but that more deer-men came and built the fire higher, he asked Dubornos and Efnís to help him braid his hair after the manner of the Eceni, with a warrior's knot at the side and a single black kill-feather woven in at the temple. Efnís gave him a necklace to wear with amber beads carved in the shapes of dream-animals; six-legged bears followed wildcats with long teeth and otters that held snakes between their jaws. Bellos had an armband in bronze that sat well on Hawk's arm and Gunovar took some red wool from the edging of her tunic and bound it about the quill of the feather to mark him as one who had saved others in battle at the risk of his own life. He looked quite different when they were done.

Dubornos said, 'They want you as Coritani, not as Eceni.'

Hawk grinned. 'Then they can change me. But they will know they have done it.'

The rite of the horned god began with three young women painted all in black spirals who played whistling pipes carved from deer horn that made low, fluted noises like night birds.

The music looped up and down, weaving laceworks of sound that encircled Hawk as a net circles the salmon, and drew him away from the others to stand by the fire. They made him stand in the north, the place of the hunter, of the warrior, of the horned god. The leader was the same one who had taken them in the beginning. He stood, and, for all his strength, was smaller than Hawk, and his hair did not gleam on his head, nor was the bronze of his skin set off by the armband of the same colour and the flowing amber about his neck. He bore no kill-feathers, red-banded or not, and was less for it, and must have known it.

Hawk said, 'The Coritani worship the Horned One above everything except Briga. Even so, we do not send unwilling life to any god.'

'Nor do we. When you understand what we ask of the gods and they of us, you will embrace your death willingly. The music and the dance alone will make it easy.'

Three young men, painted in white lines, brought Gunovar to

join him. She was lame from the Roman inquisitors and had done nothing to adorn herself and still she looked regal. With care, they removed the dreamer's thong from her brow and gave her a neck-band instead made of the backbones of deer.

The deer-warriors made a corridor, and two at the front took the skulls and tapped on them with bones to set up a rhythm, as the bear-dancers did on their skull drums, but less discordantly.

The elder took his knife and made a third cut on Hawk, who stood still and let him do it. The man stepped back and grunted and was half deer again.

'Outside. Everybody.' His arms swung wide. 'All of us, from youngest to oldest, will dance to meet the god outside, under the stars and the horned moon.'

X X X V

IN THE LAND OF THE CORNOVII, ONLY ARDACOS COULD TRAVEL safely.

The pathmakers of the Brigantes were fast and silent and left no trail but they did not see the scout who watched from a hillside. Ardacos saw him and found him and killed him and returned with a Cornovi knife, with a deer's foot hilt, as proof. Breaca thanked the pathmakers and sent them back to Venutios.

Soon after that, Ardacos left his horse on open land where it could be found by others and went on foot, ranging from side to side on the rolling heath and into the open weave of the forest, leaving marks that only Cygfa could find. Breaca followed her lead, as safe or as dangerous as it might be; she could do nothing else, nor speed their travel. Miraculously, she felt herself free of all responsibility for the first time since she had come east from Mona to the lands of the Eceni.

It was an illusion, but she accepted the gift of its freedom and chose not to think deeply on what they were nearing, or the failed quest behind, or the question that Venutios had offered as an unexpected, unwanted gift.

With Cygfa ahead and Stone at her heel, she rode fast on small paths, or no paths at all, heading south and a little west. The gritstone and heather moors of the meeting place became high limestone crags and deep clefted valleys with forest eaten at the edges by the axes of the legions, but not yet reduced all to farmland.

Near evening, under a clear sky with the sun vastly red on the horizon, they saw Ardacos for the first time since he had abandoned his horse. He sat on a fallen birch, eating flowers of cow parsley and elder, so that his lips were dusted in yellow and his thighs streaked where he had wiped his fingers clean on them. He had taken the time to braid his hair and weave in the eye teeth of the bear that were his right. His face was painted with white clay and his eyes were no longer haunted. There were three deer-handled knives newly hanging from his belt.

Breaca said, 'You have met with the bear.'

'I have. And she is content.' There was a life in his eyes she had not seen for years; he, too, was revelling in the gift of a day's freedom, whatever may come at the end of it. He met her gaze and held it and said the things without speaking that she needed most to hear.

Breaking off, he nodded over his shoulder to the forest, where the undergrowth grew to chest height and seemed impassable. 'From here, we need to leave your horses also.' He looked up the length of her, from feet to head. 'Are you fit to run?'

It was a challenge of the kind they had set each other on Mona, long before, when the world was young. She lifted one shoulder and said, 'I don't know. Shall we find out?'

She could run, which was good to know, and exhilarating for a while before it became simply hard work.

The challenge was greater than they had ever set on Mona. Then they had not been flogged, had not walked the grey lands between life and death, had not lost – and so refound – the reasons for living. Only once on Mona had they had to run and fight and hide with death all around from undiscovered sources.

Here, it was not all running: Breaca crawled along paths through dense brush that opened only barely and closed behind them; she crossed rivers on stepping stones screened by drooping hazel and river alder so that they were invisible until she trod on them; she sheltered under a whitethorn bush for the duration of a storm and then ran on.

Long into dusk, she scrambled up a narrow path by feel alone and sat for a moment at the top of the limestone crag clutching the bent rowan that had anchored her with one hand and Stone with the other and thought that, if she was not as fit as in her youth on Mona, she was no worse than she had been before the procurator's flogging, and perhaps a little fitter.

Soon after that, they saw the fires in the wooded valley down and to their right.

'Wait here.' Ardacos laid a hand on her arm. Breaca sat and watched him slide alone into the dusk.

Cygfa did not wait. She vanished and returned as a ghosted shape in the dusk; only her hair was visible, and the silvered whites of her eyes. 'Graine's there, in the valley.'

'And the others?'

'They're all there, and more than a hundred Cornovii, all dancing. Hawk is in the centre, wearing a stag skull with antlers. There's a woman with him. I think it may be Gunovar.'

From somewhere to the right, Ardacos said, 'It is.' He pushed through branches that drenched him with old rain and came close enough to let her read him in the dusk. He loved Gunovar, as he had once loved Breaca. The weight of that carved new lines in his face.

To him, Breaca said, 'If we attack a hundred Cornovii, we'll die and they may kill the others. To live, we need to reach the elders alive. If we walk in openly, do you think the scouts will kill us before they recognize who we are?'

'They know already.' She saw the tilt of his face in the part-light as he looked down at his hands. 'It is only because of who you are that we have been allowed to come this far. If they did not have orders to guide us to their elders, we would have been sent away long since.' The admission hurt; he was once the best there had ever been. He raised his voice so that the words carried to the sighing trees. 'I know of six who watch us, and have done so since we entered the woods. Another two I am less certain of.'

It was not impossible, only unexpected; Breaca had never yet felt unsafe in Ardacos' care. She said, 'If they knew you were there, why did they let you kill three of their scouts?'

The sun-lines deepened about his eyes. 'The ones who died were not good enough. The men of the deer, like the followers of the bear, test their young thus against worthy opponents. I am . . . not unworthy. Those deaths will not be held against us.'

'But they didn't kill you when they knew you were there. They, too, are not unworthy. Does the same not apply?'

He grinned, a youth again, who has won a challenge. 'They didn't know where I was, except when I was with you, and you are the Boudica who is guarded now by more than Briga and the grandmothers. You make your own rules, or the gods make them for you.'

'How do they know that?'

He shook his head at the stupidity of the question. 'Breaca, it shines from you. It has always done, just less so when you were ill. The elders of the Horned One are not so different from the elders of the she-bear. They will see it as we would. If you would stand now, and address those who are hidden, we can test if I am right.'

Graine danced for the horned god under pine made heavy by rain, to skull-drummed rhythms and pipe music and low urgent chants that the god had given to the ancestors and had never been changed.

The skull-beat was a heartbeat, calm sometimes, sometimes hunted, sometimes – and Graine shut herself away at these times – fired by the rut and the power of the god in the stag battles and the mating afterwards that was the right of the victor.

Those times apart, she danced through the sweat and the smoke and the weaving net of noise because she could do nothing else; the songs sang into her blood, the skull drums pulsed into the marrow of her bones, the whistling pipes drew her soul forward so that her flesh had to follow.

She danced in a ring of Cornovii. They were not all men but all of them except her were old enough to have had children and all the women showed the linear marks of childbirth on their bellies. They were all unclothed and no-one tried to protect her from the sight of it and she found that she no longer cared.

With Dubornos in front of her, animated as she had never known him, she danced time and again through the cycle of life that was most sacred to the Cornovii; through the growth of the small thing seeded by the stag in the belly of the hind and the quick slither of its birthing and its first steps in a world where the Horned One held the new life sacred.

With Efnís wild-eyed and leaping behind, she danced over and over the enfolding breath of the mother and the calf's first knowing of cold, first fear, first taste of milk and of green things growing and of bark in the winter when the snow hid the ground.

With Bellos close to her side, surefooted as any mountain hind, she danced and became the deer and lived and almost-died free of humanity's care and so began to touch the edges of what that might mean.

She was one of hundreds and they all danced in a ring about the horned man in the centre, who was Hawk and not-Hawk, and the woman who was more than Gunovar who met him and painted her face with his blood.

They danced and the rain dried on the grass and the stars spun and made new shapes and every one of them was carried by the magic of the drums and the horn pipes and they were no longer Eceni and Cornovii and a single Coritani, for ever at war, but one pulse, one heartbeat, one breath, one dance through life towards the inevitable death and there was not one of them who would not willingly have stepped over the precipice that their dancing made to fall into the arms of the waiting god when he called them.

Each time they came close and backed away and started the cycle again with the rut and the setting of seed, they felt envy that the one in the centre was the chosen; that his seed would remain to make new life and he would fly to the god in the moment of his perfection, and be honoured for it ever after.

Graine stubbed her toe. It was a small thing, and only came about because she was by far the youngest and the smallest of the dancers. She was a hind, or perhaps a young buck, and the hunt began and she was trying to out-leap the hounds, which meant leaping higher than Efnís and Dubornos, and she came down awkwardly and twisted her big toe and it hurt so that she hopped and lost the rhythm and thereby lost the dance.

She understood the power of it only by the shock when she stepped back. She did not stop dancing – to do so now would have been to risk being trampled by the rest – but the salt sweat on her lip was no longer the salt of birthing and the pounding heart in her chest was from exertion, not from the hunt, or the rut, or the closeness of death.

She looked about her and saw Efnís completely given to the god and, far more surprisingly, Dubornos, dancing with his eyes half closed and rapture painted on the hills and valleys of his face such as she had never seen in him in the whole of her life. He was a man transformed, aching with the fear of the hunt and the proximity of death and yet in ecstasy of a kind his troubled heart had never given him.

She looked for Bellos and found him nearby and that was the greatest surprise of all. He leaped with the others and shook his head with the pound of the beat, but when she sought him and found him, he turned his blind face to hers and smiled, quite normally, and then blinked both his blind eyes together in such an obvious signal that she stopped dancing for a moment, and havoc and discord shivered down the line.

'Don't stop.' Bellos was at her side, lifting her forward so that they could continue. 'Stay in yourself and watch and learn. It is not a bad thing to be given to the god, but the moon will rise soon and things will change and it is good for one given to Nemain to be able to step away from her when the need arises.'

'But you're given to Briga.'

'And she is mother to all things. Even the horned god. Even death. And I think, if you look now between the trees, that she has sent one who will change what was to have happened here. You may not have to watch Hawk die.'

Graine stared about, confused. She was dancing again and the fire was bright. Beyond it, the forest was a swirl of dark and other dark and none of it had shape more than a shadow except for the silver haze on the horizon that was the first cutting edge of the sickle moon. Bellos picked her up and whirled her high and set her on his shoulders. His hands held her tightly, buoyantly; he was as exuberant as the others, only with a different reason.

'Be my eyes for me,' he said, laughing, so that she laughed too, 'and tell me that I am right and that not only is the Boudica healed, but she has found the heart-song of a blade that will carry all of us past the legions.'

Breaca heard the song of her father's blade long before she came to it.

Because of Stone, she could not climb down the rock to the valley's floor.

Because there was no other way down nearby, the Cornovi scouts who had become their guides led them south along the top of the cliff, towards the far southern end where the limestone dipped away to join open heathland and a hound could run safely down.

Because of that, they came to the horses, and the packs that they still carried.

Ardacos had been right: the scouts had known who Breaca was and were in awe of her; even in the dark, they were careful not to hold her gaze for long, or to look her full in the face. He had been wrong about their numbers. There were nine scouts leading them and surrounding them and following behind in case they should lose the path; the eight that he had known of, and one he had not.

The shame of that one left unseen hung about him the full length of the silent, leaping run along the crag's head, past the fire and the dancing and the rattled drumbeats and mourning pipes that reached up from the valley's floor and snared them, almost, in the net of their rhythms.

They were not moving slowly; the scouts could run through dense forest at night as easily as in daytime and they were good guides; those who followed them were not much slower. Even so, the stars had moved a long way across the sky before they came to the crag's end, so that Breaca had begun to wonder if she should have tethered Stone and gone back for him in the morning. Then they found the path and ran down it to the valley's floor and a horse that she recognized whinnied in the dark and it was not, after all, a waste of time running to the end of the valley.

'That's Graine's mare,' she said.

It was, and with it were Dubornos' moon-grey and Gunovar's draught horse and Hawk's odd-eyed chestnut. The light from the fires stretched just so far and no more, enough to show that their travelling packs were untouched, and the weapons wrapped in oiled skin and bound to the back of the saddle.

Her father's blade was there, strapped to the back of Hawk's horse, that had been sent to Mona for safe keeping, at Eburovic's command. She felt it as a tangible presence, as if her great-great-grandfather had made it newly and lifted it from the fires and placed it in her hand, still smelling of burned iron and his sweat. She felt the roughness of his face as he kissed her, and his hands on her shoulders and his voice, speaking, but not the words that he said. He was her father, and not her father, a different part of her lineage.

The blade sang to her, as it had not done in the silent dell by the gods' pool with Valerius watching over her as if she might break, and her son setting fire to the Roman watchtower in the first attack of a war. Or perhaps it had sung just the same and she had not been able to hear it then.

The horses were hobbled by a fast-running stream. Under the watch of the Cornovi scouts, she spoke to them, and briefly to the horse-boys on guard, and the blade was hers; wrapped tight and singing. Her palm burned as it had when it was newly cut. She could have wept for the feel of it returning, when she had thought it gone beyond recall.

She knelt and laid the blade on the stones and heather by the stream. Stars gave her light. The Hunter had passed over, but the Hound remained, reflected in the running water, and the twinned Serpents that followed behind it. She sought, and found, the ties with which Hawk had bound it safe.

'Not yet. Don't unwrap it here.' Ardacos was a shadow seen in the silver of the stream. He spoke softly, so that the sound was lost in the rushing water. 'If you need to use it to fight your way out, we are lost anyway, but I think it will count for more if it is unwrapped by the fire in front of the elders under the light of the horned moon.' He came close enough to touch. 'It can sing to you wrapped as well as unwrapped.'

She had always trusted his common sense. 'Thank you.' She squeezed his arm. 'There was no shame in missing the ninth scout.'

'I should have died for it.' His voice was less bitter than she had feared. 'But for this night, I am glad I did not. Just to hear the music they make was worth living a night longer.' He tipped his head down the valley, whence the fire made the trees glow red and the music of the deer-men skittered through the branches. 'Do the skull drums of the she-bear sear so strongly the souls of those who are not part of our rites?'

Breaca grinned. 'Far worse. But you have never yet sent a man unwilling to his death. For that you can drum any kind of discord. We will have to move fast now if we are to reach the dancers before the moon rises. The bear is not a friend to the deer. Will you be safe if we go back to the fire?'

'As safe as anyone. And I'm not going to stay away. We should take the horses. It will look better like that.'

*

Her mother rode Hawk's horse, and Stone was with her.

Breaca came from between the trees and stopped for a moment where the trees stopped, so that pines stood as honour guards on either side, and the fire made liquid bronze of her hair and turned Hawk's red horse to heaving, sweating gold.

She was changed, different, cast in new colours. Graine saw all of those in the first vertiginous moments when it was all she could do to hold on to Bellos and not fall from his shoulders in the whirling madness of the dance and looking out to the trees was one thing too many.

Graine saw her mother and the horse and the hound and something lit all three from within that was greater than the fire and was not anything she had seen before. Whether it was a healing was another question.

She could not hear the song of any blade, which was a good thing.

Holding tight to Bellos' wrists to keep from falling, she spoke to his upturned face and the quantity of questions it held. 'I have never seen the wildfire in my mother. Is this it?'

'I don't know.' He was still joyful. 'But it's far more than I was led to expect. What of the bladesong?'

'I don't know. I can't hear it. I think it may be my grandfather's blade. Valerius gave it to Hawk. It's still on his horse.'

Iron clashed on iron in her head as she spoke. Not understanding, she said, 'The dance must have opened you to more than is your right. That song is not for others to hear.'

Bellos' face was open and wise. He had dreamed on Mona and was given to Briga. He sang as he swung her. 'Tonight, child of the moon, everything is for everyone to hear.'

He had dreamed on Mona and was given to Briga and she was a child and not yet fully healed. Still, she did not believe him.

The trees parted again. Cygfa came through, and then Ardacos, on Breaca's other side. Others saw them, and the dancing faltered, and then the singing and the pipes and one of the drums. Its twin kept up an erratic solo for a dozen beats, and then it, too, failed.

Hawk continued to leap and spin in the circle's centre; the god filled him and he could not stop. Gunovar matched him, so that he might not be left alone. The rest of the dancers, Cornovi and Eceni, came, sweating, to a standstill.

Bellos said, 'You should go down now.'

Graine came unsteadily to the ground, holding on to Bellos' fore-arms and then his shoulders and then his waist. She hugged him as her feet reached the earth and felt the soft whisper of his lips as he stooped to kiss her head.

About her, men and women were returning slowly to their senses. Not all of them wished to. Efnís shook his head and bent double with his hands propped on his knees, catching his breath. 'Too . . . soon,' he said. 'It should not . . . have ended yet.' He did not have breath to elaborate, but he was not a broken man, only concerned.

Dubornos was broken. He stood near Graine, staring east to where the first hard edge of the moon sliced up over the crag's head. The light of the fire did not touch him at all. He was bone white with his eyes as pits in his face and a black weight of grief about him that cast his decades of melancholy into shade by comparison.

For no better reason than that she was closest, and she cared for him, Graine slid her hand in his. He flinched and made to step away and then came back to himself and let her small hand hold him, and feel the shaking and the hollowness in his soul and the tunnel that led from it to the god, that was closing.

He looked down at her and tried to smile and failed. With raw shock, she saw the tears leak to join the sweat on his cheeks. 'It's over,' he said, and his voice had lost all hope. 'We were so close, and your mother has broken it.'

Graine let her hand drop away and did not try to comfort him further. Never in her life had she heard so much grief from any man.

She turned towards her mother and did not know what she could do, only that what had been shattered must be made whole, and only the Boudica, who had done the breaking, could mend it.

XXXVI

GRAINE.

Graine in the circle of leaping, spinning dancers, holding her own and moving among them, loose limbed and active as a hound whelp on its first hunt.

Graine swung high onto the shoulders of a blond-haired youth with eyes that shone like moon discs in the firelight.

Graine laughing – *laughing* – and looking across the open space to her mother and then not laughing.

Graine clutching the youth's arms as he set her down, and letting him kiss her head.

Graine talking to Efnís, who looked god-dazed, and then Dubornos, who looked as if he had died, only that his body waited for permission to fall. The only colour about him came from the fox fur on his arm, bright as the firelight.

Graine. Graine coming to see her, a little taller, a little more of the woman-to-be and less of the wounded child; Graine, free, finally, of the bruises and the dark shadows beneath her eyes; Graine, focused and serious, walking across the dancing ground as if it were the great-house in highest ceremony, looking as Airmid looked, or Luain mac Calma, or Valerius when his gods were with him, and so perhaps it was not too much to hope that she, too, had found healing and been made whole again.

Graine at the red colt's shoulder with one hand on the exuberant

Stone and the other on her mother's knee, with her face tilted up showing horn-streaks marked on her forehead in clay over wide sea-grey eyes, turned copper-green in the firelight.

Graine, child of her soul, not healed after all, but better, saying, 'You can't let it stop now. The seed has been set too often. It can't break before it goes to the god, or we are all broken with it, not just Dubornos.'

It was necessary, suddenly, to come down from the horse.

Breaca slid to the ground and hooked one arm over the saddle to hold herself steady after the madness of the night ride.

She needed that hold; the world was not as it had been. The beat of the deer-drums still pulsed in the land and came up through the soles of her feet. Her father's blade sang and would not be silent. Cunobelin's ring hanging on its thong about her neck pressed into the notch between her collar bones and she heard the breathless whisper of the Sun Hound, dry as old leaves, saying, *Daughter*.

Fleetingly, she saw the weave of the worlds stretch out strong and unbroken with Graine at the heart of it. The relief of that was stunning. She held the saddle more tightly that she might not fall.

She might have taken the ring off then, and given it to her daughter as evidence of that line unbroken, but that a man had come to stand in front of her, painted in red lines from heel to brow, and he had the same eyes as the ancestor-dreamer. He reached for her, and held her wrist, staying her hand.

More kindly than those eyes allowed, he said, 'Not yet. There are things you must do before you can relinquish to others the weight of all that you carry, and this daughter may not hold it all. Remember the question you have been asked.'

If it comes to it, which will you save, your land or your lineage?

An elder of the Cornovii could not possibly have heard Venutios; no scout in the world could have come close to them on top of the bare rock. Hairs rose down the length of her spine. 'Who are you?'

'Sûr mac Donnachaidh. Elder. Friend to the Boudica as she was before and as she is now, holder of the threads to past and future. You would not be here alive without my saying it.'

That much, she believed to be true. Graine was still close, and unafraid. Breaca crouched down so that their eyes were level. Stone pushed between and joined them both. 'Heart of life, what is it that's broken, that must be mended?'

Her daughter frowned. 'The circle. The dance. I don't know. Dubornos could tell you.'

Dubornos was not fit to talk. In his stead, the painted deer-elder said, 'The horned moon rises. Tonight, my people and yours have danced life into death. The life must be given or the cycle is broken. Already the weaving is fraying loose.'

Efnís was there, panting, but able. He said, 'He's telling the truth. We have gone too far to let this go. To break the circle now would bring ruin to more than the Cornovii.'

Breaca said, 'You could have stopped this before it began. Why did you not?'

He was the man named next Elder of Mona. With all the gravity of that, he said, 'I could not have stopped it. I could only have refused to take part. They wanted Graine and I am sworn to her side. Where she goes, I go. Where she dances, I dance.'

'She did not have to dance.'

'I did,' Graine said. 'Hawk danced. We couldn't leave him to do it alone.' The simplicity of a child, and all the layers and layers beneath it.

Hawk was still dancing after a fashion. The beat of the deer-drums still moved him where it had abandoned Efnís and left Dubornos bereft. He heard his name and was more able to walk than Dubornos. The stag's head crown gave him height above all of the others as he wove through the throng towards them. He carried it well. The deer-elder swayed aside to make room for him.

He was breathing as hard as a racehorse, but it was the marks on him that mattered more. From a distance, he had seemed painted as the deer men were. Close, the red that marked him was from knife-cuts, a dozen or more, a hand's breadth apart, that lined his body as paint lined the elders'. Oddly, they heightened him. He was fit and lean and his body was perfect.

His mind, too, had grown on Mona; he had lost his arrogance, and his fear. Quite plainly, he had danced to the limits of his endurance and beyond it, but he met Breaca's gaze more cleanly than he had ever done. The old pulse of the deer-drums swept through them both one last time and was still.

'I did everything I could to keep your daughter safe,' he said. 'I kept my oath.'

'I know. And are doing so still. You know what they ask of you?'

'Yes.'

'Do you accept it?'

The deer-elder flinched. Efnís sucked air hissing through his teeth. Graine put out a hand to her mother and took it away again.

Hawk regarded her calmly. 'I would not cling to life if it will bring to ruin all that you have fought for.' He had learned, too, to pick his words as did the dreamers.

Breaca said, 'But you don't seek to embrace the god in death?'

'No.'

There was a hush, and a keening somewhere that she thought was her father's blade, or possibly the ring, and then found was Dubornos, who stood swaying, and making a noise that should only have come from the lands beyond life.

The deer-elder begged, silently, his soul in his eyes. He wet his lips and looked down and then up again, framing words and letting them go. Eventually, baldly, 'If you do this, we are severed for ever from the god.'

Breaca said, 'Your warriors could kill us all. You would have your sacrifice then.'

He had considered that, clearly. 'It would be for naught; the one anointed must go willingly, or not at all.'

'Hawk is not willing.'

'He was before you came. He could be made so again.'

Breaca turned. 'Hawk?'

His eyes held hers a moment, then, with as much ceremony as any man might achieve who has danced beyond exhaustion and yet carries the god within, he bent his head and lifted off the stag's full-pointed majesty and held it out to the deer-elder. 'I'm sorry. I understand what it means, but to lie now will not help. I was never willing. I will never be so. Life is too precious to cast aside for such as this.'

Cygfa moved her horse a little closer to Breaca, as she might have done at the start of battle. She said, 'Who carries your father's blade is your son, and so is sacrosanct.'

The blade lay quiet on the back of the saddle. To untie it was a matter of moments, and then to unwrap the shroud of oiled linen.

The blade was of day and the power of the sun. The bear on its hilt was cast in bronze and came most to life under the bright light of noon. Even so, it shone in the night-place of the horned god, drawing in the firelight and spinning it out richer and redder to the far edges of the clearing.

In the shocked space that followed, Breaca said, 'Then would you, Hawk of the Coritani and now of the Eceni, accept the blade of my father, in gift this time, not only in trust, knowing that if you accept, you become as my son in all things, as Cygfa is my daughter?'

'With great gratitude.' His soul sparked deep in his eyes. 'You may have to tell Cunomar, though. I would not wish to be responsible for that.'

A little hoarsely, Ardacos said, 'That much, I can do,' and so it was settled, and the Boudica had another son, and this one not of the Sun Hound's lineage, nor of her own father's line.

It was a small thing, the giving of the blade, done with no more ceremony than that she passed it from her hands to his, and he accepted, and tested the weight again as if it were new, and became aware of the occasion and turned and lifted it high to the fire and the dancers beyond it, and let it fall again, in silence.

In silence. The appalling keening had stopped. Breaca feared that Dubornos might have lost consciousness, or that his body had caught up with his soul and fallen into death, but it seemed that he was still alive and could walk, which was a miracle, then, as he came closer, was perhaps more a curse.

The tall, gaunt singer had been melancholy from his early youth when he had first come to Mona, but this night had taken him far beyond that. Grief was etched on every part of his being, a lifetime of hurt laid bare as he had never shown it before. His eyes were tunnels into other worlds and each one of them was torment. He looked through Breaca to Cygfa, whom he had loved for ten years without hope of return, and then back again to Breaca, so that she knew before he spoke what he was going to say.

'I would go willing to the god.'

'No!'

'Dubornos, you can't.'

She and the deer-elder spoke together. Their voices clashed like blades across his head. He looked from one to the other and gained a little colour at the challenge they offered. He touched two fingers to the band of tawny vixen pelt on his upper arm. Its warmth fired him.

'Why not? I have danced under the dark of the moon in the lost time before the horned god sent his daughter to light us; I have set the seed as often as Hawk did; I have drowned in the birthing and come to life again, gasping like a landed salmon; I have found first feet, stumbling under the nine-branched hazel; I have known the first run, tasted the first milk, the first sward, the first beech nuts; I have dug for forage under first snow and seen the rain fall to wash it away in spring; I have watched the young bucks fighting at the time of the rowan berries and have fought them in play and in earnest; I have roared as the stag and cracked horns with him and won and fallen in the same breath. I have lived the life in its cycles times without number and I have danced nearer to the edge of the precipice each time, knowing what I did.

'From the first, I have envied Hawk his gift of life to the god and now I find that he does not wish to give it. I am a singer. I know what it is to speak with the gods. I understand what we need now, as well as any man might; I can ask from the roots of my soul for the help that we need to keep the land true to the gods and ourselves true to the land. I offer myself willingly in Hawk's place; to go now, in this cause, would give me the greatest of all possible joy.'

He was a singer, trained for half a lifetime in the rhythms and metres of the great-house. He knew how to cast his voice to hold an audience be they in front of the winter fires of a family or the great blazing trenches of the council house on Mona. He knew how to mould words to his purpose, and he did so bending every part of his skill to it.

He had faced the elder and all of the dancers as he spoke. Now, at the last, he, who knew Breaca as well as any man alive, turned and spoke only to her.

'This is not a final, pointless gesture of self-reproach because I failed to protect Cunomar and then Graine after him. At each time, I did the best I could, I know that and know that you know it. This is greater than any petty recrimination or guilt; it is my destiny, the pinnacle to which all of my life has pointed. Airmid would understand. She has held me in the lands of the living since the first time I tried to leave. She would not hold me back now. It is the only gift I have ever asked of you – and I do ask it, from the core of my soul. She would not let you keep it from me.'

Breaca was weeping, which was ridiculous, if a testament to his skill. Graine, dry-faced, had slipped a hand into hers and was squeezing as she had done in the days when they first moved east out of Mona. Stone nudged her leg and whined.

Cygfa said, 'You do yourselves and us great honour.' Her voice was thick with care and admiration. Still, she did not love him.

Ardacos said, 'Can it be done? You did not dance in the centre of the circle as Hawk did. You were not marked for the god.'

'It can be done, and Mona would support it. But not here and not now and not as it was planned.' Efnís answered before the deer-elder could speak. Turning, he pointed east and they all looked to where the first round edge of the sickle moon had carved its way through the white stone of the crag and was already lighting the clearing.

Speaking to the greater crowd, he said, 'It's too late to begin what the men of the Horned One would have done, but there may be a way that would join the gods of the night with the gods of the day, join the oldest of the gods, older than the Horned One, with the gods of our time. Dubornos, if he is truly willing, could carry the wish of our hearts to the gods in a way that transcends all prayer and dreaming. Such a thing has been done in living memory on Mona, but not often. It would be a very great thing if it could be done here and now at the time of greatest need in our confrontation with Rome.'

To those closer, he said, 'It would be a faster death than was planned for Hawk, and would need to be carried out at full dawn, when the sun shares the sky with the horned moon. There's time between now and then to make ready. If Dubornos truly wishes this.'

'I do.'

To the painted man in front of her, Breaca said, 'Will you allow this?'

Sûr mac Donnachaidh, elder of the horned god and friend to the Boudica, closed his eyes and consulted with the god within. Opening them, he spoke in his own tongue to the silent, painted men who had gathered closest.

At length, he said, 'It's possible. We can say no more than that. If the fox-man would give himself willingly, then the god will not refuse him. But it should not be done here, at the dancing place, on land given only to the god. We will take you to the heathland, beyond the river, where the sun and the moon may be seen together without trees in the way. There is time for that if we move swiftly.'

They built no fire on the heath. The late sickle moon hung sharp and bright and clear above them and gave more light than anything made by human hand. Beneath its light, seeding thistles drifted down onto the breeze and buttercups shone pale as milk.

Dubornos led them to the heath and across it. He was a man transformed; faced with death and so release, he had come into himself as a man does who lives his own destiny after years of its denial.

The deer-dancers followed him in a broad procession. They brought their skull drums and their pipes and their god, in so far as they were able. Hawk did not take back the antlered stag's pride, nor was it offered to Dubornos in his stead; the night had already moved beyond that.

Graine walked with Bellos between Cygfa and Hawk, who had gone from almost-dead to almost-brother with a speed that left her uncertain of where she stood. He bore her grandfather's blade in a harness across his back and that changed everything, only that she did not yet know how.

She wanted to ask if he could hear the bladesong, but no-one spoke in the long, dark trek from the dancing place through the woods and past the river where the horses were left tethered and out onto the heath where the horned moon hung so bright above.

She forgot her question after a while and lost herself in the rhythms of the deer-drums that kept her feet moving long after she would have otherwise tried to sleep, and the husky whistle of the horn pipes that drifted back on the thistledown and tugged at her blood so that she had energy enough to run and dance another cycle of life and another after it if such were needed.

The sky was lightening to the east. Graine felt it in the increasing urgency of the drums. She began to walk faster, and then to run except it was not running, but a kind of dancing. Lame Gunovar was at the front with Dubornos. She set up a chant in her deep, hoarse voice that was older in its language and rhythms than the deer-chant, more deeply rooted, more unsettling in its challenges.

They ran to that new rhythm, hitting the earth with their feet so they sounded like horses crossing the dry earth. After a while, Efnís began a counterpoint and others joined him, weaving in and through with the essences of other gods.

They ran faster then, and faster, until their blood boiled in their hearts and mist covered their eyes that was not only the morning mist. In it, indistinctly at first and then more surely, Graine saw the gods run beside them. Nemain led them, in her guise as a hare and then as Airmid, or someone close to her; Briga followed, who was death and life and birth and war and the lure of the singer's tale of the thrashing salmon under the ninefold hazel; Herne ran with them both, father and brother, lover and son: the horned god who was the deer and the wolf, the hare and the hound, the dove and the hawk, for ever part of the cycle of hunter and prey.

These three Graine knew and expected. Behind them, around them, came the ones she did not and could not fully name: Lugh of the sun-spear, and Camul, perhaps, who had been the war god of the Trinovantes who had named Camulodunum in his honour; Belin, who was the sun under a different name for a different people, and Macha, the mare-mother, who brought life to the Dumnonii with her milk and her hides and her yearly birthing of foals.

Behind them and around them were the gods of the ancestors, older, wilder gods whose names she had never heard except in the smoke of the great-house fires with their images running on the rafters; the ancestor-dreamer was there, and Ardacos' she-bear, and deer with antlers that reached to entangle the stars and hounds who bore snakes about them as they ran and a man-woman figure made of starlight and deathlight and laced with the rising dawn who was the horizon lifted upright and was older than all of the rest combined.

She should have been afraid. She was afraid, but the chant held her and would not let her go and Bellos' face was full of wonder so that it was hard to imagine him afraid and Hawk was there and he, too, could see what she could see and his hand brushed her wrist so that she could feel the life in him and hear, very faintly, the song of her grandfather's blade which was more frightening than all the rest, and exhilarating and intoxicating so that she could run and not be afraid.

They stopped. Everything stopped: the dance, the chant, the

drums, the pipes, the heart-crash of the run and the mist that came with it. The gods were there, but less substantial so that only by looking sideways out of the corner of her eye could Graine still see them, and then only fleetingly.

They stood at the edge of a moss, where sphagnum lay innocently green and bog cotton fluffed like dandelion heads and myrtle scented the air with slated mint and the very flatness of the land screamed danger.

Breathlessly, Bellos said, 'They will do it here. He will die to the earth and the water. Graine, can you see a stone? Something about as big as your two fists. There will be one close. It would be good if you could find it, not anyone else.'

She did find it: a smooth, egg-shaped rock cut through with a vein of pale crystal. Bellos took it in his hands and lifted it to his ear and said, 'Perfect. Keep it for later. You will know when. Now, we should be closer.' Hawk led them all forward through the crowd.

Cygfa followed because these were her brother and sister and the night was a time to keep together, not because she wanted to be close to Dubornos and his death. Even so, it came to the same thing; when Hawk stopped, they were with Breaca who was with Efnís, who was standing with Dubornos on one side and Gunovar on the other, and the chants were still in them and weaving them together so that they were set apart from the rest as the gods are from their people.

The moon was sharp as a blade. It cut the sky on the edge of its curve; west of it was the absolute black of night; east was subtly paler, blue instead of black, lightening by degrees to the eastern horizon.

Efnís said, 'We are in time; the night is not yet lost.' He stepped back, so that Dubornos and Gunovar were together, still breathing fast and hard from the run, still sheened with sweat. He said, 'The seed has been set over and over in the chant and the dancing. It should be set in living blood and bone now, so that life comes of death.'

If Cygfa had not been there, they might have done it, standing, lost in the godspace and the earthen urgency of the chant and the need that was clear in them both, but she was, and Dubornos' gaze settled on her even as Efnís spoke.

He loved her, he had always loved her, and he was going to die. Graine was near to him. She read the longing in him first, and then the others.

In the space where no-one spoke, Cygfa said, 'Let it be me.'

The gods and the world held their breath. Graine heard a keening such as Dubornos had made earlier and could not find its source, only heard the endless, unstoppable ache and wept for it.

Dubornos did not weep. He looked up at the moon and out to the sun and around to where the shadows of the gods lay on the land. 'No. Thank you, but no.'

Cygfa said, 'It is willingly offered.' There were tears wet on her lashes. Graine had never seen that.

Dubornos shook his head. 'I know. Thank you.' His eyes were ancient. The pain had become so vast it had turned to compassion. 'But "willing" is different from a yearning that grows from the heart's roots and I would not have it otherwise. In any case . . .' He grinned, and they could see the lightness of who he might have been if his life had taken different turns, 'there is not time for what I would want and anything less would be . . . too little.' He stepped forward and embraced her, and pressed dry lips to her cheek and stepped apart again. She stood shocked and white in his absence.

With a courage that could be tasted, Gunovar said, 'We are back, then, to what Efnís said. You and I can do this.'

The moment had gone; even Graine could feel that. Dubornos shook his head. 'Can I not go as I am? Do the gods need that I leave a seed when what I take is our asking for their help?'

It was Sûr mac Donnachaidh, the deer-elder, who said, 'The time of seed-setting is past. What we make here is something new. What the fox-man wants, he should have. The gods will not honour the gift of his life otherwise.' More than human minds knew him correct.

Dawn was growing, the night becoming less. They were measurable heartbeats away from the time when the sun would begin to outshine the moon, the day to engulf the night.

Efnís said, 'We should begin. Dubornos, how would you have us—'

Graine heard Bellos draw a breath through his teeth and felt gooseflesh rise on her arms.

Dubornos said, 'The threefold death. It must be.'

It was older than the death the deer-elders had planned for

Hawk, and honoured more gods. Bellos let out his breath again in a long, soft hiss. 'Well done. Very well done.' He said it quietly; Graine did not think she was meant to hear.

Efnís nodded and ran his tongue across his teeth and said, 'Who should do it?'

Graine had not thought he might be given that choice. The stone she had found weighed suddenly heavy in her hand so that she wanted to drop it, or throw it away, but could not. His gaze swung to his right, where she stood among the others, and her heart stopped in her chest, then began again, crashingly, as he smiled for her and his eyes said goodbye and his gaze moved on and rested on Cygfa, who turned white as the moon and seemed not to breathe for the long moment it took for him to speak his wordless farewells there, too, and then passed on to linger more briefly on Hawk and to exchange the odd shared look with Bellos' blind gaze and then the elders and Gunovar and so it was obvious, because he came to her last, whom he would choose.

He did not kneel, although the thought was there, only stepped forward to face the woman who stood a little apart from the rest, and had done so from the beginning, the one who had run just behind him all the way from the dancing ground, who stood there now, with her back to the rising sun, gathering all the light of day and night so that she stood balanced exactly on the borderline of both, and held them both, and was them both, shiningly.

With all that he asked and offered free to be read on his face, Dubornos gave the warrior's salute of the Eceni and said, 'Breaca, would you do this for me?'

She heard him speak her name through the soar of the dawn in her head.

She saw the radiance of his face and could not understand why she had never thought him beautiful before. More than a man in love, more than a winner of battles, he encompassed peace and the astounding grace of a life lived to its utmost. She matched his salute and knew that if the deer-elders had seen him thus, they would never have chosen Hawk to carry their plea to the god.

More gods than only the Horned One of forest and night stood around them, so that the air was pregnant with their waiting. The pressure of that and the rising crescendo of the dawn, as of a storm that comes to breaking, filled her head and made it hard to think.

'Don't think.' Dubornos was with her, close as a shield-mate in battle, a partner in the ultimate dance. 'Only act, Breaca. It is not for us to think now.'

Efnís was there, and Gunovar, and the beautiful gold-haired blind youth from Mona so that she was caught in an arc of dreamers. Then Graine stepped amongst them, her face smooth in its seriousness. She carried a stone the shape and size of an eagle's egg between her two hands and offered it up.

Breaca could not move.

Dubornos took it. 'Thank you. That's perfect.' He was moon-blind, his eyes wide and black. He found Breaca's hands by feel and pressed the cold stone into it. 'That is the first gift of your daughter. You need a cord or a thong for the second.'

She had one round her neck, bearing the Sun Hound's ring. She waited for someone amongst the hundreds to come forward with something better, but they were all naked and had nothing to offer.

The ring fitted her. She had not expected that. She untied the two ends of the thong and wrapped the whole round her left hand. Graine's rock lay cool and heavy in her right.

The dawn roared, as a storm near breaking. The horned moon sang a single lofting note. Somewhere in the balance between these two was a gap, a gateway when the light of each was even on the earth, when night was perfectly matched by day. Through such a gateway, a man might step who had the need and the desire, who was clearly focused in his intent to greet the gods and they open in their welcome, forewarned of his coming.

In the language of the ancestors, old as the stone, Dubornos said, 'Breaca, it must be now, or we have lost the time.'

Others sang it, who were not human. The noises converged and made a space of silence in which, blessedly, it was possible to think, and so, finally, to act.

They stood on the edge of the bog. Breaca held Graine's stone in one hand. Dubornos placed the thong round his own neck. The moon held them: all-night, all-power of the dark and the unseen and the unspoken. Then the dawn moved on and the rush of its beginning, of all beginnings, of new day and new life and new hope carried them to the place where day and night, beginning and ending, life and death were exactly even, and they were needed, one stepping into life, one into death, to keep that balance.

'Hold me,' he said, and she held him.

He was naked, but for the tab of vixen's fur round his upper arm. She felt the brush of it between her breasts, damp with his sweat and hers. She breathed in the smell of his hair, his skin, his breath. She felt the drumming of his heart, far steadier than her own; his pulse, leaping as the deer leaps, as the salmon, from one heartbeat to the next, the urgency of it, the joy. She felt the surety of his intent, the sudden, certain settling into focus, and heard him.

'Breaca, now. Please.'

With the stone, she broke his head. The egg fitted the curve of her palm. Its weight cracked open his skull. His spirit broke free of his body. He was heavier in her arms.

With the cord at his neck, she cut off his air, that his breathing might stop, as it had once started when the cord was cut from his mother.

Last, she lowered him with all care face down into the bog that he might return to the water whence he came, and the embrace of the earth beneath it. To her left, the dawn, so long delayed, soared into being.

Thank you.

His soul spoke from beyond earth and water. He shone. His eyes were the moon and the sun. Peace hung about him like a cloak, and the certainty of where he must go. Already, he was moving, backing away from her on the shining path the new sun made for him. He said, *I know what we need. With all my soul, I will ask for it.*

She could not speak. Her throat closed over the words and the air as if a second cord had been hers. He said, *Don't grieve. It was the best of deaths. The gods approved it.*

She felt that; the pressure of waiting, of watching, was gone and in its place was a quiet gratitude. The air weighed less heavily on her skin. The gateway she had seen between the dawn and the night lay open. Briga was there, and Nemain and the other, older gods. She saw the ancestor-dreamer and the Sun Hound woven together and a piece fell into place in her soul, that made sense of them both, and herself.

What had become of Dubornos said, *I should go.*

'Yes.'

Still facing her, he backed away, faster. A river came, where there had been none, and nine stepping stones across it. Ninefold hazels drooped to the running water. A crow sat on each branch. A stag waited, full-pride, at the water's edge. It raised its head and bellowed. Dubornos turned and began to run.

She had seen so many men and women fall on the battlefield and wander lost after. Never had she seen one pass without help to the river and across it. She stood a long time watching after he had gone.

'Mother?'

She thought it might be Graine. It was Hawk, naming her mother for the first time. Graine was with him, and Cygfa on his other side. She had four children, where before there had been but three. Another one added to her lineage, another to help preserve the land. It was easier to think like that than to weigh one more in the balance of Venutios' question.

'Would you like to eat?'

The smell of roasting deer sighed through the lightness of the moss and the bog myrtle and the blood from Dubornos' head. She was crouching beside him still, locked in place. Her hands were on his body, which was cold. She had thought she was standing. She stood now. Her knees cracked and were slow to unbend.

Dubornos lay face down as she had laid him. The fox fur on his arm was black with the water. His hair was the same colour. Since his boyhood, it had always been thin. It seemed thicker now, floating out around his head to weave into the moss.

'Mother?' This time, Graine said it.

'No. Actually, yes, I would like to eat. Thank you.'

They brought her food and she ate and came slowly back to the morning. The sun was far higher than it had been, the moon a pale ghosted sickle, already dropping down to the west. She sat on a rock and let the sun warm her skin and tried to come away from the sense of him stepping over the last stone into nowhere.

A young man came to sit by her, with striking blond hair and eyes that did not focus on her face. She remembered him in the dance, but not what he had done. He said, 'I'm Bellos, once of the Belgae. Your brother, Valerius, who was Bán, brought me from Gaul and made of me a dreamer on Mona. It was I who called your daughter to the island and I return her now. The Elder, Luain mac

Calma, believes her to be the wild piece of the Warrior's Dance. He sends her back, with his wish that you and she find healing together.' His gaze sharpened, disconcertingly. 'Last night, I thought you healed.'

'And now?'

'Now . . . You have passed beyond that. Can you see where you must go?'

She remembered a number of the things Valerius had told her about this young man, and saw the things that he had not. She said, 'Not clearly. Never that. Only that we must be where the legions are, and that they are moving south. They are our bane. Their destruction is our salvation, or not, if we fail. Whatever happens can happen in their company only.'

Sûr mac Donnachaidh was near, eating meat from a rib. He had aged in the night. His eyes searched her face. 'Ardacos could take you, but he might lose a day in finding their trail. My scouts have been watching the legions' progress, and those who hunt them.'

A number of youths gathered behind him who had not been present in the night. They wore knife belts, where their peers were naked, and clay paint was smeared on their faces and in their hair, making them things of the soil. He said, 'If you will take our horses and your own, you could reach them by nightfall. Your son and the Warrior of Mona have brought a thousand spears and are tracking them close behind. They will attack soon, before you can get there. They are outnumbered, but they hope to use surprise, as it was used before. I think they will not succeed.'

The dark thread in the weft took shape and form and size. Under the sun, the day felt cold. She sent a prayer to Dubornos and felt him gather it close, as she might gather a child.

She said, 'Then if your scouts can take us, we will ride whatever you have to offer.'

XXXVII

S UN ON SUN ON SUN ON POLISHED METAL, MAKING MORE SUN,
blindingly.
       Corvus rode south, at noon in the height of hot summer,
with two legions of infantry marching in full armour ahead of him
and a cloud of flies feeding about his face.

He wanted to bandage his eyes, to take away the glare. He
wanted to stuff cotton in his ears to dull the hammer of nailed feet
and the clash of harness and the interminable bloody marching
chants of the cohorts, for ever out of key. He wanted to slay every
fly in the province and then drink unceasingly of cold water from
mountain streams that splashed down through dim valleys to pools
where only moonlight reached. He wanted to be back on the straits
by Mona, or in the fortress of the XXth or in Camulodunum, even
if it had burned. He wanted to be anywhere, but not on an open
road with legionaries marching six abreast in double time ahead of
him and a baggage train moving almost, but not quite, as fast, and
himself the teeth in the serpent's tail at the back, to make sure the
rear guard could bite when – not if – it was attacked. He regretted
ever having devised that strategy, and loathed the man, whosoever
he might be, who had told the governor of it and encouraged him
to use it now.

The heatwave was in its third day. The memory of the storms
was gone from the men and the land. The flies were unspeakable

and he chose not to think of them. Almost as bad was the gritty dust that clogged the air and settled on the mane of his bay battle mare and her harness and filtered through into Corvus' neck and his waist and his groin, abrading them steadily so that already he could feel the ooze of blood where his belt sat over his mail. He checked his saddlecloth for the hundredth time and made himself believe his favourite battle mount was not being similarly damaged.

He drank from his waterskin and poured a little onto his palm and wiped his face, then leaned forward and rubbed his damp hand between the mare's ears, batting away the flies and murmuring to her all the while. 'It's past noon. The worst is over. Walk steady and all will be well.'

He had taken to talking to the mare for the past two days, since shortly after the governor's small party, riding north, had met the legions marching south with the remainder of his wing, the Quinta Gallorum, as escort.

The meeting had been welcome on both sides and the reunion joyful, but within a day Corvus had run out of things to say to Sabinius, who carried the standards and had led the wing in his commander's absence. The mare, on the whole, was more rewarding to talk to. She did not contradict him and rarely answered back while Sabinius was very likely to do both. He had been escorting infantry in hostile territory for nearly twenty years; he knew exactly how long the day was, and that the worst almost certainly was not over.

The standard-bearer grunted now and narrowed his eyes to peer through the shimmering heat haze ahead. He said, 'You have never told me how far south we are going to march. If Vespasian's Bridge and Verulamium are both destroyed, then there is nothing left to reach.'

'That's because I don't know. I don't think Paullinus knows. We can perhaps march to the west of the bridge and find another way across the river but I can't imagine we'll reach it. We face a rebel army that best estimates put at fifteen to twenty thousand warriors and we are less than seven thousand strong. Where we meet them is largely academic, I think, only that we must, and that if we march like this, so their scouts can see us from half a day away, without ever needing to come within range, then we will call them to us and won't have to go looking for them. Paullinus will have his final, glorious battle.'

'And we will all die, gloriously.' Sabinius swiped absently at a horsefly and looked up at the unsullied sky. 'As long as someone lives to take word to Rome.'

'Paullinus has pigeons that will fly to Gaul with his report of all those who should be rewarded for their courage. Our names will stand for ever in the annals of the Senate.'

'If the dreamers' falcons don't pull the birds out of the sky and eat them before they get anywhere close to Gaul.'

'Thank you. Yes. If that.'

This was why Corvus talked to his horse. It was measurably less depressing.

They fell to silence, then. Ahead, the four cohorts of the shrunken XXth legion set up a new marching chant. They were fewer than two thousand and all of them veterans of old campaigns; by sickness and nightmares and the savage waters of the straits, had the dreamers of Mona culled out the youths and the less seasoned men. Those left alive, therefore, were the fittest and the best. Sadly they were also those who had spent two decades of winters devising new words to go with the old, settled rhythms of the march.

They began rustily, until the ones who knew the words had passed them on. Surprisingly soon, all two thousand men caught on and built the volume, the better to drown out the competition coming from the XIVth in front.

Against his better judgement, Corvus listened to the increasingly coherent snatches that rose up through the billowing dust; a complex triple rhyme involving heat and dust and insurgency and all saved from ruin by the wide brown eyes of a boy from Alexandria.

Even for one jaundiced by nearly thirty years in the legions, it was clever and he grinned the first time he caught it all, and still smiled for the second and third repeats. By the tenth, or perhaps the twentieth, he wanted cotton again for his ears and, lacking it, let his mind drift to Alexandria, which was hotter, certainly, than the land through which he was riding, and dustier and quite definitely more prone to lethal intrigue and insurgency against anyone who attempted to govern the ungovernable.

It had not, in his experience, been saved by the wide brown eyes of any boy, although there had been a man, and his eyes had, indeed, been brown and a great deal of Corvus' life's path, if he thought about it, stemmed from that man and all he had offered, and the result could be considered salvation, if one chose to look at it in that light.

The day was hot and images flowed easily, borne on the beat of marching feet and a scurrilous song that managed to link every officer in both legions and both wings of cavalry by anatomically improbable methods to the brown-eyed Alexandrian youth.

A small bronze statue of Horus took wings from Corvus' pack and lifted over the mirage of the marching men. Its one jet eye winked at him and became the brown eye of an Alexandrian man, full of wisdom and care and dead so very much too early. The bird soared high. From its height a man's voice said, *What does it profit a man to serve the gods of two worlds?*

He had always spoken thus, setting riddles in his arcane Alexandrian tongue in a voice smooth as quicksilver and sweet as ambrosia. The answers were never to be found where first one sought them.

Determined not to try, Corvus let his mind drift and drift again and, as it always did when drifting, it came eventually to a black-eyed, solemn, thoughtful boy of the Eceni and the painful trail he had walked to become an officer in the Roman cavalry, feared for his ferocity by those who fought on both sides of the conflict in Britannia and named traitor in Rome because he had made the mistake of pledging oath and honour to an emperor in the days before his dying.

He thought of the man that boy had become and the sight of him on a pied horse standing over the procurator of all Britannia with murder in his eyes and something quite different shining from his heart.

To his bay battle mare, Corvus murmured, 'But Valerius is given to Mithras, the bull-slayer. He serves only him; a god of the world he has left behind. The gods of the Eceni would not accept him.'

Why not?

For five paces more, Corvus remained in quiet reverie, then his world broke into shards, as a glass that is thrown at a white marble wall. 'Sabinius! Signal alert forward and back!'

He barely recognized his own voice; out of nowhere he had found the spit and crispness of early morning and the certainty of battle command.

Sabinius' standard flittered in the breeze, twice forward, twice back. A trumpeter in the infantry took up the signal and sent it forward up the line. Another sent it back at a different pitch; every man of the seven thousand up to and including the governor knew whence came the order and so whom to blame if it were wrong.

Corvus looked about. The mirage was gone. Men marched where it had been. Already their chant sank dead in the air. They shifted their packs and loosened their gladii and the lift of their feet in the march was higher and more elastic. Silence hung about them like a shield.

His neck prickled. His palms were wet on the reins. He looked about with different eyes. The road was raised, as they always were. The land about was flat for a spear's throw on either side and should have been cleared back to the naked turf for three spearcasts beyond that. Once, it might have been; the trees had certainly been felled at least to the start of the rising land, but in the last year, the men of the legions had been occupied with other things than making safe the roads and the land was a havoc of scrubby new growth that could have hidden half the marching men and easily as many warriors.

Both sides were not the same. To the left, the land rose gently to make a small ridge which was covered in scrub. To the right, it fell away more steeply and the trees had been left to grow closer to the road; the engineers did not believe warriors would attack uphill.

Corvus thought they were right. The danger all came from the left. He looked over and through the nettles and flowering thistles and green-berried thorns and the scrub elder and saw nothing, only felt loathing and excitement and the almost-readiness to attack. He drew his own sword and shifted his shield from shoulder to forearm.

Sabinius copied him. 'Valerius?' he asked.

'I don't think so. I think I would know if he were . . .' Corvus shook his head. 'Yes, I would know. He isn't here. But there is someone . . . many. Waiting, watching . . .'

Their eyes scoured him. His guts clenched and he thought he might be sick, but he always thought that, riding into ambush. It had never yet been true.

Sabinius spat, sending precious water to the road. 'They're going to try to pick us off from back to front as they did with the Ninth.'

'I know. But we're not led by an idiot. And this serpent has a sting in its tail such as they've never encountered.'

There was release in action. The bay battle mare came round in a faultless spin and danced on the spot, perfect and beautiful and ready to fight. Loudly enough for those around to hear, Corvus said to Sabinius, 'You have command of the first two troops. At all costs, protect the mules and the baggage; I don't want to sleep in the open tonight even if you do. I'm going back to be with Ursus and Flavius at the rear.'

Ursus and Flavius were ready. The former had already deployed the nearest two dozen men as flank riders, setting them in pairs, mostly to the left, staggered out and back so that each outer man protected the side and back of his partner, and each outer pair covered the side and back of those on the inside.

Flavius had command of the archers. Since last autumn, the Quinta Gallorum had retained one dozen Scythian horse-archers, employed at insane expense, who dressed in silks and then complained daily of the cold and the mud and had to be waited on and served hot spiced beef and olives and good wine and given their own private cook and must be set to train in secret, with scouts all around to guard against spies so that now, when they were most needed, they could be brought into action against an unprepared enemy, with all the insanity of money and cosseting proved worthwhile and not a man begrudging them a single olive.

Flavius had been given charge of them, and had come to care for them as the Atrebatan hound-boy cared for the governor's blue-skinned hounds, and for much the same reason: they set him apart from the rest. He had taken the time to learn their language, which was more than anyone else had done, and he shouted to them clearly, pure as a bell, as Corvus approached.

Like the hounds, the Scythians craved release into action. At the first of Flavius' calls, they began to string their small, wickedly curved bows and chose arrows from the packs on their horses' shoulders and nocked them, quietly and unobtrusively, the better to keep secret from the watching warriors.

The rest of the troop rode forward at an even pace, not turning to look at them, or to point or do anything that might attract the enemy's attention; their orders were unambiguous in this regard. The flank riders covered them, and had orders to die in their defence.

Following his own instructions, Corvus rode past them to the rear without looking. Flavius gave him a queer, half-friendly salute as he passed. Ursus nodded, curtly. He had the same question as Sabinius, only asked with less tact. 'Is it Valerius? If it is, he'll know what we do and how we do it.'

'It's not Valerius; he isn't here. But that doesn't mean he hasn't spent the last half month drilling those who are.'

'What do we do?'

'Out-fight them,' said Corvus, grimly. 'And pray that word of the archers has never reached Valerius. Keep them facing the left; that's where the danger has to be.'

'That's Corvus, whom Valerius saw above Lugdunum. He leads the cavalry. He's a friend to the Boudica.'

'And was soul-friend once to Valerius. He is known on Mona.'

Cunomar lay with Braint in a patch of head-high nettles within half a spear's cast of the road. Even attacking the Ninth, he had not been so close. He could see the beads of sweat on the faces of the men as they marched, and black runnels of it on the necks of the horses. He could see grit and flies and the dulled eyes of men who had marched fast for days and had more days ahead of them. He heard pounding feet and the inane marching ditties and closed his ears to them so that the sudden blast of the trumpets had shocked him and he had jumped, and cursed and made himself lie still again.

Braint had not jumped, even when Corvus swung his bay mare out to the side within almost-touch of her face. Amongst all the lime-painted, grey-greased warriors of Cunomar's she-bear, she alone was unpainted and almost unadorned. She wore a single banded feather in her hair from the tail of a peregrine tiercel and two eye teeth of a wildcat hung from a horsehide thong round her neck. She had worked dust and mud into her hair so that it looked like an upturned sod of turf, but for the rest, her skin was brown from a summer of sun and wind and matt from the dust of the marching men and before the first troop of the first cohort of the first century of the XIVth legion had passed, she had become another shadow in many shadows amongst the nettles.

She lay still and silent, and seemed not to notice the flies. Except when he had agreed to attack the legion early, before the remainder of the warriors joined them, Cunomar had never seen her smile.

He remembered stories his mother had told of Braint as a girl on Mona and later in the battles of the invasion, of her grief at the death of her boy-cousin and her vitality as she came out of it, and her fearlessness so that she had lured an entire troop of Gaulish cavalrymen to their deaths, using her own body as bait.

The fire of that was still there to be seen, but grief and joy had burned away equally in its heat, leaving her unyielding as iron. She was unquestionably a good warrior, even excellent. Cunomar was coming slowly to the view that, next to his own family, she might be the best he had ever met.

Now, from his left, without moving, she said, 'Mac Calma was right. They do have archers. Look.'

For the time it took four ranks of the wing to ride past, Cunomar looked and saw nothing. Then he saw the flicker of a scarlet fletching and from that traced the outline of an arrow and so a bow and the brown-skinned, hawk-nosed man who bore it. Once seen, it was easier to find the others. 'Twelve,' he said. 'They're all here.'

Braint had told him of the hidden danger the evening before, when the fires of the legions had been hot sparks on the horizon. Their own fire had been three barely red lumps of charcoal in a pit. Leaning into it, so he could see the red on her face, she had said, 'Luain mac Calma has three informers among the Siluran scouts used by the legions. They report to him only in exceptional circumstances and then only through an intermediary. If the truth has reached us cleanly, they have been keeping watch on a dozen brown-skinned archers who can shoot a dove from the sky and the hawk that is following it and then turn and kill a hunted hare and the hound when both are going the opposite way. They can do all this standing or sitting or on horseback and in any direction.'

'How far can they shoot?' Cunomar had asked.

'Two spear-casts accurately. Three if they are aiming for a target as big as a warrior.'

'Then if we don't have more warriors than they have arrows, we are finished, and all the lives wasted.'

'No. Mac Calma has sent us with five slingers. All we have to do is to keep them alive while they target the archers. Can your she-bears do that, do you think?'

'I don't know,' he had said. 'Against mounted cavalry we are at a disadvantage. We can run in and cut the heel-strings of the horses but that's costly in lives. We can throw spears, but the archers will be faster. We can run at them, but we have not enough in numbers to overwhelm them. We could try to attack at night, but they are well fortified and have sentries at every second pace who change eight times overnight and are alert. What do you suggest?'

Braint had turned her head at last and looked at him. Warmed only by the embers, her gaze was long and cool and dispassionate. It was like being regarded by a hound; he had never enjoyed that. Eventually, she had said, 'I suggest that you ask the bear for help and do as she advises.'

He had asked the bear. The answer had not been distinct. He had danced to her under the first rise of the horned moon until exhaustion and the soft rhythm of palms pounded on the earth – they had not dared use the skull drums this close to the enemy – had lifted him out of himself and into the savage care of the beast to whom he was sworn.

He had smelled the hot meatiness of her breath and felt the brush of her hair against his face and seen a thousand bears set against a thousand cavalry horses, ripping them asunder, leaving three dead.

Somewhere in the chaos, a deer calf had died twice, and a serpent had coiled on itself and struck at the back of his head so that he could feel the puncture of its teeth in his scalp. Afterwards, he had retold it all to those who had pounded the earth, hoping one of them might see some clarity.

It was Ulla who had said, 'The slingers don't need much time, only long enough to see and kill the archers. We can do this, if Braint can direct the slingers. We have the horned god of the hunt to guide us, and half a night to make real the dreams of the bear.'

Cunomar had not been sure then. He was not sure now. He wanted glory and the death of Rome, not the annihilation of the she-bear brought about because he had failed in his first duty as a leader to protect his warriors.

The time for doubt was past. The end of the column was eight horses away. The outriders were stepping within an arm's reach of his head.

He offered his soul to the bear, knowing the value of it, and that all life was a lesson, to be mined for all it could give, even if – particularly if – that mining ended in death.

'Let's go,' he said, and reached for the spear haft that lay across the ground in front of him.

Corvus said, 'There! In the nettles! Something moved!'

All twelve of the archers fired. Arrows whistled, silk stripped fast on silk, and embedded solidly in meat and bone.

Someone, or something, died, twitching. Afterwards, the jangle of harness and pound of feet sounded as nothing, so that the air was filled with silence, and two words of congratulatory Scythian spoken by Flavius.

Hoarsely, Ursus said, 'Gods, that was close. They could touch the horses, almost, from there.'

Corvus had to swallow to speak. 'If we have not just shot a sleeping hog.'

'Hogs don't lie sleeping while two legions march by.' Ursus waited and waited and then said, 'Do they?'

Corvus said, 'They might do, if they have been fed the right plants by the dreamers. Something feels wrong. I think— Move! Cover the archers!'

The slingstone passed by his face. He felt the wind of it. In the sudden slowing of his mind, he believed that he could see the black paint that coated it. His soul shrank from the threat.

An archer died. A second was knocked in the shoulder.

'*Right!* They're on the right!'

Corvus screamed it. A trumpeter – outstandingly courageous – sounded it clearly to the troop and the infantry ahead. By that act alone, the man made himself a target. He died for it, to a thrown spear, not a slingstone, at the same time as the third of the twelve archers.

There was time to shout his name, and the promise of honours, so that his departing ghost and the men of his tent party might hear it, so that someone might survive and remember, and then there was mayhem and the howling of bear-warriors up the line as far as Corvus could see and the screaming of horses and of men and women so that no single voice had any chance to be heard and only the trumpets and the standards kept discipline and order.

Corvus killed a woman with red hair and brown skin and did not pause to see if he knew her. He ducked a stone and pushed his shield to cover Ursus, who had moved his own shield to cover Corvus. They each thrust and hit flesh and bone and tasted blood that was not their own and their world shrank to the immediacy of survival, except that they had a duty to protect the infantry and Corvus had to think also about that.

There were warriors on the left now, as well as the right. Corvus looked about and saw another trumpeter close to the knot of surviving archers who were firing from behind a human shield of cavalry, and scoring hit after hit, earning with each shot the gold and effort and tedium of their keep.

'The trumpeter . . .' Corvus mouthed it to Ursus, who nodded. They fought closer until the man saw them and fought back so that they were joined in an island of relative calm with death and wounding all about.

'Sound the two-serpent strike.'

The man stared at him, and grinned, and sounded his trumpet so that the notes flew high and pure as larks over the fighting men. They had drilled and drilled until men and mounts equally knew what to do to the sound of that, and a horse would take its own part even if its rider were dead or beyond control.

The bay mare knew it as well as the rest. Corvus felt the bunching of muscles beneath him and the straining for air and the kick of acceleration as she saw a gap and went for it. He made himself sleek and lay tight to the mane with his blade in one hand and his shield covering the horse as much as his own body and let her carry him to relative safety.

Ursus was behind him, and the trumpeter, and a growing band of his men. He swung round and felt the judder as the mare jumped off the road and began the curve that would strike at the backs of the attacking warriors. Ursus peeled away from him and rode the other way, to the right. Every second man followed him round.

For a moment, all Corvus had to do was ride. He did so, and ignored the still, small voice in the deeper part of his mind that wanted to know what it was the archers had first killed that might not have been a sleeping hog, but he dearly hoped was not a certain man.

There were fewer warriors on the left side and they were not experienced against horses. They died without fuss. Corvus saw a movement in the shrubs to his left and directed his horse towards it. The trumpeter followed, sending silver lark-notes cascading behind. Flavius and two of the archers abandoned formation and came with him.

The deer calf had died only once, when Cunomar threw his knife into its chest.

The wound had been small, easily stuffed with dried grass and moss so that there was no smell of fresh blood that might alert passing horses. He had sewn shut its anus and prepuce with sinews so that they did not leak and similarly give it away. He broke its forelegs and worked them until they moved through the death-stiffness. Braint had found and woven the birch bark to make ropes long enough and strong enough to reach and not to break.

Pegging it in position without crushing the nettles had taken half the night so that the sky was pale and the sun roaring red on the eastern horizon by the time they backed away, laying the bark ropes along cleared lines so that a stone would not cut or block them. They had time for a single test, with Braint on the roadway and Cunomar in the far elder scrub, watching as much to see if he could be seen when he tugged on his end of the spear haft as whether the movement it made was enough to catch the eyes of passing horsemen.

So much had hung on it. So much had succeeded. So much was so close to failure.

Corvus rode directly at him. Braint came up to a crouch. Without any sign of urgency, she picked a stone from her pouch and fitted it in her sling. Cunomar had not known she used that. He regretted never having learned it himself. For no clear reason, he said, 'He loves Valerius, and is loved by him.'

She smiled, thinly. 'I know.'

They were close enough to smell the horses. She stood and drew back her arm.

A brown-skinned man in red silk moved with the same certain speed.

Frozen, Cunomar said, 'Archers! He has two of the archers!'

For the rest of his life, however short or long, Cunomar would remember the pain in her face as Braint picked one target from the three that were possible, and the startling accuracy of the stone, and the venom with which it was sent, as if by killing the man who posed most danger she might damage the others whom she hated most.

She died, not knowing if she had succeeded.

Cunomar would also never forget the impersonal death of an arrow, of three arrows, sent with such speed that they might all have come from the same bowshot, so that there was not time for her parting soul to dally or consider the life that had been lived.

She was alive, and then she was dead and the only reason Cunomar was not likewise was that Ulla had thrown a spear and three others of the she-bear had come from the other side and none of them was a slinger, but one was lucky and knocked the remaining archer from his horse, so that the immediate threat was over and Cunomar could reach for the bear and fail to find her and still drag his spear clear of the birch ropes and leap from the elder, and fight, and try not to die, and not have to think yet, at all, about how he was going to break the news of Braint's death to Cygfa.

He saw a flash of movement on the edge of his vision; in a moment of bear-inspired madness, he hurled his spear.

Corvus watched the second slingstone pass his face and did not need to look to see if this one was painted black, the better to send his soul to utter annihilation, he could feel the hatred in it as it passed. He heard the impact and the slump of a man falling and jinked the bay mare sideways in case there were more slingers and swung with his sword for a warrior who came at him.

He missed, and missed again, and saw Breaca's son leap from cover and knew he had been recognized. A spear passed him, harmlessly, and he pushed the bay mare forward into the melting maelstrom of warriors.

He had more men and more horses and they were, with all due modesty, manifestly better drilled than any native warriors. Even so, lesser men, more poorly drilled, had won against odds in the past and horses are only valuable against infantry if those on the ground are afraid of horses, and do not know them.

The Eceni against whom he fought now lived and died and took their first steps on horseback. He fought, moreover, the warriors of the she-bear who did not care about living, but only death in the embrace of the bear, and honour afterwards for the life lived complete.

As if in proof, the Boudica's son broke through the guards round the archers and drove his knife into the chest of one of the horses. Corvus watched him leap onto the back of the falling beast and take its rider down with him. Cunomar's blade flashed red. His face was frozen in a scream of pain and triumph that no sane man could stand against. No officer would ask it of those who trusted their lives to him.

Except that there was a way, for men who had drilled to perfection and who trusted their commander.

Corvus shouted to the trumpeter, 'Line! Call for a line! Back here. Form on me!'

Silvered larksong burst high over the carnage – and ceased.

The trumpeter curled up like a leaf, clutching his right shoulder from which a thrown knife protruded. His trumpet hung from the thong on his forearm. Corvus hacked once more at the shrieking banshee that assailed him – he thought it was a woman but did not stop to look – and pushed the bay battle mare forward to the man's side. He used his own blade to cut the trumpet's cords and was grateful that he kept it sharper than was necessary and that the kills of the day had not blunted its edge, more grateful still that he had learned the skills of sounding the horn, and the basic tunes of command.

Half of his men had heard him shout in any case. They were already grouping into pairs and then threes and then sixes and eights to form the line that would sweep the flat ground and trample into the earth those who thought to stand against them.

Corvus wet his lips and lifted the shining weight of the trumpet and drew breath and sought the first note, shakily – and was drowned by the brasher, louder sound of ten horns braying in unison from the front of the column.

'No! Gods curse you, no . . .'

He could have wept. The trumpet call was redundant. His men were on either side of him, only six were straggling to catch up, one of those wounded, two assailed on both sides and unlikely to live. Eighteen men were with him and they could have swept the broad, flat land from one end of the column to the other.

'We could still do it.'

Corvus looked to his left. Flavius was there, flushed and breathing hard and caught on a wave of victory. Their eyes met. Flavius grinned and did not hate him. He said, 'We didn't hear it.

The horns are too far. We can only hear you. Tell us to charge.'

Eighteen men wanted to believe that. Not one of them would have spoken against him later. Even the governor would have acknowledged that in battle not all commands can be heard. The deified Caesar had once failed to call back his men and had sent instead a second signal for luck when he knew they had run on to victory against his command. Against such a precedent, what general could discipline men who had fought and prevailed?

Corvus lifted the trumpet to his lips. He had no need to call the line, they were already with him, drilled to perfection, sweeping round the fulcrum that he made, turning like the arm of a wheel to face south, so that they could run parallel to the road. The warriors were scattering. Two more had died. The Boudica's son was calling, calling, to no avail . . .

The horns brayed again, louder. The great bull-horn of the governor's own cavalry contingent that took two men to carry it sounded a single, long, earth-shuddering note. The standards of both legions and the Quinta Gallorum swung hard to left and right.

'No, damn you! *Not now!*' Corvus hurled the trumpet at the hard ground. It bounced and his bay mare shied and he kicked her, which was unforgivable. His men swept about him, hard-faced, protecting him in the depth of his folly, when he was too lost in rage to guard against the slingers or spear throwers who still assailed them.

He cursed again and closed his eyes and swallowed and brought himself back into balance. Never in his life had he lost his temper in the field. He did so now, and turned the battle mare and swung his arm for want of a standard and, with a bitterness that stayed with him for the whole of the fast, hard ride back to the column, led his men away from victory to follow the governor and protect the rear of the now-running legions wherever they might lead.

'They're gone,' said Ulla. 'Why?'

'The governor's horns called them back in a way they couldn't ignore. Why that should have happened is anyone's guess. Maybe Valerius has arrived early and attacked the front of the column and they see him as more of a threat than us and need their better troops to set against him. We can't catch them on foot. They must know that.'

Cunomar knelt by Braint's corpse. His own body was lacerated with cuts and bruised all down one side where a horse had fallen on him. He felt nothing. He leaned over Braint and put a hand to her throat to feel her pulse as if she might still be alive, which was ridiculous, but he did it all the same.

The arrows had passed into her chest in front and out again at the back, only lodged by their scarlet and black fletchings. Like that, she was unable to lie flat, but was arced, as if in agony, with her chest reaching to the sky.

She had not stiffened yet. Gently, Cunomar lifted her to sitting and propped her against his knee. He broke each of the arrows at the haft and laid her back again to rest. With his thumbs, he closed her eyes and held them shut for a while, that she might not stare so at the evening sky. Numbly, 'She was Warrior of Mona. We should take her with us. Those she led will want to mourn her.'

Ulla said, 'Cygfa will want to mourn her.'

'If she comes back. She went with the Boudica and we have heard nothing. It may be they are not coming back.' The thought rose unbidden from the formless fears of Cunomar's mind and was spoken before he could force it down.

Ulla stared at him and opened her mouth and closed it again. She said, 'She will come back and the Boudica will come back, and then we have the legions trapped. Valerius isn't ahead of us; he'd have sent word with the scouts if he were. The legions aren't running towards war, they're running for safety, to somewhere they can defend better than an open road. All we need do is wait for Valerius to bring up his sworn spears and we have them trapped like sheep in a fold. Tomorrow, we will set the war host on them and by evening the land will be free of two more legions.'

Tomorrow . . .

Unheralded, the old nightmare returned to Cunomar, of the bear turned at bay in its den, ready to savage the first fumbling fool who came near. This time, he was in no doubt that the she-bear had sent him the image, with all its portents of danger.

Afraid to name it aloud, Cunomar made himself smile for Ulla. 'Tomorrow is too far to think of. First, we need to take the wounded back to the meeting place and hope that Valerius has reached it. He has Theophilus with him who can look to the injuries. When that's done, we need to build a pyre for Braint that will show everyone how great she was. Will you help me carry her?'

Ulla put the flat of her thumb across his mouth and smoothed away the false smile. Her gaze peeled away the layers of his falsehoods. 'Of course; I'll always help you. Why do you have to ask?'

XXXVIII

CUNOMAR AND VALERIUS LIT BRAINT'S FUNERAL PYRE TOGETHER, at dusk, before the assembled warriors of the war host and within sight of the camped legions.

Insects made black the evening air. Swifts and bats scythed through them, shrilly. Camp fires by the thousands, and tens of thousands, sent smoke to the still-blue sky.

A low ridge separated the two armies, a wrinkle in the land less than the height of a man.

West of it glowed the fires of the legions, set out in perfect lines, rank upon rank in the settling dusk.

They were so few, and so crisp in their arrogance. As Ulla had said, they had found safety. A blind-ended valley held them secure with steep walls of green earth rising on both sides and behind to pen them like sheep. It helped Cunomar to think of them still as sheep and therefore helpless; too many terrors lurked in the image of a trapped bear turning against those who hunted it.

East of the ridge, the fifty thousand warriors of the Boudica's war host prepared for war in the Boudica's continuing absence. Genial chaos abounded at scattered family camp fires as those too young or too old, too frail or too afraid to fight vied to bring forth tales of how they would turn the tide of a battle with a skin of water handed to a warrior at a crucial moment, or a horse held and brought forward when it was most needed.

To the southern side, more orderly fires blazed for Civilis and his Batavian cavalry, newly summoned by Valerius to join in the war host. Left and right of these, the Boudica's brother had set his own warriors, who followed him now as if none of them had ever doubted his value as their leader.

At the front of them all, Braint's fire touched the sky. If the height of a pyre was testament to the honour and courage of a warrior, this was the worth of half a legion.

Days of hot sun had left dry wood by the armload and the refugees from Verulamium had discovered in their wagons supplies of pitch pine and lamp oil and whole fleeces of crisp brown wool and given them freely as gifts to the departed woman and to the gods, that the Warrior's fire might light the sky and reach to the Roman legions with its foretaste of doom. They, at least, were confident of tomorrow's victory.

Cunomar was not at all confident. The enormity of what had happened grew on him slowly through the day until, by the lighting of the fire, he was hollow and sick.

Before he had ever arrived bearing Braint's body in his arms, Valerius had begun to hold the war councils and to sketch out a strategy for the battle that must now happen. To Cunomar, when the spear-leaders had left, he had said, 'We should never have turned them at bay. It's my fault; I asked you to harry them and didn't know the valley was there to offer them shelter. I'm sorry.'

Any question of a bone thrown to a hound was gone. The Boudica's brother and son were united in the need to salvage victory from catastrophe, or at least to avert defeat. Cunomar had said, 'We could ride away and leave them. They won't risk coming far off the road.'

Valerius had pinched the bridge of his nose. 'If we were fewer, we would certainly do that, but we have thirty thousand refugees now that yours are come from Verulamium; we can't leave them to the slaughter that would follow. In any case, the warriors are convinced that the gods will send a miracle and the Boudica will appear out of the setting sun to lead them to victory; someone has said it and they hold it as truth. We could no more persuade them to leave than we could persuade them that they might not win tomorrow. There's no point in trying. They need to believe that we believe in them.'

Cunomar had said, 'Do we not believe in them? We outnumber the legions five to one.' There was still room for hope. He did not want to abandon it.

'The deer outnumber the hounds at the start of a day's hunting but they still die,' Valerius had said. 'This is a time when training and experience matter, not numbers. We're against the Fourteenth and the Twentieth who have fought through every summer and drilled through every winter for the past twenty years. We have perhaps two thousand warriors of Mona who have a decade's experience of battle. Your she-bears are dedicated but they have only ever fought in towns and in woods. Do you remember fighting the veterans in the garden behind the temple? It would be like that, but worse. To fight in open country against a standing legion is like trying to sail a small-boat into an ocean in full storm after paddling it across a placid lake. For the rest, we have forty thousand enthusiastic amateurs most of whom have been forbidden to hold a blade since the first invasion. We need luck, a great deal of it, to stand any chance at all.'

Valerius had not been smiling; all hint of the dry, self-mocking humour was gone. That was at least as worrying as what he had said.

Grimly, Cunomar had said, 'Then we need to make that luck happen.'

'I know. If your mother would join us, it might make the difference. In her absence, you and I must do what we can.'

'Is she coming back?' To his own ears, Cunomar sounded like a child. Just then, he did not care.

'I hope so. But the scouts have yet no word of her.'

Thus had the evening begun, making others believe what could not be believed, and hiding a growing dread. For want of anyone better, Cunomar had helped to light Braint's fire, not because he had a right, or that she would have wanted it, particularly. Wishing himself elsewhere, he had touched his pine torch to the tags of tinder at the margins and stood with it as the flames licked up past his face.

He wanted Cygfa to be there, so that she could rage at him over Braint's death and he could tell her how much he was sorry. He wanted the Boudica there, a walking miracle, to prove that such things were possible. Very badly, he wanted Ardacos, simply for the old warrior's presence.

417

Because none of these was there, because he was not even sure that they were still alive, Cunomar had spoken aloud the words of invocation to Briga, for the sending of a Warrior of Mona into her care. Then, on Valerius' advice and in the presence and hearing of the gods and assembled warriors he had named Huw of the Ordovices to be Braint's successor, unless or until the Elder of Mona should choose to appoint another in his place.

His voice was deeper than he ever remembered, as if Braint's death had broken the last bridge to his childhood, when he had thought it all gone long ago. The echoes of his words fell away and were burned with the moths in the leaping flames. A bat shrilled past his head, drifting cooler air at the place where his ear had once been. He had combed lime paint through his hair in her honour, and stained it with berry juice so that it stood black like the spines of a hedgehog in the long ridge from brow to neck. He felt it stiffen in the heat, stretching his scalp. The old scars of the bear on his shoulder itched as they had not done since they were first cut in the caves of the Caledonii. He tried to read a message in that and failed.

He closed his eyes and watched the flames fan red on the inside of his lids and opened them and turned to his left, to where Valerius stood, dark-cloaked and dark-haired, with his fine-etched nose and high cheeks, a perfect mirror to Luain mac Calma, his father, who was Elder of Mona, and yet somehow still Roman for all that he bore not one stitch of Roman dress. The flames dealt kindly with him, washing smooth the lines of care about his mouth and eyes, raising the cloak of bitter humour to leave him simply a man, exhausted almost beyond endurance, but trying still to do what he believed to be right.

It was possible, then, to see his mother's brother clearly as a man unwillingly divided, lodged in the un-gap between two nations; for the first time truly to admire, rather than despise, his daily struggle to reconcile the opposites within him. It was possible – and suddenly overwhelmingly necessary – to understand that exactly this paradox was the key to winning an otherwise impossible battle.

Formally, in the language of the great-house, because the moment required it, Cunomar said, 'There is one thing left un-spoken in our plans for tomorrow: in the event that the Boudica does not ride out of the sunset, we will need a leader to take the war host into combat. I name you now as that leader. The warriors of the she-bear will follow the Boudica's brother into battle. You only need give the order and we will give our lives to make it happen.'

'No.'

Something punched a hollow space in Cunomar's chest. 'You won't let us fight?'

'Not at all. I will do whatever I can to persuade you to fight short of holding you at sword point. I was going to say that the sworn spears of the Boudica's brother will follow the Boudica's son wherever he leads, that you only need give the order and we will die to make it happen.' Now the fire etched new lines on Valerius' face. 'I have set out the battle plan because I have rather more experience of the legions than most and know what's needed, but I will not lead the tribes into battle.'

There was stillness and a crackling of fire. Braint's hair took light and burned in a sudden dandelion puff of flame. The air smelled briefly rank and then sweetly again, of pine resin.

Cunomar said, 'I don't understand. Why not? Are you unwilling to attack Rome?'

The sharp, self-mocking smile returned. 'Hardly. I've been attacking Rome for years. I will lead the right wing in the wedge and be honoured to do so. But I will not take full leadership of a war host that has gathered in the Boudica's name. That place is rightfully yours, and I believe that you are capable now of taking it. In any case, they wouldn't follow me.'

'We would,' said Huw, quietly. 'The warriors of Mona will follow you anywhere. Where we go, the rest will follow.'

There was a curious satisfaction in that. Cunomar nodded. 'Thank you. The she-bear will be honoured to follow the grey cloaks of Mona wherever they may lead.'

A muscle twitched under Valerius' eye. He said, 'Then they will all follow your banner.' There was a set to his jaw that was exactly like Breaca's when she was at her most stubborn. Cunomar had never seen it in any other living person besides his sister, Graine. He had thought that he shared the same intransigence, and that it would outmatch any man's. In this, too, it seemed he was outdone by Valerius.

He turned back to the fire. The flames had reached Braint's body, flowing over and down like sunlit water so that it was possible to imagine them cool and pleasant. As he watched, her face scorched red and then black and began to melt. Her sword lay along the length of her body. The hilt pulsed red in the drifting heat. Cunomar remembered her alive, and the cold spark in her eyes, and how that changed at the prospect of battle. She had never needed to seek the she-bear, or read a message in the tug of old scars, to know what to do and how and where.

He set aside the last remnant of his pride. 'I can't lead,' he said, quietly. 'I don't know what to do.'

Valerius regarded him for a long, cool moment. He opened his mouth to speak. On his unreadable face, Cunomar thought he read pity. Above all else, he did not want that.

Forestalling whatever might come, he said, 'I'm not saying this only because I need to make recompense for Braint and this is my only payment. I am saying it because you were fighting for Rome before I was born. You have led more men into more battles than I have led hunts and all of them successful, whichever side you were on. I don't want to die for no reason. Tomorrow I will do so if you can't tell us how to win against the trained men of the legions. It's not enough to have set the battle plan; we need you on the field to tell us what to do if – when – they do something we haven't planned for.'

Night had come while he was watching the pyre. The sky was darker than it had been, and the fire brighter so that it consumed all of the horizon. To the west, the sun broke open and bled onto the silhouette of the ridge.

Valerius swept a hand through his hair and pinched the bridge of his nose. He said, 'There is such a thing as god-luck and it's as necessary in battle as any amount of training. All the things you say are true. We face annihilation if we are not disciplined and the tribes have never fought with discipline. It takes years to make a legion of the calibre of the Fourteenth. We have one night and if we have any sense at all, we'll spend most of it sleeping. Lacking that, the warriors need instead a figure they can follow and believe in. Someone whom the gods will openly support, and who has the ability to swing the course of battle by the power of his presence. In the absence of the Boudica, the Boudica's son is the only possible replacement.'

'Not at all the only replacement, but perhaps, now, a worthy one.'

Cygfa's voice reached them from the darkness beyond the fire. She had always moved as quietly as the she-bear. Cunomar jumped, and hated himself for doing so. Valerius, he thought, came close, which made him feel better. He held the other man's gaze and saw his own sudden ache reflected.

There was a moment's held balance. Valerius nodded, very slightly, and took a half-step back, leaving the space open and all that it implied.

It took more courage than Cunomar had ever mustered for anything, more than facing the bear-elders and their knives, more than the two different mornings of his own crucifixion, to turn to his sister now and say, 'Braint's dead. It was my fault. We didn't know you were coming. We lit her pyre without you. I'm sorry.'

He saw Cygfa through a veil of flame. Her face was blurred, softened, so that she looked again like the half-grown girl he barely remembered from their childhood on Mona.

Presently, she asked, 'How?' She was looking at Valerius.

Cunomar said, 'Arrows. The cavalry had archers. Two of them came at us. She killed one with a slingstone. The other shot her. She knew it would happen. She gave her life to kill the better of the two and so give us a chance to kill the rest of the troop.'

The fire-soft eyes turned at last to him. She was still a thing of flame, outlined against the growing dark. He thought the ice at her core had melted, but did not know what was in its place, only that she was stronger for being less brittle. 'Did you kill them?' she asked.

He should have done; better to have died trying than to live and have to admit failure. Cunomar said, 'No. That is, I believe I killed one, but can't be sure. The rest . . . they were on horseback. They were set to ride over the top of us when they were recalled. They ran one way and we ran the other. They will be waiting for us tomorrow.' His own blood ran to ice with the saying of it. The words came like dry straw from his throat.

Astonishingly, she smiled. 'Then we'll greet them as Braint would wish us to. At least the fire you have built for her will show them who she was. Thank you for that.'

She took a moment to watch the flames and then looked equally at Valerius and Cunomar. 'If it helps,' she said, 'I would have followed either or both of you willingly in tomorrow's battles.'

Neither of them wanted to speak. It was Huw, new Warrior of Mona, who said, '. . . *would have . . .*? Then you are not alone?'

Cygfa stepped back. Other shadows moved where she had been. Cunomar thought he had finally stepped over the line into dreaming because Graine was there on her small, fat cob, looking as close to whole as could be imagined, and then Ardacos and Hawk and Gunovar and Efnís and a gold-haired dreamer he did not know and last – it should not have been last; Dubornos was missing and the gap he left was astonishing for its size – his mother rode out of the sunset, as someone, somewhere, had said she would, and came to a halt in front of him.

His mother. He stopped thinking then, and simply looked.

For every night of his childhood and most of his growing youth, Cunomar had seen his mother by firelight. Better than daylight, the dance of living flame opened her to him, as moonlight opens the hunter's trail. From the first opening of his eyes, he had watched the softening light play on her hair and thought it a live thing, a river of copper, cascading onto the rock of her shoulder just for him.

Later, older, he had watched the wildfire come alive when she was near battle, had seen, and not yet understood, the quite different fire that filled her when she was close to childbirth, had watched, and mourned, the progressive damping of the flame through their last years on Mona and their time in the Eceni lands as she had grieved over the loss of the land and the exile, for ever, of Caradoc mac Cunobelin, his father. Always, it was at night that he had best understood what had touched her.

He studied her now by the light of Braint's pyre and her hair was a river of fire again, and the wildfire shone in her and she was all that she had been and still everything was different so that he had no idea at all what had touched her, only that he regretted with every fibre of his being that he had not been a part of it.

He stepped forward, ignoring the heat, and reached up for her. Behind, scores of thousands of gathered warriors and refugees saw the Boudica's bear-son greet the Boudica, framed by the Warrior's fire and the night beyond, and the thunder roll of their cheering reached as high as the flames and joined the two horizons.

It was impossible not to be moved by it. Impossible, also, to speak. After a while, when they had shouted themselves hoarse and the waves of it were dying away, so that he thought he could be heard by her, but no-one else, he said, 'We shouldn't be here. I know that, and it's my fault and I'm sorry, but I can't undo what's done. We need you now to find the victory within it.'

XXXIX

*I*CAN'T UNDO WHAT'S DONE. WE NEED YOU NOW TO FIND THE *victory within it.*

Nobody could undo what had been done and Breaca had no idea if she could find victory, only that it was needed or the land was lost. Thus were the dark weft and the bright woven together; a war host of fifty thousand facing at best eight thousand legionaries, and the advantage all with the enemy.

. . . there is such a thing as god-luck . . . it is as necessary as any amount of training . . .

Valerius had said that, and had gone on to set a battle plan that was as solid as any man might devise. It was clean and easily learned and had the twists in it that might yet confound the enemy. He had given himself the most dangerous part of it and Breaca had not taken that from him, believing it their best hope of success.

She spoke to him of it, sitting by the fire when the spear-leaders had departed and the camp was settling to sleep. 'Dubornos openly gave his life for this, to carry our need to the gods. Are you thinking to do the same in the battle tomorrow?'

He was leaner than when they had parted in Camulodunum, and his skin had seen more sun. His humour had become freer, too, so that she could see the many parts of him, dreamer and warrior, boy and man, Eceni and Latin, Nemain and Mithras in the dryness of his smile and the solemn quiet that had followed it.

Leaning forward, Valerius gave his attention for a moment to Stone, who lay across their feet, then said, 'The gods guide, they rarely demand. It is up to each of us to listen to the whispers and make what we can of them. Dubornos has told them of our need and our sincerity with the magnitude of his gift. I would not presume to follow him. I will do what is needed tomorrow. As will you.' He paused and she thought he might leave and then, quite differently, he said, 'In Camulodunum, you said that I should bring you the serpent-spear if you were whole when you returned. You're as whole now as I have ever seen you. If you are ever to have it, tonight is the time. Shall I bring it?'

He was shy then, a boy offering his first-made carving to his older sister. The box he brought to her was as long as he was tall, but light. He laid it in the fire's light and sat back, watching her.

She would have admired the box for its workmanship, but the night was short. Opened, a spear lay within, with a haft as long as her body of white ashwood and a long, narrow blade in the shape of a leaf.

Her heart had skipped a beat and come back to its rhythm faster. 'Is this a true heron-spear, as the Caledonii use? I would not wish to cast one of those lightly on the morning of battle.'

'No.' He lifted it for her, balancing it across two fingers. For the first time in her presence, the maker in him shone through, eclipsing the dreamer and the warrior. 'The blade isn't silver and I have made no feathers to bind at the neck and alter its flight. Airmid carved the serpents of the haft.'

'And you have brought the sun into the iron of the blade,' she said, in wonder.

Such a gift she had never received. She held it closer to the fire and saw the curls of sun-red copper beaten into the blue iron of the blade, so that it drew in the fire and made it brighter. She saw the serpents that curved in living patterns along the wood, and the smooth running lines of the hound beaten in copper into the iron of the blade.

She stood and tested it; the balance was perfect. The song was subtle and took some time to hear over the crack and spit of the fire. When at last she reached it, or it her, it was the song of her own soul, set in counterpoint.

She said, ' "Find the mark that is ours and seek its place in your soul." '

'I'm sorry?'

'The ancestor's prophecy. This was the third task: I was to gather and arm a war host, then find the warrior with the eyes and heart of a dreamer; both of these are done. The final task was to find the mark that is ours – mine, the ancestor's, Briga's – and seek its place in my soul. I thought I was to come to understand it more and had been struggling to do so. Now . . .' Breaca lifted the blade and let its light glow soft before the fire, 'you have given it to me.'

She sat down, feeling weightless. 'I don't have the words.'

'You don't need any.' His smile came from his own soul, shorn of all irony.

They sat with the blade and the hound and the fire. A long time later, Breaca said, 'Three tasks and three answers. A life might end on the completion of that.'

'Or it might be only beginning.' Valerius lay back with his hands laced behind his head and one knee cocked up. His eyes sought hers and held them. 'Tomorrow is the culmination of all that we have lived for, you and I. It is still possible that we may all come through it alive.'

He was the brother she had lost and was only now beginning to find. He was balancing better the two broken halves of himself. His own hound had returned, the dream of Hail that ran at his side. She was coming to learn that it was only there to be seen when he was in most danger, or had opened his soul most widely to one or other of his gods. It lay between them both, a long, warm, intangible shape made of uneven light and shadow. She rested a hand on her knee and could feel the coarse hair that ran the length of its neck.

She said, 'It is true that the gods guide and do not demand, but they also protect, I think, or give each of us the means of our protection. Don't forget that in the heat of battle.'

A while later, when the hound was less easily seen, Valerius said, 'And the gods give us their luck, which is in you. Don't forget that, either, in the heat of battle.'

He rose some time after that, and went to talk to Longinus and Theophilus, who were waiting for him with news of a tent that the refugees from Verulamium, or Canonium, or Caesaromagus had found in their wagons. Thinking to honour him, they had erected it and lit a brazier inside, so that the once-Roman who had burned their towns in the name of freedom could sleep in comfort as did the legions' generals.

Breaca and Airmid joined them in the ring of others admiring aloud the fine-dressed hides and the neat double stitching of the seams and the way the light from the brazier made shadows on the walls. It was a good way to end the night, to laugh with friends and to come away again after, to sleep by the last heat of Braint's fire.

Or not to sleep, but to sit with Stone at her side and think.

. . . the gods give us their luck, which is in you . . .

Breaca stared into redness. The pyre fell in on itself again. The heap of ash was down to shoulder height. She let her gaze soften until all she could see was red.

As if he asked it again, she heard in the flames Venutios' question and wondered whether she might yet escape its answer. As if she held it again, she felt the stone that had crushed Dubornos' skull and released his soul from his body. As if it were real, and knowing it was not, she watched the horned moon become full and saw the hare that was on its surface step down onto the earth. Soft wind breathed on the embers that had been Braint. Fire soughed and sighed and became, distantly, the belling of hounds, picked for their voices, and their speed. They hunted without cease, but did not kill.

Stone raised his head and whined softly and laid it down again to rest. From behind, Airmid murmured, 'You should sleep. The battle will need you sharp and awake.'

'Maybe later.' Breaca was as sharp and awake as she had ever been in her life. Impossible to imagine ever sleeping again.

'Do you want help to reach to the heart of the fire?'

To have the understanding even to ask that question was a gift beyond measure. She reached back and found Airmid's arm and squeezed it. 'Maybe later.'

They sat in silence in the circle of their family. Graine lay curled in her cloak. After a while, Stone joined her and she made him her pillow, never waking from sleep. Cygfa sat up talking to Gunovar somewhere near a small stand of hawthorn. Hawk slept with the bear-blade of Eburovic as his companion. Cunomar and Ardacos

427

and those who followed them were gone; somewhere within earshot, the skull drums of the she-bear played their discordant rhythm, just far enough away not to disturb the rest of those who needed to sleep.

Valerius was still awake, sitting up with Longinus and Theophilus. She could see his outline in silhouette, and the growing tension that lacked any obvious reason. He shifted a little, and she saw that the hound had left him again and he sat alone staring out into the night as if waiting for something, or someone.

She had thought that, and then who it might be, and was going to go over to speak to him when the night stirred and she was too late.

'Valerius?'

A voice called it from the dark beyond the fire. Breaca watched her brother stand, slowly, as if, now it had come, he would rather have continued to wait. Huw came into the light, the young slinger with the scarred face who was now Warrior of Mona. Brilliant metal flashed between his two hands.

Valerius did not take what was offered: a small statuette of the falcon, Horus, dented on the head, with one eye made of jet. He stood with his head bowed, staring at his clasped hands, and did not move.

It was Longinus who asked, 'Where is he?' He had no need to give a name; he, too, had been waiting.

Huw said, 'On the other side of the ridge. The scouts have him. They'll kill him if you give the order.'

'No!' Breaca said it, standing now. 'Valerius, is it Corvus?' and then, when he gave no answer, 'Go. He was a friend before this began. He may be again when it's over. It's not for us now to turn our backs on friendship.'

And then Longinus said it again, kindly, and with other threads in the weave, 'Go. I'll wait here, where there's warmth. There's a long night yet before the day begins; we can mend then whatever might be broken,' which was enough finally to unglue her brother's feet and set him moving into the dark beyond the fire.

He felt sick, which was ridiculous on the eve of battle. He had thought Theophilus might offer to come with him and had not been sure he could find the voice to send him back. He was grateful that had not been needed. He followed Huw through the dark, blindly, and chose not to think of where he was going or why.

They came to a place where a small stream ran along the base of the ridge, and a hazel stood on either side. He had marked them for the spear-leaders for the day to come; not because they were useful for cover – there was no cover to speak of in the open plain in front of Paullinus' valley – but as rallying points, easily seen by all the warriors.

'Here.' Huw pressed the small Horus into his hands. 'I'll not be far,' and faded back to the shadow of the ridge.

The night was empty. He might have been alone under the stars, except that there was a faint scent on the breeze that he would have recognized anywhere, at any time, in the blind heat of battle, on the cold of a winter's mountain, in a throng of drinking legionaries in a filthy tavern in a Gaulish sea port – or here, at the edge of an ordinary plain on which the future of a province would be decided at daybreak.

He said, 'Why are you here?'

'To see you.' Corvus was sitting on a rock with his bare feet in the stream. Coming so recently from the firelight, it took some time for Valerius to see him. The water was first, making silvered furrows around his ankles, then the slow revelation of a man.

He looked more tired than he had at Prasutagos' steading, when he had sent the procurator's veterans away and so saved Breaca's life. His hair carried more silver than it had done in the years of his youth and he was, perhaps, a little thicker in the waist. Beyond all of those, he was the same man who had been shipwrecked on the Eceni coast twenty-three years before, the same officer who had lifted a boy from slavery and brought him into the cavalry.

They stood on opposite sides of the stream, and words would not bridge it.

After a while, Corvus cleared his throat and asked, 'Do you still have your mad horse?'

'Yes. And Cygfa has his grandson. He has the spirit of his grandsire, but isn't quite as mad.'

'Gods . . . With two of those on the battlefield . . . we should leave now.'

'Will you?'

'No.'

The false levity withered. The river ran yet between them. Valerius leaned in and set the bronze Horus on a rock mid-stream. Its jet eye glared at him. He said, 'This is yours. You should have it back.'

'Thank you.' Corvus made no attempt to take it. 'It's travelled a long way to be here.'

'From Alexandria?'

'Yes.'

'You never told me his name.' Valerius had no idea why he said that. There had been years when he could have asked and the answer would have been given freely.

Corvus said, 'I am not sure I ever knew his real name. He called himself Alexandro.' He said it in the soft, southern way, sliding the consonants across the root of his tongue. He smiled, thinly, so that the river caught the reflection of it. 'I was his Hephaistion.'

'You loved him that much?'

'I thought I did. Love was . . . very different then. Simpler.' Corvus reached to turn the falcon round, his fingers tracing the dent in its head. 'I was nineteen. I thought I knew everything there was to know of life and love and all the things between them.'

'And now?' Valerius asked it softly.

'Now I know nothing and know that I know nothing. No . . . that's not true.' Corvus drew a short breath and hissed it out, shaking his head. 'I never know what to say in your company any more. For gods' sake, must we sit like this with a river between us when it will all end tomorrow?'

It was hard to speak, but necessary. 'There's room here,' said Valerius, 'and equally on your side. I can cross or you can. I don't think there's room for both of us and the Horus on the stone in the middle.'

'No.' Corvus barked a laugh. 'No, there isn't. So then, shall I cross or will you? It seems to matter. What do your gods tell you?'

'That it should never have come to this.' Valerius' voice snagged in his throat. 'Wait, I'll come over.'

He got his feet wet, and stubbed his toe, and landed like a thrown fish on the far bank and lay laughing, shakily. He was weeping, which felt better than he might have supposed.

With the heel of his hand, he smeared the wet from his eyes and sat up. 'I'm supposed to be leading the right wing tomorrow. I doubt they would follow me if they saw this.' He could say that, and lose nothing; it would be obvious from the opening of the battle lines.

Giving as little away, Corvus said, 'Then we'll meet. The Quinta Gallorum are set to hold the left.'

'There is still time to change it.' Valerius thought about that. 'But we won't. We will do what we must because there is no way now to change the things that really matter.' He sat up. Tears leaked down the line of his nose, as if a tap had opened and could not be closed off. He reached out, fuzzily, and took hands that waited for him. 'Quintus Valerius Corvus. I loved you more than I knew. I would never have thrown it away so lightly if I had known what it meant.'

The hands that lay in his were still and cool and only a small tremor betrayed them. Corvus said, 'Someone told me once that men are doomed to learn through pain until they can find a way to learn through joy. It seems we have a lot to learn, each of us.'

'We do. Was that from him?' He nodded to the Horus.

'No. But it was of that time. A woman. She was to Isis what you are to Mithras. And now, I think, to Nemain? Or is it Briga?'

'Nemain.'

'It must be hard to hold true to them both at once.'

'Impossible. I am still two people in one skin. I imagine I will always be.'

'But one soul, and that Eceni and that is where the treasure lies.' Corvus lifted Valerius' hand and traced the lines of the palm with one finger and said, 'You know that if I could restore to you all that is lost, I would do it.'

'I know. Thank you.'

Without speaking, they had moved, and sat close, so that it was possible once again for Valerius to tip his head sideways and find a shoulder waiting, as it had always waited, and the weight of a cheek on his crown and to feel an arm round him and the steady – so very steady – rhythm of a heartbeat that sang to his own. The gods were there, quietly, without conflict, so that it was possible to be young again, and know nothing except the simplicity of love, and at the same time to be older, and know that there was everything still to know.

'Luain mac Calma.' Corvus spoke the name into his hair; a

blessing, or a curse. 'I asked him if we would meet in death. He promised me that we would meet once more in this life. I didn't believe him at the time.'

Once more. The words cut them both, and were believed.

Valerius said, 'He's my father, did you know?'

'Yes, he told me. I had always thought it, only when Eburovic was alive, it seemed impolite to ask. He was there in the beginning, at the first shipwreck. Will he be here now, at the end?'

'I don't know. He thinks Graine is the wild piece on the board. He sent her back to Breaca so she would be here. It may be he thinks that's enough.'

'For the sake of your people, it would be good to think so.'

'Yes.' The weeping had stopped and there was, after all, no need to talk. Valerius sat still, listening to a heartbeat and feeling the press of a cheek, and of lips on his head. Then he sat a little higher, and the head was beside his, and it would have been a small thing to turn inward and seek the kiss and the solace that had been ten years denied.

A part of him wanted to. The greater part, god-connected, did not. The gap between the two ached with an old, familiar yearning.

Unsteadily, Corvus said, 'I think this is enough. To have met, to have spoken—'

'To know that there is no hate.'

'And never was?'

'Never.'

The night was cooler than it had been. The glow of Braint's pyre was a setting sun on the wrong horizon. It was hard to part. Harder still to imagine leaving. Hardest to imagine battle, and the endings it might bring. They came apart, slowly, making the moments draw out beyond their span.

Corvus picked up the Horus and wiped the water from it with the hem of his cloak. He said, 'Luain mac Calma knows the things we don't. If anyone can rescue sense from nonsense, it is him. He spared my life on Mona. I like to think there was a reason, and that it was not for the destruction of us both, or our people.'

The stepping stone was free. Valerius crossed the stream again with dry feet and did not stumble. From the far bank, which was Eceni at least until morning, he said, 'Whatever comes, know that I am sorry for all that I said and did that hurt you.'

'I always knew that. I was just not always able to let you know that I knew.'

The joy of that would have melted him if he had stayed on the Roman side. Valerius gave the salute of warrior to warrior and said, 'Until tomorrow then, and whatever comes after. If I cross the river to the gods first, I will wait for you, however long it takes.'

'Will your gods allow it, when they are not mine?' Corvus had never dared voice that doubt before, to himself or anyone. He watched Valerius pause on his own side of the river and search within in a way he had never done in his younger years. The answer, then, when it came, was quiet and solid and certain, and settled in Corvus' heart as a bandage ready for expected pain.

'They will always allow it. It's only men who need ownership. The gods allow more freedom.'

The message came from the gods, and was for all who could hear it. The smile was for Corvus alone, and he treasured it.

X L

VALERIUS WALKED ALONG THE SIDE OF THE STREAM. WHEN HE could no longer hear the sound of footsteps going the other way, he bent to wash his face.

Nobody came to join him or to ask unnecessary questions. There was no moon, yet, to open wide the pathways to Nemain. No bulls grazed near the two armies to bring him closer to Mithras. Even so, a boundary had been crossed that was more than the wetting of feet in a river and a last remembrance of love. The night was crisper than it had been, so that the stars were punched holes in the void and god-light leaked through. He turned in to walk across the open plain towards the camp, and set himself open, waiting.

Cygfa met him, who was the last he had expected. She stood alone, in night so black that only the brilliance of her hair gave her away, and even that was a strange, muted pewter, not the corn gold of her father's daylight legacy. She had changed since the battle for Camulodunum and Valerius did not fully know why. Guessing, he said, 'I'm sorry about Braint.'

'Thank you. So am I, but it was a good death and a good day to die. Few of us are privileged to cross the river under the same moon as Dubornos. Did you hear of that?'

'Yes. Airmid told me, and then Breaca.'

'How much did they say of what passed between him and me?'

'That you offered yourself to carry his life on after his death, but he . . .' Valerius struggled to find words that would suit and would not further offend the sudden stiffening, and the edge of something else he still could not read. She had not been stiff in his presence since they had left Gaul on a ship when he had still thought he fought for Rome. He did not want to remember that. He had grown used to the ease of her presence, and her acceptance of him for all he had been. It would hurt to find it lost.

She turned and he led her closer to the camp, to where the fire-light might let him read her. She took his lead, but pushed him a little eastward, towards the tent that the refugees had given him, and the red light of its brazier.

There, she said, 'Dubornos wouldn't accept what I offered. He couldn't. Perhaps I should not have offered, but I felt it right at the time.'

'Then it was right.' Luain mac Calma would have said that better, so that it sounded less glib, or Efnís, or Valerius himself if he had been less raw.

'I know. And he said what he needed aloud in front of everyone. They will have told you that.'

They had reached the tent, close enough to smell the charcoal that filled the brazier, and the rosemary oil someone had sprinkled on it. Valerius gave thanks, fervently, that he had not smelled that before he saw Corvus. In the years when their lives had been lived as one, they had often set rosemary oil on the fire before love; it would have been far harder to leave if the memory of that had filled his head. He brought his attention back to Cygfa and what she was saying.

'. . . will not have told you what he said to me alone, as he held me.'

'What was that?'

It mattered. It mattered enough to have made her stay awake on the night before battle and come out to the dark to find him. It mattered enough to turn her face the same bloodless white as her hair, both given colour only by the brazier. He knew that, and even so it was hard to think through the scent of rosemary oil and the sudden havoc of twinned god-space that had opened within him.

He held on to one of the guys of the tent and clenched his hand on it until the hide dug a groove, knowing that he would regret it in the morning, and through the day's battle.

Cygfa was no more free of the chaos than he was, only for other reasons, that he could not yet see. She closed her eyes and the effort she took to speak was clear. 'Before he gave himself to the gods, Dubornos said, "You are bed for other seed than mine. When the time comes, do not let it past." '

She had been raped in Rome and again at the end of winter by the procurator's veterans. If she had ever desired a man, he could not imagine it might happen now. It was not good to think ill of a man who had just given himself to the gods, but Valerius cursed the dead singer for a fool and did not retract it after.

He said, 'Dubornos was already walking with the gods when he spoke. He may have been talking as they do, in the images of dreams and half-thoughts. To be a bed for seed does not always mean that one has to bear a child. Men, too, can nurture ideas, or followers, or—'

'No. I knew him as well as anyone. He was not talking in dream pictures. I've been talking to Gunovar. She was there and was part of it with him. She felt what he felt. She saw what he saw.'

A certain dread came over him. He held the guy rope and had no care for the damage to his hand. 'What?'

'That there is more to this than a single tribe or a single people. What matters now is not whether we win or lose the battle to-morrow, or whether you or I live or die in doing that. What matters is that the lineage we carry continues beyond us, that children are born and nurtured who can hold the power of the gods and join it to the land. Breaca was told in the first dreaming of her long-nights that what mattered was the children and that is still so; without the children – *the right children* – we can win tomorrow and still lose. With them, we can lose and still win.'

He had walked across ice and the ice had broken and he was falling through endless, black, ice-frozen water. His hair stood on end and his tongue had swollen in his throat. He tried to remember Corvus and could not. Longinus was within shouting distance. He could not find the breath to shout.

'No.' Valerius said it flatly, and found it in himself to step back. 'You don't want it. I don't want it. If it must be done, let it be by others than us.'

'Who?' Cygfa looked like her father, when scorn was his weapon. 'You think I should send you to Graine perhaps?'

'*Don't!*'

She had come close and he must have tried to push her away. Her hands were on his wrists, holding them. Her face was close to his, so that he could smell her breath and her sweat and none of it was what he had just left by the water's edge.

It was not what he wanted. He could not imagine ever wanting it, except once, and that had been Nemain, which was different . . . He remembered river water and the run of it over his skin and the memory was sacred, and would not be pushed away.

Nor would Cygfa. She was the stronger and the gods lit her eyes. She was her father made woman, or simply come again to earth in different form. Valerius had never loved Caradoc, only respected him and envied his life.

She was too close, too earnest. 'Valerius, listen to me. Our two lines must continue. Graine is of the Sun Hound, but she's too young. Cunomar could get a child on someone but he is only one part of it and there is no-one to match you. You are son of the Elder of Mona, one of the greatest, possibly the greatest there has ever been. Macha was his match; if she had stayed, there is every chance she would have been chosen in his place. If your life had been different, it would not be Efnís who was named his successor.'

Uselessly, 'I don't want to be Elder of Mona.'

'I know. And you don't want to father a child and I don't want to bear one, and yet it must be done. *It must be done.*'

Cygfa swayed back, so that she was not so close and yet still held him. Her eyes challenged, as they had once done on a different riverbank in Gaul. He had been so arrogant then. Both of them had. She said, 'Ask your gods and see if they accept what I say. If you can truly say they don't, I will leave you.'

That was the fear and the desperation: he already knew what they wanted. If he spoke it aloud, she would not have to leave him.

Cygfa felt his resistance end. He saw the sudden upsetting of her balance, as if she had been depending on him to outmatch her and, now that he had failed, did not know what to do.

She gathered her courage, a smaller figure now, following a path she had never wanted to tread. They were near the tent. She still had hold of him, and tugged him towards it. 'In here?'

They were too close to hide from each other, and had shared too many battles. He could feel her fear, and the courage it took for her to keep to what she believed was needed.

'No,' Valerius said. 'This child should have nothing of Rome. Come with me,' and he led her away from the stitched hides and the red glowing charcoal and the too-strong scent of rosemary oil and back to the water's edge, upstream from his meeting place with Corvus.

The river curved round to the east and swung back again in an oxbow. The apex of the curve was a point halfway between the two competing armies. There was just enough light from the fires of both camps by which to see the ground and each other.

Here, elder, heavy with hard green berries, made a stand with drooping willow. The grass was ankle deep and untrodden as yet by war. Water hissed smoothly; no crossing stones stopped the river. They disturbed a roosting crow that flapped raggedly away; its feathers cracked in the dark.

Thinly Cygfa said, 'Briga blesses us? Or not?'

Valerius said, 'Or Mithras. The raven is the first of his beasts, before the hound and the bull and the serpent.'

Cygfa forced a smile. 'If we meet the others, it could be an interesting night.'

She was so deeply afraid, and striving so hard not to show it. It was easier, then, to find some strength in what they had been given.

Valerius searched his own soul for compassion, and found it, and a kind of love that was rooted in respect for all she had been; enough to let the two gods within bring some sense of passion.

He held only her hand. 'I have no experience of this.'

'And I have too much.' Her body was rigid as a cornered deer.

'Then will you guide me, that your experience might be different from what it has been?'

'I can try, but if I fail, you have to finish.'

'I can try.'

They lay down together under the berried elder, and moved slowly, and were gentle each with the other so that there was time for compassion and duty to become passion and something approaching need.

Near the end, while he could still speak, Valerius said, 'If we do this, will you stay out of the battle, to keep the child alive?'

He felt her smile stretch the skin of his shoulder, where her teeth had just grazed it. Her voice rolled into his marrow. 'No. Nothing will keep me out of the battle, any more than it will you. But I may not do as I had planned and follow Braint across the river if it seems that we are losing.'

'Good. Very good. It would be very hard indeed to lose you.'

He surprised them both with the sincerity of that, and the depth of feeling. It was enough, evidently, for them both to climb the last hill and find release and rest, believing that a child had been made, that would carry the lineage of moon and sun and build a life in a future yet to be fashioned.

XLI

FOR THE FIRST TIME IN BREACA'S LIFE, THE TORC OF THE ECENI ancestors settled easily about her neck. The ancestor-dreamer did not hiss warnings of hubris from the cave of her mind; the Sun Hound did not burden her with foretellings of doom if she let his line or hers fall into ruin; the weight of ceremony of a hundred generations did not settle on her, demanding that she be their equal.

The end-burnings of the fire that had once been a friend glowed red in the dark and she sat with it, the only one awake in a host of thousands and tens of thousands on the almost-morning of battle. The torc lay warm as a living snake against her skin, but there was no threat in it. She felt its presence as she felt Valerius' hound, a thing that hovered on the edge of understanding but nevertheless gave comfort and a measure of protection.

'The hound is his dream.' The voice came from behind her, rich with the currents of sleep. 'The serpent-spear is yours. Each of you carries that which you need most to hold it close.'

'I thought you were asleep?'

'I was.' Airmid sat up and eased round beside her. 'Efnís is leaving at dawn. He'll take word back to Luain mac Calma of what we plan. I should speak to him before he leaves, but not yet. There's time enough before the light comes.'

Time enough to be together. They leaned against each other in the dark, shoulder to shoulder, warmth to warmth, breath to breath. They had never said goodbye on the morning before battle, only their closeness was more tangible, and time was slowed for a while, then too fast.

It was still slow now, near dawn, as if the pulse of the earth yet slept.

They sat quietly, healed and healer, and watched the fire. Presently, Breaca took off the torc and balanced it on the joined tent of their knees. 'When you gave me this after 'Tagos' death, I felt it as a living thing, the serpent of the serpent-spear, filled with the power of the ancestor-dreamer.'

'And now?' Airmid's head was on her shoulder, a heavy, necessary weight. Impossible to imagine it gone, or that other mornings might not see them joined like this.

'Now it feels empty. Not dead, simply empty, like a vessel that has been drained, and is waiting to be filled again.'

'It is,' Airmid said. 'All that was in it is in you. Can you feel that?'

'Yes.'

Breaca turned the torc between her hands. The workmanship still left her breathless. The ancestors, having more time, had learned to work gold in ways smiths working under Rome could never do. In its simplicity was its beauty, in the unsullied purity of the red Siluran gold and the weaving of the wires and the open loops at the end for the kill-feathers. There were no feathers on it now, nor had been, since the first year of the legions' invasion.

Airmid ran her fingers along, bridging the gap with her fingers. 'If you're going to wear it in battle again, there should be something here, for who you are. Wait . . .' and she reached for her own pack and brought out a feather cast in silver, one-third the size of a real crow's feather, battered, with one end bent.

Breaca said, 'I thought the procurator's men stole all of those.'

'So did I.' Airmid held it out flat on her palm, so that the fire could make it gold. She had red thread with her and began to bind the shaft. 'Gunovar found this afterwards in the ruin of 'Tagos' hut. She gave it to me to hold until you were well again.'

'Thank you.' More than the newness of the torc, the feather was the confirmation of her wholeness.

Breaca watched Airmid's long, fine dreamer's fingers weave the thread to the feather and the feather to the gold. 'I thought they might come, now, at the end; the elder grandmother, the ancestor-dreamer and the Sun Hound and all those who came before and since. I have sat half the night awaiting them.'

'If it were truly the end, they might do so. There is a battle first, before any endings come. Would their presence help you fight?'

'No.' The thought made her grimace. 'I can live without help from past ghosts.'

'But you know something of what is needed before the fighting starts?'

'Last night, when I was watching the fire, a hare stepped down from the moon, and there were hounds that were not Stone who followed it. Graine was there. She helped.'

'Can you bring that into being?'

'I think so. Later, when we must.' She did not mention Venutios' question, nor had she done so to anyone.

Dew had formed on the grass around them, beyond the heat of the fire. In the trees behind, a kestrel fed mewling young. Somewhere too close for comfort, the skull drums of the she-bear started up again, maddening as biting flies. Even so, it was dark and the line of the eastern day had not yet begun.

Breaca reached out, and took the half-bound feather and the torc and laid them aside. 'It's still night,' she said, 'and we have time to be together before we must be all that we have become. I think we can make better use of it than this.'

This much, at least, had not changed. They did not say goodbye, but they lay together in the dark beyond the red wash of Braint's fire and let drop the last boundaries that divided them, and shared the stretching time when the pulse of the earth was still slow and they could watch each heartbeat, and savour it.

The hare raised its head and snuffed the air.

Graine froze in her forward movement. She lay face down in long grass with morning mist curling round her like fire smoke and her hair sodden with dew.

She could feel the hare's presence as a second heartbeat in her chest, and nurtured it, as she might a new flame in too-damp tinder. Warily, afraid to crush it with her own clumsiness, she attended as lightly as she could on the dry, tickling sensation that teased the roots of her mind, on the spiking sense of urgency that did not come from her, or from her mother a spear's throw to the left, or from Stone, close by on the right, but from the hare ahead.

These four – herself, her mother, the hound and the hare – were all part of the hunt, and Graine the centre of their web. Her own heart hammered too hard and would not be quiet. She had not *felt* like this since before the procurator's men had assaulted her, possibly not even then. It was as if sight had been given back to her after long months of blindness and the world held more colour than it had done before. She wanted to tell Bellos and was not sure that it would be fair.

The hare relaxed. The distant sounds of the war camp were no longer as unsettling as they had been. The skull drums of the she-bear, begun long before dawn, were no longer driving it mad.

Graine edged forward. She had never wanted to be a hunter, but her mother had asked it, the dazzling stranger, infinitely familiar, who had woken her with a hand on her ankle and an offering of fresh oat bannock and river water flavoured with dried elder-flowers. Her mother who had held her close and pressed her lips to Graine's hair so that her breath warmed her head and there had been a moment's safety in the unsafe world, and that, too, had been something to nurture before the morning snuffed it out.

'Would you help me find a hare?' her mother had asked. 'A strong young doe, in young, but not too heavy so that she can still run fast. We're not going to kill her. I have an idea of something that may help us today.'

Breaca had been with Airmid, clearly; the legacy of that hung around her like a cloak and made sharper her gaze so that she looked like the elder grandmother, except that the care was more evident, and that had made the morning brighter and less frightening.

There had been the challenge, then, of finding the right hare, and the unquestioning belief that she could do it, so that, rising from sleep and strange, intricate dreams, Graine had not questioned it, only splashed her face with the water and drunk a little, and tasted things other than elderflowers and then let out the web of her mind until a young, strong and pregnant hare was within it, and she had walked and then crawled and then slithered within reach of it.

Her mother had a net. It was already set, hanging up on forked hazel twigs, so that it would fall and fold onto anything that ran into it. Graine had decided she did not want to rely on it. She marked the line in her mind, and moved on through the grass.

The hare could feel her, as she felt the hare. The moment of joining was a physical thing, the rebridging of an umbilical cord that each had sought, but not known how to find. Fear and hope came together; its fear was her fear, her hope was its hope, and the certainty of safety. She sang to it in her mind and it sang back high silvered notes, like the music of the moon.

The moon hung old and sharp and fading in the sky, but was still there to be seen, running ahead of the sun. They reached for it separately and together, the beast and the child of Nemain, two sides of a triangle that, once made, was not to be broken.

The hare lay down in its form and laid its ears to its head and sang. Graine sang and slid forward and gathered it, warm beast held safe in sanctuary against her warm skin, heartbeat to heartbeat, breath to breath, soul to soul with the moon between.

A long time later, she stood up, and walked through the drying grass to her mother, who said nothing, only reflected the sun in her honour and whistled Stone in to heel and led her back to the war camp where warriors who did not know what had been made sang their battle songs and braided their hair and the chattering skull drums of Cunomar's she-bears had finally come to rest.

Airmid met them with a doeskin bag for the hare and sat with Graine by the last embers of Braint's pyre and they sang to the beast of an ancient battle between the ancestors and the eagles in the days when the world was young.

Bellos came to sit beside Graine and she did not need to talk to him of the un-blinding and the new colours in the world. Instead, she said, 'I don't understand what has happened.'

'You have been to Mona and that is no small thing.' He had combed his white-gold hair and set a raven's skull in it, for Briga. It looked like a jewel in the morning. 'And then you were required to find the stone for Dubornos. He healed more than himself with the gift of his life.'

He turned his face to her, in the way she had come to recognize on Mona, so that although his eyes were in the wrong place, his attention was on her. 'When it was needed of you for Dubornos, how did you know you had found the right stone?'

'I felt it.'

'Did it call to you? As the hare called? And join as the hare joined?'

The hare was still joined. She could feel the tug of it against her belly and could not imagine a child being joined any more strongly. The joining to the stone had been less, a thread thin as spider's silk. Without the more tangible feel of the hare, she would not have recognized it.

Bellos put a hand on her shoulder. 'Don't hold that sense too hard, or chase the feel of it. Just stay with it and know how it is and be ready to know it again when it comes.'

He rose, smoothly. The hollow eyes of his raven's skull stared down at her from his height. 'You should stay here while the rest prepare for battle. I need to find Cunomar and then Hawk. Can you point me to one or the other?'

Her old brother and her new were together, which was a miracle in itself, although there was no clear peace between them. She showed Bellos where to find them and set his feet on the right path and settled back with the warm weight of the hare heavy against her and watched the warriors make themselves ready for war.

Cunomar said, 'You are my brother.'

'Yes,' said Hawk. He bore the bear-blade of Eburovic on his back, and had set his hair in the Eceni way, with the warrior's braid at the side. Someone had given him the small antler of a young buck and he had fixed that at his temple in place of kill-feathers and painted the serpent-spear on the top part of his sword arm. Everyone, by then, knew why.

One should love one's brother, or at least not hate him.

They were evenly matched. If they had fought, Cunomar believed he would have won, but only because he had the advantage of the bear. New claw marks bled freshly on his shoulders, as on the shoulders of the two hundred others who had danced with him in front of Ardacos to the rhythms of the skull drums and given their souls afresh to the bear.

Hawk was not one of those, but he had sat on the margins, by Ardacos' invitation, and had seen some of the mystery. Only the Boudica and Cygfa had been so permitted before. More even than Eburovic's blade, it had affirmed Hawk's place within the family.

Around them, the singing of the warriors had halted. Some were mounted, ready. Valerius' cavalry was moving into a mass and beginning to organize into a semblance of squadrons, as he had shown them on the ride up from Lugdunum. Cygfa was a shining spear, drawing warriors behind her, like gulls behind a ship. The Boudica was talking with her honour guard. The horses were gathered and already sweating.

There was no time left for indecision. Cunomar was still undecided.

Hawk touched two fingers to the hilt of Eburovic's blade, and then the serpent-spear on his arm. 'I didn't ask for this. It was freely given.'

'I know.'

Cunomar had heard it first from Breaca, and then Ardacos, and then Cygfa. Standing by Braint's pyre with his mother newly returned, there had been too much havoc in his heart and head to make sense of yet another new strand. In the brisk morning, with the mist clearing and battle close, he still did not know which way to turn.

A new voice said, 'If you would be a match for each other in combat, how much would you both combined be a match against the legions?'

Bellos spoke from Cunomar's side, the bright-haired Belgic youth whom he had met as a frightened slave boy in Gaul and who had become, it seemed, a dreamer of Mona, given to Briga; and blind; he had been told that in the night, too.

Hawk knew him, and respected him. He gave the salute of warrior to dreamer and then, unexpectedly, turned to Cunomar and gave the salute of warrior to warrior, and shield-mate. 'If you would accept it, I would swear to fight as your shield-mate, to give my life for yours, to the ends of the earth and the four winds.'

The hair stood upright on Cunomar's arms. The bear scars on his shoulder pulled tight, as if they were cut and then scabbed over and healed, all in one movement. He heard the harsh breath of the bear, and felt the moment of its death, as he had killed it. He said, 'That oath is too old. I would not hold you to it.'

'But it's an oath made within families. I offer it, knowing what it means.'

Bellos said, 'You can't accept it if you hate him, but you don't yet have to love. Can you find something between these two?'

446

Cunomar thought about that. At length, he said, 'I can respect and honour the courage of one who danced for the deer-elders, who would have given his life.' He still regretted not having been there. He looked to the last warmth of Braint's fire and saw Graine. 'Are you not already sworn to my sister?'

Hawk said, 'The dreamers will stand together away from the battle and Graine will be with them. They'll be behind the battle lines. If we're lost, they are lost, but they know that. I spoke to your sister last night and she set me free to fight in the battle.' He offered a tentative smile. 'On Mona, I taught her to fight. The legions should be more afraid of her than any of us.'

Graine was so small. If the tip of Eburovic's blade were placed on the floor between her feet, the hilt would have reached almost to her chin. She would have been hard pushed to lift it, still less wield it, even had her grandfather not expressly forbidden her to touch it years before.

The absurdity of it reached a place beyond love or hate. Cunomar grinned fleetingly. 'Then we can leave the dreamers in their safety.' With due gravity, he returned the warrior's salute. 'I accept your offer, but release you from it also so that you might fight with our mother. I'll be on the left wing, while she leads the centre. She should have at least one of her children with her.'

'I accept. On the understanding that if the dreamers are in danger, you and I will come back alone or together to protect them, whatever may be happening elsewhere.'

Bellos said, 'Thank you. We are all grateful for that.'

It could have been done just by the saying of it in the presence of a dreamer, but they clasped arms, hand to elbow, in the old way, so that they felt the mettle of each other for the first time since they had met.

Cunomar thought he was right, that he would have won if they fought, but that it would have been closer than he had imagined and it was better by far to fight together against Rome. In the knowing of that, his nightmare of the bear turned at bay haunted him less.

Stepping away, he wanted to give something that would match the moment. 'You should meet Ulla,' he said. 'Come to the bear's fire. There is time yet to introduce you before the final gathering begins.'

The Boudica addressed her war host from the back of the white-legged colt that was Cygfa's heart-gift to her on the eve of battle.

She stood to the west, with the rising sun in front and Braint's pyre rebuilt behind and all the Roman army gathering for its own address behind that.

She had not slept for two days, and felt as brisk as if she had just risen. The sun was within her, and the horned moon. The pulse of the earth was her own pulse. The gods walked within and without and death was all around, so that she could have stepped down from the colt and crossed any one of the unseen thresholds into the lands beyond life without any need for a battle, or even a stone hammered down to break open her head.

She was not ready to die, and might never be; life held too much promise.

Ahead was her hope for that promise. Fifty thousand warriors gathered, all given to her. All tribal marks were gone; Coritani fought alongside Cornovii and both beside Eceni and the sign of the serpent-spear was on everything. Once, the ancestor-dreamer would have been with her, behind or to one side or echoing snake-dry in the cave of her mind, declaring the mark as her own. There was no cave now, and no echo; she had claimed the mark for herself, and all that it had been and was and would be, and the gods did not gainsay her.

The warriors were silent, waiting. They had their backs to the east. Only she saw the moment when the sun broke free of the land, and parted the shadowing cloud as it had done at Camulodunum, but sooner, so that the fire of the gods met the fires of the warriors, and she the gateway between.

She raised her arms to her war host. A forest of spears stabbed the sky in silent answer. A great wave of polished shield bosses caught the sun and sent forward an ocean of light that flowed round her and emptied into Braint's pyre.

She did not try to speak to them; she could speak to a thousand, three thousand, possibly ten thousand, but not to the fifty thousand who faced her and as many refugees who waited beyond them with any hope of being heard.

Even so, they needed something from her to carry them into war. Her family were around her; Airmid and the dreamers on one side, her sons and daughters on the other and Valerius at the meeting point between. The sun was their signal. Unpractised, but planned, Valerius and Cygfa moved forward on foot, carrying one of the great round war shields of the Votadini between them. They held it flat at shoulder height as a platform. Hawk and Cunomar brought Graine to it and, between them, they lifted her onto it, so that she stood level with her mother, in sight of the full fifty thousand.

Her balance was good; astonishing in fact. She had dressed carefully, in a tunic of undyed wool with edged hemming in Eceni blue. Her hair was a rich, dark ox-blood and hung flat down her back, sleek as polished wood. She said, 'Now, while they are quiet,' and held out her hands.

In view of the full fifty thousand, with the children among the throng all reared on stories of the heroes, and of how children had brought them water in the heart of combat, and so enabled them to rise again and win the battle, Breaca of the Eceni and of Mona, Boudica of the tribes, lifted the torc of her ancestors from her neck and placed it in the waiting hands of her daughter.

They had not planned clearly what came next. Graine's face became still. In front of thousands, she closed her eyes and dipped her head and pressed her brow to the arc of the torc, then raised it to the sun as if she might drain the sky of light and hold it in the gold. Last, she slipped it about her own neck.

It was too large, and she too small, and they were both radiant.

Slowly, the Boudica raised her blade. Ardacos came, with the bear-warriors of his own choosing, who had been with him since the days on Mona, and Ulla and the others of the younger she-bear, and Civilis with a handful of his Batavians and half of Valerius' cavalry, so that she was surrounded by warriors on foot and on horseback. Together, they made the salute of warriors to a dreamer, all for the Boudica's daughter.

In the profound quiet that followed, there was some chance of being heard.

Facing an ocean of light, with her daughter at her side, Breaca raised her voice and cast it to the thousands. 'This is what we fight for, and why we must win. Never forget it, however long the battle lasts.'

She finished, and sheathed her blade, and then Stone rose up and planted his forefeet on either side of her leg and raised his head and gave voice to the belled tones of a war hound, in the way of the heroes' hounds in the winter tales, and she had not planned that at all.

For perhaps two heartbeats more, there was silence. Then the roar began, loud, and louder and louder yet, because it mattered that they rock the earth and the sky with the power of their voices, that they tell the legions what they already knew: that they were outnumbered and outmatched and would spend their last hours fighting a losing battle against a war host that was unassailable.

Behind them, starting slowly and growing, the legions and cavalry wings of Rome did their best to out-match them; and failed.

They waited a long time for the shouting to cease, and the hammer of blades on shields to die away.

The sun was higher, and the shadows sharper. Valerius said, 'Graine? It might be good if we set you down.'

With difficulty, Graine brought her mind back from the far distant place where the torc had taken it. The hare in its sack sang to her quietly, so that she had a thread to follow home. She smiled for her mother's brother, who had fathered a child in the night and did not yet know how that had changed him.

'Yes, thank you.' Her voice was not her own, but in the clamour of almost-war, it was barely noticed.

They set her to earth gently. The sun was blinding. The moon sang too loudly. She swayed and Cygfa held her up. Being on the shield had been easier.

Her mother said, 'Graine? Is it the torc?' That voice came more clearly through the siren calls of the other worlds.

She turned to where she thought Breaca might be. 'I don't know.'

The gold was lifted from her neck. The singing stopped and she could see. Her mother had dismounted and was crouched in front of her, settling the torc round her own neck. She kissed Graine on the forehead and the ground ceased to heave.

'We are learning,' Breaca said. 'This is not for you yet.' She stood back and studied her daughter. Her face was Briga's face, mother of all life and the compassion of death. 'We have to begin

450

the battle shortly. Are you well enough to help me with the hare?'

'Yes.' Nothing would have kept her from that.

They began very soon. Valerius, who had been to the top of the ridge and back, said, 'The legions are gathered. He has the cavalry at the wings and the Fourteenth are standing shoulder to shoulder across the width between. The valley's mouth is a line of iron. There is no way to come at them but from the front.'

Breaca said, 'Thank you. You said they would do that. Does he have the hounds with him?'

'Of course. He knows this is his day to live or die. He wouldn't be without them now.'

Graine had never been at the forefront of a war host. Her mother's arm was on her shoulder, shielding her as a hawk shields her young. Even so, moths fluttered at her diaphragm and her mouth was stickily dry.

Breaca looked down and smiled the same, tentative smile she had offered once, on a dawn morning, before they had really come to know one another. 'Shall we go, heart of life? I think this day is better started.'

Her mother mounted. Valerius swung Graine up before her on the black colt with the white legs and Airmid handed her the hare in its sack. It was too late for talking. The colt swung round to face the enemy. The last murmur of the war host halted. In silence, Breaca of the Eceni, Boudica of nations, raised her blade, and in silence sent her colt forward. Two spear-lengths behind, her war host followed.

The ridge was barely the height of a man; enough only to shield the armies of both sides from each other.

At the crest, they dismounted. Nemain's beast was of the earth, and must not be sent to battle from horseback; her mother's dreams had shown that. The legions waited, as Valerius had said, locked within the safe walls of the valley so that none could come at them but from the front. They stood in perfect rows; shield met square-edged shield in a band of red and black, while polished helmets, sun-welded each to the next, made a brazen line that blurred the faces of the men beneath so that each man was the same, a grain of sand in the ocean of the army. On either side, the cavalry waited, set out in squares on horses that were carved from stone.

Suetonius Paullinus, governor of Britannia, was in front of them all, mounted on a red horse half a hand higher than any around it. His cloak was black and flowed over its haunches in the way of the statues in Camulodunum. His helmet plumes were white and stuck upright, as straight and high as the limed hair of Cunomar's she-bears.

His two smooth-pelted running dogs were leashed and held by a young and very striking warrior of the Atrebates, who bore clan marks that could be seen from halfway across the field. It mattered, clearly, for Rome to be seen to have at least one ally among the tribes.

It was impossible not to stop, faced by that. It was necessary to go forward. Graine felt her mother's hand light on her back and heard her mother's voice say, 'Shall we show them who we are?' and they walked down the ridge on foot, with only Stone for company so that, for a moment, it must have seemed to the waiting legions that the Boudica came to face them with only a child and a lame hound and no warriors at all behind her. The cheer then was of derision and the waves of it battered them, as a storm batters a ship.

They were at the foot of the ridge when the entire line of the Boudica's war host crested the ridge.

The legions fell to silence as if their officers had commanded it. The quiet was of a sucked breath, and a cramped hand clenching.

Against all pride, Graine glanced over her shoulder. She faltered and was still and so Breaca, too, had to turn and look and even she, who had called her war host into being, drew a breath at what she had made.

Warriors and warriors and warriors stood poised in an endless, beautiful, wild and savage row: men and women, naked and armoured, painted and plain, gold-haired and black, unmounted and mounted on horses of every height in a havoc of clashing colours, of skin, of hair, of tunic and cloak, in Mona's grey and the gorse yellow of the Trinovantes and the dusk-sky blue of the Eceni and stolen white messenger-cloaks that had once belonged to the enemy, bearing the great-spears of the Votadini and the axes of the Dumnonii and the ancestor-blades of the horse warriors and the wicked, two-edged knives of the limed and painted she-bear.

They were magnificent in their disorder and the power of their self-belief and on every shield, turned to the fore, was the serpent-spear of the Boudica, painted in red the colour of newly shed horse blood, set on and never allowed to dry.

For the two of them alone, Graine said, 'It's your dream from the ancestors' cave: the Roman eagle crushed and the serpent-spear flying over in victory.'

The Boudica was all of them, made one. Her smile drew the gods from their watching place and made them flesh and blood on the earth. She laid her arm on her daughter's shoulder and Graine could have become a warrior then, with the power it gave her.

Breaca said, 'Then come with me and make it happen,' and they walked together the last few steps towards the long sloping plain at the foot of the ridge.

XLII

THE PULSE OF THE EARTH WAS HER OWN PULSE.

Sweating under the growing sun, the war hosts of both sides watched her. They would not move now until she had done what she must do; there was that much honour, at least, between them.

A small river ran to her left, winding snake-like beyond the end of the ridge. Stubborn crows sat in the drooped branches of a hazel there and would not move, whatever the noise. To the right of these, she found a good place to begin it all, nearly opposite the Roman general. His hounds sat still, not yet tense on the leash. He was glorious in his black cloak and white plumes, on his burnished copper horse.

Breaca had no idea how she looked, only that the torc lay at her neck warm as a living snake and she could feel its brilliance reflected in her daughter's eyes. Her own hound, Stone, was crippled and it showed in the way he walked. She believed him noble beyond anything of Rome.

Dew lay still in the shadows of the ridge. Spiders' webs hung heavy with it in the grass, bejewelled ropes slung from bending stems. It seemed a pity to crush them early, before the war host swept them dead. She stepped over their threshold and onto the open ground beyond.

'Have you the hare?' she asked.

'Here,' Graine said.

In the wide space between the armies, the Boudica and her daughter bent together over Airmid's doeskin hunting bag. It smelled faintly of woundwort and hemp and stuffily of warm hare's breath.

The beast was sleek and fit and lay still, as if tame. Graine crouched and ran the knuckle of her first finger down its back, crooning.

Breaca said, 'Can you hear her song? In the way the warriors hear the bladesong of their weapons?'

'I think so. I can hear something.' Graine's eyes were focused elsewhere, as if she watched things her mother could not see. 'She's pregnant. You said you wanted that. I can hear the beginning-songs of the young, but they're small. She can still run if she has to.'

The gods very rarely grant perfection. In this, they came so very close.

Breaca said, 'Can she hear you? Could you ask her to show us the line we must take, to attack the legions and yet stay safe?'

A single line creased Graine's forehead, deepening. Her eyes were wide and grey and focused fully on her mother. 'The Roman general has hounds,' she said. 'They'll hunt her, two against one so she has nowhere to turn. She'll die.'

There had been a hunt once, a single hound set against a young buck hare. The hare had died. Breaca had not been present for that, and had regretted it since.

Now, she said, 'I think she'll live, but I can't be certain. If she dies, there might yet be time to bring the war host away without bloodshed. With an omen so strong, they would accept retreat, even now, and it's possible the legions wouldn't dare to follow us, thinking it a ruse to lure them from the safety of their valley.'

She crouched, and spoke to the yellow eyes of the hare, and through them to her daughter. 'Can we take that risk, she and I? You and I? Would the hare offer her life as Dubornos did, in the name of all that we have worked for? If not, we can take her back and let her go somewhere behind the host, well away from Paullinus and his hounds. Airmid will know where.'

Graine was the Boudica's daughter. She had lived all her life with the need to fight Rome. There was no chance she would renounce it now, however much she hated the hunt. She bit her lip and closed her eyes, frowning. Eventually, 'You need to hold her up to the moon.'

She looked like Airmid or Valerius when they were dreaming; enough to trust that the god-luck was with them. *Luain mac Calma believes her to be the wild piece of the Warrior's Dance.*

Breaca said, 'You do it. I'll hold Stone.'

The moon was fading by the day and by the heartbeat. It was closer to the sun than it had been for Dubornos, smaller, and thinner and paler in the sky. Still, it was there; Nemain's watch on her people.

Graine turned, and walked forward a little, so that she could clearly be seen by both sides. The hare lay placid across her hands. She lifted it high, so that one could imagine it moon-blessed, and then turned and clearly spoke to it, and placed it on the ground, and stepped back.

Cygfa said, 'Airmid says the hare is pregnant. Did you know?'

Valerius did know, but not because Airmid had told him. Ever since waking, a substantial part of his awareness had resided with Graine, the hare, and the thin threads by which these two were bound to each other and the moon. The whisper of Nemain had never been loud within him, and there were times when he could barely hear it at all. Now it was a single steady note, like a flame seen in darkness, that blurred to fog the rest of the world.

Cygfa should not have been close enough to speak to him; the understanding of that came hazily. Without taking his eyes off Graine or the hare, he said, 'You can't ride with me. We agreed that.'

'No. You said it and I didn't argue. Longinus the same. But I didn't know about the hare then. Valerius, it's *pregnant.*'

'That doesn't mean that you can go where it goes or do what—'

It was impossible to speak longer. The hare felt him then, as he felt it. It rose up on its hind legs and snuffed the air. Nemain stretched through him, striving to reach to it. Too much of himself was in the way, caught up with the trappings of responsibility and care.

He faltered, and tried again and was joined by others, tenuously. He knew Airmid by the sense of Breaca within her, and Efnís for the vast chorus of Mona that touched the edge of what he sent; the profound resonance of Bellos he knew for himself alone.

None of them touched him consistently, and none of them could reach the child or the hare except through him. He had no idea why; he was closest, perhaps, or shared her blood, however distantly. Nothing in that told him how to reach Graine, only that he needed urgently to do so.

Cygfa was still there. Longinus had moved silently to his other side and both of them should have been safe on the left side of the battle lines, away from the cavalry wedge that Valerius had so carefully built on the right.

Civilis and his Batavians waited behind him as the iron-hard point of that wedge, with Madb and Huw and three hundred hand-picked warriors of Mona on their flanks. All of them had fought with him either in the charge against the IXth or on Mona and in the battles since; they trusted him as he trusted them, and understood how much rested on the success of their charge.

Longinus and Cygfa trusted him equally, if not more, but they were too precious to risk in a wedge. He wanted to tell both of them to leave, and could not find the shapes of the words.

Longinus said, 'You have no way to send us back. Enjoy that we are here and do what you must with the hare. It matters now more than anything.'

The hare did matter more than anything. She was running, and the hounds had been loosed. Valerius felt the beginning of her indecision and the need to reach her consumed him. Lacking the time or will to argue, he closed his eyes and gathered to him all those whom he had tried before to reach and did all that he could to stretch forward to the child and so the beast on the plain.

There had been a hunt, once, and the hare had come to her for sanctuary and she had failed it. When all Graine's other dreams had gone, the memory of that had haunted her sleep, not fully a dream and not fully a memory.

Every part of it came back in full as she stood alone on the plain: the crisp sharpness of Mona's dawn light, the lift of the hare's head at the strange scent on the wind, her own movement that sent Stone, in his prime, coursing forward, to hunt and hunt and turn and turn the hare until it doubled back to her, desperate for life, and she had been powerless to save it.

She was not powerless now, only that she did not know what to do, except to hold the whispering hare-song in her mind as this new hare lopped erratically forward and paused to nibble grass in the broad plain between the armies.

The war host recognized what she was trying to do before the legions; word passed like wind in corn. The enemy saw it after, and some understood. In ones and twos, they began to strike the pommels of their swords on their shields, taking it up along the rows, thinking that the thunder would drive the hare back in an omen of abject retreat.

The hare paused and rose up on her hind legs and surveyed the source of the noise.

Across the plain, the governor's two coursing hounds saw her and came tight on the leash. The Atrebatan hound-boy wound the leather round his wrists and leaned back against a double pull that threatened to haul him off his feet.

The hounds belled musically, a semitone apart. Their hides were the blue of fire-fresh iron, heads narrow as snakes, with sleek pelts and ears laid flat in their baying hysteria and long whiplash tails. They reared on their hind legs like bad-mannered colts, and the Atrebatan traitor held them on pain of death if they broke loose too early.

The hare turned and looked at Graine, who did not know what to do. Once, she had sent a hound against a hare. Never had she imagined she would send a hare against two hounds. She did so now, hurling her own hope and the yearning for victory along the fine thread of the hare-song.

If she had thrown a spear, it could not have gone so hard, or so fast, or so straight towards the enemy. Seeing it, the governor gave an order. The hound-boy loosed his leashes and the hounds came fast as missiles towards the running beast.

There was quiet for the hunt. Once the hounds had been loosed, not one man among the legions dared hammer blade to shield for fear of diverting them.

The Atrebatan had cast them out cleanly, so that they went together, blue matching blue, silent in their intent. They kept a man's breadth apart, running straight at the hare, ready to turn if she turned, to drive her from one to the other between them until she tired and was lost. Only Rome used two hounds thus in a hare hunt; the tribes did not think it fair to match more than one against Nemain's beast.

Calamity came before they reached their quarry. Graine felt the wave of panic as the hare saw the two hounds, and slowed, and did not know which way to turn. She tried to reach the beast and could not; the singing thread that bound them was swamped by the raw, red terror. Worse than that, fear reached back to her, a clawing, panting, annihilation coming so fast and so hard and so—

'Don't let it touch you.' Breaca was at her one side, Stone on the other. Between them, they held her up. 'Graine. Is there anyone else who can help?'

She felt it then, beyond the clamour of the hounds and the soul-destroying fear; Valerius was there, with others behind him, less clear. Like reaching across a broken bridge, she stretched for him and for Nemain, who stood behind. Sensing her, Valerius stretched in return.

They stretched, and could not touch.

The hare faltered. The hounds saw it and increased their speed.

On the ridge, Cygfa reached for Valerius' hand.

In the core of his mind where Corvus remained, Valerius, who had been Bán, heard a questioning voice ... *what you are to Mithras. And now, I think, to Nemain?*

The bull-slayer stood on the threshold of his awareness, kept safely distant by the need to be true to Nemain. A hound ran at his heels and a serpent drank the blood of the dying bull.

Valerius saw the moon rise with a bull on her horns, and a bull stand at a gate with the moon lighting its eyes and late, but not too late, he understood. With relief rushing over him, he opened the last gateways to his soul to let the music of both of his gods reach through him equally, and so pass at last unchecked to the child and thus the beast on the plain.

It was over so fast.

Thread-straight, spear-straight, god-straight, the hare ran between the two hounds. They were the best Roman gold could buy; each one turned in tightly, in a perfect arc – and met in the centre line where the hare had been, and slammed one into the other so that the one screamed and the other fell silent as a killed sheep with its neck snapped, to lie lifeless on the turf.

The hare ran straight and true through the Roman ranks, between Roman legs to the debris of their camp behind and not one of those who bent over with grasping hands managed to catch her.

She was gone to freedom, beyond the Roman lines.

A single horse stamped at flies in the silence. Its harness clashed softly. Breaca reached, fumbling, for her daughter's hand. Graine dared to look and found that she had been right to think her mother wept.

'You should go now,' said the Boudica. 'Take Stone to guard you, and you to guard him. Airmid will take care of you both. We'll meet again at the battle's end.'

She kissed her daughter lightly, in front of both armies. Graine turned to go. Hawk was there, bringing forward the black colt with the white legs that had been Cygfa's battle gift to the Boudica.

Graine walked with her crippled hound up the ridge and the war host parted to let her through. As with Airmid, as with Cygfa and Valerius, with Cunomar and Hawk and Ardacos, as long ago with Caradoc, her mother never said goodbye to her before a battle, for the ill-luck of it: never.

The first wave of warriors ran, screaming, over the place she had been.

XLIII

ALREADY THEY WERE RIDING. THE RIDGE PASSED IN A JOLT OF hammering hooves and a war howl that wrenched the last crows from the trees. The shocked ranks of legionaries were lifting their javelins; their training was solid, if their belief in victory was not.

From Valerius' left, and a little behind, Cygfa shouted, 'We should drive through where the hare went!'

'We will!'

Wind whipped at his eyes, his blade was level, his shield solid, the Crow-horse was as fit and eager as it had ever been, the hound of his dreaming ran with its head by his knee and he had found balance at last with both gods. Longinus was to his left and Cygfa to his right behind and if they died in the first moments of the wedge, all three together, even so, the world was perfect.

Corvus had not yet unleashed his cavalry against them. He had no doubt it would come, but even that was perfect; they had discovered peace and death offered a re-joining that life had made impossible.

The hare had run more to the centre. Valerius let the Crow-horse veer very slightly to his left, away from the place he had first intended to point his attack.

Civilis, Madb, Huw and the combined eight hundred of the cavalry wedge followed him. The legions raised their javelins to shoulder height, long, light needles of death, ready for the command to throw. Valerius could see the trembling of the ends and the slight tilt in the cross wind. He raised his shield and held it to cover his horse and himself. Behind, eight hundred warriors did the same.

They were in reach. He knew a moment's pain that he had come to find his soul's peace so late, and had so little time to savour it, but such time as he did have was a gods' gift and he treasured it. At the last, just before they came within javelin-strike, he raised his voice in a wild, open-hearted paean to both of his gods and all they had given him, and heard his honour guard echo it, joyfully.

He saw the trench too late, as he passed its end.

It was dug at an angle across the plain, coming obliquely in from the valley's end to narrow its mouth; if he had led his wedge as he had first intended, swinging wider from the right, he would have run his horse straight at the centre and would have died, and all eight hundred who followed him.

The hare had shown him a path to safety, but not those on his right, in the wider wing of the wedge, who hurled themselves across treacherous turf that gave way without warning to reveal a ditch as wide as six men, with rocks and stakes in its base that broke limbs and necks and pierced flesh and guts and chests and broke apart the perfect instrument of his wedge.

Horses and warriors fell, screaming, in a havoc of rending flesh and breaking bone and unsheathed swords that impaled the warriors who held them, or those who tumbled onto them afterwards.

Half of the eight hundred fell and the rest could not stop, pushed on by their own momentum. They were slowing, with Valerius at the lead, when he heard the light whickering wind that every legionary knew to his marrow, and feared; the javelins had started.

Hail fell, of hard, penetrating iron. It stuck in shields and made them useless; it pierced leather armour and iron and skin and flesh and bone. Men and women died by the dozen.

'Valerius!'

By a miracle, Civilis was still alive. Half of his band were still with him, riding to Valerius' right. The old warrior raised his blade to the sky and his voice to the heavens.

'Go left! We are your shields!'

Valerius felt wind graze his skin, but no iron. He would have argued, but there was no time, and the offer was there and it was right.

On an instinct that was as deep-drilled as the legions' raising of their weapons, he swung the Crow-horse hard to his left. For three suicidal strides, he veered broadside across the line of the legions, and waited for the moment's shock of impact, and did not feel it, because Civilis was there, and his men after him, a solid wall of flesh and bone and iron that took the first impact of the javelins and held it fast, in front of the men with whom they had so recently served.

Five hundred Batavians found death in blazing glory and their horses with them, that the rest of the wedge might have life and fight on.

'*Civilis!*'

Valerius shouted it as a battle cry and a thanks and an outpouring of grief for which there was no more time. The Crow-horse kept him safe, turning tight as a coursing hound, to race back over the place they had come, where the hare had gone before him; the only place on the battlefield they could be sure was solid earth.

The ranks upon ranks of Breaca's warriors who had followed the wedge came forward still. He spun sideways, to give them room, and made the Crow-horse slow and turned it back to face the legions and found that Cygfa was with him and Longinus, and Huw and Madb and Knife and two-thirds of the warriors of Mona, for which he should have been grateful, but was not; he had lost Civilis and his entire wing of Batavians, and the battle had not yet fully started.

He could have wept, but there was not time for it. Panting, high-coloured, Cygfa said, 'Did Corvus do this?'

'I don't know.' He had asked that of the gods in the first moments and not found the answer. 'It must have been done before our scouts found the valley, which means the engineers and pathfinders did it when they first came here, and laid out the camp later. If he didn't do it, he knew of it.'

'And said nothing.' She would have killed him for that.

'This is war. Why would he?' He said it aloud and his heart keened and did not believe it. *To me, he should have said something.*

Cygfa thought the same; it was etched into her face. She said, 'What do we do now?'

'Fight where we stand. Try not to die. Keep the right flank safe as we planned. This is not the end.'

Cunomar felt the shock of the breaking wedge from the far side of the field.

The she-bear were on foot and so slower and he had time, just, to understand the catastrophe of the trenches, and to realize that they might face the same in mirrored image – and to see it, and shout a warning inward to Ulla and Ardacos who ran on the far side with his older bear-warriors, and to jump the trench, howling, and to hurtle on towards legionaries who were distracted by the carnage on the far side and had not yet cast their javelins.

The bear was with them, clearly; under blazing mid-morning sun, they ran beneath the arc of the late throw so that the lethal, singing hail passed over their heads and landed harmlessly beyond, and then they were in, hurling themselves at shields and half-drawn blades and men were dying, and they were not of the bear.

Cunomar dodged a shield that smashed for his face, and tasted blood where the edge caught his cheek, and stabbed for an exposed eye with his knife and felt the puncture and grate of the socket. If the man screamed, the noise was lost in the chaos around him. The Boudica's son screamed his mother's name and heard Ulla echo him and then Ardacos' deep bear-howl. His nightmare was as nothing, banished by the force of their intent. Without fear, he immersed himself in battle. A small part of him, cold and quiet in his core, listened for the trumpet calls of the enemy.

It mattered that the Boudica be noticed, and known.

She was dressed to catch the eye: for the first time in years, she rode into battle wearing a cloak in the late-sky blue of the Eceni, not Mona's grey. The sun-serpent torc of her ancestors blazed at her neck. Her hair was a banner of spun copper made gold in the high, hot sun. She bore the broad-bladed spear, made for her in hope and love by Valerius and Airmid in the days before they left Eceni lands.

Copper whorls along the blade caught the morning, brightly, as if she held aloft a rod of flame. Its balance was perfect, and its song caught the strings of her heart, calling in echoes of Briga and the full panoply of ancestors. She was the warrior with the eyes and

heart of a dreamer. In final and complete fulfilment of the ancestor-dreamer's prophecy, she led the central mass of her war host
into battle.

In the matter of being noticed, she had succeeded; already the
javelins of the centre ranks converged on her. Beyond that, it
mattered also that the governor should have personal reason to
unleash his legions against her.

She knew her enemy now, and had an idea of what would hurt.
After the destruction of Valerius' wedge, she had no qualms about
doing it.

As she rode, she dipped from her horse and thrust her spear into
the body of the injured hound, putting an end to its pain. Someone
in front of her shouted at that; it might have been the Atrebatan
hound-boy but she believed not; she did not rise up in time to look.

Hawk, riding close behind, bent further and cut an ear and
threw it to her as they rode. She impaled it on the bloodied end of
her spear and held it high like a legionary standard. A great many
men shouted at that. The first javelins flew, loosed by rage, not
reason. They fell five horse-lengths short.

Two strides on, almost within javelin range, she brought the
spear to her shoulder and waited until its song rang in resonance
with the rhythm of her horse, and of her heart.

Suetonius Paullinus, governor of all Britannia, sat ahead of her
cloaked in his arrogance and dignity with his white plumes making
a perfect aiming point above his head.

The spear sang. The white-legged colt ran its heart out. Breaca
lifted herself high from the saddle and hurled the spear as high and
as fast and as true as she had ever thrown anything.

It passed into and through the unarmoured chest of the
Atrebatan hound-boy, who fell dead.

The rage of the legions shook the earth. Javelins made white the
air and treacherous the ground on which they landed.

Already the war host was slowing. The second volley fell a long-
step closer and more of the javelins were targeted on the Boudica;
it had not been only the governor who had favoured the hound-
boy and the grey-blue snakeheads he kept. As the third volley
began to hit shields and drive past their heads, Breaca threw up her
arm and shouted, 'Back! Get back! They'll finish us!'

Throughout the evening of Valerius' orders and all the morning's preparation, the men and women who had been chosen to follow the Boudica and so hold the central brunt of the Roman attack had been schooled in two things. The first of these was that the Boudica's spear throw was the preparation for retreat and that the rearmost ranks must be ready to turn about and run, or Breaca and those who rode closest to her would be driven onto the Roman sword points and certain death.

They were not a standing army; the warriors were not used to drill and discipline, so took a long time to slow down and longer to stop. The legionaries ahead took another long-step forward and raised their arms for their fourth volley. Breaca swung up her shield and felt the crows gather in the other worlds and Briga breathe close.

Hawk shouted, 'Come! We're clear!'

The pressure behind her was less, and then nothing at all. The colt had been schooled by Civilis and Valerius had showed her all it could do. She spun it rearing and sent it forward and the leap was of a hare before a hound, or a stag from a clifftop.

He brought her clear. They scaled the ridge and down the other side and there was room to stop and turn and a moment to pause, to drink from the hundred skins passed amongst them, to slide a hand down the sweat-soaked neck of the horse and to thank him, to be still and hear the songs of the weapons and of the horses and the deep, thrumming call of Briga's crows, not yet drowned out by the shouts of five thousand men pushed past the limits of their own exertion.

Then the flood gates opened, and the legions came.

Men and men and men in full battle armour, shining as silver in the sun, crested the ridge and flowed down it, like the foaming edge of a wave. In their midst was a red horse with a white helmet plume rising above.

The leading ranks saw the war host in front of them, and tried to stop and failed. As Valerius had predicted, the weight of armour, and of men behind, pushed them on in growing disarray. He had drawn what must happen next half a dozen times in the ash of the fire, so that its creation now seemed inevitable.

'Go!'

The shout came from her left and right together. Breaca threw up her arm and held the centre still while the remains of Valerius' wedge hurtled forward on the right flank and Cunomar's she-bears sprinted forward on the left. Within moments, the entire front line of the war host curled in like the sickle points of a horned moon, drawing the running legionaries on into a void of iron where they could be crushed together and slaughtered without room to swing their blades. All that mattered to make it happen was that the Boudica send the centre forward at the right time.

Five spear-lengths. Four. Three . . .

'*Go!*'

She launched the white-legged colt forward, and her warriors followed in a great solid wave.

The two sides came together in a splintering of bone and flesh and armour. Death rode attendance, and reaped a fast harvest. Breaca sat a colt of black lightning and it rose and killed as her blade rose and killed and she heard the songs of both and saw Hawk still alive at her one side and Gunovar at the other and there was room, then, for a fierce, abiding hope in all the chaos.

'We're winning. More of theirs are dead than ours by five to one.'

Bellos said it, and neither Airmid nor Theophilus argued, which meant it might be true.

Graine stood above all three, on a bale of part-cured sheepskins on the headboard of a wagon with Stone shivering his tension at her side. In theory, she had a crow's view over the battlefield. In reality, she looked beyond, to where the hare had gone, showing the way to freedom.

She dared to look now at the battle. On the field, the brazen heads of the legionaries flowed into the crescent of the war host as blood flows into water, thinning as they went. The wings of the moon folded inwards, Valerius' horse-warriors on one side and Cunomar's bears the other. The bronze mass of men was crushed between, and began to crumple at the edges. She said, 'Valerius' horned moon has worked.'

'So far,' said Airmid, distantly. 'There's danger far out to the right. I can feel it.'

That was the cloud on the day. Under full sun, Graine was cold. She said, 'Then Valerius will feel it too.'

'We can hope so.'

XLIV

T RUMPETS RANG FRANTICALLY, TUNEFUL AS BIRDSONG.
Three notes ripped and ripped again. Before they could
sound for the third time, Valerius spun the Crow-horse on
its hocks. Longinus was with him; he had drilled as often, as hard
and as long; the trumpets sang to his heart's blood. Cygfa was
slower.

'Come on!' Valerius screamed it over the crush and pulp and
then, quieter, when she was close enough, 'It's Corvus.'

It was Corvus, stationed out of sight on the right, who had waited
until they had committed to the field, and then come at their backs.
Because it was what Valerius would have done, he was ready for it.
His honour guard followed him, as fast as they might. He had less
than two hundred now, against a full cavalry wing of five hundred.

Led by Huw, who used his sling with startling efficiency,
Valerius' horse-warriors broadened out in a line as they fought
their way free of the melee. It took longer than it should have done;
the footing was cluttered with the pulp of dead men and no room
to fight easily free from them.

'Come *on*!'

A line of cavalry came at a gallop, curving back in a bow's arc
that let the front ranks meet first, and the rest hold back to circle
the outskirts if needed. The cavalry manuals offered two standard
ripostes to that and Valerius had neither the time nor the trained

men for either, only warriors who would give him their hearts and horses that he believed – that he had to believe – were faster and stronger and had far greater stamina than the enemy.

'Left!'

He swung his own blade and his own horse and they followed, as geese follow the lead bird, as fish the eye of the shoal, only slower, because some were still fighting.

He led them over the ridge and back down and the slope gave them speed and momentum as it had done to the legionaries. He did not run headlong into a waiting horde, but turned hard at the bottom so that all who followed him swung out wide and back in again and came in at the right hand side of Corvus' arched bow of riders, the sword side, where the shields were no use, against men whose focus had been in front, and whose vision had been blocked by the ridge.

The clash was short and sharp and light and only six of the enemy died. Valerius pulled the Crow-horse far out to the side and back in again, stinging now at the rear of Corvus' men as a hornet stings a horse.

To live, the cavalry had to turn and fight, leaving Breaca and the central mass behind them. Valerius darted in again, and killed, and danced back, saving his horse's strength for when it was needed.

Even so few, they made Corvus' wing spread out, and forced men to fight one on one when they were better in solid ranks. It was not perfect, but it was better than he had hoped for and, after the disaster of the ditch, far more than he deserved.

Cygfa fought beside him, a shining beacon in the noon sun. She struck and swung and pulled her colt back, and shouted, 'We can do it! Valerius, your name will be sung at every winter fire for generations. What a father this child will have!'

They were killing and not dying. In the centre, Breaca held her warriors together and they, too, killed more than they lost. On the understanding of that, a battle hinges. Valerius saw desperation grow in the expressions of those he faced and, for the first time, began to believe the war host might win.

He was thinking that when the trumpets blew again, differently. In the valley, where the governor held his reserves, two thousand rested men moved into formation and marched forward, ready to fight.

The last two cohorts of the XIVth legion came over the ridge in a slower wave than those who had come before.

They descended the slope steadily, in fast, tight order, with their shields together and their blades poking between. On reaching level ground again, the men at the sides turned their shields outwards, making a grid of wood and iron that only a long, fast cavalry charge might fracture.

There was no way to withdraw before them; discipline among the warriors had long since been lost, and any chance of retreat in order. As far as Breaca could see was a boiling mess of battle and all behind her.

If they come at you in tight ranks and you can't go back, break out to the side. Don't give them a front to come in at.

Valerius had said that twice in the evening and again in the morning. Knowing what might come, he had used his warriors to give her room, luring the cavalry out to the side. She thanked him for that, alive or dead, and saw the way she could go.

'Out!' She shouted it over the tumult. 'Out to the sides! Make them spread out to reach us!'

Her voice was lost in the clash of living and dying. Gunovar heard her and the two dozen of her closest honour guard. They passed the message on. It moved sluggishly through the fighting mass, slowing to a standstill in pockets where to live mattered more than to pass a message of things that happened too far away to be seen.

Five spear-lengths to the legionaries. Few of these bore javelins; most carried the short, stabbing gladii, knifing out between the shields. Breaca looked around her and saw no enemy close. Taking a risk, she drew the colt high into a rear and raised her sword arm high.

'The sides! Go out to the sides.'

They heard her then, the hundreds who were close, or they saw the flash of sunned metal and knew her and the colt who had become a second Hail, and fought for her with the heart of a hundred warriors. The war host opened, slowly, like a stick untidily cleft, ready to absorb the oncoming men.

The enemy heard her too, or knew her by her hair and the torc and the cloak; it had mattered to be seen and known.

Somewhere nearby, she heard her name shouted, in Latin. A trumpet sounded a rippling clarion that held her name somewhere within it, and was the cry of the huntsman to his hounds, on finding a greater and better quarry. The whole mass of the legion swayed her way.

'*Move!*' That was Hawk, at her side. His colt was married to hers, shoulder to shoulder, hip to hip. 'Get out! If they catch us here, against the mass of the battle, they'll crush us as a hammer crushes tin.'

Gunovar came to her other side. The honour guard closed on her, a shield of living flesh. Together they cut across the grain of battle, fighting towards clear land at the edge.

They were within sight of clear land when the javelin hit. Iron punched her left arm, high up, above the ridge of her shield. She grabbed at the colt's mane and held her breath against the flooding blackness and a long, cold wait before the pain.

Jubilation followed her from the legions' ranks behind. In the blurring confusion was a memory of Valerius by the fireside, dry in his humour, in the time before he gave her the spear. *If you're hit, nothing will stop them. Even so, I think it would be better if you were not.*

She felt the touch of his mind, and of Airmid's, and there was cool and a sense of running water and it mattered only to stay mounted and to fight a way out across turf churned to blood and thick with the dead and debris of both sides: corpses and armour and weapons that made every footfall treacherous.

Somewhere a crow called, and the deep bass tones hummed through her chest. She threw her shield away and felt better, and pushed the white-legged colt towards clear land.

Graine had sat with the warriors as they planned a strategy that made her mother a visible target and had hated it and still had not found a good reason to argue. Death came in war; if Briga sought a life, no amount of care would save it; if Briga chose to spare a life, no amount of risk would end it.

It was Briga, then, who had put a solid line of horse warriors in the way when the Roman governor in the white plumed helmet recognized her mother and directed the javelins of his men against her.

His order had seen the fury of the battle redoubled, when it was already as hard and as hot and as murderous as anything Graine had ever seen. Blades flashed brilliant in the sun and the screaming wounded drowned the war howls of tiring warriors. For too-long moments, it was impossible to know who lived and who died.

Graine looked away, to the farther side of the field where Ardacos held a small knot of the bear-warriors and guided them as a warrior guides a thrusting-spear. Beyond him, Cunomar was recognizable even across the field of battle by his white limed hair that stood proud from his head and the king-band he wore on his arm. He and his bear-warriors were engaged with the flank of the enemy and had withstood one cavalry charge, melting away to let them through and running in after to cut the horses' hamstrings from behind. They had learned that from the Batavians in the battle for the invasion, and put it to good use now against them.

The front had become skewed and they were fighting with their backs to the ridge. Graine watched her brother sprint up to the top of it, to gain momentum in the run down so that he could better leap for the back of a passing horse and haul the rider to the ground. He had endless energy. His third run was as fast as the two before it – only that he stopped on the ridge and looked across to where the Boudica was enmired in the spreading mass of the XIVth legion.

Or, perhaps, had broken free.

Airmid said, 'Hawk's alive,' and so Graine had turned back to look and saw the moment when the white-legged colt broke free of the battle's edge out into the clear ground beyond.

Theophilus, physician of Athens and Cos, said, 'That wound won't kill her,' and it mattered a great deal to believe him.

Those who fought with the Boudica were not of the same opinion. Gunovar was there and Hawk and they were clearly trying to persuade her to put aside the late-sky cloak and put on a helmet and make herself less of a target.

There was a moment when it seemed she might have agreed, but it was already too late for that; a hammerhead of legionaries had broken free of the melee and was coming for them in disciplined formation and Valerius and his honour guard were fighting Corvus' cavalry just behind, so that even if they had managed to render her ordinary, there was nowhere left for them to run.

They made a stand, therefore, because there was nothing left to do.

Graine watched Hawk lean down to wrench a shield from a dead warrior and pass it up to Breaca with something that looked like a salute and then Gunovar found a spear and they set their horses in a line, with the honour guard finding order at the sides, just in time to meet the first of the oncoming men.

It was not possible, then, to look away.

Finally, Corvus was close enough to be seen.

His presence burned through the necessary concentration of battle, until the flashing blades and sweating, crashing masses of horseflesh became thinly grey. Valerius fought and lived by instinct, not thought, and that instinct drew him forwards, to the man on the bay mare who battled in a halo of god-given protection close to the edge of the main fighting.

A cavalryman came at Valerius and died and it occurred to him that he, too, lived in that same halo, where men died because he did not have to waste time in thinking, only needed to let his body act.

He was within almost-reach of the black colt when something sighed in the midst of battle. By chance, the fighting mass ahead of him swayed open, and by chance he looked through.

'*Breaca's down!*' Someone screamed it. Later, he found it was himself.

Corvus turned before anyone else. His standard-bearer turned a little after, and a trumpeter after that, who sounded a single note, as of the hunt that has found fresh quarry. The bay mare leaped high as a deer and came down nearer to Breaca.

The Eceni had the better horses; Valerius was sure of that. He set the Crow-horse racing, and did not care who came with him or who might try to get in the way.

The new shield was too heavy, which was why Breaca dropped it too low, which was, in turn, what let in the blade that smashed across her back so that only the mail shirt she wore kept her living.

Her white-legged colt was twisting away even as the blade was coming in, but the dead on the ground made the turn unsmooth so that the arc of it threw her off balance and the force of the blow sent her down.

She rolled, and did not hit any loose blades, which was a miracle.

She rose and Hawk had thrown himself from his own horse and was beside her, helping her up, and then Gunovar too had dismounted and pushed in tight on the other side and they were fighting on foot with the horses behind them and the honour guard desperately trying to keep the legionaries at bay.

They failed, and drew back to the flanks so that the Boudica's three could fight unhampered, and yet not fear attack from the sides.

In an odd way, it felt better than riding above the battle, working strategy against the legions. Breaca tasted her own sweat and the blood of dead men and savoured them, and raised the too-heavy shield again to block a strike that came for her head and knew that she could count on the fingers of her one good hand the number of times left she could do that.

She wanted to tell Hawk and Gunovar to leave her and knew she had not the breath and that if she had, it would be wasted. She blocked another blow, badly. The edge of the blade flashed by her face. Hawk struck at the man who had delivered it and did not hit him. They were all tiring now.

Breaca said, 'We should . . . stand back to . . . back.' She had learned that on Mona a long time ago as the way for warriors to die who knew there was no future.

Hawk nodded, and licked his lips and waited until the smash of the next shield pushed him round. Gunovar stepped back and fitted in the space between. Breaca slipped on spilled guts and came up again and Hawk was still there, pressing his shoulders against hers, solid and sure and dependable. Of all her children, she had never thought to die in the presence of the newest. It left hope, at least, that the others might live.

The thinning ranks of the honour guard gave way. Two legionaries came at her at once.

Breaca struck back with her own blade and was lucky; it glanced off one helmet into the cheek of the man beside, who reeled back, holding his face and screaming.

Blood splashed in her eye, blinding her. She blinked hard and when she could see next, both of the men in front of her were dead and Valerius was where they had been, protecting her bodily with the Crow-horse, slashing frantically on both sides. A dozen warriors of Mona followed him, spreading death in their wake.

Very quickly, where had been mayhem was a circle of quiet.

Breaca felt Hawk sag against her and tried to remain standing; to fall now would humiliate them both.

Her brother threw out orders as a green-stick fire throws sparks; Huw and three other slingers took position in front of her, and warriors behind; Longinus and Cygfa came up on either side to support the three standing warriors. Valerius turned in and she could not read his face. 'Breaca, can you mount?'

The white-legged colt was too far away to reach. It was hard to think clearly. She said, 'Your horse won't take us both.'

He stared at her blankly, then, 'I know. I didn't mean that. I just need to know if—'

'*Bán!*'

She screamed the wrong name. The gap when he did not know himself nearly killed him. Someone else knew it first and faster. A bay mare that she had reared from a foal slewed round in a perfect turn. A blade came for her brother's head, swung by a man who had once been a friend.

She screamed that name, too, and did not expect him to answer; Corvus brought death and, this time, would not be deflected.

Corvus brought death; Valerius answered him.

There was no respite in the fighting about them, no quarter given from either side to let them settle it alone, only one more man to fight in the disintegrating chaos of the battle and others coming in at either side. From the edge of his eye, Valerius saw Huw fit a slingstone and shouted 'Don't!' and did not know why he had done so.

Iron flashed in the too-hot sun. Corvus' blade came murderously for his head. The Crow-horse spun out of the way and reared and slashed, because Valerius had thought it, or the beast had thought it and Valerius had followed its lead; in battle, there was no distinction between these two, and never had been.

Corvus' mount was almost as good. A bay mare marked with the brand of the Eceni on its shoulder, it skittered sideways, avoiding the dead on the ground, spinning to send its rider forward with his shield high, protecting them both, and his blade coming up in an underhand stab that reached for Valerius' heart.

His face was clear above it, framed by a helmet that bore dents on either side with the black hair fringed below and the wide black eyes and the runnels of sweat and the lucid, focused concentration that had lasted through the day and would last on as long as was needed.

They could have spoken, perhaps, between the sobbing breaths of battle, but there was nothing left to say.

If I die first, I will wait for you.

Neither had said, *If you kill me, I will still wait*, but it had been there, and was again, thick in the air between them.

Valerius countered the stab and turned his open shoulder in to give a target and danced the Crow-horse back when the invitation was not taken and the edge of a shield came instead for his face, and then his arm. He swung his own sword at an exposed flash of brown skin and saw blood spring fresh to the surface.

The surprise of that slowed his shield so that he, in turn, was wounded on the thigh, and a long scrape up the neck of the Crow-horse who screamed its own anger and high-stepped over a wounded Siluran and rose and lashed out and came down again too soon, stumbling: for all its heart and hate, the Crow-horse, too, was tiring.

Valerius had never thought to sit on this horse and find it tired. Shock clove his heart as Corvus had not done. The doors to his mind fell open then, and the hallways were empty of everything; of gods and love and past and present; of a child unborn and a sister newly healed; of strategy and tactic and basic battlefield survival; everything but the impossibility of losing this horse and finding a life worth living beyond.

Despair dragged at him, heavy as death. Through a rising red mist, it came to him that he was tired and beyond tired and, because he had seen it in others, he knew that this killed more men than stupidity or arrogance or bad luck together.

He and his horse slewed round, avoiding another strike by too small a margin.

If I die first . . .

We could die together, which would be fitting, and good. A glimmer of that, and how it might be made to happen, probed through the fog.

Searching for open ground, he dragged the Crow-horse back. Corvus followed, as if joined by birth-cords neither could break.

The rest of the battle had faded to nothing; after Huw, no-one among the war host had attempted to intervene, except to keep killing the legionaries and the cavalry and make space for Valerius to do what he must. To his left, Breaca had not yet found a horse. He wanted to shout to Cygfa and had not the time nor the breath.

Valerius feinted and feinted and each time let his shield drop, because he was tired, and Corvus, who knew him best, saw it, and came in harder. Valerius struck and was countered and the back stroke cut him again, on the neck this time, where the armour ended. He jerked his head back and swore and let the Crow-horse dance sideways as well as it could and waited for the next cut, which should come high, above his shoulder, and did, so that he—

'Valerius! Move!' That was Longinus; in time, with the right name and still too late.

The Crow-horse was already turning. He owed his life to that. The blade sang with his soul's name and shaved hide and metal from his back. He had nothing ready to counter the stroke, and the horse, which might have done so, was spent. He used his knees to turn it and it answered more slowly and the backswing this time was aimed not for him, but for the horse; a broad, arcing sweep that took its neck as the god took the bull at slaughter, opening vessels and windpipe down to the bone so that it fell as if pole-axed and only the fact that they had been turning threw him clear.

'NO!'

He screamed for the horse, which could make no sound. The Crow-horse lay thrashing in a mindless gallop. Its life blood flooded the earth, whipped to foam by its ending breath.

Life was still in its eyes. Valerius threw himself bodily for its head and lay along it, weeping.

They gave him space for that, the men and women who lived and died around him, because to grieve for a horse mattered more than the battle. Or perhaps they left him for Corvus who had brought his own horse to a standstill and watched, white-faced, above.

There were no words. Corvus said them anyway. 'I'm sorry. It will wait for you, as I would have done. It's better like this. Your war host is losing. The reserves of the Fourteenth have broken them. When the Twentieth are sent, it will be over.'

477

They had trained together so often in how a mounted man might make a sure kill of the enemy on the ground. Valerius made himself stand, because he would not die lying down. The gods made his world slower, that he might seem to live longer. In a timeless infinity, he saw the beginnings of the sweep that would finish him, and mapped its progress, back and round and down towards his head—

—which was not there, because once, in a long winter on the banks of the Rhine, they had put some effort into finding a counter to this move, and just once, in a thousand times of trying, it had worked.

The gods had slowed the world that Valerius might seem to live longer, and he moved fast within it. In a move like the warrior's mount but harder, he threw himself at Corvus' horse, ducking the arc of the incoming blade and fighting for purchase on a beast that bucked at the new weight, and reaching for a handhold on an armoured man who half knew he was coming, but still could not quite shake him off.

For two strides, he struggled, then instinct and the need to win won over fear and exhaustion and he was riding behind Corvus as he had once done on the banks of the Rhine, except that now he had a blade in his hand, and a reason to use it.

Not a good enough reason. Assailed by a smell he had known all of his adult life, that was least when a man came from the baths and most when he was in battle, or had spent the night in another's company, Valerius could not make the final strike.

They had tried one more thing, in that long, tedious winter, with the snow hock-deep on the ground and ice over the river thick enough to ride a horse across, and to practise cavalry manoeuvres. Valerius reached up with one arm under Corvus' armpit and thrust with his knee and twisted with all that was left of his strength and his grief.

'I'm sorry,' he said, as the other man fell. 'I will still wait for you, however long it is, and know that you wait for me.'

The mare was Eceni; she knew the words that he spoke to her and answered the nudge of his knee. She turned when he asked, so that he was in time to see a man in a foul wolfskin cape throw himself from his horse and crouch beside the body that lay crooked on the ground.

Corvus might have been breathing. There was room, still, to believe that.

The mare turned away again, and came up when Valerius asked her to, and reared high over the battle so that he saw the whole lie of it, and the emerging pattern, and then found Breaca, who was with Hawk in the heart of a boiling knot of fighting, and losing, as her war host was losing.

He had been wrong. He did, after all, have a reason to live. Valerius set the new horse forward and raised his blade, asking the gods for help to reach his sister.

XLV

GUNOVAR SOLD HER LIFE HARD, TAKING WITH HER THE MAN who had killed her, and the one who stood at his side. She fell forwards, and her body, for a while, blocked the incoming men.

Breaca had no time to grieve, only spoke the three words that took the dead dreamer safe to Briga, and those with little enough breath to spare. Beyond the ones who had killed Gunovar more came; the string of legionaries had become a flood and the horse-warriors of Mona were barely holding them.

They were two, she and Hawk, standing in a crescent of horses and cavalry with armoured men coming in from the front.

Breaca had found a lighter shield and someone had passed her water and she had found that she could breathe again without her throat's feeling as if it were on fire and she could at least hold her shield arm steady, if not lift it well, and even if death were certain, there was a joy in meeting it openly, in full awareness, in the company of those she loved.

She fought as well as she had ever done; life and care were narrowed to the cut of a blade and the block of a strike and the spray of sweat and blood and the greater picture mattered not at all, nor did she want it to.

There came a moment's respite, when one man fell dead and

others had not yet stepped over the growing clutter of bodies. Hawk was still with her, a sentient shadow.

Breaca said, 'Ready?' and he had the strength to grin. She picked a man and stepped forward into a sudden gap and struck at him, and he fell at the first touch, which was entirely surprising, and then Valerius was there, brilliant and savage and furious. He was no longer riding the Crow-horse, but mounted instead on a bay mare that had been her gift once to Graine and Graine's to Corvus and she had not seen him take it. She spoke Briga's invocation for Corvus, because he, too, must be dead, even if she could not see him.

Valerius was as welded to the mare as he had been to the Crow. Together, mare and man reaped their own harvest among the legion. Men fell back, replaced by others, who saw glory in the killing of those in front of them and cared nothing if their lives were the cost.

Even so, his passing created a space where it was possible to think and to realize that it mattered to be mounted, and so to look about for her own white-legged colt, and find that she could no longer see it, nor were any of the growing number of loose horses within reach.

'Up.' Valerius was there, just in front of her, stinking of horse sweat and breathing hard. He pushed the mare across broadside towards her and reached down to take her arm. 'Up behind me. Now. Cygfa will take Hawk.'

He was her brother. He was an officer in the Roman cavalry whose orders were not given lightly and had only rarely been ignored. For both these reasons, she did as he asked and grasped his arm at the elbow and made a passable leap to the rump of his horse.

Behind, in the ranks of the legions' reserves, six legionary trumpets pealed a short, repeating sequence.

'Not now, damn you!'

Valerius spun his new horse on its hocks. Breaca grabbed for his waist with her one good arm and held on. He set the mare to climb the ridge, and they rose for a moment above the field on the parting it created. Spread below on the eastern side was the carnage where the untrained mass of the war host battled the precision of the XIVth legion and were manifestly losing. Unable or unwilling to move to the margins, they were crushed tighter in on themselves, unable to find the space to swing their blades or use their horses or draw back an arm to wield a sling.

West of the ridge was peace and order. Ranks of unsullied blades waited there, held by men who had stood quiet and watched their brethren die, saving themselves until the time when their coming could turn the battle.

That time was now. The trumpets promised and demanded, equally. As Breaca watched, rank upon rank of legionaries detached smoothly from the lines and locked their shields and drew their blades and began the short march to the ridge. They were silver-white in the afternoon sun, a long rippling line of iron and bronze and unwavering intent. The trumpet calls clove them in the centre, separating them out into two moving wings, to make a horned moon of their own, with all the devastation of their weight behind it.

Valerius had already set the bay mare down the ridge. To stay on was a challenge; success and survival one more gift from the gods.

Breaca shouted over his shoulder, 'We have to get the warriors out of the way. They need room to regroup.'

Her brother shouted something back, but it was lost in the sudden clash of iron as Cygfa and Hawk came up alongside and then Longinus and Madb and Huw and the others of Mona who bunched around her and broke through the thinning ranks of Corvus' cavalry and were riding as she had asked, out to the farthest reach of the wagon line, where Graine waited, with Airmid and Bellos and the Greek physician who must, by now, be thinking he had picked the wrong side to support.

A white-legged black colt with the brand of the Batavians on its shoulder came to a halt in the open land near the wagons. Finding no battle around, it dropped its head to graze.

Graine waited for someone to notice and when they did not, she stepped down from the wagon and walked to it, churring quietly as she had heard Valerius do. Stone was with her and all the Batavian horses had grown with hounds from when they were foals. The old hound flopped onto the floor and lay on his side, savouring the sun. The black colt eyed girl and hound equally and chose not to run.

Her palm was heavy with salt sweat. Graine let the beast lick, and then offered the crook of her elbow which was as wet. It tasted her, and she took hold of its bridle and then grew bold, and tried to lead it. It paused a moment, to show that a choice had been made, and then followed to the place behind the wagons where the water was kept. She splashed some into the bowl of an upturned shield and it drank and grazed again and she held on to the looped ends of the reins, and prayed to the ancestor and the elder grandmother that Breaca should look across and see that her daughter had found her horse.

Quite soon after, Airmid walked past and caught a bright red colt bearing the brand of the Eceni and Hawk's mark of the fire lizard and so it was certain that the gods had sent these two to be with them, and not simply that they had smelled the water, or knew the people on the wagon and had come by half-chance to known faces and voices they trusted.

Cunomar saw the first movement of the legions as he ran up the ridge.

He stopped and raised a hand and hollered a name. Ardacos joined him in moments; his father-in-spirit had never been far away.

Cunomar said, 'We could attack them before they reach the ridge.'

'And throw our lives for nothing.' Ardacos was looking north along the ridge's line, to where the horse-warriors of Mona fought, to where Breaca had been unhorsed and was now, astonishingly, riding doubled with Valerius. As they watched, the pair crested the ridge and down again.

There was no need to speak further; amongst the bear, some things were certain and the first of those was that the need to protect the lives of the Boudica and those who attended her was set before the immediate needs of battle.

Cunomar nodded at a question that had not been asked. Ardacos put his two fingers to his lips and whistled a soaring note that fell away at the end. The pierce of it was sharp as any trumpet. A winter's training was paid in that one moment. Forty of the she-bear broke away from their killing and came to join him on the ridge. The remaining dozens fought on as if there were no change.

Cunomar led them. Ulla was a lithe shadow at his side. Ardacos and his older warriors held the rear, against possible attack.

Light and unarmoured, in full view of the advancing legionaries, they ran down onto the Roman side of the ridge, and along the free ground, where the fallen dead were fewer, to the far edge of the combat. There, they rose up again, behind the Boudica and those who attacked her.

At the crest of the ridge, Cunomar wiped his palm on his tunic and regripped his knife and raised his hoarse voice in the bear-howl, that the men of Rome might know on whose blade they died before Briga came to take them.

A shining tide of legionaries crested the ridge and flowed down towards the battle. Trumpets moved them, spreading them out as they came, so that half went to one side and half to the other of the massed ranks already fighting.

The two parts joined together neatly, as the hilt fits the pommel of the sword, leaving no gaps. The killing began at once, and was neatly efficient; the legions' reserves were fit and rested and had drunk water before they marched and had trained for half their lives in the slaughter of untrained men and women.

Graine stood holding the white-legged colt, and watched half-trained youths fall like corn at harvest, and felt sick. Stone began to whine, so that she had to take hold of him with her other hand, to keep him from running into the fray.

'They're coming.' Airmid said it; the first time she had spoken since Breaca fell from her horse. 'He's bringing her to the horses.'

Graine dragged her gaze from the slaughter and looked instead towards the boiling mass of horse-warriors and cavalry from which burst, galloping, two doubly laden horses and a surrounding guard of Mona.

Urgently and with emphasis, Bellos said, 'Airmid, she's alive,' as if there had been doubt, and might be so still.

Then Theophilus said, 'Cunomar's coming over the ridge, and Ardacos,' and it was true.

The Boudica's son and the Boudica's brother arrived together, so that the two parties almost clashed, and swayed back, eyeing each other as if they might be enemy.

Valerius said, 'It's over. We need to get out and back. We have to sound the retreat.' It came almost as a question, as if he was still unsure of his right to give commands.

Cunomar said, 'The she-bear follow where you lead,' and then Breaca, 'The battle plan was yours, and the retreat. Do what you must.'

Valerius nodded his thanks. Orders flowed from him without cease. 'Hawk, Breaca, mount your horses. Cunomar, Ardacos, call in as many of the she-bear as you can reach. Madb, Cygfa, gather the horse-warriors. We'll need to make a rear guard to cover those leaving the field. Huw – sound the horn for the retreat.'

Graine passed close to Huw as she brought her mother's colt to be mounted; for that reason alone, she saw the anguish on his scarred face and understood what was happening.

Huw had borne the horn of Mona for less than a day. For a thousand years, it had sounded attack. This once, at Valerius' insistence, they had saved it for the one sound every fighting man and woman would recognize and was oath-sworn to obey: the signal to abandon the fight and run, in whatever order they could; to separate and keep on separating, making space and clear ground between them, until the ranks of legionaries had thinned so that the power of their togetherness was lost.

Huw brought the horn up and hesitated. Never had it been used thus.

'Do it!' Valerius snarled at him, savage as any hound. 'We've lost. If Paullinus calls Henghes' Batavian cavalry in at the wings, we'll never live to fight again.'

Huw wet his lips raggedly and blew.

The sound of the horn was the song of the hare, made loud as a bull's bellow. Thrice and thrice again, it rang silver-strong over the field. Legionaries and warriors hesitated in their bloodshed; the one side because it was a sound they did not know, the other because they knew it intimately, and had not expected to hear it ever, and so were not prepared.

They were not trained, either, in the art of disengagement. Graine watched men and women die who did not know how to walk backwards in battle and live. Those of Cunomar's she-bears who had been left made a living wall for those they could reach at the far side of the field. Elsewhere, others less skilled made a wall of corpses that had much the same effect.

Unsmoothly, with overwhelming sorrow and astonishing numbers of dead, the warriors of the Boudica's war host obeyed the command of the horn and abandoned their fight.

The white-legged colt danced on the spot, ready again for battle. Just for a moment, Graine saw Valerius' soul stand awake in his eyes, purely Eceni, alive with the love of a horse. Then a veil dropped and he was half-Roman again, throwing out brisk orders as if all those around were his cavalrymen and he the officer.

'Mount. Everybody mount. Now.'

They were settling in the saddles when the men of Corvus' cavalry wing broke through the lines of Mona to reach them; big men, fit and angry and led by a black-haired savage with a stinking wolfskin across his shoulders who screamed his hatred as shrilly as any she-bear. That one came for Valerius and struck at him and would have killed him if Longinus had not been there to block his blade. Graine saw nothing after that but fighting and no sense to be made of any of it.

'Get Graine out!' A man's voice: Valerius.

Cunomar stuck his knife in a passing horse and saw it fall and then turned at Valerius' command and went back for his sister. Hawk was already there; his brother, oath-sworn to family. He stood by a flashy grey filly with a brand on its shoulder that said it had won three races. His hands were looped in a hammock for her to mount.

'Graine. Up.' He was like Valerius, giving urgent orders, not understanding her fear of fast horses.

Cunomar said, 'Graine, you must take this one. The pony isn't fast enough. Please. We'll help you.'

She looked at him, her face a picture of horror, then she opened her mouth and screamed, not at him, but at his brother.

'Hawk!'

The blade missed both of them, but only because of Graine. Hawk rolled and came up without his shield but wielding the blade of the she-bear, Eburovic's blade, two-handed, as it was made to be used.

The savage with the rancid wolfskin across his shoulders turned his black colt on its hocks and came back again, howling as loud as the she-bear. Hawk shouted, 'See to Graine!' and stepped in to meet him.

For Cunomar to set Graine on the horse was the matter of moments. The grey race-filly was battle-trained and stood solid as stone with mayhem around her.

'Go.' Graine whispered it, from the depths of terror. 'He needs you.'

Wolfskin was good. At another time, Cunomar might have admired him. He used his horse as a weapon in the ways of the best Eceni. The she-bear were trained to overcome that, but not Hawk, who had only been brought to the edges of what the bear could give.

Even so, Hawk, too, was astonishing in his skill. He stood full on to the oncoming horse wielding the great, broad war blade as if born to it. His hair was woven in a warrior's knot and crow feathers fluttered damp with his sweat at his left temple. He was Eceni to the roots of his hair and his soul and he fought with a grace that would have left singers weeping as they told of it round the winter fires, were there any left to see it.

There were none, only Cunomar, watching as his brother-in-soul faced down the black colt and made it swerve, slicing for its head and bringing the blade round and up to graze the back of the rider even as he spun and came back for a second pass. Each move was fluid in its economy and Cunomar could believe that he was the only one who saw that Hawk was fighting on the last of his reserves and that each controlled swing of the blade took him closer to an ending beyond which death waited draped in a stinking wolfskin, with no care for the beauty it destroyed.

The end came faster than he had thought. The black colt could turn on one hock and not break stride. Its rider spun it in a curve round Hawk and this time had the measure of the two-handed, two-looped swing. He ducked the first arc and brought his own blade back-handed across the line of its flight, flicking upwards so that his blade caught in a notch that an ancestor of Cunomar's had created in single-handed combat against a white-haired warrior of the Coritani in a dispute over a boundary line.

Cunomar had never heard who won that fight, so many generations ago. Now, the fault in the blade cost Hawk his life, or seemed to. The great blade leaped from his hand like a salmon at spawning, and sailed high, spiralling, to come to rest three strides from where he stood.

Three strides, and it might as well have been three days' ride. Hawk stood unarmed before the wolf-caped rider and smiled at him, as a true warrior smiles facing death. He drew his knife, which was a brave thing, and pointless; even the she-bear would have had trouble against such as this.

He threw a smile at Cunomar, said, 'Take care of Graine for me!' and stepped in to face his end.

Three strides. The blade was within Cunomar's reach. He had almost taken it up, for the ease of it, and the chance to give it back to Hawk, that he might at least die with his brother beside him and the ancester-blade in his hand.

The shade of Eburovic stopped him, solid as the earth, as the sky, as the sweating, blowing colt and the black-bearded man who rode it. His grandfather stood before him, so close that Cunomar could see every wrinkle and line in his skin, could see the brown eyes and their care for him, could feel the eternal cold that wrapped him, could hear again the words that had been cut into Cunomar's soul since before he returned to his homeland. *If my grandchild ever wields my blade, know that the death of the Eceni will follow,* and then, newly, *Is one man's life, even your brother's, worth so much loss? The she-bear is your god and my dream. In her name, I ask you not to do this.*

There was nothing he could do. His oath was to the bear, his soul given into her care in the caves of the Caledonii. The binding was complete and for life and there was nothing and no-one who could override it.

He was caught in the living reality of his nightmare, but that it was Hawk who was under attack and by a wolf-man, not a bear. He could still fight, though. He had his knife and his courage and his brother had need of him. Cunomar turned, ready to help, and found that he was already too late, and that the nightmare was made complete.

'Hawk!'

No-one heard her shout this time; the noise of battle was too great. Graine watched her brother's blade fly high from his hand and gouge a line in the earth less than a spear's length from the back of her horse. Dubornos had been sworn to her, and she had let him die, because he wanted it. Hawk was sworn to her before all the others and so she to him and he manifestly did not want to die; he had said so to the deer-elders on the night of the horned moon.

The grey race-filly stood still as stone. Graine slid to the ground and was running even as Cunomar was running. He might have reached the blade before her, but he faltered and she did not. The thread that drew her to the weapon was the soul-thread that had bound her to the hare, only brighter, because now they were in battle. She lifted it and heard the song at last.

The hilt swamped her hands. The blade had its own balance in the way the practice blades on Mona had never done. The feeding bear on the pommel offered its own weight and its own momentum. It dipped down, so that the long sweep of blued iron that was the blade rose without effort; and all she had to do was let her hands be the balance point between the two.

The ease of it was uncanny, so that she stared at the blade and the old marks made by the ancestors, and the new ones hacked by Hawk in his endeavours and—

'*Graine!*' Someone screamed her name, from beyond the end of the blade. She looked up, remembering the battle. Wolfskin came at her, grinning, and another man at his side.

She heard the wolf-caped one shout, 'Flavius! This one's mine! Her life for Corvus!' and the earth rolled with the hammer of their horses and their blades sang for her life and somewhere the elder grandmother said, *Now is the time of choosing. Which matters most, your line or your land?* which made no sense even as she saw Cunomar leap for the man, Flavius, with his blade bared and Hawk at his side and together they might reach him, but that still left Wolfskin, who had proved himself in battle, and now came directly for her, grinning, with his blade swept back.

She tasted death and tried not to be afraid and failed.

Then her mother was there, throwing the white-legged colt forward in all her terrible fury, and Stone was at her side, where he had wanted to be all through the battle.

The grandmother smiled and said, *Good*, and the world was made right.

She felt her father close.

He had been there from the moment she had slithered from the

489

back of Valerius' horse; a silent presence, watching. He was not alone. The grandmother was there, and the ancestor-dreamer and the Sun Hound and his lineage; they stood all around, these ancestors of her line, in the place where their children's children lived or died. She listened for the deep bell-note of Briga's crow and did not hear it any louder than it tolled for all the other dead.

Hawk fought brilliantly. Even as she saw him lose the blade, she knew that she had seen something exceptional and that others had seen it, enough to be sure the memory of it lived on after his death. She began the keening to Briga as the blade fell from his hands, and then stopped, because Cunomar had stepped close and she heard her own father, as clearly as she had first heard him, saying, *If my grandchild ever wields my blade, know that the death of the Eceni will follow. I trust you to see it does not happen.*

Cunomar heard him too. She saw him stop, and put his hand to his face and turn away from the blade and draw his knife instead. Relief left her weak, and not looking beyond so that it was too late when she shouted.

'Graine! *No!*'

I trust you to see it does not happen.

Far, far too late. The world hung on a blade's edge and was falling to destruction. Graine, slim, slight, fragile and as recognizable as her mother, had walked onto the field of battle with a blade in her hand, and was about to die for it. Distantly, she heard Venutios set his question again. *If it comes to the choosing, which matters more, your line or your land?*

She had no idea if it had come to the choosing, only that Graine must not die. There was a poor spear's throw between the oncoming cavalrymen and the child who carried all hope for a future in the light of her smile.

Two men came at once, each seeking the glory of having slain the Boudica's daughter. Her two sons dealt with the incomer, Flavius, and killed him. The gods gave her the other, the wolf-caped savage, as their gift. She set the white-legged colt into a leap that halved the distance and brought him up alongside. Stone came from the other side, running almost as sound as he had done through his youth. Her heart leaped to see him.

The wolf-man did not swerve. He saw the woman, the horse and

490

the hound and deemed them no threat. His blade was within reach of Graine.

He was right; she was too far away to stop him, except there was a move that her father had taught her, lifetimes ago, when the names of the heroes were still sung by the fire, and the ways they had died in the certain saving of others. She had never practised it; even in play-fights, the risk had always seemed too great. She set the parts one by the other in her mind now, and they were perfect.

She had less than a horse's length to make herself ready, to leap for the neck of the oncoming horse, cutting up for its throat even while her weight pulled down and round as a bear does in the kill, so that it stumbled and fell and she heard the crack of its neck and the scintillating havoc of an armoured body slamming into the ground at a speed that must surely be fatal, before she let herself know that a sword blade had already hit her, quite hard, somewhere under her bad arm. That was always the risk: the heroes had all died making this move; it was why they were heroes.

She heard Graine, and Valerius, and her father, all say her name. Somewhere nearby, Stone howled, and Hail with him.

The world closed into black.

XLVI

Valerius rode in the memory of a dream become a
nightmare. He rode a white-splashed black horse at speed
from a battlefield, but it was Graine who clung on behind
him, not Breaca. His sister was on the race-bred grey filly, held on
by a wrap of her own cloak that bound her and kept her from
falling.

Her family surrounded her; an honour guard of blood and spirit
sworn to shield her with their lives. Cunomar rode on one side with
Stone slung across his saddle; in the midst of battle, as they shouted
orders for the rear guard, he had stopped to pick up the hound his
mother loved. Ulla followed him, with Hawk and Cygfa on the
sword side. Airmid, Bellos and Theophilus came bunched together
behind.

They galloped fast, but not fast enough to outrun the blood that
Breaca was losing, nor, possibly, the half-wing of tiring cavalry
who followed, led by Sabinius, who had been standard-bearer even
in Valerius' time and, like Civilis, should have died long since. He
drove his men like one possessed, screaming Corvus' name.

Ardacos was there to stop him, standing in a circle drawn in the
dirt, oath-sworn to remain there until death forced him out, to take
as many of the enemy with him as he could, knowing those who
died on either side would serve as worthy companions in the long
trek through the other-forests to the welcome of the she-bear in

whose care they might rest and hunt and fight and rest again, for ever blessed.

He was not alone. Fifty of his own warriors, old, scarred men and women who had lived two decades in the care of the she-bear, drew their own circles in the earth and made the bear-line on either side of Ardacos. Behind them, in a second row, stood Scerros and the younger warriors who had followed Cunomar.

One other was there, newly come to their ranks: seeing them make their stand, and only barely understanding, Knife had swung off his horse and joined them, swearing his soul to the bear as had only ever been done twice before on the field of battle; and now a third time.

They were of the bear and the bear was in them and Valerius had no doubt they would sell their lives dearly, but that the cavalry would still overwhelm them. To buy more time than they alone could manage, Longinus drew together the horse-warriors of Mona to stand on either side of this line of living shields. Thus was Valerius' oath to him broken; to stay now in the chaos of the retreat was to die. They had both known that in the frantic moments of parting.

'I will wait for you in the gods' care,' Longinus had said, 'however long it takes. Don't forget me, when you meet the others who will be awaiting you.'

Valerius had clasped him close and kissed him. 'I won't forget. Beyond life, there are no limits to love. I will come to you, and there will be time, then, for all that has never been said.'

'It would be good to hear that.'

They had parted then, and not too soon. Huw had stayed to help Longinus, and Madb and all the horse-warriors of Mona and of the Eceni, and there had been no time for a proper parting from any of them. The trumpets were calling and those who remained faced more than the remnants of the Quinta Gallorum; the last cohorts of the XXth were coming from where they had waited through all the long day for their moment of triumph.

The battlefield was a slaughterhouse, and the refugees in their wagons were as sheep awaiting the cull. Between and beyond, warriors stayed to fight, or ran, as their instincts drove them; whichever they chose, most of them died.

There was room for hope that Ardacos' bears and the

horse-warriors who fought under Longinus' command were better led and better trained and so might live, but numbers did not tell in their favour.

They were giving their lives so that the Boudica's honour guard might live; it mattered to remember that. Valerius ran his hand along the black coat and it came back wet with sweat and other men's blood as it had in all the repetitions of his dream. His horse jumped a log. A long-practised part of him waited to fall off as they landed, and did not.

Airmid came up alongside. Breaca's blood stained her tunic. Clotted streaks of it painted her face. She looked more fearsome than the she-bear had ever done.

Over the thunder of running horses, she said to Valerius, 'In the dream of your childhood your left hand was cut off at the wrist. If you have altered that much with the changing paths of your life, we can be grateful.'

He shouted back, 'I would rather lose a hand than lose Breaca.'

'We're not given that choice. We can't change what has happened, only keep Graine safe, and Cygfa, and the child she will bear. Do you know of anywhere we can go so that Breaca can be quiet at the end? A god-space would be good, if there are any in the mountains that will hold us.'

Thus did Airmid of Nemain give Valerius of Nemain and Mithras the key to all that was of the other part of him. He looked for a peak he knew, and measured the distance to it.

'If we can ride hard, there's a cave that I know of, given in recent years to Mithras, but other gods were there first. It's near the fortress of the Twentieth but that's empty; Paullinus pulled every last man and servant out for the attack on Mona.'

'Can you get us there in time, do you think?'

'Yes.' His horse was fresher than any of those who might follow, and it had been trained by Civilis, who was one of the greatest horsemen of his age.

Valerius set his courage and his mount to the first of the slopes that led to the mountain and heard the others follow him. They were nine, and one of them dying, and they left behind a battle whose loss spelled the ending of a nation.

*

The rider walked his horse out of the trees near dusk, as they made the foot of the mountain. Valerius swung his blade at the misted shape, and then drew it back again, hissing through his teeth.

'You're late,' he said. 'The battle's over.'

'If the battle were what mattered most, then I would, indeed, be late,' said his father, Luain mac Calma, Elder of Mona. He moved his mare alongside the white-legged colt so they rode head to head up the track. 'Are you going to the cave of the bull god?'

'Unless you have something better.'

'Not at all.'

'Will you come?' It surprised Valerius how much he wanted that.

'I think not. You can do all that is needed. I'll wait here, and guide you to Mona after. The island is safe for now, and when it is no longer so, we have a welcome in Hibernia for everyone who survives the battle. There will be more than you fear and less than you hope.'

Valerius did not have the heart to think of more dead. 'Will Rome make Mona unsafe?' he asked.

'Yes, and eventually Hibernia too, but not in our lives, or our children, or our children's children, and there will be time before that to do what is needed so that the line may survive while the land is in thrall to the descendants of Rome. Go now. Breaca needs you more than a future that may never happen.'

They came to Mithras' cave at dusk, exhausted and riding spent horses, and found the place abandoned to the gods of stone and water.

The waterfall outside with its spreading hazels was thin with a summer's lack of rain. A winter's rock fall had partly obscured the entrance. A jar of honey had been stuffed into a crevasse, and someone had offered a child's toy sword, not yet rusted. Otherwise, Valerius could see no sign that anyone had been up since he had so rashly removed the false trappings of the god.

He was too tired to think. He let the colt slow to a halt and dropped to the ground on legs that would barely hold him. The grey race-filly slowed with him. Breaca lay along its neck, pliant as a child in sleep.

'Is she still alive?' That Airmid had to ask made the question more urgent.

'Yes.'

He left them and used his hands to scoop aside the worst of the rubble from the entrance. All the way up the mountain he had thought of the tight, snaking passage and the last difficult drop into the cave. Cygfa, Cunomar and Hawk had joined him by then, clearing stones. Theophilus filled waterskins from the river. Bellos and Airmid held Graine safe between them, and kept Stone holding to the last threads of life.

Valerius said, 'The way in is hard even when you're awake and whole. We'll need light inside. I'll go in first, and light a fire and come back.'

He lit more than a fire. In their haste to abandon their shrine, the officiates of the bull god had left behind reed torches hung on iron wall brackets and a handful of honey-tallow candles and a miniature brazier, still heavy with old charcoal, and a cache of tinder lodged beneath.

He lit both from the ember-pot Airmid had given him and crouched, breathing life into the flame until the light loosed its rippling, incandescent magic across the god's lake at one side of the cave, and lit to brilliance the eternal shining wetness of the walls and ceiling that arched above.

Once, he had been blinded by the magnificence of the god's fire laid across water in the utter darkness of the cave. Now, he stood surrounded by jewelled light and his heart was a black cavern, filled with too much fear to acknowledge beauty, or remember awe.

From the numbness of utter loss, he asked the favour of both of his gods to remain in this place that had been most recently given only to one of them. Mithras did not walk to him across the water with his hound at his heels as he had once done, but Valerius allowed himself to feel a sense of welcome, and carried it to those waiting outside.

The way in was hard, and harder with Breaca, who was cool by then, and slippery with her own sweat. They carried her to the lake's edge, where the brazier had settled to glowing coals and made the water a sheet of lost blood. The blushing scarlet gave her colour, so that she looked almost well, as if she slept in the wake of battle and could rise again, and fight again and this time win.

So that she might be warm and comfortable, they made a bed of folded cloaks and a pillow from the sheepskin saddle pad from

Graine's pony. They set Stone alongside and he had life enough left for his warmth to reach her. Airmid sat by her head, Bellos by her feet, Valerius held one side and Cygfa the other. Graine sat near the brazier, silent and white. Hawk kept vigil near the entrance, and left after a while, to set signs for Cunomar and Ardacos, in case they should survive and should track them this far.

He came back and nothing had changed but that more blood had seeped from the wound in Breaca's side, staining the pale blue of her cloak. He took his place again in silence.

Then there was nothing to do but wait.

'Graine?'

The voice was a sigh on the wind, although it was easy to hear her mother within it. No-one else heard it, or they had the sense to know it a product of the tumbling air within the cave, or they were simply too focused now on the death that was coming.

Graine did not know how to call the gods as they were needed. She had watched Airmid from the beginning. The tall dreamer had called Nemain so close that she and the god were one, and still she was beyond weeping. Bellos was watching Briga as if he alone might keep her at bay. Valerius had not yet called his gods, as if to do so in this place was sacrilege, or an admission of defeat. Hawk had called on no-one, only asked whosoever might listen for a miracle, and did not expect it given.

'Graine!'

Sharper now, and louder. No-one else moved. Graine touched the back of her hand to the brazier to make sure she was awake. The burn made her swear. The blister began to swell even as she sucked it. Without asking permission of those who sat with her mother, she took up one of the flickering beeswax candles and went to find the voice.

She sought darkness, away from the flowing blood of the brazier. At the back of the cave was a torn gap around an altar carved from the living rock. The wind did not settle there. She turned away from it, towards the blank wall, and found that her candle sent light into a sucking space from which no reflection came back.

The entrance to the inner cave, when she found it, was narrow and reached to the roof. She passed through it sideways and stood in a blackness so profound she might have lost her sight and become blind as Bellos, except that she could see the uncertain light of the candle, and so herself.

The wind snuffed the candle out. She felt a pressure, and a testing and was not unwelcome.

'*Graine. Come.*' It was a kind wind, or she chose to believe it so. She walked forward with her hands stretched out.

Presently, she felt a wall and turned to her left and walked with her shoulder against it, so that when it bent again the other way, as the waves of a snake, she was able to follow, slowly, in case the ground fell away.

She saw the light then, a grey feathering in the absolute black. As dawn that comes soon after midnight, her eyes feasted on it, taking in fine ridges in the rock, and the wear on the floor, as from the passing of many thousand feet over many hundreds of generations.

She followed the grey round another sinuous curve; and stopped.

The kind wind smoothed her face. The grey rock was steady behind her. Ahead, a vent in the towering roof let in the late evening light. To either side of that vent, down the steep, arched angles of the roof, the rock was not grey, but the colour of late winter ice, streaked and cracked and imperfect, but still sharp-edged as knife blades so that the million facets took the faint light and bounced it forward and back and out and down and made of the grey a rainbow of monochrome shades.

There was light enough to see the extent of the new chamber, to walk across it and find the place where a fire, or many fires, had once scorched the plain stone of the floor and sent smoke to streak the flawed brilliance of the roof; to scramble up on a rock bench and find the place where the wall folded in on itself to make a bed, and so to find the remains of the body that had been left to lie there, so long ago that the flesh had melted and the skin had dried onto the bones and the torc that had once lain so cleanly round the throat had fallen askew and was twisting the neck and the great blade that had kept guard for so long had dipped down between the arched bones of the pelvis.

On a day of so much grief, that seemed too much. She reached for the end-loops of the torc to straighten the thing, and let the dead lie in better order.

'Graine?'

The voice was very clearly not the wind. She turned fast, as if caught in some wrongdoing; and stopped again, for a second time, frozen.

Her mother was there.

The world broke apart, and was remade, perfect. Graine sagged against the stone. Relief flooded over her in scalding waves that left her damp and shivering with slick skin and hair that pricked on her scalp. 'You're better,' she said. Her voice came out as a whisper.

Her mother opened her arms and Graine came to them, and it was as it had been, before the procurator came with his veterans and his endless harm. Here was a haven of warmth and comfort and strength and the heartbeat of a warrior who could take on Rome and beat the legions back into the ocean and free the land for ever for the gods and the people. Before all of that, she was Breaca, daughter of one Graine who was dead, mother to this Graine, who was so very alive.

She sat now near the place where the fire had been, and seemed a little tired, but not more than anyone who has spent all day in battle and has not slept for two nights before. She pressed her lips to Graine's head and blew a long lungful of breath so that the perfect heat of it passed down through her crown to the soles of her feet, shivering. Graine reached up, and took a handful of fox-red hair that was still rough with dried sweat. She combed it, gently, with her fingers.

Her mother said, 'Did you find the torc? The one in the stone chamber?'

'Yes. I didn't move it, though. I was going to, but I didn't.'

'You should. It's yours. You can take it now.'

'But—'

Don't argue now, child. There isn't time.

Graine looked up. The elder grandmother was there, brisk and sharp as she had ever been. Her eyes gleamed like a hawk's in the strange light. She smiled, which was never a comfortable thing.

Take the torc. You'll need it. The other can be left here after.

'The other . . . ?' There was only one torc, which was her mother's. Graine looked at the elder grandmother, who smiled as if she had done something particularly clever, and nodded.

And so she knew, and the world was not perfect, but broken beyond all hope.

She fell back against the wall, and reached for her mother, who was not truly there. 'I'm not ready,' she whispered. 'I'm too young. The elder grandmother came to you like this on your long-nights, after she was dead. I'm not old enough for that, you can't leave me, you can't . . .'

'I know. I'm sorry. I shouldn't, there's too much to do, but I can't stay. All I can do is leave you a gift, and the torc is it. Will you take it now, while I'm here?'

'What about yours? And the blade lying on the bones in the stone cleft?'

'The blade in the stone is for Hawk, to have in exchange for Eburovic's blade, which must be left here with me. You do understand that? I am to lie here in the place of the ancestors, with the bear-blade and the torc of the Eceni. Tell Airmid. She'll know what to do.'

'How can you leave her? She loves you.'

'Unfair, light of my soul, unfair . . .' Her mother leaned over and kissed her. The breath did not reach to her scalp, still less to her feet. She sounded sad, but not bereft, as she should have done. 'I will wait for her, as we all do, on the river's far bank. She knows that, too. I will wait for you, also, and for your children and your children's children; I will be their strength to the ends of the earth and the four winds; tell them that as they are growing so that they might always remember. But for now, I must go. Will you take up the torc? Please? I would see you have it before I leave.'

If Graine could have slowed time by standing with the torc untaken, she would have stood for the rest of her life and beyond. Already, others were gathering; the ancestor-dreamer was there, and Macha, who had sent Valerius to her in the dream, and her grandfather, whose blade she had touched and so had brought ruin to her mother, and a man she did not know, with blazing yellow hair and the sign of the Sun Hound on his signet ring. When she saw Dubornos, standing near with the crows of Briga on either side, she knew she could not wait longer.

The ancestor's torc was narrower than her mother's, and had white gold in the nine-wired weaving alongside the rich Siluran red. It settled on her own neck as if moulded for it, with the open end-pieces hanging solidly over her collar bones. She took her hands away, and waited for the world to become void, as it had when she wore her mother's torc.

Nothing happened. She was disappointed, and surprised. Then she felt the light press of her mother's lips and the breath reached again through her crown to her toes. The light of the cave became richer and the ghosts within it more solid. The elder grandmother tipped her head to one side and eyed her critically.

A lot of learning still unlearned, for one so gifted. Do not begin to think you have the answers. If you ever do, hubris will kill you.

She wanted to say she would not care what killed her if she could join her mother, but Breaca was there, kneeling in front, taking the silver feather from her own neck and fastening it to Graine's, looped across the two end-rings so that it balanced between. 'The feather is my gift alone, not from the lineage or the gods or the past. Tell Airmid I said so. She'll make it happen.'

Breaca stepped back. The other ghosts had gone, except Dubornos, who waited, and the shade of a god, of all gods, that waited with him.

'You should go back now,' she said. 'You are all of the future, and all of the past. Live for that, and never forget that I love you,' and was gone.

EPILOGUE

O F ALL THOSE WHO COULD HAVE COME, IT WAS VALERIUS WHO followed her to the river's edge; she was surprised about that.

'Airmid is tending Longinus,' he said, by way of explanation. 'Madb and Huw found him lying on the field, and brought him as they fled. He may follow you yet, but not if we can hold him with us a while longer.' He smiled the wry, familiar smile. 'It would be very hard to lose you both in the same battle.'

I am not lost.

'No. I have walked with the dead long enough to know that. But I will grieve none the less. And wake and know the pain of each day without you. The world is made lesser by your passing.'

You can make it better, if you try.

'We can't defeat Rome. The spirit of the war host is broken. There is no Boudica now, to hold it together.'

And will not be for years and generations. We were privileged to see the last of the daylight; now we are at dusk, in a time of mourning, the onset of winter before the next spring. Night follows day and there is cold and grief in the darkness, but there will be dawn again, when Rome is gone, and all that follows from it.

'I won't be alive then, or our children, or our children's children.'

No, but you can set the seeds for what can grow when the night lifts and the sunrise brings hope. The gods know nothing of time.

They will be here, when those who need them come again, but to reach them again, the children must know what they have been, and what they can be. That is the task for now: to make sure the seed lies ready for the daylight.

The river lay broad in front of her, and the stepping stones, and the welcome on the far bank. She saw Dubornos there, and the crows that would guard her passage over.

Bán, I must go. He did not flinch at the name. She said, *Call your daughter Bán if you would not keep the name to yourself. It is as good for a girl and a woman as a boy and a man.* She leaned in and kissed him and said his other name. For the first time, it did not stick in her throat. *Valerius, you must go back, and find what it is to live with both of your souls in balance, holding the two gods within you. That is the gift of all you have been.*

'I know.' He was weeping, silently. His tears fed the river, and made it fast and beautiful and safe, that kept the lands of life separate from the lands of the dead.

She felt the brush of his caress as he left her, and returned it.

The river called her, and the land beyond it.

'Breaca?'

The voice was one she knew, and had known, and would always know. She turned, and Airmid was there, at the end, a singular presence, indistinguishable now from Nemain as she herself was indistinguishable from Briga, who had guided her life.

They met in a place where time had no meaning. She said, *I will wait for you. I always have, through all the lifetimes.*

Airmid's smile was the radiance of the moon. 'Sometimes I have waited for you, and will do again. I will be there when you call me.'

They parted, in no-time, and she stepped out across the first stone.

Her mother was there, and her father, and Stone came, young again and joyful, and brought Hail, the hound she had loved first, and an old grey battle mare, and she saw, finally, what she had not seen when Dubornos stepped off the last stone; that the land beyond was the land of her heart, open, untouched, unsullied by human endeavour, and that the gods waited there, those she had followed and those she had not, offering the gift of their care, equally.

AUTHOR'S NOTE

THERE IS VERY LITTLE LEFT TO SAY NOW, AT THE END.

This final part of the Boudica's story is the simplest and the best known. It is almost the only episode of early British history with corroborative archaeological evidence: Colchester, Chelmsford, London, St Albans and a host of smaller towns did all burn to the ground some time in the first century AD.

The detail of how and why and in what order comes from Tacitus and is as plausible as the rest of his writing, which is to say it seems likely that the base facts are correct, if one allows for the hyperbole of the victors' side.

I have deviated from the customary accepted reading of his account in a few places. Most notably, I have the IXth legion march straight down Peddar's Way in their effort to relieve Colchester. There seems reasonable evidence that the Wash did not extend as far inland as it does now and this was therefore by far the most direct route.

Beyond that, I have the Boudica's forces divide to assault Lugdunum and Verulamium (London and St Albans) rather than looping back on themselves, simply because it seems to make geographical sense. More controversially, I have set the final battle rather further west than is the currently accepted location of Mancetter, near Leicester.

Of all the myths and suppositions surrounding the Boudica, it would seem to me highly unlikely that tens of thousands of warriors did meet ten thousand legionaries in the particular valley the historians have identified; if they had, the metal detectors would have recovered at least a belt buckle or a harness mount by now.

Finally, I have given the Boudica an ending in war as befitted her spirit; neither the poison of Tacitus – the standard means by which a good Roman matron might take her life – nor the 'illness' of Dio Cassius were worthy of her, nor did they seem particularly plausible.

The other characters are largely fictional, although the two Roman commanders bear mention.

Petillius Cerialis, the impetuous legate of the IXth legion, did, apparently, survive an almost total annihilation of his forces and escape with his standards and a small company of his cavalry to take refuge in his fortress. He later became governor of Britannia, which suggests his action was not condemned in Rome.

Suetonius Paullinus' actions as governor are more or less as described: he was in the process of assaulting Mona when he heard news of the revolt. He took ship south and rode inland to view the situation in London, decided it was hopeless and rode away again, leaving the population to face the Boudican war host undefended.

In the wake of the revolt, he scoured the land in apparent vengeance. Nero finally recalled him on the grounds that he was treating the natives too harshly, and installed a more moderate governor, Turpilianus, who dealt with the remaining tribal leaders by more diplomatic methods – or as Tacitus would have it, 'veiled [his] tame inaction under the honourable name of peace'.

On the native side, Dubornos' fictional life and death are based on the discovery in a bog of the corpse of a young man described as a 'druid prince'. He had undergone the threefold death of a blow to the head, strangulation by a cord and drowning in the peat bog. He was naked, but for a band of fox fur round his upper arm. He was well fed and fit and had the remains of a burned bannock in his stomach.

All of these have led archaeologists to assume that he was a sacrifice to the gods of the place and time. Our culture tends to deride that but it has always seemed to me that the willing gift of a life, to take a message directly across the river to the lands of the dead, provided no-one else is harmed in the process of sacrifice, is quite different from the mindless slaughter of beasts or of unwilling victims and is not necessarily something to abhor.

The writing of this series has been an extraordinary personal odyssey in which almost every aspect of my life has changed, most of it attributable to the deepening dreaming brought about by the Boudica and all who surround her. I doubt very much if the characters who inhabit my dreaming will choose to leave quietly and already they are knocking at other doors in other ways. If life and times permit, I will look back first at the pre-history to this series in Alexandria and on Mona and then forward a little towards Rome in the aftermath of the revolt and then forward further to the end of Rome in Britain. Those readers who are already familiar with the Arthurian legends will have seen the seeds of something similar threaded through the narrative since the first book of this series. I have no idea where that might lead, but it would be interesting to find out.

The wider world has changed in ways far more dramatic than my own. When I began writing *Eagle*, the new millennium had just begun, full of hope for a different future. Since then, war and natural disasters have plagued the earth. In particular, I have watched the governing powers of my country launch a war against a distant state that, whatever one thinks of its legality, bears remarkable resemblance to the Roman invasion of Britain nearly two millennia ago. From the shifting reasons for invasion to the attempt to harness local resources for distant profit, to the failure to imagine insurrection amongst the native population, the invasion of Iraq has in my view mirrored the legions' progress in Britannia.

We don't, of course, have to follow the path laid down two thousand years ago. History does not have to repeat itself unless we choose it, or allow it to happen by default. Our land may be ruled by the natural inheritors of Rome. They may have spread their influence across the globe, with their need to control all that they do not understand. But those of us who dream with and of the land can believe that their grip is beginning to loosen, and that there is hope that a different way of seeing the world might emerge; that we could learn from who we were and so change who we might be.

The world would be a very different place if Boudica had won her final battle. She lost and we live with the consequences. It is too late to go back and remake history. It is not too late to go forward differently.

Suffolk, autumn 2005

For those interested in the dreaming, the author's website, http://www.mandascott.co.uk, carries details of contemporary dreaming workshops, recommended reading and other resources.

CHARACTERS AND PRONUNCIATION OF NAMES

THE LANGUAGE OF THE PRE-ROMAN TRIBES IS LOST TO US; WE HAVE NO means of knowing the exact pronunciations although linguists make brave attempts, based on known living and dead languages, particularly modern and medieval Breton, Cornish and Welsh. The following are my best attempts at accuracy. You are free to make your own. The names of characters based in history are marked with an asterisk.

Tribal characters

Airmid of Nemain – Air-med. Frog-dreamer, lover to Breaca. Airmid is one of the Irish names of the goddess.

Ardacos – Ar-dah-kos. She-bear warrior of the Caledones. Former lover to Breaca.

Bellos the Blind – Bell-oss. Former slave boy of the Belgae. Brought to Hibernia and then to Mona by Valerius. Now a dreamer of Mona.

Braint – Braynt. Warrior of Mona who fought with Breaca in the invasion battles. Lover to Cygfa.

*Breaca – Bray-ah-ca. Also known as the Boudica, from the old word 'Boudeg' meaning Bringer of Victory, thus 'She who Brings Victory'. Breaca is a derivative of the goddess Briga.

*Caradoc – Kar-a-dok. Lover to Breaca, father to Cygfa, Cunomar and Graine. Co-leader of the western resistance against Rome.

Civilis – Kivilis. An officer of the Batavian wing of the auxiliary cavalry who fought with Valerius in the invasion battles.

*Cunobelin – Koon-oh-bel-in. Father to Caradoc, now dead. Cun, 'hound', Belin, the sun god. Hence, Hound of the Sun or Sun Hound.

Cunomar – Koon-oh-mar. Son of Breaca and Caradoc. His name means 'hound of the sea'.

Cygfa – Sig-va. Daughter of Caradoc and Cwmfen, half-sister to Cunomar.

Dubornos – Doob-ohr-nos. Singer and warrior of the Eceni, childhood companion to Breaca and Bán.

Eburovic – Eh-boor-oh-vik. Father to Breaca and Bán, now dead.

Efnís – Eff-neesh. Dreamer of the Eceni.

Eneit – Enate. Soul-friend of Cunomar. His name means 'spirit'.

Graine – Granya; the first 'a' is pronounced like the 'o' in bonfire. Daughter of Breaca and Caradoc.

Gunovar – Goonavar. Daughter of Gunovic and a dreamer of the Dumnonii.

Huw – Hugh. A warrior of Mona, renowned for his skills with the sling. Fought with Valerius in the western wars against Longinus Sdapeze's cavalry.

Lanis – Lan-is. Mother of Eneit, and a dreamer of the Eceni.

*Longinus Sdapeze – Long-guy-nus. Formerly of the auxiliary cavalry, now fighting for the Boudica's war host. Lover to Valerius. His cracked and broken gravestone was found in Camulodunum (Colchester) during excavations.

Luain mac Calma – Luw-ain mak Kalma. Elder of Mona and heron-dreamer. A prince of Hibernia.

Macha – Mach-ah; the 'ch' is soft as in Scottish 'loch'. Bán's mother, now dead. Macha is a derivative of the horse goddess.

Madb – Maeve. A warrior of the Hibernians.

Valerius – dreamer and warrior. Breaca's half-brother, son of Macha and Luain mac Calma. Until recently an officer in the auxiliary cavalry. Formerly known as Bán.

Roman characters

Latin is rather closer to our language, although we would pronounce the letter 'J' as equivalent to the current 'Y', 'V' would be 'W' and 'C' would be a hard 'K' in all cases. However, this is so rarely used that it is simpler to retain standard modern pronunciation of these letters.

*Decianus Catus** – procurator of all Britannia under Nero.

Flavius – standard-bearer to Ursus' troop.

*Lucius Domitius Ahenobarbus**, a.k.a. Nero, emperor of Rome.

*Petillius Cerialis** – legate of the IXth legion.

Quintus Valerius Corvus – prefect of the Ala Quinta Gallorum.

Sabinius – standard-bearer to the first troop, directly under Corvus' command.

*Suetonius Paullinus** – governor of all Britannia.

Ursus – decurion of the Ala Quinta Gallorum, serving under Corvus.